The Hampton House

SWEET ROMANTIC WOMEN'S FICTION

THE HAMPTONS
BOOK ONE

JESSIE NEWTON

ISBN-13: 978-1-63876-374-1

Chapter One

Mandie Kelton took a sip of her coffee, now lukewarm, and told herself to go dump it out and get some water. She'd been experiencing heartburn more often than not on days when she drank the entire cup of coffee she picked up on the way in to work.

She set the to-go cup further from her and reached for the next file in the pile. Part of her job involved looking through prospective properties, and she really enjoyed browsing through the "slush pile."

At tomorrow's meeting, she'd be expected to have her top three choices for the next clean-up project, appropriately labeled CUP in her department, and literal tally marks went up on the white board as the team reviewed their personal favorites.

Mandie had two files in her favorites folder already, but she told herself to have an open mind as she looked at the picture of the mansion on the first page in the new file.

"Ten thousand square feet," she said. In all honesty, most mega-mansions approached ten thousand square feet, with multiple bedrooms, twice as many bathrooms, and ornate staircases.

Her heartbeat pumped out an extra beat, because she absolutely loved taking the abandoned and restoring it to full glory. That, and her phone had just sparkle-chimed with her husband's assigned ringtone.

Charlie had said, *I'm so going to pass this Pharmacology final*, with a smiley face emoji. *To celebrate, I'm stopping by Lin Chu's for dinner. You want those chickeny noodles?*

She grinned at his use of "chickeny noodles," abandoned the file, and reached for her phone to answer him. *You're finished with the final already?*

Piece of cake, he said, which was Charlie-code for *yes, I'm done and leaving campus*. He only had the one final today, and Charlie hated staying on campus when he could leave it. She'd find him in their one-bedroom apartment when she got home, and he'd most likely time dinner to arrive only a few moments before her.

She and Charlie had been married for almost five years now, and he took very, very good care of her. Mandie loved him with her whole heart, and they'd even started talking about starting a family.

Everything Mandie did required her to go through a minefield of thoughts, and she often felt like she'd made the wrong turn and gotten blown back to the beginning. She envied others who could made quick decisions with confidence, because that had never been Mandie's strong suit.

See you at home, she texted Charlie, and then she went back to the file in front of her. She had to have her choices done for tomorrow, and then she had some appointments to make with a restoration company for an apartment building here in the city that had sustained some flooding damage.

She loved her job at PastForward Restoration Company—PFRC—because they helped people who needed it while showing respect to the history of the dwellings and buildings on the East Coast. Some properties here were hundreds of years old, and Mandie felt a sense of reverence every time she went out on a field assignment.

The house in the file intrigued her, and Mandie leafed through the floor plan, read the story behind its abandonment, and embraced the growing excitement within her. She didn't often make her choices based on pictures, checklists, and facts. She relied on her feelings, and she reached for a green sticky note, which she attached to the front of this file.

It got placed in the yes-pile, and Mandie sat back. She loved learning about old things, and since she hadn't been on a field assignment yet this year, she muttered, "So you'll bring it up in your meeting tomorrow."

Part of her yearned to get out of this office building, though she'd once been tickled and thrilled to be riding the subway from Brooklyn, where she and Charlie lived, to the Flatiron building every day.

She still was, but she definitely felt like some of the glitter that had first coated her job had started to flake off. She stood and stretched her back, glancing across the partition that separated her desk from the one in front of her.

The man who worked there had various camera equipment littering his space, and Flint Rogers looked up. "Hey." He leaned back in his chair. "My eyes are starting to cross."

"Editing your latest film?"

"Final edits," he said. "It's due to production by tomorrow night, and it should air next month."

"That's awesome," Mandie said. By "air," he meant the complete walk-through of one of the abandoned mansions. He led the film crew on field assignments, and they documented everything from the first step the team took onto the property to the final walk-through when a place went up for sale.

If he was lucky, he could work on one project per year, as his post-production was far more detailed than Mandie's. She was involved on field assignments from the first step to the sale, and that was it. She didn't then have hundreds of hours of film to go through and edit into a ninety-minute documentary.

"I can't believe the Maryland Mansion is almost done," she said.

"Hopefully, there will be something new at tomorrow's meeting," Flint said. He wore a neatly trimmed ginger beard, with a full head of hair to match. He was what Mandie would call a "clean hipster," as he showered regularly and didn't wear his hair long. His emerald eyes always seemed to see more than Mandie could, and he wore loafers everywhere he went, even into dangerous, abandoned houses.

He rolled his khakis at the ankle, always wore tapered pants and skin-tight tees—if he didn't have on a too-small polo.

"You think you'll get another assignment right away?" Mandie asked. She leaned against the chest-high divider and took in more of his mess. How he worked in those conditions, she didn't understand. He had yellow legal pads filled with notes and numbers in black pen she couldn't read. But Flint somehow knew what it all meant, and she supposed that was all that mattered.

"Jo Ann's quitting," Flint said. "Which means they'll have to promote up another film lead, and last time Candace needed to do that, it took four months for me to go through multiple interviews, present my portfolios, and get named to the position."

Mandie drew in a breath. "Jo Ann's quitting?" She'd just finished a huge project that had sold in less than a week—the Mountain Manor, a gorgeous log cabin in Massachusetts.

Flint swore and looked away. "I guess that isn't common knowledge." He looked at Mandie with puppy-dog eyes. "Don't say anything, okay?"

"Yeah, of course not," she said.

Flint stood and stretched his arms above his head, his tiny shirt pulling up over the waistband of his khakis. "You haven't been out in the field in a while."

"Tell me about it." Mandie rolled her eyes. "I think Candace thought I'd get pregnant, and she didn't want to assign me to anything."

"So you're not pregnant?" Flint grinned at her, and Mandie smiled and shook her head.

"Even if I was," she said. "That shouldn't exclude me from field work. It's pregnancy discrimination."

"Sometimes those old houses are full of mold."

"We have protective gear for that." Mandie folded her arms, becoming more and more determined to get an assignment tomorrow. She'd had enough of desk work, phone calls, and file browsing. She swatted at Flint's chest. "Plus, you tromp through those sites in shoes with barely any soles and no socks. It's a miracle you haven't contracted gangrene or something."

Flint bellowed out a laugh, and Mandie allowed herself to smile. As he quieted, she said, "All right, Flint. Tell me how to get assigned to something tomorrow."

"Step into my office," he said, and Mandie scrambled to go around the dividers and into his disorganization. If it would help her get a field assignment, she could sit among cameras, flash lights, and micro SD cards.

"So the final went well?" Mandie asked as she entered her apartment. She tapped the door with her foot to close it, then noticed the candles on the table. She froze. "What anniversary did I forget?"

Charlie turned from the back counter, a plate of orange chicken in his hand. "Final went amazing. There's no anniversary."

"There's something," Mandie said as she got moving again. She'd brought home her top three files so she could obsess over them while she and Charlie watched TV tonight. He sometimes had her quiz him, especially with anything math-related, but he'd already taken that final, so she anticipated an evening filled with some sort of action-adventure movie, and she could easily keep up with the plot while she looked through her files again.

"There's me finishing another year of school," he said. "That's it."

"Only one more," Mandie said as she dropped her bag over the back of the couch and shrugged out of her jacket. Springtime in New York could still be chilly, and Mandie hated nothing more than being cold on the subway.

She wrapped her arms around Charlie once he'd set down the plate of chicken. "You're amazing, baby. One more year of pharmacy school." She kissed him, glad she got to spend her evenings with her best friend in the whole world.

"Tomorrow, they're making assignments for the next major field assignment, and I want it so badly." She whispered the last few words, almost afraid to speak her desires.

"You'll get it," Charlie said. "You haven't been out of the office in a while."

"For six months," she said. "And I know Candace just got a whole heap of new funding. She might even schedule two projects."

"Where are they?"

"My favorite one is in the Hamptons," Mandie said as he pulled out her chair and she sat down. "It would be a dream to work on it. It's close, so I wouldn't have to live on-site. My other two favorites are out of the city. One in South Carolina—a really old plantation that would be pretty cool—and one up in Cape Cod."

"Mm." Charlie sat down too. He dished up some of her chickeny noodles, and Mandie simply watched him.

"Did you hear about the internship?"

"Another interview next week," he said casually, but Mandie knew he hated the multiple interview process. *Honestly*, he'd said. *If they don't know by now, I don't know what else to do to win them over.*

She smiled at him. "So we'll both have amazing new by this time next week."

"You'll have yours tomorrow." He grinned at her and took orange chicken and ham fried rice for himself.

"What if I don't get it?" Mandie let her vulnerability show. Only for him, and Charlie heard her and looked right at her. "She's been passing me over for some reason, and I just—what if I've gotten my hopes up and I don't get it?"

"You're going to get it."

She sighed, because frustration frothed through her. "Thank you, baby." She did like his confidence in her, but they'd been together long enough to see that sometimes confidence didn't always equate to getting what they wanted.

He hadn't gotten into the Pharm.D. program at Rutgers, for example. He'd had to settle for his second choice of St. John's, and while he loved his program there now, Charlie had definitely been disappointed.

"And if you don't," he said. "I'll have mint chocolate chip ice cream here tomorrow night, and we'll go away for the weekend. Go see your mom in the cove." He raised his eyebrows. "Okay? It won't be the end of the world."

"It'll just feel like it," she said miserably.

"Hey, let's be positive," he said. "You've got a strong case for getting assigned, and they've picked your top choice the last four times."

"Yeah." Mandie twirled up some noodles and stuck them in her mouth. Salty, savory deliciousness moved through her. "Mm."

Charlie grinned at her, and suddenly everything was okay.

"And hey," she said. "If I do get it, I know I won't have to work with The Bulldozer."

Charlie choked on his chicken as he started to laugh. Mandie smiled too, though she truly didn't like working with Suzette Paxman. She'd been nicknamed The Bulldozer by everyone in the office, because she rammed through old houses like one. She held a degree in Anthropology, and she acted like she was the only human being alive who did.

In some cases, working with her meant Mandie didn't have to get her hands and feet as dirty, as Suzie wasn't afraid of anything. She'd go into any room, any broken-down pool house, over any surface, to get the footage and information they needed.

She giggled with Charlie, because suddenly everything felt lighter. "I'm going to get it," she said, mustering up all the optimism she could. "And I'm going to have the best team ever, and it'll be the house in The Hamptons, and when we go home to Five Island Cove this weekend, it'll be to celebrate my new field assignment."

"There you go." Her husband beamed at her, and Mandie reached over and covered his hand with hers.

"Should I really get us tickets for the Steamer?" she asked.

He nodded. "Yeah, my mom would like it too. She'll take us to lunch to celebrate another semester done."

"Free food," Mandie mused. "I see how you are."

"Hey, I never say no to free food." Charlie grinned, and Mandie did too. She suddenly had so much to look forward to in the next few days, and her stomach flipped over tomorrow morning's meeting.

She just had to get a field assignment. She simply had to.

Chapter Two

Alicia Halverson stepped onto the elevator ahead of Mandie, and when she turned, she gave the other woman a look that spoke volumes. Thankfully, Mandie could understand looks where words weren't spoken, and she edged behind a tall African American man to position herself closer to Alicia.

"What have you got?" she whispered on the third floor, when half the people in the elevator exited. "Lish, don't hold out on me. I'm here an hour early to go over files I have memorized."

"Please." Alicia half-scoffed and half-laughed. "You're here early so you can pace in the bathroom and pitch yourself to your reflection."

Mandie's shoulders shivered back and forth, her way of conceding to Alicia without words. Alicia laughed, because she knew Mandie so well. She reminded her of her younger sister, and a powerful wave of missing rolled through Alicia completely unbidden.

"My thumbs are aching from how much I texted last night," Alicia said as the elevator struggled to get moving again.

"It better have been with Michael." Mandie sighed, and Alicia felt her frustration. She hadn't been assigned a field trip in months either, and once Mandie had texted last night, Alicia had taken it upon herself to figure out how to get the two of them assigned to whatever went up on the board today at PastForward.

"Michael, I wish." Alicia rolled her neck, and the day hadn't even started yet.

"He's going to ask you out. You just need to keep stopping by for those chocolate croissants."

"Yeah, and then I have to run fifty miles on the treadmill." Alicia shook her head now, the ends of her long, dark hair brushing against her elbows. She'd braided it into pigtails today in an attempt to make herself look younger. Candace seemed to discriminate on any grounds she could, and only she knew what those were.

Alicia and Mandie had brainstormed that they changed all the time too, and it could be because Alicia left her food in the microwave too long or that she'd just turned thirty-five. No one really knew, and she wished there was a system for how people got selected for field assignments.

"Rory says there's no way Suzie will get picked," Alicia

said once they'd passed the seventh floor. "She's still finishing up with the New Hampshire mansion."

"So we'll need another bulldozer," Mandie said, her eyes glued to the numbers above the doors. They were nearing ten now, and had five more to go. "Who?"

"Rory says the two of us would make a killer research and checklist team, with Flint behind the camera."

Mandie only hummed, but that said so much. Alicia knew she wanted this field assignment more than anything, and she'd known before Mandie had texted last night. She knew, because Alicia needed this assignment like she needed oxygen.

"You love Flint."

"Flint's the best," Mandie agreed. "So John as the third?"

"Could be." Alicia nodded as the elevator made another stop and then continued up. She and Mandie got off on the fifteenth floor and went past the ritzy real estate firm to their private historical restoration and reconstruction firm.

They both worked in the Preservation and Conservation Department, but they both also handled local clients who needed help getting natural disasters cleaned up when they weren't working on historical cases.

"I'm so bored," Alicia whispered as she opened the glass door and held it for Mandie.

"I might scream if I don't get assigned today," she whispered back. "Just right out loud, in the middle of the meeting."

Alicia laughed lightly. "I doubt it. Assignments always come at the *end* of the meeting."

Mandie scoffed and veered off into her desk area while Alicia continued down another two rows to hers. She quickly put her purse in her bottom desk drawer, grabbed her files, and went back to Mandie's desk.

"Top three. We have to be in perfect alignment."

Mandie already had her folders out too. She loved sticky notes and color-coding, which was why she'd be perfect for any field crew. The woman literally never missed a detail, and she had three folders, one each labeled with a green note, a yellow one, and a pink one.

"Is pink above green or below?"

"Pink is the prize, my friend." Mandie smiled as she slipped the marked folder to the top.

Please let it be the Hampton House, Alicia prayed as Mandie seemed to fall into slow motion. Alicia really couldn't leave her children for an off-site field assignment, and she wondered if Candace had somehow found out about her recent divorce.

She commuted from Queens, from the tiny two-bedroom apartment where her kids shared a room while she slept in the other. She'd had to leave behind the house she'd shared with her husband, and the longer commute would make it difficult to be on-site for any amount of time. She'd chosen the Hampton House simply in the hopes that it would be selected, and she could get the field assignment.

She earned more when on assignment, as they received

a per diem for food for every day worked out at the site. Plus, the house held a magic to it that leapt off the printed page and permeated the air.

"I knew you'd like the Hampton place too." Alicia grinned widely when she saw the pillared mansion on the front page inside the pink-sticky-note-marked folder.

"It's the best property," Mandie said. "Though I did like that one in the Appalachians."

"The Appalachian Jewel?" Alicia fake-swooned. "Isn't it amazing? Even full of someone else's stuff and those ghastly all-terrain vehicles. I can't even imagine the views." Alicia could admit she was somewhat of a romantic, but the images of her eight-year-old's and her five-year-old's faces grounded her. Brought her back to reality, and that meant she couldn't run off to Virginia even for an amazing mountain mansion.

"I didn't put it in my top three," Mandie said. "I don't really want to travel for the field assignment." She tucked her honey-blonde hair behind her ear as she bent over the Hampton House. "I'm worried that if it comes up a lot, Candace will choose it even if it doesn't have the most votes."

"She is so unpredictable," Alicia complained. "That's what I dislike the most. If I knew how things could go, if I could predict it, I wouldn't be so nervous." She flapped her hands a couple of times, then told herself to stop it.

She got to her feet. "Look, you're the natural choice for the researcher. I'm the perfect fit for the financial advisor. All we need is a bulldozer and a film crew, and this is going to be the best summer and fall of our lives."

Mandie clapped her hands together. "Yes! This is the kind of pep talk we need."

No one else had come into the office this early, and Alicia had psyched herself up appropriately. "Okay," she said, pacing to get out some of her extra energy. "We are going to pitch ourselves today. I *want* this assignment."

"I *need* it," Mandie said. "I'm tired of assisting on research and then staying here while the team goes out."

"This is ours."

"What's yours?" someone asked, and Alicia's gaze flew past Mandie to another blonde, this one more strawberry than not and so not someone she wanted to talk to this early in the morning. Or ever, really.

"Hey, Suzie," she chirped in a falsely bright voice. "You're here early."

"I've got to get this last form filed for the West Hills Monster."

Mandie got to her feet, her irritation like a scent on the air. Suzie barely looked at her, as if Mandie didn't hold any importance at all. Alicia reached out and grabbed onto her forearm, and that stopped Mandie. Thankfully.

"Leave it," she hissed as Suzie went by them. "We'll play our cards in the meeting."

Several seconds passed while they both waited for the blonde bulldozer to get out of earshot, and then both she and Mandie sat down in Mandie's desk area. "She thinks she's going to get another assignment," Mandie said. "Unbelievable."

"She's not going to get it," Alicia said. "There are so many deserving people—like us."

"Like us," Mandie agreed with a nod. "Okay, more people are starting to come in. We can't be seen conspiring, or Candace will for-sure give the assignment to someone else."

"Right." Alicia squeezed her friend's hands, then stood, and made her way over to her desk. The office started to fill, and before she knew it, Candace had stepped out of the conference room, the silver bell in her hand.

"Let's go, people," she called as she started to ding the bell over and over and over. *Ding! Ding! Ding!*

Everyone got to their feet like dogs, like the bell had triggered something Pavlovian inside them. Alicia joined them, her three folders and her notebook in her hands. She deliberately didn't allow herself to migrate to Mandie's side. Candace didn't like it when friends tried to get on the same teams, and Alicia panicked that her friendship with Mandie—which was well-known around PastForward— would suddenly hinder her.

Fourteen people crowded into the room, and Candace indicated the three trays in the middle of the oblong table. "First, second, third," she said, indicating a tray with each one. "Folders in."

Someone swore, and Jackson—another accountant with a degree in construction management—jumped to his feet. "I forgot my folders."

"Door's closing in ten seconds," Candace called after him, and though he was one of Alicia's main competitors for this field assignment, she hated seeing him humiliated. Candace had locked people out of meetings before, so her ten-second rule was not an empty threat.

Ten seconds later, Jackson sprinted into the room just as Candace said, "Doors, please."

He practically threw his folders into the trays. Candace glared at him as she pulled the first tray toward her. "Paula, please tally."

Another woman scrambled to her feet, and Alicia wondered why they all kept showing up here, day after day, to be ordered around and treated subserviently. Paula uncapped a blue white board marker, and Candace flipped open the first folder.

"Hamptons," she said, and Alicia shot a look over to Mandie. She sat very still, her gaze trained on Candace. "Cape Cod." Another folder. "Hamptons." She continued on until all the folders in the first pile had been read, and it was obvious that the majority of people in the office wanted to work on the Hampton House next.

Candace turned and looked at the tally marks. "Nine, wow." She smiled as she turned back and picked up the second stack of folders. She read through those, and the Cape Cod Complex came in second.

Their boss didn't even turn to get the remaining pile of folders. She steepled her fingers and considered the board. "I'm a bit surprised more of you didn't pick the

Appalachian Jewel." She simply let the words hang there, and Alicia had learned not to justify anything.

If Candace asked her a direct question, she'd answer. Otherwise, she wouldn't. If she didn't get an assignment today, Alicia wasn't sure what she'd do. Screaming, like Mandie had suggested, sounded about right.

She looked down the table to her friend again, and this time, Mandie's eyes darted to hers too. Then Candace spun, and Alicia jerked her attention back to her. The tension in the conference room pressed against the ceiling, against all the walls and windows, straining to get out. Alicia could barely get a decent breath, and she wondered if anyone but her felt that.

"We might as well go over what's third." Candace started reading through those, and Paula dutifully tallied them all up. Candace, in all her bleach-blonde-bunned glory, turned to face the board again.

She never went out in the field, except to check-in once, maybe twice, during a project. She demanded detailed reports which she religiously read, and she'd email questions or call private meetings with teams. Alicia had never seen her wear anything but skirts that fell precisely to her knees, heels, and fluttery blouses.

Todays was pale blue, with a navy skirt and navy heels, and perfectly matching robin's egg blue earrings in the shape of dragonflies.

"Ah, there's my Appalachian Jewel." She grinned at the board, then swiveled back to the group at-large. "Thank you, Paula. Please take your seat."

Paula did just that, and Alicia looked down at her notebook, almost afraid to make eye contact with Candace. She forced herself to look up, because she couldn't show her boss any weakness.

"We have enough funding for two teams to get started," she said. "I'm going to send some of you to Virginia and this mountain mansion. I think it's the best in the bunch, and I'm honestly surprised it's not number one."

No one said anything, because it sounded like Candace had just started a lecture. Alicia gazed at her, and Candace looked her way.

"Let's start down there." Candace looked down at some notes in front of her. "Jackson." Alicia's heart started to pound through her whole body. If Jackson got the Jewel, she'd be the most logical choice for the Hampton House.

"Vanessa, I need you on point," Candace said.

"Yes, ma'am," Vanessa said.

"Chevy." Candace glanced over to him, and he was a bulldozer like Suzie.

"You got it, Candy," he said, and he was the only one who'd ever called Candace such a thing. A thread of horror moved through Alicia, but Candace only laughed.

"And on film..." She paused and sighed. "I'm going to pause on that for a minute. I want you guys to clear your afternoon on Monday. We'll meet to go over everything then."

Murmurs of assent moved through the group, and the tension in the room skyrocketed. Alicia shifted in her seat, and Candace looked at her. Her eyebrows went up, and Alicia's did too. That was about as big of a challenge as she could lay down, and she hoped the message had gotten across.

"The Hampton House," Candace said, consulting her notebook again. A few seconds went by, then a few more.

"Ma'am?"

Every eye flew to Mandie. She'd half-raised her hand, and she'd gone pale, like she might throw up. Candace looked at her, blinking rapidly a few times.

"I'm in love with this house," Mandie said. "I'd love to take point on it. I've already sketched out a few things to get started."

"You have?" Candace folded her arms and considered Mandie, her gaze sharp and hooked. Alicia's mouth had gone dry, and she had no idea how Mandie had the nerve to speak up in a meeting where people didn't do such things.

"Yes, ma'am," Mandie said. "And I'm completely available to meet with you and whoever else you appoint to the team anytime."

"Anytime." Candace nodded, though something cold definitely emanated from her. She leaned back in her chair and appraised Mandie for several long seconds. Then a couple more. Right when Alicia thought the air would snap, she said, "All right, Miss Kelton. Oops, I mean *Mrs.* Kelton. You can have point."

"Thank you, ma'am."

Alicia couldn't speak up now, but she wasn't a bulldozer, nor on film. If she didn't get named next, she wouldn't have an assignment. A voice started shrieking in her head, an internal monologue that left her feeling desperate, irritated, and hopeless all at the same time.

She had to get out of this room.

Now.

Get out. Get out. Get out!

She stayed right where she was, and Candace looked at her notes and then right at her. "Alicia, can you keep *Mrs.* Kelton within budget?"

"Yes, ma'am," she said, her voice grating like rusty nails against cement. "Absolutely, I can."

Candace nodded and looked around. Alicia's heartbeat now bobbed somewhere outside her body, but she still had enough wherewithal to pray, *Not Suzie. Please, not Suzie.*

"Brandt," she said. "You'll be on bulldozer, and Flint, I know you're just barely finishing up the Maryland Mansion, but I need you in the Hamptons."

"Sure thing," Flint said.

"Apparently, *Mrs.* Kelton has some notes already for us," Candace said dryly, and Alicia thought Mandie might blow her top. She'd turned bright red now, and since Alicia sat on the same side of the table as her, she could see her fisted hands.

"Mandie's the best," Flint said. "I'm sure she and Lish can get started without me. We're more of the on-site crew." Flint threw Alicia a smile, and that settled some of the acid boiling in her stomach.

"I want the Hampton House team in my office first

thing Monday morning." She got to her feet. "I'll have my own notes to go over." She gave Mandie a pointed look. "All right. Back to work."

She started stacking the folders, and Alicia filed out of the conference room along with everyone else...except Mandie. Alicia met her eyes and gestured for her to *come on! Don't stay in here with the Big Bad Wolf!*

Mandie shook her head slightly, her jaw set and her eyes filled with pure determination. Alicia moved out of the way, wondering if she needed to stay and back-up whatever Mandie said.

But Mandie said, "Miss Ewing? Can I speak to you privately for just five minutes?" and Alicia ducked out of the room. She'd hear all about this five-minute meeting soon enough, and she didn't want to step on her friend's toes.

She closed the door behind her and practically rammed into Flint.

"What's she doing?" he murmured.

"It's suicide," Alicia said, turning to face the conference room. All of the blinds were open, but Mandie stood with her back to the office.

"So we'll be going to lunch today," Flint said easily. "If she's still alive, we'll hear all about it." He nudged Alicia with his elbow. "And hey, you guys got Brandt."

Relief filled her again and then again, and she finally felt like she could breathe properly. "Yeah," she said. "We got Brandt." Her gaze went back to the conference room.

"And if Mandie doesn't get fired, we pretty much have the dream team for the Hampton House."

Then she turned and walked back to her desk, praying for her friend in a constant internal stream of words.

26

Chapter Three

S uzette Paxman wrinkled her nose as the scent of lemongrass and fish sauce hit her like a wall as she stepped off the elevator on the sixth floor.

"Phil's making dinner again," she grumbled, her own grocery bags swinging from her hands. The plastic cut into her skin, and she hurried past her Vietnamese neighbors to her apartment with the paper-thin walls.

She'd started taking some foreign language classes just to figure out what Phil and Angelica argued about all the time. Turned out, they had the same problems everyone else did—a lack of time, money, and who they should spend their holidays with.

Suzette dropped the bag with the fresh produce in it so she could key her way into her apartment, the weight of the weekend settling onto her shoulders. Most people looked forward to Friday night.

TGIF and all that.

For Suzie, it simply meant she had two more days before she could get back to work. Friday night mocked her every week, reminding her of how utterly alone she still was. Forty years in, and she still had an empty apartment welcoming her home each evening.

"Meow." Oh, and a gray and white cat named Jackrabbit.

"Hey, Rabbit," she said to the cat as she bent to get her groceries. The scent of potstickers had already seeped into every corner of her tiny apartment, the perfect complement to her terrible week.

She sighed and toed the door closed, then lifted her hand with the lighter bags of groceries to lock it behind her. Jackrabbit followed her, rubbed against her legs as she unpacked the things she needed to make dinner that night, and then meowed again.

"I'm getting there," she told him, as she fed him in the bathroom—which she kept closed while she went to work. Now, she stepped the few feet down the hall to the bathroom and opened the door.

Jackrabbit darted inside, and Suzie followed the feline to refill his water fountain. She did leave that in the kitchen, but it sputtered if it didn't have enough liquid in it.

With her cat fed, Suzie returned to the kitchen to get herself something to eat. Cutting, chopping, and slicing helped Suzie pound out her frustrations with her personal life—or lack thereof. Her job. Pretty much everything about her life made her reach for a sharp knife and hack a head of lettuce into tiny pieces.

With her pork chop seared and in the oven, Suzie mixed up the slaw and put it in the fridge. Only then did she turn to her laptop, determined to finish watching the initial documentary on the West Hills Monster project.

Everyone on the team had to provide notes once things came in from the videographer, and Suzie wanted to get hers done. The West Hills Monster had turned out to live up to its name, and she just wanted this project behind her.

The sooner she wrapped this up, the sooner she could start on something new. She reached for her wine glass, a sigh pulling through her whole body. "You didn't get assigned to a new project."

Truth be told, Suzie had not thought she would, but that didn't mean the disappointment and frustration stemming from her job stung any less. Since she hadn't gotten a new assignment, she wouldn't until next quarter.

That meant she'd be stuck in the office for the next three months, and Suzie hated everything about working inside every day. Her reputation at PastForward got her outside the bland office walls more than others—that, and Candace had a shortage of people willing to bulldoze their way through old mansions.

Suzie lived for it.

She wanted something to challenge her and showcase her skills at the same time, and she loved that she'd found a way to combine her love of demolition of something old and rebuilding it into something new, and her fascination with the culture of people throughout time.

"And there's nowhere as nuanced and faceted as the Hamptons." Suzie drained the last of her wine and set her glass down, ready to work now. She had wanted to get assigned to the Hampton House, though she knew Candace had been fair.

And what about Mandie Kelton speaking up the way she had? Suzie had always overlooked the younger woman —she'd only been at PastForward for a couple of years— and they'd never worked directly together on a project before.

Suzie could admire someone who spoke up for themselves, and she loved the cultural history of the Hamptons. That mansion there would be a pure gem to work on, as well as something personal for her, but Suzie pushed it out of her mind as she watched the opening pan of the camera as it moved over the West Hills Monster.

The house screamed that it had been neglected, with the vines and overgrowth all around it. Suzie loved old buildings with everything inside her. She also loved transforming them into something new.

She wished she could work on herself for six months and come out a brand new woman on the other side. Maybe then she could get a date that would lead to a second one. Maybe then she wouldn't be the first person in the office, the last to leave, and find herself working when she got home too.

As the video played, Suzie made a list of the things she

was good at. Tearing out cabinets and hammering into old walls.

Keeping her apartment clean and fixed up.

Cooking. Baking. Eating ice cream sandwiches.

She smiled at the list, which meant it had accomplished what she'd needed it to. Whenever Suzie got down on herself, she just needed a few minutes to remind herself that she had good qualities.

Just because one of them wasn't keeping a boyfriend didn't mean she didn't have value. Sometimes she felt like her life was being held together by sheer willpower and duct tape, but the lists helped.

She did wish she had friends she could go out with, and she picked up her phone to see if someone had texted her. She'd worked with Hailey and Alex on the West Hills Monster, and they'd gone out for drinks after a long day on-site.

But they hadn't texted. No one had, and Suzie should be glad her mother hadn't asked about the guy she'd gone out with last weekend.

Her pork chops came out beautiful, and Suzie enjoyed her gourmet-meal-for-one in front of her laptop.

By the time Monday morning dawned, Suzie had run ten miles on the treadmill and put together five pages of notes for her meeting later that day. She arrived at the Flatiron building, rode the elevator up with a crowd of people, none of whom spoke to her.

Suzie existed in pure isolation, surrounded by a sea of lives around her. She had no idea why she seemed to have this wall of waxed paper around her, where people could see her, but no one wanted to speak to her or interact with her.

It honestly felt worse than being invisible. If no one could see her, then the way she got ignored had a reason that wasn't simply her personality.

She pushed her way through the luxurious glass doors that led into the office, unsurprised to find the lights on but no one there. Suzie could go through her physical mail and start on her email before another soul walked in.

Moving past the other empty cubicles, Suzie nearly tripped over her feet when she saw Mandie sitting at her desk. Part of her wanted to stop and say hello, maybe ask Mandie how her weekend was.

Something clenched in Suzie's stomach, and she walked right on by, her ankle boots making plenty of noise against the industrial carpet. Mandie surely heard her, but Suzie didn't look behind her.

Mandie seemed nice, but she was at least fifteen years younger than Suzie and already married. She came from Five Island Cove, which meant her family had plenty of money, and Suzie honestly didn't think they could really be friends.

Maybe if you tried, she thought as she arrived in her cube and sat down. Mandie could try too, and she'd only ever glared in Suzie's direction.

She'd just sent her notes to the printer—which sat clear across the office—when her phone buzzed and then shrieked as it started to ring. She'd assigned that ringtone to Candace, and Suzie quickly swiped the device from her bag.

"Hey," she said crisply.

"Where are you right now?"

Suzie hesitated, because she'd been told to work normal hours by the hardnosed woman on the other end of the line.

"Suzie, I don't have time for this. If you can't answer me—"

"I'm sitting in my office," she barked out.

"Great, I need to see you right now."

"Are you—?" Suzie got to her feet and twisted toward the offices along the back wall, the ones with windows. "Here?"

"Yes, I'm here. Come now." Candace ended the call, which sent a full-on shiver down Suzie's spine.

Part of her wanted to deliberately take a few extra minutes to gather her printouts, then head to the restroom to make sure her hair hadn't been disturbed by her subway ride from Brooklyn to Manhattan.

Down the row, Mandie got to her feet too. She visibly gave herself a little shake, ran her hands through her hair, faced Candace's office, and marched with decided determination toward it.

Suzie's heartbeat swept through her body as if it had lost all its peaks and valleys. Flat-lined. Mandie had been called into Candace's office too?

To make matters worse, someone pushed their way through the glass doors fifteen yards from Suzie, her phone stuck to her ear. Alicia Halverson looked like a million bucks, as always, though a bit harried as she too beelined for Candace's office without even bothering to stop by her own desk space.

Suzie watched as the second woman entered their boss's office, her feet somehow still glued to the floor. Her phone chimed again, and Suzie's body jolted. Thankfully, her mind got the electric pulse too, and she started for the office as well.

Candace's office had windows flanking both sides of the closed door, and she'd fired people for entering without knocking. So Suzie paused at the door to rap on it, feeling a measure of stupidity she hadn't in a while.

She told herself she was far too old to have so much anxiety over who she was, and when Candace yelled, "Come in," Suzie pulled the same move as Mandie and squared her shoulders.

The scene in the office opened up, and she found both Mandie and Alicia seated in the only two chairs in the room. All three of them stared at her, and Suzie distinctly told herself not to tug on the bottom of her jacket.

"Good, you're here." Candace did not say anything about where Suzie should sit or stand, so she simply moved far enough into the office to close the door behind her. She glanced at Mandie, who snapped her mouth closed and narrowed her eyes. She then turned back to Candace, Alicia mirroring her.

Suzie cleared her throat and moved to stand behind and between their chairs. Candace clicked on something on her computer, a pair of glasses perched on her nose. She didn't seem to be in such a hurry now, and a silent scream gathered in Suzie's throat.

Candace clicked one more time and sighed as she swung her attention to the three of them waiting for her. "Brandt broke his leg."

"You're kidding," Mandie said.

Candace gave her a withering look that Mandie didn't wilt from. Good for her. The boss's eyes came to Suzie's. "I know you're not done with the West Hills Monster, but these ladies need a bulldozer."

"You're—" Alicia glanced at Suzie and then Candace, but Suzie couldn't look away from her boss. "She's going to be the new bulldozer."

"Yes," Candace said. "If Suzie can handle the double load for a little bit."

Suzie's heart throbbed in the back of her throat, caging her voice there, keeping it mute. She knew everyone around the office had nicknamed her "The Bulldozer," though others had the same job as her. All men, and they didn't seem to get any flack for what they did on the abandoned mansion restorations.

She tried to soften her expression from one of pure shock—and yes, some complete fear at having to work with the two women seated in front of her—but she didn't quite pull it off. She'd spent so long establishing her tough exterior that she wasn't sure how to let it down anymore.

Maybe, just maybe, she could show Mandie and Alicia a different side of herself. To prove that she could be more than just the abrasive, no-nonsense worker bee everyone thought she was.

"Can you do it?" Candace asked. "What is wrong with you this morning?" Her eyes swept down to Suzie's shoes and back. "You're acting weird."

"I'm fine," Suzie said, her voice just as short as ever. "I can handle the load for a little bit. It's mostly prep in the beginning anyway."

"I'll make sure she has everything she needs," Mandie said.

"I'm sure you will," Candace said with the tone the same humidity as the Sahara Dessert. "Since you're all here early, I want the three of you to pow-wow before our regularly scheduled meeting."

"What time is that?" Suzie asked.

"Nine," Candace said, which gave them more than a few minutes to "pow-wow." Suzie didn't even know what that meant, but she wasn't going to say anything.

She felt so out of place standing there, and the shiver of anticipation and maybe a little fear turned to dread. Mandie and Alicia clearly didn't like her, not that she'd ever given them a reason to.

So give them a reason to, she told herself as Alicia stood. Candace had handed her a folder, their meeting clearly over. Alicia turned and nearly came chest-to-chest with Suzie, who stood in her way.

She blinked, the moment lengthening and turning awkward and weird before Suzie clued in that she was the problem. "Sorry," she muttered, and then she spun on her heel and marched out of the office ahead of everyone else.

Some life had started to crawl into the office, and Suzie fed off the buzz of the extra people.

"Should we meet in the conference room?" Mandie asked, and she sounded a tiny bit timid.

"Sure," Alicia said easily, and Suzie wondered why she couldn't be friends with them. In that moment, all she wanted was to be friends with these two women, as oddly paired as they might all be. Alicia was somewhere in her thirties, and Suzie didn't feel nearly as threatened by her as she did Mandie.

That also made no sense, but she simply nodded at the other two women. They exchanged a glance that said something not-great about Suzie, she knew that, and then they headed for the conference room.

They suddenly felt like the golden girls of PastForward, always so effortlessly perfect and popular, while she was the older, uglier duckling.

She'd never worked directly with either of these women, but PastForward wasn't a big place, and people talked.

Mandie's first project had been the Millbrook Estate, and when things had gotten heated with one of their structural decisions, all of the bulldozers had gotten together to brainstorm some ideas for Mike, who'd been on the team.

Suzie had pushed for a more thorough investigation of the property's foundations, while Mike had two reports already and was satisfied he knew what to do.

The argument had escalated, with Suzie's blunt words and forceful demeanor clashing against his more diplomatic approach. In the end, Suzie had been right about the foundation issues, but the victory had felt hollow. She'd overheard Mandie, Alicia, and Mike talking about her later, using words like "impossible" and "nightmare to work with."

Taking a deep breath, Suzie moved after them. She'd faced down rotting floorboards and rabid raccoons in abandoned mansions. She could handle a couple of coworkers who didn't like her. Still, a small part of her ached for acceptance, for the easy camaraderie she saw between others in the office. What would it be like to have friends like that? To grab coffee together, to share stories and laugh over inside jokes?

As she approached the conference room, Suzette caught a glimpse of her reflection in the glass. For a moment, she saw herself as others might see her: tall, imposing, with that perpetual scowl etched on her freckled face. "The Bulldozer," ready to plow through anyone who got in her way.

Her heart crashed to the soles of her feet. She didn't want to be that person.

Perhaps this was her chance to change that. To show them who she really was, beneath the tough exterior. Suzette thought of her passion for historical architecture, her meticulous attention to detail, her genuine desire to preserve the stories and cultures of the past. If only she could find a way to let that side of herself shine through.

Inside the conference room, the air crackled with unspoken judgments and pure tension. Mandie turned to face her as Alicia set the folder on the table, and Suzie wasn't sure if she should blurt out an apology to begin or let the other women lead.

Since she'd never been much of a follower, she took a breath and prayed her words would come forward in the right order.

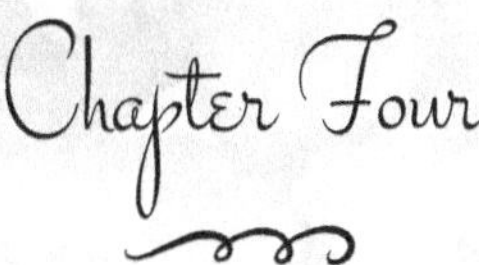

Chapter Four

Mandie's stomach clenched as Suzette Paxman entered the conference room. The older woman's imposing frame seemed to fill the doorway, her face set in its usual stern expression. She looked like she'd rather be anywhere but in the conference room with Mandie and Alicia.

Mandie glanced over to her best friend, who arranged and rearranged the papers from the folder Candace had given her, pointedly avoiding eye contact with Suzie. So she wasn't going to get any help there.

The air in the room held a charge, so high that Mandie could barely breathe. Her mind raced. She was the point person, the one everyone would look to for the duration of this project.

Including, supposedly, Suzette.

"Listen," Suzie said. "I just want to say I'm sorry." Her

blue-green eyes flicked over to Alicia, who'd likewise frozen.

Mandie had started to take a deep breath, and it choked in her throat. She coughed as heat rose through her face. "I—"

"I can maybe come across a little strongly sometimes." Suzette pulled back the closest chair and sank into it. "I know you guys call me The Bulldozer." She wore an accusatory glint in her eye now.

Mandie cleared her throat as Alicia blinked and blinked and blinked. "You're...a good bulldozer on a project," she came up. Her words sounded ridiculous to her own ears. "I just—you weren't even on the Millbrook Estate."

"I know." Suzette nodded and brushed her strawberry blonde hair out of her eyes, while Mandie expected her to argue. "I know you're team lead, and I know what my job is."

"You're very good at your job," Alicia said, which painted relief through Mandie.

She nodded. "Yes, Lish is right."

"Lish?" Suzette's eyebrows went up. "If we're going to use nicknames, you guys can call me Suzie."

Mandie took a seat too, glad when Alicia did as well. The three of them sat there, and Mandie glanced around at them. "Suzie." The name didn't sound quite right as it moved across her tongue, but she forged onward. "You've been here the longest out of all of us. Has there been an all-female team on a project this size before?"

Suzie tilted her head and looked at Mandie thoughtfully. "I don't think so." Her expression lit up, and she folded her arms on the table in front of her. "I can look into it."

Mandie nodded at her and said, "Too bad about Brandt," then wanted to crawl under the table and hide.

"What happened?" Suzie asked. "Did Candace say?"

"He went Upstate," Mandie said. "Water skiing."

Alicia smiled. "Bet Candace loved that."

Mandie allowed a tiny smile to cross her face. None of Candace's texts indicated that she liked Brandt going water skiing over the weekend. "So, the Hampton House."

"Yes." Alicia cleared her throat. "We need every duck lined up before nine a.m."

Mandie nodded, grateful for the shift to business. "Good idea. Suzie, do you know a bit about the house?"

"I read the same proposals as everyone," she said. Another flash of a smile graced her lips. "And I have a slight obsession with the Hamptons."

Another round of silence filled the room, while Mandie tried to formulate a response. Alicia finally broke the quiet with a little giggle. "I do too. I can't wait to spend my days out there."

"I have ties to the Harrington family," Suzie said, once again tucking her hair. On-site, she no doubt wore it up.

"Ooh, fancy," Alicia said, and Mandie relaxed into the more casual atmosphere. Maybe this project wouldn't be a complete disaster.

Of course, Mandie would never allow it to become

such. This was only her second field assignment, and she wanted to prove to Candace that she had the chops to handle anything thrown her way.

Including a broken leg and the reassignment of a bulldozer who steamrolled everyone she came in contact with.

"What if we approach the restoration from a cultural perspective?" Mandie suggested. "There's so much history in the Hamptons."

"We could plan to tour the historic mansions there and make some notes on the styles, from the prominent families of the time." Suzie glanced over to Alicia, and Mandie loved working with people who loved culture and history as much as she did.

Alicia had an accounting background, but she had an excellent eye for historical document preservation as well. "We could incorporate elements from different eras, showcasing how the Hamptons, its residents, and thus its architecture, evolved over time."

Despite her initial reservations about working with Suzette, a flicker of excitement tickled inside her. "I like these ideas." Mandie had her own notes on the house—she'd prepared extensively for the meeting this morning.

She tapped to open her phone and started adding the things Suzie and Alicia had said. Mandie didn't know all the intricate history of the Hamptons, but now she wanted to learn more—and this project just took on a whole new meaning for Mandie.

Her excitement doubled. Now, she just had to make it

through this morning's meeting and the next couple of weeks of prep before the on-site work began.

———

SEVERAL DAYS LATER, SHE BREATHED IN THE scent of the salt air as the ferry pulled into the dock. Other passengers had started to move closer to the exit, but Mandie stayed in her seat with her hand in Charlie's.

"Are you going to tell me what's going on before we meet up with our parents?" he asked as the boat bumped into place.

She glanced over to him, and she didn't have to ask what he meant.

"We've come to Five Island Cove two weekends in a row," he said. "Your mom is going to have a million questions, and I feel like I should know the answers too."

"You know all the answers." She snuggled into his chest, a sense of safety and comfort running through her when he put his arm around her.

"You let work too far in."

"I just want to be good at this," she said.

"You *are* good at this," he said. "You're so amazing you got the biggest house your company has restored in the past several years."

"Suzie will change the moment we get in the field."

Charlie drew in a breath, his chest rising as he did. Mandie had dominated their evening conversations this week after finding out Brandt had been injured and Suzie would be on her team. He'd been patient with her, and since his classes were over, and his internship hadn't started yet, Charlie had been working around their apartment, going through their closets, and making sure dinner sat on the table when Mandie walked in the door.

"This project is going to be amazing," he said as he stood. He pulled her to her feet and looked her straight in the eye. "Because you're amazing."

Mandie melted into his arms, a smile filling her from top to bottom and side to side. "Maybe we should just stay on the boat and go home."

"Too late for that," Charlie said dryly. "You told Ginny we were coming, and she and Bob came last night so we can spend today at the beach with them."

"I just—we haven't seen them in a while." Ginny had married Bob several months before Mandie and Charlie had tied the knot, and they'd been living in Boston while he finished law school and started at a prestigious firm in the city.

Mandie loved Ginny like her own sister, and as much as Charlie calmed her, his twin sister did the same.

She moved with Charlie toward the exit. "We love beach day with everyone."

"Yeah," he said, and Mandie simply let him take care of everything from there. He carried their bags; he got them a RideShare to the beach; he led her toward the red umbrellas that always marked the spot where their parents met with their friends for beach days.

Mandie tugged on his hand to get him to stop. "Charlie."

He stopped and turned toward her, and she loved the compassion and worry mingling in his expression. She stepped into his chest and leaned into her palms there. "You know I love you endlessly, right?"

He ducked his head, but gone was his long hair that would fall down over his eyes. "Yeah, sweetheart. I know that."

"And sometimes I just need my mom, but it has nothing to do with how I feel about you."

"So you've said."

"Ginny comes to see your mom all the time," Mandie pressed. "It's just what we women do."

"I know you're close with your mom, Mandie." Charlie leaned down and kissed her. "I love you too, you know, and *I* want to be the one to help you."

"You do help me," she murmured against his lips. "You're everything to me."

He nodded slightly, touched his lips to hers again, and said, "All right. Let's go join them. I'm sure your mom already knows you're here."

Mandie smiled at him as she stepped back. "She knows *we're* here." She faced the three red umbrellas again, and sure enough, her mom ducked underneath one a moment later. Mandie's chest shook with emotion, because she did sometimes simply need her mother. She needed to hear her voice tell her she was smart, and capable, and that it was okay to feel all the frustrating things she felt.

So, even though Charlie had always given her that space, told her the same things, and gave her the same permissions, Mandie grinned and headed toward her mom at a much faster pace than before.

"You're here," Mom said as she opened her arms to Mandie.

She stepped into them, sinking into her mother's embrace, and she knew what Charlie had been telling her was true: The Hampton House was going to challenge her—but she was ready for it.

Even with Suzie on her team. Even with her limited field experience. Even with everything else going on in her life.

She was ready for this, and she was going to conquer it.

"All right," Mom said as she stepped back. "Come tell me everything." She faced Charlie as he moved to Mandie's side, and Mom grabbed onto him too. "Oh, it's so good to see you again, Charlie. How's the city?"

"It's good," Charlie said, because he far preferred the hustling, bustling city to the slower pace of Five Island Cove. Mandie loved them both for different reasons, and today, she craved the low-key beach life she'd once exclusively lived.

Mandie let Charlie and Mom go ahead of her, each of them now carrying a bag, and she simply stood in the hot sand and faced the vast water. "I can do this," she told herself, her voice barely more than a whisper.

Now, she just needed to hope and pray she actually could take the dilapidated mansion and turn it into a historical gem—oh, and stay within budget, complete the project on time, and work with personalities she'd never gotten along with.

No wonder she needed this beach day, because she, Alicia, and Suzie had a trip planned to the Hamptons for Monday morning.

Once she ducked under the umbrella, Mandie's heart felt like she'd just sunk into the warmest, calmest water possible. She loved her family—and everyone here, whether they shared her DNA or not—felt like family.

"Hello, dear," Alice said. Charlie's mom folded her into a hug. "We've got lunch over here."

"Thank you." Mandie pulled back, all smiles. She followed Alice over to a stack of coolers, where Charlie had opened the top one. He held three sandwiches in his hand, and he looked at her when she stopped beside him.

"Ham and cheddar," he said. "Turkey and Swiss. Or Arthur made salami, pepperoni, and provolone." He made a quick face, and Mandie giggled. No way he would choose that one.

"There's roast beef too," Alice said, but she didn't join them at the cooler. She simply moved over to the chair she'd obviously vacated.

"Ham or turkey is fine with me," Mandie said.

Charlie handed her a couple of sandwiches and said, "I'll get drinks and chips."

Mandie grabbed a bag of homemade brownie bites too, because Kristen had made those, and they made a party in her mouth. She sank into the chair beside Alice, her mother just on the other side of one of her best friends.

"So," Alice said. She lifted her soda can to her mouth and took a shallow sip. That wasn't good, and Mandie's defenses automatically rose. "I hear you're working in the Hamptons now."

A smile spread through Mandie, chasing away some of her anxiety. "Yeah," she said. "A big mansion there. Rumored to be from the late eighteen hundreds, owned by a shipping tycoon." She looked past Alice to her mom, who grinned at her.

In front of them, children ran and played in the sand, with still others out splashing in the ocean. Mandie missed the lazier days of her youth, with her sister and both of her parents here. But her dad had been fishing in Alaska every summer for years now, and Jamie, her younger sister, was off at college in Maryland.

"We're going out to see the house soon," she said. "It's been delayed a little, as we had to wait on our videographer."

"No need to rush out there," Alice said as Charlie sat beside Mandie. His mother glanced over to him. "Do you guys go out to the Hamptons a lot?"

Charlie took his sandwich from Mandie and shook his head. "Nope."

Alice seemed happy about that, her nods more enthusiastic. "Good," she said. "You've got to be careful in the Hamptons."

"Careful?" Mandie looked over to Charlie and then

back to Alice. They both simply gazed out at the water. "What am I missing?"

"The Hamptons can consume a person," Alice said.

Mandie reached over to Charlie and took his hand. "It's not going to consume me." She did tend to get ultra-focused on things she was passionate about, and she'd already spoken to Charlie about making sure she didn't do that with this project.

It's just a house, she'd told him.

It's just a house, he'd echoed back.

Mandie hadn't even been out to the house yet. She leaned closer to Charlie. "We should take a cab out to the Hamptons to see your old house and the mansion."

He looked at her out of the corner of his eye. "We should?"

"Can we?" She leaned her head against his bicep, and he sighed.

"I suppose."

"It's not going to consume me." She lifted her head and looked over to Alice. "It's not."

Alice gave her a kind smile and patted her hand. "I sincerely hope not." She gazed out to the water again. "The Hamptons...just beware of what feels like magic there."

Mandie heard her, but she didn't believe her. "This is my job," she said. "There's not going to be anything magical about it." Those words felt right as she said them, and Mandie nodded for good measure, as if to solidify her feelings.

"That's not what she means, sweetheart," Charlie murmured.

"Then what does she mean?"

Charlie simply put the last bite of his sandwich in his mouth, and when he finished his sandwich, he leaned over and pressed a kiss to her temple. "We'll go out and see the houses this week."

"Okay." Mandie finally unwrapped her sandwich and took a bite of the ham and cheese, with the creamy mayo and tangy mustard. They'd go see his house, where Charlie had lived for the first fourteen years of his life, and they'd go by the Hampton House.

They're just houses, she told herself. She wasn't going to get sucked into anything magical or consumed by the job in the Hamptons.

She wasn't.

Chapter Five

Alicia keyed her way into her apartment, pure exhaustion pulling through her shoulders.

"Mama! Mama!" her daughter called, and Alicia put a smile on her face for Lily. Something smelled good in the apartment, which meant her mother was cooking. Alicia wasn't going to be upset about that.

"Hey, baby," she said as she knelt down and took her five-year-old into her arms. She didn't see Lily's brother anywhere and asked, "Where's Gray?"

"Gram-Mary put him in timeout," Lily said soberly, her dark eyes like a sad puppy dog.

Alicia looked to the back of the apartment, where her mother pulled a pot off the stove and started pouring the boiling water down the sink. She was probably making macaroni and cheese or spaghetti, which were two of the kids' favorite meals.

Alicia had been relying more and more on her mom

for babysitting help since her divorce had been finalized. Ryan had moved across the river to Jersey, making coordinating custody difficult, as well as childcare. He had a full-time job as well, and they'd struggled to make sure all their bases were covered when they were together. Now that they had to manage things separately, everything in Alicia's life felt like it was being held together by dental floss.

Still, a bubbling excitement entered her bloodstream whenever she thought about working on the Hampton House. She couldn't give it up, though she knew the days would be longer, her commute harder, and she might have to rely on people more than she wanted to.

Her last three texts to Ryan had gone unanswered as she'd tried to coordinate getting the kids to him on Saturday evenings and then picking them up on Tuesday night. That would give her two days that she didn't have to coordinate childcare while she worked. Something needled inside her, telling her that she needed to talk to Mandie and probably Suzie to let them know that Wednesday, Thursday, and Friday would be harder for her to be on-site early or stay late. But Monday and Tuesday were hers. She could be there from dawn till dusk—if she could get Ryan to answer her texts.

So you'll text him after the kids go to bed, she told herself. With that plan in place, she straightened and moved toward the kitchen. "Mom, how'd it go today?"

Her mom twisted to look over her shoulder, acting as if she didn't know someone had entered the apartment. "Good," she said. "Well, good enough."

Alicia glanced down the hall that led to the two bedrooms and single bathroom in this apartment in the Bronx. "Gray got in trouble?"

Her mother turned her back on her and lifted the pasta out of the sink to pour it into the saucepan. She started to mix it all together—the steaming red sauce, the hot ground beef—and Alicia's stomach roared.

"Oh, he just sassed me a little bit," her mom said. "It's no big deal. You can go get him out. Dinner will be ready in a few minutes." She pulled open the oven. "I'm just waiting on this garlic bread."

Alicia's gratitude for her mother knew no bounds, so she stepped over to her mom and gave her a quick side squeeze before saying, "I'll be right back."

She went down the hall, noting that someone had lined the baseboards with marbles—her son, of course. Gray seemed obsessed with building things, and that included racetracks for marbles. His grandfather had given him a side-by-side racing track that he'd built as a boy, and Gray loved it with his whole heart.

Alicia knocked on his door a couple of times and then pushed it open. She found Gray kneeling on the floor in front of the track, two marbles poised and ready to go. He looked over his shoulder at her, something nervous in his eight-year-old expression.

Alicia folded her arms. "Let them go," she said, smiling to let him know he wasn't in any trouble with her.

Gray released the marbles, and they rolled down the track. Ryan had told him many times about gravity and how technically, the marbles should arrive at the bottom of the track at the same time. But inevitably, one always made it before the other.

Alicia entered the room and knelt down on the floor next to her son just as the marbles reached the bottom. A big blue one with a cloudy white streak through it won, and he grabbed it before it fell off the track. He nabbed the other one too, more of a golden-green cat's eye, and handed it to her.

"I get the losing one?" she asked.

Gray shrugged one bony shoulder and reached to pick up a couple more marbles.

"You sassed Gram-Mary," she said next. "What was it about?"

"Just something stupid with Alan," Gray said. "I wanted to go over there and look at his baseball cards. Gram-Mary said we didn't have time."

Alicia didn't want to be the heavy when she came home from work. She barely saw the kids as it was, and now that they didn't have school, she didn't have to be on his case about homework all the time. Of course he wanted to see his friends, not be stuck in this apartment with his grandma.

"Well, Gram-Mary probably knows what time you guys need to be places," she said. "You've got to find a better way at communicating than getting upset."

"I know," Gray said, and Alicia pulled him into her chest and hugged him.

"We can go to the beach this weekend."

Gray's face brightened. "Can we?"

"Yes." Alicia smiled. It didn't cost much to put together a picnic lunch and head down to the beach. She could even go to the Hamptons, probably drive out by the big mansion where she was going to be working, and show the kids. She had to feed them anyway, and sitting on the sand and listening to the waves was free.

"Dinner!" her mom called. Alicia got to her feet and extended her hand to Gray.

"Come on," she said. "You know you have to apologize to Gram-Mary."

"All right," he said, suddenly sullen again, but he went down the hall and eased right into his grandmother's arms, hugging her tight around the middle. "I'm sorry, Gram-Mary."

"Oh, it's okay, you sweet boy." Alicia's mother pressed a kiss to the top of his head and served everyone dinner. She only stayed for a few more minutes, not even eating the spaghetti she'd made, before she shouldered her purse and headed for the door. Alicia went after her, her heart pounding in her throat.

"Thank you so much, Mom," she said, hugging her. "You help me so much. I really appreciate it."

Her mom pulled back. "Anytime, dear. Do you know what your schedule will be like next week?"

"I haven't gotten in touch with Ryan yet," Alicia said. "His custody days are Sunday, Monday, and Tuesday. So."

Everyone knew that, as they'd been living this custody schedule for the last six months. It was easier while school was in, though Ryan had complained about crossing the river to take Gray to his school here in the Bronx. But really, Alicia didn't care what Ryan didn't like.

He'd chosen to move to New Jersey. *He'd* chosen to cheat on her. *He'd* chosen to go with his mistress instead of fighting for his marriage. That meant he could cross the river to take their children to school and pick them up on Mondays and Tuesdays. She had the kids the other sixty percent of the time. And yes, it was easier to live three blocks away from the school and be able to finish her work from home once they got out.

But again, choices had been made, and they had to be lived with. It wasn't her job to make Ryan's life easier. Not anymore.

"I'll let you know," Alicia said, feeling a weight settle on the back of her neck. "Thanks for dinner, Mom. You're the best."

Her mom smiled, brushed a kiss across her cheek, and left. Alicia turned and faced the apartment. It wasn't the little house she and Ryan had purchased to raise their family. No little backyard, no single car driveway with a detached garage in the back, no plans to finish the basement and have more kids.

But Alicia couldn't afford all that on her own. And while Ryan did pay spousal support and child support and she had a full-time job, this was the best she could do right now. The kids shared a bedroom, which was fine because they were only five and eight. But Alicia knew as they grew up, she would have to provide them with their own rooms.

Worry rained through her, and she pushed it away the best she could. She sighed, pulled her hair out of its ponytail, and returned to the kitchen.

"Tell me three fun things you did today," she said brightly, pointing her fork at Gray. "You go first."

That got the kids talking, and Alicia spent the next couple of hours focused solely on them—their needs, what they'd have tomorrow for lunch with her mom, and planning a beach day for the following day, Saturday, when she'd then take public transit to Jersey and drop them off at their father's. Lily needed her laundry done before then, and Gray had a baseball game on Sunday, so he'd need his sports bag.

Once Alicia got the kids to bed, she sat down at the dining room table and started to make a to-do list for the next several days. At the very top went *Work out childcare for the summer.*

Her ex had to talk to her, but Alicia put off the task by walking around the apartment and picking up toys, putting shoes on the rack in the closet, hanging up sweatshirts, and organizing her work files.

Two warring emotions ran through her with every task she did and every item she put away—guilt that she was neglecting her children and excitement that she had work files for what was going to be an amazing project.

She, Mandie, and Suzie had been getting along pretty well for the past couple of weeks, and they'd make their debut trip to the Hamptons on Monday. When she couldn't put it off any longer and the clock ticked closer and closer to ten, she finally settled on the couch and started texting.

Ryan, she said, *I really need you to text me back. I have to know what we're doing next week. You said you might have a work trip, and I'm going to be out in the Hamptons on a project. Will you be able to take the kids on your regular days?*

She read over the words, proud of herself for setting a limit. Her therapist had told her she hadn't established enough boundaries in her marriage, and now, in the divorce, she had to do better.

If you don't text me back in the next ten minutes, I'm going to call you until you answer and we work this out.

He worked a busy job in construction management, and he got up early and got off early. It was also not her problem if he was already in bed. She'd given him three days to answer her previous texts, and he hadn't done it. He could do so in the next ten minutes, or she'd wake him up.

Then, feeling bold and brave, she opened a text string and included Mandie and Suzie on it. She hesitated, wondering if she should add Flint. He was still putting the final touches on his latest project, but he would go with them on Monday and do the drone flyover of the Hampton House.

They always took before shots, a lot of them. Flint would work in the Hamptons every day next week getting before shots while Mandie, Alicia, and Suzie finalized their plans for the on-the-ground renovations that wouldn't start until the next week

Flint and his crew also went through the mansion early and then didn't come back for a while. Most of the projects PastForward did showcased two or three major items in the mansion to go through in detail, and then the video showed before and after shots of the enormity of the project. With something as big as the Hampton House—almost sixteen thousand square feet—there would be a lot of before and after shots.

In the end, Alicia decided not to include Flint. She liked him. They went to lunch a couple of times each week, and she'd known him for a few years—long enough to trust him. But Mandie was her best friend at work, probably her best friend in her whole life besides her mother and her sister, who lived in Kansas.

Alicia hadn't even told Mandie about her divorce yet. She swallowed, not quite sure why she felt like it was her fault. She hadn't been the one to cheat with a high school girlfriend that she'd reconnected with through social media. She hadn't been the one to lie to her spouse and break her marriage vows. And yet, something thick in her throat made it hard for her to tell anyone about her separation and subsequent divorce.

Only a few neighbors in this building knew, and Alicia actually found great relief in not living on the same street, in the same house, where she and Ryan had started to build their life together.

Hey, guys, Alicia typed out. *I just wanted to let you know that I recently got divorced. My ex is living in New Jersey now, working on a big project there, and that makes childcare hard for my five- and eight-year-old. I don't have them on Mondays and Tuesdays, which means those are the best days for me to put in long and extra hours on our project. The other days of the week are a little bit harder, but I'm working on childcare and shouldn't have a problem being where I need to be.*

She swallowed and read through the message again, then added, *I just wanted to let you guys know, but I haven't told anyone else yet. Not even Candace. Please don't tell anyone.* She stabbed at the send button before she could second-guess herself, and the message went flying through cyberspace. She couldn't call it back now, and somehow, the invisible weight and burden that she'd been carrying lifted right off of her shoulders.

She hadn't expected that, but it sure felt good. Not only that, but a text from Ryan came in. *I can take the kids on our normal custody days next week and the week after that. I do have a work trip that got moved to the third week of June, and I won't be able to take them at all that week. But I can take them all of the week after.*

Relief pounded through Alicia's bloodstream. That was a whole month of childcare worked out in a simple text, and she sent back, *Thank you. Let me type up the dates, and you can see if they're right.*

She quickly did that, giving him Saturday night to Tuesday night for the next couple of weeks, nothing for the week after that, and then Saturday night to Tuesday night—almost ten days—the week after that.

Is that right? she asked.

For several moments, she waited. Thankfully, neither Mandie nor Suzie responded immediately either. She wasn't sure what Suzie did. If she lived with roommates. If she was married. If she had a boyfriend. Alicia had no idea.

But Mandie was married, and she seemed to be more of a morning person than a night owl, so Alicia wasn't surprised that she hadn't answered.

That looks fine, Ryan said. *I'd like to keep them all the way through the next Tuesday after that. My mom wants to see them for the Fourth.*

The Fourth fell on a Thursday this year, and she'd be getting them back the Tuesday before. But if he kept them through that week, all the way through to the following Tuesday, that simply gave Alicia less to worry about.

That will be fine, she said. *Thank you, Ryan.*

Their divorce hadn't been terribly ugly. He hadn't wanted to go to therapy. He hadn't wanted to work things out. He'd made his choice, and it wasn't her or the kids, though he claimed to love them. And he did agree to the custody as she had suggested it. She worried about them when he got up and had to be on-site by six a.m., but he had a brother in Jersey, and his mother lived here in the city as well.

With that done, Alicia moved over to the calendar in the kitchen and updated it for when the kids would be with her and when they would be with Ryan. She could text her mom in the morning, as suddenly her emotional exhaustion caught up to her physical exhaustion.

She worked full-time outside the home and always had plenty to do at home with the kids. As she looked at the days, at how long Ryan would have them this summer, relief and guilt chased each other. Alicia didn't want to be relieved that she didn't have to take care of her kids. She loved her kids. She'd never had to battle these emotions when she'd been married.

Tears pricked her eyes, and she brushed them away quickly, focused on cleaning up dinner, something she hadn't done yet. There was always more to do, both at work and at home. By the time she made it down the hall to her bedroom, Alicia had decided to simply let the tears win.

She cried for the things that she'd lost. She cried for the things that she'd gained: her freedom, her dignity, some measure of control. She cried for her children and the fact that they had to go back and forth between two houses, between their mother and their father.

But what she didn't cry over was this assignment. She was going to knock this out of the park, prove to everyone at PastForward, especially Candace, that she was good at her job and deserved more recognition, more assignments, and more responsibility.

Now all she had to do was get out there and earn it.

Chapter Six

Mandie felt like she had swallowed an angry nest of hornets. They'd suddenly realized they no longer had access to the sun, flowers, or fresh air, and they started to sting through her insides, desperate to get out.

Perhaps it was the erratic way Suzie weaved in and out of traffic as they made their way from Manhattan to the Hamptons. Or perhaps it was the fact that they were going to the Hamptons for the first time as a team.

Alicia had texted over the weekend with some pictures of the house from the road behind the gate when she'd taken her kids to the beach. Mandie had driven by the Hampton House too, but only on a bus, as she and Charlie didn't own a car. They really didn't see the need in the city. Anywhere they had to go, they could get there on public transportation.

She rode in the front passenger seat with Alicia behind

her, and Mandie really wished she had someone to give her some words of encouragement about now.

"We're almost there," Alicia said. There weren't that many roads out here in the Hamptons. It was an island, a finger that branched off the city of New York. It wasn't like there were a lot of congested roadways and different turns where they could get lost.

Suzie slammed on the brakes and yelled, "Do you not see me?" which only set Mandie's nerves further on edge. She ground her teeth together and wished that she'd found a different way to get to the house. But the mansion waited today, and Henry Swinton, a member of the Hampton Historical Society, would be there to unlock the gate and let them in.

He was a local historian with some expertise in restoration. He'd worked with PastForward on other houses in the New York area, and Candace loved him. That meant Mandie needed him to love her so he would give a good report to her boss. She felt like so much rode on what was happening right now, and she really didn't need Suzie slamming on the brakes and yanking the wheel to the right, as if she might ram the truck in front of them.

Mandie clutched her clipboard and clenched her knees around her backpack, which held her lunch and all the files she needed for the Hampton House. She had them memorized but had brought them along anyway, including the work permit that she needed to show Henry that morning.

"You missed it," Alicia said from the backseat.

"I'm aware," Suzie griped back at her. She flipped on her blinker, and Mandie reached up to hang onto the handle above the window as Suzie pulled over and flipped around—without a proper gap in traffic.

"It's right there on the right now," Alicia said once Suzie had made a U-turn without killing them and started back down the road.

"I see it," Suzie snapped back at her.

Alicia showed great restraint by not bickering back, and Mandie pressed her lips together as Suzie made the turn onto a quieter road. A couple of houses sat here, one on each side of the short road, their destination down at the end, where a huge, ornate gate stood.

Mandie started to relax for some reason. She loved old things, fancy things, and expensive things. This house had it all. She couldn't wait to get inside and see what hung on the walls, what had been left in the cupboards, where all the nooks and crannies were, and if there were any hidden staircases or passageways.

Old mansions like this from the late eighteen hundreds often had them, and the Hampton House was rumored to have belonged to the Harrington family. The Hamptons had once been a playground for the rich and famous, the elite of New York City's society life.

Mandie could imagine herself back then, getting dressed up in sequined gowns and feathery hats and attending the most lavish parties away from the city. Summer was when the Hamptons really came alive, and they still had a vibrant restaurant community with soirées and parties, and a vibrant beach atmosphere where one could expect to see celebrities on any given day of the week.

"This is it," Alicia said, and her voice carried the same excitement that ran through Mandie.

The hornets still stung, but Mandie had been nervous about other things in her life that she'd done anyway. Going to college, telling her mom she was going to marry her high school boyfriend, actually getting married to her high school boyfriend, moving from apartment to apartment, looking for a job.

She may only be twenty-five years old, but she'd done some hard things in her life—hard for her, anyway. This was simply one more. She was the team lead at the Hampton House, leading two women at least a decade older than her and reporting to another woman who had fired people for walking in five minutes late, forgetting a folder, or having their appendix burst and not being able to finish a project.

Nerves still stole through her like a thief in the night. Mandie didn't think she'd be able to get rid of them until she finished this project.

Another car sat in front of the gate, and Mandie locked eyes with a man across the hoods of the two vehicles as she stood and straightened.

"You must be Henry," she said pleasantly.

He wore a suit—a crisp black suit in the summer— with a burgundy pocket square and a tie that matched.

Mandie could not imagine what his job was like, or his life for that matter. She rounded the hood with a smile, her hand outstretched.

"I'm Mandie Kelton, team lead on the Hampton House project for PastForward."

"Yes," he said. "Candace sent ahead your bios and pictures." He glanced at Suzie and Alicia as they both got out of the car as well. "Suzie is the blonde," he added.

He smiled as he took Mandie's hand and shook it. Suzie stepped over and saluted him, such a Suzie thing to do. Mandie very nearly rolled her eyes but managed to refrain at the last moment. Then Suzie stuck out her hand and pumped Henry's a couple of times.

"Nice to meet you," he said, clear shock in his tone and moving across his face.

"And Alicia Halverson," he said, his eyes zeroing in on her as Suzie backed up.

Alicia followed Mandie around the car and shook his hand, her smile pleasant as well. "It's great to meet you, Henry," she said. "I think we worked together on a mansion in Upstate New York, but I came in at the very end after another one of our team members got ill and couldn't finish."

"Oh, right." He smiled widely. "Right," he repeated. "That was a beautiful property. On a lake, if I remember correctly."

Alicia smiled back at him and gathered her hair into a ponytail. "It was; you're correct."

That project was before Mandie's time, so she made no

comment on it. In fact, she simply wanted to get into this house, past this gate. Her fingers itched for it. She wished she had eyes that could see through solid objects.

"This place is rumored to have gardens and walkways," she said. "How long has it been since you've been inside?" She pulled her gaze away from the gate and looked at Henry again. He hadn't looked away from Alicia yet, though, and in fact, he still held her hand.

Alicia cleared her throat and pulled away, which seemed to jolt Henry back to the present situation. "I'm sorry, what?" he asked in his regular refined, dignified voice.

"I asked how long it's been since anyone's been inside," Mandie repeated. "Do you do any sort of groundskeeping or anything like that?"

June had arrived, and that meant things had started blooming and growing around the city. Trees had all leafed up, flowers and bushes had revived, and people had planted their gardens on the rooftops, in their community plots, and in little pots on their balconies.

"It's been a while since anyone's been on this property," Henry admitted. "And no, we don't do any sort of upkeep on our historical sites."

"Well, this isn't a historical site," Suzie said, folding her arms. She too faced the gate. Mandie wouldn't put it past her to have superhuman vision that could see through solid objects. "This is private property, so of course they haven't come to keep it up."

Mandie suddenly felt foolish, because that was true.

PastForward partnered with local historical societies for PR reasons, to make sure everyone was happy with the work they did. They had to bring in heavy machinery and construction vehicles, and that annoyed neighbors.

Out here in the Hamptons, where those neighbors had plenty of money and as much time as they wanted to do whatever they wanted, that led to calls to municipalities, police stations, and yes, the Historical Society.

Alicia had filed all the proper paperwork. They'd gotten the work permits. They'd proven that they'd bought the property and had the right to work on it. Now Mandie simply needed to *see* it.

Her heartbeat thundered in her chest as Henry reached into his pocket and retrieved a jangling set of keys. "Let's go in, shall we?"

Mandie could barely breathe, let alone speak, so she simply edged forward, following Henry. Alicia came to her side, and Suzie, in typical bulldozer fashion, actually stepped in front of her.

Annoyance sang through Mandie, but she kept quiet. Henry unlocked the padlock around the ornate handles on the gate, and Mandie's vision went white for a moment. Then the gates started to roll open—then they stopped.

"These wheels are a little rusty," Henry said, and while he probably stood six feet tall, he didn't have much bulk. He strained against the left-hand side door, but the gate didn't move.

Mandie saw the grounds in the gap, and sure enough, the property boasted plenty of green. Overgrown green.

"I have a pulley in the car," Henry said, and he wiped his brow, where he'd started to sweat in the summer morning.

"Oh, come on," Suzie practically yelled. She stepped forward in her steel-toed boots and khaki cargo shorts and gave Henry a withering look. "I can do it without your silly pully."

"Suzie," Mandie hissed at her. Henry looked like he'd been personally insulted, because he had been. Suzie muscled him out of the way, and he stumbled as he fell back.

His face flamed red as Mandie's pulse sped up—and as Suzie put her impressive bulldozing to use and opened the gate. The wheels shrieked as the gate opened in an old-fashioned style, the track clearly needing to be replaced or updated. Oiled at the very least.

Mandie wasn't here to make notes on the property today. They'd do that over the course of the next several days; today, she and the team wanted to get their first impressions of the place, meet Henry, and get Flint onto the property to start the before shots.

Still, she carried her clipboard, and she'd write down notes from memory once she found herself alone. As she stepped from the driveway to the private lane, she sucked in a breath. "This place has a mosaic on the driveway."

She hadn't seen this in modern culture, but some wealthy members of ancient culture had done this to show their importance in the society. She'd seen some ornate mosaics come out of Pompeii, and wonder simply held her motionless for a moment.

This mosaic wasn't made of words like some others she'd seen. Restored, this would be a colorful and vibrant art display of waves along the bottom, with an anchor rising from the sea.

The Harringtons had owned fleets of ships, and they'd hailed from Northern Italy. When they'd come to the United States, they'd thrived by expanding their shipping empire to include the railroad.

Mandie couldn't wait to see what other artifacts she'd find inside, but for now, she drank in the art as Alicia came to her side. "Wow," she murmured.

Mandie slipped her arm through Alicia's and squeezed. "I can't wait to see this whole place."

Behind them, an engine sounded, and Mandie took a long look at the tree-lined lane, with a dry fountain down at the end of it. She could only imagine that restored and bubbling, but the picture-perfect image shattered as a door slammed.

Mandie turned to find Flint there, and she turned quickly to introduce him to Henry. "This is our videographer," she said. "Flint Rogers. Flint, this is Henry Swinton, from the Historical Society."

The two men shook hands, and Flint started unloading his equipment. Mandie took another look at Henry just as Suzie did. The other woman opened her mouth to say something, and Mandie darted in front of Henry.

"Hey." She felt breathless, and her mind couldn't quite come up with the right thing to say. "He's going to do quite a bit of filming of the outdoor area today, and he'll be here all week to do the interior."

"Of course," Henry said, extending the keys to Mandie. "I'll pass these to you." He shot a look to Suzie. "You guys clearly don't need me here."

Mandie refused the keys. She curled her fingers around his, palming the keys into his palm instead of taking them. "Henry, I was counting on you to give me a tour of this place. All the insider information." She gave him her best smile. "I want all the secrets you know about this place that no one else does."

"Do we have time for that?" Suzie asked, and Mandie threw her a death look.

"Yes," she said. "Suzie, I want you to assist Flint with his equipment out here while Henry tells Alicia and I about the grounds. When we're ready to go inside, we'll go together."

Suzie frowned, and she looked around the group as Flint arrived with his camera equipment. She wore a look of displeasure, but she must've been able to read something in Mandie's expression, because she said, "All right. But I want to see it as a team."

"We will," Mandie said, as they had discussed that. She returned her attention to Henry, who literally straightened his pocket square and then his tie.

He held his head high and said, "I'd love to give you a tour of the grounds and tell you about the mansion."

Mandie grinned even wider. "Thank you so much, Henry."

He shot a look over to Alicia as she came to Mandie's side again. The buzzy whine of a drone filled the air as Flint launched the device up to get the aerial shots. "Can I get the individual phone numbers of each member on the team?"

Henry pulled out his phone, swiped, and looked up. But not at Mandie. At Alicia. The flush that had crawled into his face when he couldn't open the gate returned in full force.

Mandie actually took a step back as he asked Alicia how to spell her name. "But you go by Lish?" he asked, clearly interested in her. Mandie grinned as Alicia gave him her number, and then Mandie pulled out her phone and recited the numbers of Flint and Suzie.

"Okay," Henry said, back to his dignified historian voice. "Let's go take a look at the beautiful gardens, which are rumored to look like the landscape of Northern Italy, where the Harrington family hails from."

"Genoa, right?" Alicia asked, and she fell into step with Henry. Mandie went with them, giving Alicia the space to walk next to Henry. As he spoke about the lemon trees, the olive trees, the fig trees, and the abundance of lavender that Lady Harrington had wanted to mimic the vegetation of Italy, Mandie simply basked in the glow of this project.

Now, if she could keep Suzie's mouth under control and smooth over any other mishaps that happened because of her tactless actions or words... Mandie definitely needed to figure out how to do that.

As Henry reached the fountain and said, "This terra cotta-lined fountain adds a touch of Mediterranean charm to the courtyard," Mandie couldn't wait to see what opulence waited for them inside.

Chapter Seven

Mandie waited as patiently as possible as Henry finally—*finally*—led her, Alicia, and Suzie down the ornate walkway toward the double-wide and double-tall front doors of the Hampton House.

"These doors came from another mansion when it was torn down," Henry said. "They were purchased from the Vander-Buys house by the last owner, only a few days before that mansion was torn down and rebuilt." He flashed Mandie a smile over his shoulder. His eyes wandered to Alicia, and he nearly tripped over the first stair as he reached it.

That got him to stumble forward and go, "Oopsie."

Mandie grinned and she reached for Alicia's arm. She threaded hers through Alicia's elbow, and she glanced over to Suzie on her other side.

Taking a chance, she linked her arm through Suzie's too. The blonde woman looked at her, her eyes wide.

Mandie gave her a small smile as they went up the steps together.

"This is our house, ladies," Mandie said as Henry fitted the key into the lock. He talked about the glass in the front windows, but Mandie couldn't even stand to look up to see it.

She wasn't sure how she was going to take in everything at once as it was, and then, Henry pushed through both doors, casting them wide open.

Mandie stood in the middle of Suzie and Alicia, a wall of hot air coming out of the yawning opening.

"There's electricity," Henry said, and he disappeared around the corner of the doors for a moment before the lights snapped on.

It spilled from the chandelier hanging somewhere Mandie couldn't see, and it danced in rainbowed colors across what looked like white marble floor.

Henry said, "The floor is white marble," which solidified Mandie's suspicions. She'd looked through and memorized all the photographs from the last sale, which had been eight years ago.

Since then, the owners had abandoned the house in favor of returning to Spain for an unknown reason, and PastForward had bought the house several months ago.

The three of them stepped across the threshold of the house, and Mandie took a deep breath of the stale, stagnant, hot air. Dust and dirt and darkness scented it, and Mandie loved it.

The foyer expanded in front of her, with the ceiling

rising two stories above her head, and plenty of light coming in from the back of the house on the second floor. Arched doorways led off both the left and right sides on this floor, the contents of those rooms hidden behind darkness. An enormous staircase rose from the middle of the foyer, and the stone on it shone with a pink pearlescent quality that made Mandie catch her breath.

"Wow," Alicia said on her right.

Mandie couldn't believe places this large existed so close to her tiny one-bedroom apartment in the city. At least four of those could fit in this foyer alone, and she listened to the rapid beating of her heart as the three of them continued to gaze around.

"The ceiling is domed," Henry said, and Mandie did look up this time. "Though you can't tell from outside. A false roof was added to hide the dome, as the second owner of the home didn't want it to be seen from the road." He smiled pleasantly and checked his watch.

The dome glinted with gold, reminding Mandie of the pictures she'd seen in big cathedrals and churches in ancient Europe.

"I'm afraid I have another appointment." He clasped his hands together the way a proper English gentleman would. "I'll leave you ladies here." He crossed back to them and handed Alicia the keys. "Great to meet all of you." He said the words while only looking at Alicia. He cleared his throat and his black, shiny shoes clacked against the marble as he left.

Suzie dropped Mandie's arm and said, "I'm going to explore over here on the left."

"Be careful," Mandie said, just so she could report to Candace—and any EMTs who might be called—that she had. "Some of the reports of this place say the floor has rotted through in some places."

"I got it," Suzie said, already on her way. Mandie stood several yards from the staircase, wanting to go up it. She wanted to know what it felt like to wear a fancy, purple dress covered in sequins and gems as she stood at the top of it, Charlie in a midnight-black tuxedo waited at the bottom.

The magical scene danced through her mind, and a smile filled her entire being as she stepped toward the stairs. "I'm going up," she said.

"I'll go right," Alicia said.

"The kitchen is in the back," Mandie said. "I'll meet everyone down there." She split from her friend, pure adrenaline spurring her footsteps forward. When she lifted her foot and put it on the pink stone, a zing of electric excitement shot up her leg.

She smiled as she climbed the steps, counting them as she did. Behind her, one of the other women yelled something Mandie couldn't make out. She didn't slow or stop but kept going until she'd climbed the twenty-four steps to the second floor.

A room stretched in front of her, while a hallway forked left and then right to the wings of the mansion.

According to the blueprint which she'd studied, the room in front of her had been labeled a lounge.

As she stepped over to the glass doors and pushed them in, she imagined it full of potted plants and leather chaises. She could do that, because the furniture still sat there. It had been knocked askew, like someone had been in the house and played a game of tag here in the lounge, run into the single-person loungers, recliners, and wing-backs, and tilted them out of position.

Of course, they should all be facing the wide, curved wall of windows in front of Mandie. She couldn't look away from the scene beyond, which showed a lawn so much like the one that extended behind the White House.

She pictured it in its heyday, with everything made of emeralds, the pool below a sparkling turquoise oasis instead of the empty, dirty, slab of concrete Mandie saw in reality.

"They left everything," she whispered. She turned, finding the pots which had held the trees and vibrant bushes she'd made to bloom in her mind. In real life, they held withered, dry skeletons of branches and twigs, as their owners had left without a way to water them.

Mandie pulled out her phone and started snapping pictures, some of the awe and shock wearing away. She loved the projects where the previous owner had left in a hurry, because it provided such a fascinating glimpse into the past.

A picture of a moment in time where the ultra-wealthy

showed how they'd decorate a massive space, filled with high-end materials.

Mandie had never aspired to be rich. She wanted to have enough to have a house for her and Charlie and their family, and she'd never had grandiose dreams of where she'd live and raise her family. She'd never even considered the Hamptons.

She and Charlie had already started talking about what they'd do when he graduated, as they both liked living in the city. Charlie had spent the first fourteen years of his life living in a big house in the Hamptons, and he didn't want that.

He wanted something bigger than Five Island Cove too, and Mandie could agree with him on that. She liked having somewhere to go home to visit, and she liked having more options than one grocery store, so she pictured her and Charlie settling down somewhere close enough to a ferry that could get them back to their parents easily enough, but where they could still have all the perks of a bigger city.

She straightened and moved right to the middle of the pinnacle of the windows. She took a picture of the grounds beyond, and she sent that to Charlie. *We're in the house! It's amazing, and the previous owners left so much.*

Now that he'd started his internship, Charlie wouldn't be able to answer until his lunch break, so Mandie moved out of the lounge and into the hallway. She felt like she could fly, what with the sunshine pouring into the back windows and only the thinnest of railings lining the hall on her left.

She walked around the curved hallway to the very last door, which stood closed. It bore dark wood, obviously hand-carved, and Mandie reached out and traced her fingers down one of the raised lines of handiwork. The part of her that could feel the past hummed, and she closed her eyes, imagining the craftsman who'd been responsible for such beautiful work.

Her phone chimed several times in a row, and Mandie looked at it, giving herself a moment for her eyes to come back into focus after she opened them. *The library is huge and completely stocked*, Suzie had said. She'd sent a picture with the message, and Mandie felt like she'd been transported to the castle in *Beauty and the Beast*.

Huge dance floor in the ballroom, Suzie said. *The grand piano is still here!* More pictures followed, and Mandie could feel the other woman's excitement over finding the house in such a preserved state.

At the same time, Mandie almost wished the Hampton House was completely empty. It would speed the project and make it far easier to focus on structural issues within the historical building instead of going laboriously through old books and documents, junk drawers and cupboards full of dishes that had to be researched to find out if they were family heirlooms or just a set from a regular department store, or closets full of clothes and shoes and personal belongings.

But she did want the historical snapshot only left-behind items could tell, and Mandie tapped to open her phone camera again before lifting the device and snapping a picture of the door.

She wanted to keep that. She wanted to recover and restore everything she could—and Alicia's budget would appreciate that.

The rooms up here had been labeled as bedrooms—six of them, with two master suites on the bottom floor—and Mandie clasped her fingers around the cold, gold doorknob, and opened the door.

"IT WAS SO INCREDIBLE," MANDIE SAID AS SHE peeled back the corner of the comforter on her side of the bed. She'd just brushed her teeth and changed into her blue silk pajamas, the day long but oh-so-amazing.

Charlie peeled his shirt over his head and tossed it onto the pile of clothes on their dresser. He smiled at her from the other side of the bed. "You're going to love this house, aren't you?"

"I love it," she gushed as she sat down, one leg tucked underneath her.

Charlie pulled the blanket down and crawled into bed, reaching for her. Mandie laid down in his arms, pure happiness pulling through her. "We got *so* many pictures today. I haven't even had time to go through all of them."

"Did you go through the whole house?" He kissed her temple, then slid his lips down the side of her face.

"Yes," she said. "I walked through all of it, but Alicia and Suzie did pictures of their assigned areas. We'll spend this week in the office, making plans while Flint gets his before footage."

Charlie hummed as he kissed her neck, and Mandie's cells buzzed and vibrated—especially as her husband's warm hand slid under the hem of her pajama top and along her bare skin to her back.

"How was your training this afternoon?" she whispered. The incredible sights and experiences of her day had dominated the conversation over dinner, as well as all the way through their evening time together, and a twinge of guilt stole through her.

"Just fine," Charlie whispered right before he matched his mouth to hers. Mandie enjoyed being with him, and she pushed the other pieces of her life out of her mind so she could focus on him right now.

After all, the Hampton House would still be there tomorrow, and Mandie was determined not to let it grab onto her, drag her under the current, and drown her.

So she kissed her husband back, wanting and absolutely *needing* a multi-faceted life where work was only one part of what made Mandie who she was.

Chapter Eight

S uzie's fingers trembled as she fitted the key into the lock of the Hampton House's back door. The sun barely remained in the west horizon, casting long shadows across the overgrown lawn. She glanced over her shoulder, half-expecting to see Mandie or Alicia step out of the shrubbery. Or to hear a cab pulling up to the gate, though intellectually, Suzie knew she wouldn't be able to hear a car that far away.

No one was there. No one would be coming, and Suzie took a deep breath, and faced the house again. The blinds in the kitchen had been broken, and she could see right into the house. With everything so dark, her skin crawled with a creepy vibe.

"Should've come a little earlier," she muttered to herself. But she, Mandie, and Alicia had been working until she'd caught a cab and came here, as it was Monday, and Alicia could stay late on Mondays.

The door creaked open, and Suzie slipped inside, closing it quietly behind her and relocking it. She stood in the grandiose kitchen, her heart pounding as the dusky sunlight glinted off the metallic appliances. The house seemed different in the waning light, insanely mysterious, and far too silent, and much, much more alive.

She reached into her pocket and pulled out the compass-shaped brooch, its weight familiar in her palm. The tiny anchor right in the middle, where the hands extended from, nearly matched the one out in the mosaic driveway.

When she'd seen that splayed on the driveway last week... Her breath still stuck in her throat whenever she examined the picture of it, and her anticipation of what she might find here tonight made her stomach roll.

Suzie had always known she was distantly related to the Harringtons, but her parents didn't have much proof. Nothing from the past. Not a journal or any titles or documents. Since this house had come up at PastForward, she'd been wondering if it could be the key to unlocking her family's past.

Her own personal past.

"I have to know," she whispered to herself, her voice echoing in the empty space.

Suzie slowly walked through the kitchen, which at first glance, seemed nearly perfect. But a house that hadn't been used in years possessed a weary spirit, and Suzie could simply tell that everything needed a lot of tender, loving care. As she passed through the dining room, she noted water damage on the ceiling and the way Alicia had dragged her fingers through the dust on the twenty-four-seat table. Out in the foyer, the floral wallpaper peeled in strips around the doorways, probably because of the lack of temperature control for so long.

She ignored all of that, for the library drew her like a magnet.

She pushed open the heavy double doors and paused though she'd been inside this room before. Floor-to-ceiling bookshelves lined every wall, even the one with the doorway, and on this side of the house, the evening twilight didn't shine as brightly.

The scent of leather-bound volumes tickled her nose, but she breathed it in deeply. A thick layer of dust covered everything, but Suzie could still sense the room's former grandeur. She took a moment to drop her hands to her sides and imagine this place completely clean, with every book catalogued and accounted for.

Every one opened to check for any trinket, a letter, a long-long envelope of money that had been tucked into the pages.

She flipped a switch, sending pockets of light throughout the library from the carefully positioned lamps on side tables. Overhead lights filled in the rest of the darkness, and Suzie moved over to the desk standing only a few paces in front of the doors. It sure seemed like someone might have sat here at some point, simply waiting for the owners to come in and request a book.

"This is incredible," she murmured, running her

fingers along the spines of the books that had been left stacked there. One was a first edition, its gold lettering barely visible beneath years of neglect.

As she moved deeper into the room, Suzie's well-trained restoration eye caught on the perfect alignment of the bookcases that had been hand-built just for this house. She could estimate the cost of this much wood in today's market, but to think it had been built over a century ago made everything more opulent and valuable.

No one would ever peg her to be the woman to take a couple of jogging steps and leap onto the library ladder, sending it sliding as she breathed in the scent of books. She was no Disney princess, after all.

And yet, Suzie loved books, and she loved old things, and she felt such a kinship with every project she'd done for PastForward.

The Hampton House possessed something special to be sure, and Suzie once again found herself reaching into her pocket for the piece of jewelry her grandmother had given her before she'd passed away a few years ago.

She didn't run through the library, show tunes blaring in her head, but merely stepped up onto the ladder. It hadn't been moved in years, and when she'd been here last week, she'd tried to slide it along the ground and found it needed a good oiling.

When she'd gone up a few steps, she turned carefully on the thick rungs and surveyed the library from this new angle.

The lamp in front of her threw light up while the overhead chandelier rained light down, and together, they made shadows go in different directions. Across from her and slightly to the right sat the fireplace, and Suzie could think of nothing more she wanted to do than sit in one of those puffy, comfy recliners with flames flickering in front of her while she read a really great romance novel.

Her heartbeat had settled into its normal rhythm, and Suzie wasn't sure why she'd come here tonight. Especially without telling Mandie or Alicia. She'd simply taken the keys, knowing she could get back to the office in the morning before them so they wouldn't know.

Almost in the corner, Suzie's eyes stopped. Confusion ran through her, and she couldn't make the angles and lines—almost all of which were straight in the bookcases of the library—line up.

For the lines there weren't straight.

Rather, they were, but they didn't match up. The twelve-foot bookcase that ran from the floorboard up didn't meet the one above it.

Suzie jumped down the three steps she'd climbed, sure she hadn't seen anything off. Sure enough, from the floor, the lines looked like they met just right. She approached the corner bookcase, frowning while the brooch in her pocket seemed to grow heavier.

Suzie ran her hands along the left edge of the bookshelf, where it met another one, feeling for any irregularities. Nothing.

She turned and looked over to the ladder. If someone had been living here and using this library, they'd be able to slide it around the two corners to this spot, and she could climb up and see the teensy gap more clearly.

As it was, she already knew the ladder wouldn't make it that far. Suzie couldn't reach up high enough to feel the top of the bookcase, and she turned to find a chair she could stand on. High-backed, sturdy chairs sat at a study table only a few paces away.

Suzie retrieved the chair and climbed up on it in her two-inch wedges. Cursing herself for not planning better for this undercover operation, she managed to steady herself on the chair enough to lean forward slightly to feel along the higher recesses of the bookcase.

Dust and grime and cobwebs coated her hand, but she didn't pull away. About two feet from the top of the book-case, her sensitive fingertips caught against the barest of bumps. Heart racing, Suzie slowly moved her hand back down.

"Something's there," she said out loud to the empty library. She centered her pointer finger right over it and pushed, not really expecting anything to happen. How could it?

Secret passages only existed in movies.

Besides, no one could reach this high to get to this tiny bump without using the ladder—or the chair like her —and that didn't feel like something anyone would do, especially if they needed to get out of the library in a hurry.

But a soft click met her ears, causing her to yank her hand back. The bookcase moved toward her slightly, and

Suzie pulled in a breath and held it. "That didn't just happen."

Ever the bulldozer, she reached out and pushed against the bookcase. Sure enough, it clicked back into place—which meant it could be moved out of its place.

She found the button—and Suzie wouldn't even use that word to describe the blemish in the wood—and pushed it again. The bookcase bumped out again. Her feet tingled, and Suzie breathed, "No way."

She scrambled down off the chair and moved it back. Facing the bookcase again, she reached out tentatively, took hold of the outer edge of it, and pulled.

The bookshelf creaked and groaned as it moved, but all Suzie could focus on was that it was *moving*.

Darkness gaped behind the now open doorway, and much cooler air filtered into the library. She hesitated for only a moment before taking the first step, pulling out her phone to use as a flashlight as she went

The passage spanned the width of the single bookcase, maybe four feet. A musty smell came from the stone walls, and cobwebs brushed against her forearms as she moved forward. The floor stayed flat and level, and Suzie's pulse raced ahead of her, anticipating a dozen different things.

This wasn't the first mansion she'd found a secret passageway in. The rich and famous were well, famous for them, and Suzie had gotten really good at looking at the outside of a house and finding places that didn't match up with the interior.

The windows lingered several yards down the wall, and

if there was going to be a secret room in this house, Suzie would've picked this corner of the library for it.

"Still unbelievable," she said as the hallway opened up into a boxy room. Suzie swept her flashlight across the space, revealing shelves filled with old documents, photographs, and artifacts.

Two desks sat in the room, facing one another, and they still held filing trays, the ghost of a potted plant, and even an old coffee mug.

Suzie couldn't breathe properly as she searched the walls nearest her for a light switch. She found one and tapped it. Lights blazed to life from can lights in the ceiling. A single-story ceiling—not two-stories like the library.

"This is it," she whispered, her voice trembling with excitement. She pulled the brooch out again, determined to find anything that looked like it. Then she'd have definitive proof the Harringtons had built and owned this place.

Then she'd know she stood somewhere her ancestors once had.

She approached a large portrait hanging on the far wall. Even through the layers of dust and smoke and grime, she could make out the features of a man who bore somewhat of a resemblance to her grandmother. Same sloped nose, at least. Beneath the portrait was a plaque: *Edmund Harrington, Founder of Hampton House, 1875.*

And on the plaque sat a compass.

Suzie's hands shook as she held up the brooch next to

the portrait's plaque, comparing the two pieces. It was an exact match.

A mixture of triumph and awe chased each other through her system. "This really was their house."

As she turned to examine the rest of the room, a leather-bound journal on the nearest desk demanded her attention. Suzie went around to where the owner of the desk would sit, and being careful not to touch anything, she leaned in to read the faded handwriting.

April 15, 1925 - Our family has always cherished the Harrington fortune, a legacy that we have preserved through generations. True value lies within our family name, and I've taken our most prized possessions and preserved them deep within the walls of our ancestral home. The crown jewel of our heritage lies—

Suzie's brow furrowed as the writing cut off, nothing else after it. "What secret?" she wondered. "Harrington fortune?"

She'd never heard of any fortune, that was for sure. She reached into her pocket and slid on a fingertip glove, one she always took everywhere with her. It had come from her first aid kit at home, and it provided a non-slip way for her to flip the pages of the journal in a delicate way.

The rest of the pages contained nothing, but the two dozen before it told a story of the first few months of 1925. Nothing of note, as the author of this journal seemed to be neck-deep in planning the fiftieth anniversary party of the construction of the mansion.

"I need to look through the family history again," she

muttered as she pulled out her phone and started snapping pictures of the journal. Deep inside, she wanted to keep them to herself, but she knew she'd have to confess to Mandie and Alicia that she'd come here tonight.

And she'd have to tell them what she'd found.

"And who you are," she muttered.

A clomping noise from somewhere in the house made her jump. It sounded like a door closing. Or someone dropping something.

Or a footstep. Just one.

Panic seized her. She shouldn't be here, and she certainly wasn't supposed to know about this hidden den. Quickly, she finished taking photos of the last few pages of the journal, then hurried back to the passageway.

She pressed her back against the wall there, wondering if someone had come into the library. In that moment, she couldn't remember if she'd pulled the bookcase back into place behind her.

Of course you didn't! her mind screamed at her. She would've never trapped herself like that, not knowing if she'd be able to open the bookcase again from this side. She peered around the edge of the doorway, the light from the library filtering in from.

Relief sagged through her, but every cell in her body remained at high alert. Without another exit in this room, she had to get out of this den and the passageway. Now.

She practically ran in her wedged shoes, and as she emerged into the library, Suzie's mind raced. Was she alone in the house? The lights in the library would surely be shining through the windows, and she cursed herself for turning them on.

She'd only heard the one sound and not another one, and her experience told her that old houses settled all the time. They groaned and complained in the weirdest of ways, and she couldn't let her imagination and her fear get the best of her.

Breathing hard, with every second feeling like an eternity, she managed to get the bookcase back in place. She dashed over to the wall and flipped off the light. This far from the road, she couldn't hear any traffic—and it wasn't even the main highway that veined its way through Southampton to the other neighborhoods in the Hamptons.

She couldn't hear anything. Not a sound.

There's no one here, she told herself.

Well, except for her, and she needed to leave. Immediately.

Employing every ounce of bravery and courage Suzie possessed, she drew a breath and held it as she exited the library. Her eyes scanned in every direction—over to the other arched doorways that led into different rooms, up the stairs to the second floor, toward the front door—as she strode toward the kitchen.

She reached the back door without incident, and she twisted and yanked on the doorknob to get out. She spilled into the night, and while it wasn't quite dark yet, twilight had claimed the dusk.

The back door closed quickly, almost crashing into her

she pulled it after her so hard. She hissed out her frustration with herself, and fumbled for the keys in her pocket.

As she re-locked the back door, her mind shouted and shouted at her.

She'd keyed her way into the house and locked the back door behind her. But as she came out...she hadn't had to unlock the door.

It had already been open.

Her next breath stuck in her lungs, and tears pressed behind her eyes. She finally got the door locked, and she ducked away from all the windows. They had so many eyes, and Suzie couldn't help feeling like someone tangible and human was watching her.

She faded into the night, moving straight back from the house to press into the darkness along the side of the pool house. She still had to call a cab and then get down the lane to get in that car. Whoever was here would surely see her then.

Her shallow breathing didn't help order her thoughts, but one managed to emerge. She didn't have to hide. She could be here, no questions asked. She had keys, and her company owned this property.

That knowledge allowed her to pull out her phone and text for a ride. It took several seconds, but she got a message that said, *Twelve minutes*, and the cab's license plate number.

She looked up and shoved her phone away. She didn't want to be night-blind by looking at her bright phone and not be able to see someone coming toward her.

Twelve minutes felt like a lifetime, but Suzie pushed herself away from the pool house and walked straight across the sunburnt lawn. She cut a glance to the side wall of the mansion as she went by it, a healthy distance between her and it, knowing the library and hidden den sat on the other side of it.

She reached the lane and walked on the far side of it until she reached the automobile gate. She hadn't opened it but had gone through the pedestrian gate in the corner instead. She exited the same way, relocked the gate behind her, and stood still while she took in the road in front of her.

Only two properties sat here, one on each side of the road, and they were the regular kind of Hampton mansion. Probably situated on an acre or two of land, with homes set back behind trees and gates.

The wind whispered through the tree branches around her, and Suzie checked the time. Six more minutes until her ride arrived.

She had found the proof she was looking for, but her heartbeat wouldn't calm while she stood so close to the house. The mansion suddenly possessed secrets, and Suzie imagined them to be deep and dangerous.

And someone else might know about them too. They might know about her. The secret passageway.

Suzie's fingers closed around the brooch in her pocket as she made a decision. She had to tell Mandie and Alicia everything—about her heritage, about the hidden den, and about the unlocked back door.

Whatever was happening here, it now felt bigger than just restoring an old mansion from one of the wealthiest families in New York.

As her cab arrived and she dove gratefully into the back seat, Suzie couldn't shake the feeling that she had just stumbled into something far more complex and perilous than she even knew.

The weight of her discovery—both personally and professionally—settled on her shoulders like a heavy cloak. The Hampton House held secrets, and now, for better or worse, Suzie was part of them.

Chapter Nine

Alicia's hands trembled as she pushed open the front door of the Hampton House. The meeting with Candace still echoed in her mind, the promise of a management position tantalizing yet terrifying.

Now, more than ever, everything hinged on the success of this project.

"As if it hadn't before." She just hadn't realized Candace was considering her for an assistant director position—until this morning.

As she stepped into the foyer, the newly polished marble floor gleamed beneath her feet. The chandelier, now sparkling and clean, cast a warm glow over the spacious entryway, despite it being unlit right now.

Pride swelled in her chest at the transformation they'd achieved in just a couple of weeks. It was amazing what a cleaning crew could do, as well as a team of five construction men who knew what they were doing and simply needed to be pointed in the right direction.

Of course, the construction manager had argued plenty with Mandie already, and Alicia marveled at her best friend's ability to stand her ground, give better explanations, and listen at the same time.

They'd started in the parlor, a room just off to the right of the foyer, and they'd done that at the suggestion of Carl, their construction manager for this project. Mandie had wanted to start in the kitchen, as it had seemed the neatest, with very little work that needed to be done. But Carl had gone through the mansion too, and he said they should do the rooms arching back toward the kitchen first, and they should be finished with the smallest pieces today.

Candace had demanded something gorgeous to show the community, the Historical Society, and everyone at PastForward—a check-in for the project, so she said. Flint had been scheduled to come in that afternoon, when the light would be golden and glorious in the parlor.

Voices drifted from that direction, and Alicia followed them, her heels clicking against the floor in time to her pulsing heartbeat. She wouldn't be able to keep the secret of her possible promotion from Mandie.

She didn't even want to. She wanted to tell Mandie, because she'd taken the news of Alicia's divorce and childcare issues and exhibited pure kindness. She'd told her to simply be communicative, and she'd take the heat for anything related to Alicia's personal problems with Candace.

She reached the doorway and paused, taking in the scene before her.

Mandie stood on a ladder near the window, watching as one of the construction workers hung a restored oil painting above the fireplace. Alicia and Mandie had gone through the painstaking process of cleaning the painting and then sending it to a professional to touch up the parts that had stripped the paint.

From a distance—and even close up—Alicia couldn't see a single blemish, and the golden frame shone with all the glory of the stars.

Suzie knelt by an antique side table, polishing its brass handles. The room had come alive with new, era-appropriate, jewel-toned wallpaper, and the hardwood floors had been cleaned and re-stained to match the original coloring —which they'd found when they'd pulled out the fireplace stones and found the wood underneath unblemished by sunshine, wear and tear, and neglect.

Her heart fell to the soles of her feet. She wanted to talk to Mandie alone, but that wasn't going to happen without calling enough attention to herself that Suzie would ask questions.

The woman didn't like being left out, that was for sure. Alicia couldn't blame her, and she actually found herself softening toward the blonde bulldozer as she scrubbed and scrubbed to make sure everything gleamed for their presentation to Candace

"Hey, you're back," Mandie called out. "Come over here and help me make sure this painting is straight."

Suzie looked up, a smudge of something dark on her cheek. Could've been furniture polish caked with grime. "How'd the meeting go?"

Alicia's stomach churned as she moved toward Mandie. Their eyes met, and Mandie got the message. Something big had happened in the meeting. She immediately threw a look over to Suzie too, and as Alicia turned around to face the fireplace, she said, "It was... interesting."

She certainly wasn't going to say anything in front of Carl. So she forced a smile as Suzie got to her feet. "The parlor looks amazing, you guys."

Relief filled her with the statement. She needed this first look at the work they'd been doing inside the Hampton House to be perfect. So much more rode on the pictures and video coming out of this room than Alicia had known when she'd left her apartment this morning.

Mandie climbed down from the ladder, dusting off her hands. "It really does." Her eyes traveled to the window between them and Suzie. "We just need to get the right finish on the hardware for the curtains, and I think we can let Flint in here." She exhaled heavily and wiped her bangs back off her forehead.

"Good?" Carl called.

"Good," Mandie called back to him, and Alicia gave him a thumbs up.

"If Henry and Candace aren't impressed by this," Suzie said as she stood and stretched out her back. "I don't know what will do it." She came to stand beside Alicia and Mandie while Carl got down off the ladder.

"I'll go call Rodger," he said as he folded it up. The metallic clanging of the ladder berated her ears, and Alicia flinched away from it. "Hopefully, he's got those brass fixtures."

"Hopefully," Mandie said. She walked toward him. "Thank you, Carl."

"We're gonna head out on lunch," he said.

"Great. Us too." Mandie lifted her hand as he left, and then she turned back to Alicia and Suzie.

Alicia saw her opportunity, but still she hesitated. The upcoming unveiling sent a fresh wave of anxiety through her, and her tongue felt so thick in her mouth. She glanced at her watch. "Can we huddle up?"

Suzie immediately turned toward her, forming one side of the triangle they made when they'd huddled up in the past.

Mandie turned toward them, her brow furrowed. "Huddle up?"

That was the term everyone at PastForward used when they needed to have an impromptu meeting about something serious. Team leads usually called them, and Alicia swallowed as she looked over to Mandie. "I met with Candace."

Mandie joined them, something eager in her eyes now. As if he knew the absolute worst time to text, Alicia's phone buzzed—a text from Henry. Her heart skipped a beat for an entirely new reason now, and she quickly flipped her phone over, hoping the others hadn't noticed.

She looked at Mandie and found her eyes coming up from the device. So she'd seen. Great. Just another secret Alicia needed to tell her.

"We have a few minutes before I hear about the hardware," Mandie said.

Alicia nodded, getting the hint. This couldn't take long. Flint was probably on his way, and they still didn't have the curtains up. In fact, the quilted, Brocade-fabric, burgundy curtains, with silver and gold threaded through the designs, lay over the back of the couch.

The inner lace curtains, done in a creamy ivory, rested on top of them, and Alicia couldn't wait to see it all with the wallpaper, the fixtures, the deep, rich, dark wood floors.

The beauty of the mansion soothed her, and she took a breath that only wavered slightly as it entered her lungs. "There's something I need to talk to you both about."

Mandie and Suzie exchanged glances before tightening the huddle. She'd not seen them do that before—usually she and Mandie could communicate with just a look. But they'd both been getting to know Suzie better, and she wasn't so bad.

Of course, Mandie was an expert at smoothing out the tactless things she said or did, and then she spoke to Suzie about them privately. The woman could work, and she worked hard, and Alicia's list of faults had dwindled to only a couple.

"This project...I know the Hampton House means a

lot to all of us." She looked at Mandie and raised her chin. "Candace told me you got the initial appraisal, which means you know what your bonus could be if this goes well and sells."

Mandie's hazel eyes blazed with fire. "Yes," she said simply, not volunteering any more information.

After a swift look to Suzie, who'd locked her jaw, Alicia decided to just rip off the bandage. Spit it all out. "Candace offered me an assistant director position, but it's contingent on how well this project goes."

The words landed in the parlor amidst heavy silence.

"We have to stay under budget," she said. "It's non-negotiable. Everything has to be immaculate." An edge of desperation started to creep into her voice. She swallowed to try to contain it. "I need the promotion."

She didn't have to say more, and to her eternal credit, Mandie reached out and took her hand. Her eyes still burned, but with a brighter, happier fire. "Alicia, that's amazing. No one deserves a promotion more than you." She glanced over to Suzie. "Right, Suzie?"

The older woman's jaw still jutted out, almost making a square. "I've been at PastForward longer than you."

"True," Alicia said slowly. She shouldn't have expected the same reaction from Suzie that Mandie had given her. She hadn't, not really. Before she could say more, all the tightness in Suzie's face and eyes relaxed.

"I know those director positions don't go to bulldozers." She sighed and looked away. "Candace views us as part of the construction crew half the time."

"Hey, now," Mandie said. "You're not part of the construction crew."

Suzie still wouldn't look at her, and Mandie glanced at Alicia. She nodded, encouraging her to go on.

"Even if you were, you're still an extremely valuable part of this team," Mandie said. When she still stared off toward the painting that had just been hung, Mandie reached out and put her hand on Suzie's forearm.

The other woman flinched and pulled back, finally swinging her attention to her with a disgusted look on her face. It took a moment, but then she relaxed again. "Thank you, Mandie." She cut a look to Alicia. "You'd be a great assistant director."

"Thank you, Suzie," Alicia murmured.

Mandie cleared her throat. "My bonus—if the house sells, which could take years, you guys—would be more than six-figures." She swallowed hard. "Charlie and I could really use that money. He only has one year of pharmacy school left, and then we're going to be looking for a more permanent place to live. A better place. Like, a real house."

Her hands went round and round each other, the way they did when Mandie got nervous. She seemed to know she was doing it, and she dropped her hands to her sides. "We do have a lot riding on this project—all of us."

They both looked at Suzie, who gave them a wary look. Several long moments passed, and Alicia said, "Okay, well—"

"I have a confession too," Suzie blurted out, her voice bulldozing right over Alicia's. She didn't immediately follow that with the confession, but Alicia had learned to simply wait, and the silence would force it out of her.

"I'm...I'm a Harrington." Suzie reached up and pulled her ponytail out. She started to gather her hair back into it before she started speaking again. "By blood—Edmund Harrington is my second cousin twice removed."

"I—what does that mean?" Mandie asked.

"My grandmother was his second cousin," Suzie said. She stuck her hand in her pocket and pulled something out. Something silver and shiny, yet fairly small. "And there's a secret den in this house that I found two weeks ago."

Shock coursed through Alicia. "Two weeks ago?"

"When?" Mandie asked. "We come to the mansion together."

Suzie's booted feet shifted, and she dropped her gaze to study them. "I came alone one night."

"You came here at night?" Mandie demanded. "Alone?" She folded her arms. "Suzie."

"I know." She threw Mandie a glare as noise echoed toward them from the foyer. The three of them turned in that direction, effectively breaking up the huddle they'd been standing in.

Flint led the way into the room, holding his recording equipment as two more people followed him. Isabella and Ryder—his film crew.

"Worst timing ever," Alicia whispered, which caused Mandie to smile.

Suzie said, "No kidding," which made Alicia grin at her. She too reached over and squeezed Suzie's hand as Mandie went to greet the film crew and get them up to speed on what was happening in the parlor that afternoon.

"You're taking us to this secret den," Alicia whispered to Suzie.

She wore steel in her eyes, but she nodded. The weight of their collective secrets hung in the air, thick and oppressive, as Flint approached. "We can get a lot of the room's details without the curtains, but I can't delay this. Candace—"

"We know what Candace wants," Mandie said, shooting a look to Alicia. "We'll have it ready. Carl's going to come through for us."

Flint nodded as Alicia's phone vibrated in her pocket. Probably Henry. When she read back through their conversations, she couldn't believe some of the things she said. She'd forgotten she could be fun and flirty, and Henry—as stuffy and proper as he'd been when he'd met them at the Hampton House that first day—was surprisingly witty. He also seemed to be very, very interested in her.

Alicia had not agreed to a date yet, at least not one where they went out together physically. They'd done a couple of phone dates while the kids were with their dad, or after they'd gone to bed, and she did like talking to him.

But Alicia hadn't advanced things too quickly. In fact, she'd told Henry she couldn't go too fast, and she'd told him about her recent divorce when so many others still didn't know.

Alicia's chest tightened, the pressure of everything pulling on her and threatening to overwhelm her. She took out her phone while Mandie texted with Carl, and Flint went to direct his film crew to get the parts of the room unaffected by the unhung curtains.

Henry had texted several times. *I want all the pictures from your parlor today.*

Just when you get a minute.

Oh, hey, there's a new Chinese place up in Queens.

I'd love to meet you there for dinner one day.

When you're ready.

A smile graced her face, because Henry flattered her with his interest in her. She did want to go to dinner with him, and she had nights where she was alone...

"Everything okay?" Suzie asked, eyeing the phone.

Alicia couldn't hide the messages now. Nor the one she'd started to send back to him. *You know what? I'd like*

So she finished the text with *that*, and sent it. She met Suzie's eye and then Mandie's. "It's Henry. We've been... texting."

Suzie's eyebrows shot up, but before she could respond, Mandie said, "Carl's got the hardware. They'll come get it done after lunch."

The construction crew was union workers, and it wouldn't matter if the hardware was here. They'd have to hang it for them. Alicia didn't mind that, though the payments to the union ate up a huge amount of their budget for the renovation.

Mandie glanced over to Flint. "If we're going to sneak away to this hidden den, we better go now."

Alicia's stomach growled, but she could prolong lunch to see a secret room in this mansion. Her mind raced, torn between her career aspirations, the weight of Suzie's revelations, and the growing complexity of her feelings for Henry.

"Let's go," Suzie said in her authoritative, bossy voice, and she led the way out of the parlor. Alicia hung back with Mandie, who hadn't seen the texts between her and Henry yet.

"Help me with this, would you?" She slipped her phone into Mandie's hand. "Read through some of that and tell me what he really wants."

"He's a man," Mandie whispered as she focused on the phone. Her steps slowed as they crossed the foyer and she read at the same time. "I already know what he wants."

Alicia's chest felt like someone had wrapped her in a giant rubber band. She didn't need to see Mandie's wide eyes to know what she was reading. She'd read all the messages and sent so many too—a mix of work-related discussions and increasingly flirtatious banter.

"Alicia," she breathed. "This man wants to be your boyfriend badly." She handed the phone back just as they reached the library entrance, memories of lazy afternoons spent exploring its shelves flooding back through her.

She loved old documents and books, and the library

would take months to go through and restore—and Alicia couldn't wait.

"What are you going to do?" Mandie asked, neither of them moving into the library to follow Suzie.

Alicia shook her head, at a loss. "I don't know. What do you think I should do?" Henry almost felt like a co-worker, though he definitely wasn't.

"You're going to go out with him," Suzie said as she bluntly returned to them. She glared at Alicia with a malicious edge in her eyes she didn't understand. She actually flinched back from her.

"I'm—sorry?"

Suzie took the glaring down a notch. "Sorry," she muttered. "It's just—" She looked between Alicia and Mandie. "I don't know how to meet men."

Alicia's adrenaline sent her pulse pounding, and she had no idea how to answer. Thankfully, Mandie was a fun-loving, hard-working extrovert, and she swept right into Suzie's personal space. "Oh, you'll find someone," she said.

"Yeah?" Suzie stood there stiffly while Mandie hugged her. Then, reluctantly, she put her arms around their team lead. "How? Can you help me?"

Mandie stepped back, her eyes wide as she searched Suzie's. "Well, we can—get you on some dating apps." She glanced over to Alicia. "Go out for drinks one night after work. That kind of thing."

"Yeah," Alicia said. "I'd be in for that."

Suzie didn't seem to believe them, and she said, "Yeah, I'm sure your husband would like you going out for drinks with your girlfriends." She rolled her eyes. "What if someone tries to hit on you?"

Mandie only smiled. "Won't happen. We'll make sure *all* the attention is on you." Her grin widened as she looked at Alicia. "Right, Lish?"

"Totally." She smiled at Suzie too, then switched her gaze to further into the library. "All right, Suzie. Time to show us this hidden den you found in the middle of the night when you came here alone."

Suzie scoffed and rolled her eyes. She spun and marched away. "It wasn't the middle of the night," she said over her shoulder. "But I do think someone else was here that night."

Alicia had only taken one step before she froze again. "Someone else?" she asked at the same time Mandie demanded, "What does that mean? Someone else was here?"

She scampered after Suzie, peppering her with questions, and Alicia hurried to catch them. Suzie told them about the lock on the back door, and then she pulled over a chair and got up on it. Her fingers traced along the left edge, and then the bookcase sort of bumped out.

"But I didn't see anyone," Suzie said.

Alicia gasped as Suzie pulled the bookcase out, seemingly without any trouble at all. She forgot her hunger now that this hidden passageway stood open. And the mystery of possibly someone else in the mansion when they shouldn't be. Her mind reeled at the implications.

"This way," Suzie said, and she stepped down the dark hallway.

Mandie looked at Alicia, and Alicia looked at Mandie. Then Mandie took a deep breath and followed her. Alicia had once again only taken a couple of steps before Suzie's voice echoed down the passageway.

"You guys, come on! There's stuff missing from last time I was here."

Chapter Ten

Mandie could barely feel her fingers as she stepped into the hidden den, her eyes adjusting to the dimmer light. The musty scent of old books and secrets filled her nostrils, and she didn't know where to look first.

Suzie flipped on a light switch, illuminating the small, squat, square room. It felt stuffed full, though it only had a couple of desks—no chairs—and a couple of bookcases against the wall to the left.

No windows. The doorway she stood in was the only way in or out.

"The journal was right here," Suzie said as Alicia crowded into Mandie's side. She pointed to an empty spot on the desk on the right. "And that painting—" She gestured to a bare patch on the wall straight ahead. "It was hung when I was here last. Now, it's been knocked down."

Mandie found the painting on the ground beneath the spot where it had been assumedly hung, and it hadn't been done nicely. It seemed like it had simply been discarded, and it rested on the corner of an ornate frame, pitched diagonally up the wall.

Alicia gasped. "There's a safe there."

"What?" Suzie turned toward the wall, and Alicia crossed the room quickly.

"Look." She wiped her bare hand along the dark patch of the wall, and sure enough, a shinier silver came out.

Mandie's gaze locked onto the metal door embedded in the wall. Her mind whirled with possibilities, with all the facts staring her in the face.

"Someone else knows about this place," she said, her voice barely above a whisper. Not just the house either. This secret den, behind a closed bookcase, in an abandoned library.

Why had they just now decided to come here and get whatever they wanted?

Suzie nodded, her face pale and her blue eyes twice as bright as usual—with fear. "Someone else was here that night."

"And they've been back." Alicia turned to face them. "How are they getting in? We have the only set of keys."

"We own this property," Mandie said, her leadership instincts kicking in. "We need to secure this house, and this room." She pulled her phone out, not sure what she would do with it. "How much will it cost to put up some security cameras around the exterior of the house?"

She had to stay within budget for this project at all costs, as she would not jeopardize anything for Alicia. At the same time, Candace would be livid when she learned someone else had been entering the property. She'd authorize the extra money for security cameras, no problem, when she discovered that.

But how to tell her without disclosing how they knew? For some reason, Mandie didn't want to tell Candace about this secret den quite yet. Why, she didn't know, but it had something to do with Suzie, and Mandie was still getting to know her.

"We can put up security cameras for a few hundred dollars," Alicia said. "I can put in the work order for them." She lifted her eyes in a silent question, and Mandie came back to the present.

She nodded at her best friend, and then turned her attention to Suzie. "You're a Harrington?"

Suzie blinked and seemed to come into herself. "Yes." She held up a piece of jewelry. "I got this from my grandmother before she died. She told me that her grandfather was Edmund's brother. That her mother and father lived here in this mansion for a few months when they came from Italy."

Wow, Mandie thought, but her voice didn't quite say out loud. She hadn't done a lot of research on where the Harrington's had gone over the years, or how many were left. But if Suzie was one of them...this house surely meant a great deal to her.

"And the journal?" Alicia asked, joining Suzie at the desk. "It was here?"

"Can you see the dust outline?"

Mandie moved over to join them, and the trio of them gazed down at the desktop. An old, weathered pad covered most of the desk, and it looked like the owner of it would show up at any moment. Possibly with lunch and a fresh cup of coffee.

A rectangular spot shone up from the desk—clearly something had been taken. Mandie even saw the faint swipe of where the person's fingers had slid under the book before lifting it up.

Her blood turned to ice, and she glanced over her shoulder as if she'd find the culprit standing there. He'd lock them in this room and... She pulled back on her thoughts, because it was broad daylight, and the mansion held other people right now.

She faced her friends. "All right," she said. "No one is to be here alone. Ever." She pierced Suzie with a look the other woman took well.

"Absolutely not," Alicia said.

"Understood," Suzie muttered.

"We'll put up cameras," Mandie said, glancing back to the desk. "I wish I knew what was in that journal."

Suzie sucked in a breath. "Wait. I took pictures of the journal pages. Here." She fumbled her phone and started swiping. "There were a lot of pages, but I got photos of all of them." She handed Mandie the device.

Another round of shock moved through her as she looked at the screen. Her eyes widened as she read. She couldn't read it all and understand it right now. "Give me the Cliff notes."

"There's a hidden Harrington fortune somewhere," Suzie said.

Mandie looked up from the phone, unable to handle any more revelations. "A hidden Harrington fortune?"

"This is huge." Alicia took the phone and started reading.

"I want all of those pictures," Mandie said. "Send them to both of us."

Alicia handed the phone back to Suzie, who nodded resolutely. "And Candace?"

Both women looked at her, and the weight of four eyes shouldn't be so heavy. Mandie blinked, trying to think. "I... Let's hold back on sending them to her quite yet," she finally said. "I want this parlor reveal to smash it out of the park, and we can tell her in a few days, once we have our first victory."

Her throat felt so dry, and she could use one of those drinks she'd suggested she, Suzie, and Alicia go get. "I'm starving," she said. "Let's go to lunch." Mandie cast another look around the room, trying to find other details that might have been disturbed. But she hadn't been in this room before, and Suzie hadn't indicated anything else.

"Lunch sounds great," Alicia said. "Suzie?"

She looked around the room for several more seconds too. "Yes," she said. "I don't see anything else." She met Mandie's eyes. "We need a break."

Mandie nodded, because they sure did. "Nothing we can do here right now, and we deserve to eat at a normal lunchtime." She led the way out of the hidden den, and she decided not to even stop by the parlor to tell Flint they were leaving.

She'd already done that, and she simply marched out of the front doors of the mansion, ready to leave behind the musty scent, the dusty touch of everything, and the enormous pressure that seemed to radiate from every surface in the house.

Twenty minutes later, they sat at a cozy table in a nearby café, steaming plates of seafood in front of them. The Hamptons had amazing restaurants, and PastForward would pick up the tab for this meal.

Some of the tension left her shoulders as she lifted one of the perfectly spiced mussels to her mouth. Growing up on an island, Mandie had eaten copious amounts of seafood in her life, and there was nothing she liked more than mussels.

"So," she said, glancing at Alicia with a mischievous grin as she put the shell in her discard bowl. "Tell us more about Henry."

Alicia blushed, running her fork through her krab salad. "There's not much to tell. We've just been texting."

"But you like him," Suzie said bluntly, as usual.

Alicia stared back at her as the pinkness in her cheeks faded. "It's complicated with the kids."

Mandie didn't have children, and she couldn't even imagine trying to date if she did. She reached out and squeezed her best friend's hand, which brought Alicia's dark eyes to hers. "You deserve to be happy, Lish. If Henry makes you smile even a little, that's a good thing."

Suzie nodded in agreement, then sighed. "I'd kill to find someone who made me smile."

Alicia laughed and finally took a bite of her krab salad. "Suzie, you've got to change your vocabulary. There's no *killing* in dating."

Mandie giggled too, and Suzie's shoulders softened. She stabbed a shrimp from out of her pasta and stuck it in her mouth. Mandie and Alicia simply watched her, and she finally swallowed. "Fine. You're right. I need to...be less...myself." She sighed and twisted her fork through the scampi again.

"No," Mandie said quickly, shooting a look to Alicia. She wore one of shock and surprise, mirroring the way Mandie's heartbeat jogged through her veins. "You don't have to be less of yourself. You just need to find someone who appreciates who you are."

"I'm forty years old," Suzie said with some measure of bitterness. "I don't know if anyone will ever appreciate who I am."

"Well," Alicia said. "I believe everyone has someone out there." She looked up as the waiter refilled her water glass, and when he walked away, she nodded to him. "What about him?"

Suzie turned her head slowly and looked at the retreating form of the waiter. "I'm sure he's not interested."

"You don't know that," Mandie said, picking up on the pieces Alicia had set down. "He might be. He was very smiley."

"Yeah, because it's lunchtime in the summer in the Hamptons," Suzie said dryly. "He wants a good tip."

"Maybe he wants a good date," Alicia said, her smile wide and playful.

"Stop it." Suzie stuffed way too much pasta in her mouth, and Mandie shook her head as she laughed.

"Honey, you don't put so much food in your mouth when you want a man to talk to you."

Suzie glared at her, a noodle still hanging from her mouth. She said something, but Mandie couldn't understand her past all the pasta. She only laughed harder, and Alicia joined in.

Just as Suzie swallowed and they quieted slightly. "Oh-ho." Alicia cleared her throat and glanced at Suzie. "He's coming back."

Suzie immediately swiveled her head toward the waiter, and Alicia hissed. "Don't look."

"What?" Suzie barked as she looked back at Alicia.

"I've got the mac-and-cheese bites," he said as he held the plate. The tiny table already held too many plates, condiments, and glasses, and he searched for a place to put it.

Mandie kicked Suzie under the table, and she grunted and glared at her. Their eyes met, and Mandie moved only her eyes up to the waiter, a man named Donovan.

"Oh," Suzie said—really, it could've been classified a shout. "You can put those right here." She started making room for the extra plate.

"Sorry they came out after the mains," he said. "We've

got a new chef in the kitchen this summer." He smiled from ear to ear as he set down the plate, and he glanced at Mandie, Alicia, and then focused on Suzie. "Can I get you ladies anything else?"

Yeah, Mandie thought. *Your phone number for my friend.*

It still startled her slightly that she labeled Suzie as a friend, but as the blonde's face pinked up, Mandie definitely thought of her as a friend. Warmth spread through her chest as Suzie mumbled something that sounded like, "No, we're fine."

But Alicia said, "You know who you should go out with, Suzie?"

That drew everyone's attention, even Donovan's. "Who?" Mandie asked when Suzie simply sat there openmouthed.

"This guy at work." Alicia started tapping on her phone. "He's just your type: Dark hair and eyes. Good job." She'd literally just described the man still standing at their table. Alicia looked up to him next, and oh, she was so fluid and easy. "Hey, where's a good place for a first date around here? Are you from the Hamptons?"

"I live in Long Island," he said. "But I've worked out here for years." He looked at Suzie. "First date material?" Donovan grinned at her. "You look like you like the outdoors."

She does? Mandie thought, but she let him carry on without saying anything.

"A little," Suzie said, almost defensively.

"There's a great State Park out here," he said. "Lots of hiking and stuff."

"Do you hike?" Alicia asked, drawing the man's attention.

"Yes," he said simply.

"Maybe you two should go on a few so she knows if she can do them before she goes out with Shawn. He's... pretty athletic."

Mandie held back her laughter by pressing her lips together and picking up her water glass. Suzie looked like she'd been hit with a two-by-four and then tased, and she simply looked back and forth between Alicia and Donovan.

"About like you," Alicia continued effortlessly. "If she can keep up with you, I bet she'll be fine with Shawn."

Yeah, because Shawn didn't exist. Mandie set down her glass, snuck a look at Suzie, and reached for one of the fried mac-and-cheese bites. "Sounds fun," she said. "My husband and I like to go on walks in the city. I didn't know there was a State Park out here."

"Oh, maybe you have a wife to go hiking with." Alicia set her phone on the table and picked up her fork again. "Sorry, I should've asked."

"I'm not married," Donovan said, and he zeroed in on Suzie. "I could show you some of the hikes."

She simply blinked at him, and Mandie nudged her under the table again. She physically bounced up an inch or two, blinked, and said, "Yeah, that's probably a good idea."

Someone called his name, and he looked over his shoulder. After a nod and a quick, dismissive wave, he faced Suzie again. "I'll just…" He plucked a pen from his apron and leaned right over and wrote his number on the paper tablecloth. "There's my number. Text me, okay?"

"Okay," Suzie said without moving her mouth.

He turned and took a couple of steps away, then spun back. "Oh, what's your name?"

"Suzie," she said, and Mandie had never been prouder.

Donovan grinned and grinned. "Suzie, nice." Then he turned and got back to work.

Mandie couldn't contain her laughter anymore, and giggles just poured from her. "You're good," she said over them, grinning at Alicia.

"That was incredible," Suzie said, pure awe in her tone. "I don't even know what happened."

Mandie pointed to the scrawled number on the table. "Alicia got you that handsome man's number. That's what happened."

With the blue sky above, and the sea breeze drifting over great food, Mandie forgot about all the troubles and snags back at the mansion. She, Suzie, and Alicia laughed through the rest of their lunch, and just when she couldn't take another bite, her phone buzzed.

"Flint," she said when she saw his name there. "You guys, he sent a video." She tapped on it to get it to open, and she held her phone in front of her as Alicia and Suzie leaned over to peer at it.

The video swept through the parlor, now complete

with the hung curtains, that gorgeous floor, and a flickering fire in the hearth. The room looked absolutely stunning, every detail perfect.

Mandie's breath caught in her throat. This was going to go over amazingly well with Candace, the Historical Society, and all of the Hamptons. She was just sure of it.

"It's beautiful," Alicia breathed.

"We did that," Suzie said, a note of pride in her voice.

Mandie nodded, a swell of emotion moving through her. Despite the mysteries and challenges they faced, they were creating something truly special at the Hampton House.

The video ended, and she pulled her phone back. As she looked at her friends' smiling faces, Mandie knew that whatever secrets the mansion held, whatever obstacles they might face, they would face them together.

As friends.

With renewed determination and motivation, Mandie raised her almost-empty water glass. "To us—and to solving the mystery of the Hampton House." She glanced to Suzie as she reached for her glass too.

Alicia and Suzie clinked their glasses against hers, and as they laughed, drank a sip of water, and replaced their glasses back on the table, Alicia's phone chimed.

She dove for it, and her whole countenance glowed as she read. She looked up, equal parts worry and joyful anticipation in her expression. "Henry and I are going out this weekend."

"Yes, you are." Mandie held up her hand for Alicia to

high-five, which she did. She grinned, but she blew out her breath like she'd just done something really hard.

She probably had, and a swell of pride for her friend filled her. "Good job, Lish. If it doesn't work out, it doesn't work out." She gave a little shrug as she stood up, hoping to put Alicia's mind at ease over going out with Henry. "We better get back to the house. I want to see the parlor in person now that it's completely done."

"Yes," Alicia said, getting to her feet too with another sigh, this one clearly weighed down with the thought of the Hampton House. "Let's go get what we need to impress Candace like she's never been impressed before."

Chapter Eleven

Alicia walked into the Chinese restaurant where she'd agreed to meet Henry for their first date, her heart a steady drumbeat in her ears. He'd wanted to come pick her up at her apartment, but Alicia had hesitated on that. For some reason, meeting him felt more casual and less like they'd become something serious.

She'd been texting with him for weeks now, and she hoped she hadn't run out of words, or that the conversation tonight wouldn't just be a rehash of what they'd already said to one another.

She paused just inside the glass door with gold accents and cast her gaze around the dimly lit interior. Lanterns hung from the ceiling, casting a warm glow over the red and gold décor. Patrons laughed and chatted at small, intimate tables crowded with bamboo steamers and porcelain teapots.

She took a breath, trying to shake off her nerves. She'd

left the apartment ten minutes late and made the four-block walk slowly, so she wouldn't be sweaty when she arrived.

This is insane, she thought. She hadn't been on a proper first date in oh, twelve years now. Far too long to know how to do things these days.

Part of her shouted at her to *flee, and flee now*, but then a man rose from a table about halfway down the window from her. Henry stood there, wearing a pair of dark brown khakis, with a pristine leather belt that surely came with the shoes. His polo reminded her of the inside of a blueberry—not quite purple or blue, but a kind of watery mix of both.

He'd tucked it in neatly, and while he wasn't wearing his three-piece suit, every part of him still sat in the perfect place. He lifted his hand in a wave, and Alicia couldn't leave now.

Taking another fortifying breath, Alicia approached. "Hey," she said, only sounding half like herself.

"Alicia," he said, stepping forward to pull out her chair. He grinned at her, and he'd never been shy about his feelings for her. "You look great."

She glanced down at herself to remind herself of what she'd put on after work today. A short-sleeved sweater that had been labeled as "berry," the pink bringing out her dark features nicely. She'd paired that with a loose pair of navy pants and a pair of sandals—nothing too special.

Still, she always appreciated a good compliment, and she smiled at Henry as she sat down. He took the seat across from her, and a waiter materialized almost immediately, offering them menus before slipping away, already yelling at someone in the kitchen.

The restaurant had a vibrancy, but not the same type as the cafes and bistros in the Hamptons. Alicia honestly wasn't sure which she preferred. *A meal you don't have to cook is a win*, she told herself as she spread the napkin over her knee.

"Have you been here before?" Henry asked, breaking the silence that had settled over them while they studied their menus.

"No, actually," she said, closing her menu and wondering how much to disclose. "But I've heard good things. It's only a short walk from my place." She gazed at him, knowing he didn't live in this borough north of Manhattan. She refrained from saying "my new place," because she'd already told Henry about her divorce. That indicated lots of changes, and she hadn't gone into detail about what all of those were, exactly.

Henry didn't scoff and say he would never eat in the Bronx. Instead, he smiled and said, "I haven't, but I checked out the reviews. Seems like a hidden gem."

"Given my love of Chinese food, I think 'barely passable' will satisfy me." She grinned at him, noticing he didn't go back to his menu either. "What are you going to get?"

She hadn't exactly set any conversation rules for tonight's date, but she didn't want to spend it talking about work, historical sites, or the Hampton House. A little would be fine, but she really didn't want her relationship with Henry to be *only* about work.

"Pork potstickers," he said. "I love them."

"That's an appetizer," she teased.

"You know, my mom has a thing she does." Henry leaned into his arms on the table. "When she wants more than one thing, she just orders both."

"Mm hm." Alicia felt like her vision sparkled as she looked at him. "So you're going to get two things?"

"I sure am."

"Maybe I will too."

He chuckled and looked up when their waiter returned with two glasses—gold-rimmed—of water. No ice. Henry didn't reach for his, and Alicia simply looked at hers too. "You ready to order?" he asked.

Henry took a breath and said, "Yes, I'll have the pork potstickers with the soy-based sauce." He didn't look at the menu at all. "The beef with broccoli and an order of sweet and sour chicken."

"White rice, brown, or fried?"

"White," Henry said, and he looked over to Alicia.

"I'll take the green bean chicken and the teriyaki pork," she said, ordering two main dishes too. The waiter jotted things down, nodded, and left.

"I'm a food-sharer," Alicia confessed. "You can have anything of mine you want."

"I suppose I can allow you to taste my food too," Henry said, and he reached across the table and covered her hand with his.

"So..." Henry squeezed her hand and pulled his back. "We haven't talked about the parlor in the Hampton House." He actually reached for his water glass and took a sip. He made a face, coughed, and said, "Nope. I knew that would be a mistake."

He put the glass down and pushed it further from him, while Alicia's stomach tried to turn itself inside out. Candace had been thrilled with the pictures of the parlor, and Flint had put together a brilliant, ten-second clip to release to everyone at PastForward, as well as the media.

Their social media manager had been flooding their accounts with the photos and video, and Alicia could admit her hopes had soared at the positive feedback the team had received.

"The house is coming along," she said carefully. "Mandie, Suzie, and I have been working really hard on it, and we have a *long* way to go."

Henry nodded, his eyes softening with understanding. "These projects take forever, don't they?"

"Seem to," she said, though they only had a six-month timeline on the Hampton House.

"Do you guys, like, make decisions on things as a team?" he asked. "Or...?"

Alicia searched his face, trying to find his true opinion without him saying it. Did he not like the parlor? And if not, what wasn't to like?

He said nothing, and Alicia didn't want to *ask* for bad news. Her phone buzzed, and she practically dove on it to get away from this particular topic.

Even her ex-husband's name on her phone provided some relief, and she wasn't sure what that meant for this date, or for her potential relationship with Henry. "It's Ryan," she said.

"Ryan?" Henry asked.

Alicia flicked up her eyes to look at him. "My ex." Her fingers flew over the phone screen to unlock it and see what he had to say. "He's got a work trip in July." She didn't have her calendar right in front of her, and it wouldn't have mattered anyway. She had to work Monday through Friday, and with a potential promotion on the horizon, Alicia couldn't be late or take unnecessary time off.

I'll call you later, she tapped out to him. *I can't talk right now.*

Another text came in before hers finished sending, but she set the phone facedown on the table and refocused on Henry. "Sorry." She half-reached for the water glass, then pulled her hand back before making that mistake. "Tell me what you thought of the parlor."

He watched her for a moment, which only sent Alicia's pulse skittering up into the rafters. "I love that house," he said. "I've studied plenty about it."

"You're not saying what you think," she said.

"I...think it could benefit from some...modern touch-es." He sighed and looked away. "I think that...I mean, that's what a restoration and renovation is. No one wants to see the mansion exactly how it was a hundred and fifty years ago."

Alicia folded her arms, trying to keep her heart from flying out of her chest. She'd found Henry to be polite, funny, and smart in the past few weeks since she'd been texting him, but hearing his careful, slow criticism of the Hampton House struck her ribs like someone swinging a baseball bat.

"We wanted to maintain the historical integrity of the house." She spoke in the same slow, measured, diplomatic voice as he had, trying to mask her defensiveness. The project was already a balancing act of budgets, deadlines, and now, apparently, aesthetic compromises. Could she really afford to rethink their design choices at this stage?

And talking to Mandie about that...Alicia wanted to keep both eyes in her head, thank you very much.

"Of course," Henry said in that proper way he had. "You guys sell the houses, though, right? They're not historical markers or being donated as museums."

"The drapes are era-appropriate," she said. "It is the drapes you don't like, right?"

He grinned at her. "It's the drapes."

"Which a new homebuyer can easily replace," she pointed out. Thankfully, their food arrived then, and it took two waiters to bring over their plates. The tiny table barely held it all, and Alicia's mouth watered with the variety of proteins and sauces being placed in front of her.

She'd just picked up her chopsticks to take her first bite when her phone buzzed, but not with a text. It was ringing, and she flipped it over just in case it was Candace calling to say she'd gotten the assistant director job.

Ryan.

She sighed out her frustration.

"Everything okay?" Henry asked, moving several pieces of chicken onto his plate with a healthy helping of white rise.

"It's my ex-husband again." Alicia's heartbeat bobbed in the back of her throat when she saw he'd texted several times since she'd told him she couldn't talk. She honestly didn't know how to balance being a mom, being on a date, and working full-time.

"I just—" The phone stopped ringing, and she'd missed her chance to answer it. She felt torn in six different directions—work, Lily, Gray, Ryan, Henry, and her own personal need for food and sleep and sunshine on her face.

She silenced the phone, so she couldn't even hear it vibrate, and this time, she shoved it into her purse. "I don't want to talk about work anymore," she said as she pinched up her first bite of chicken and green beans. "So, what else have you got?"

She could catalog the idea to do some modern touches on the little details of the mansion for later. Mandie was reasonable, and she did ask for opinions all the time. Alicia could maybe bring it up during one of those sessions.

"No work?" Henry pushed his plate of beef and broccoli toward her. "How about the food?"

Alicia put the first bite in her mouth, enjoying the richness of the sauce and the crisp bite of the green bean. By the time she couldn't take another bite, she'd tried all of the dishes and eaten half of Henry's potstickers.

She groaned as he opened the glass-and-gold door for her, having enjoyed a conversation about the upcoming Independence Day festivities, her kids, and Henry's time in college.

"So," she said as they started down the street. Henry came to her side, and she bumped him with her hip. "I'm gonna need a ballpark of your age."

"My age?"

"Yes," she said. "You speak of college like you just graduated, and I have an eight-year-old and a five-year-old."

Henry's hand brushed hers, and he cleared his throat and caught hers on the next step. "Can I hold your hand, Lish?" he whispered, the words landing like a shout in the quiet evening.

"Seems like you already are." Lightning strobed up and down her arm, all the fire originating from where his skin touched hers. She hadn't had a touch like this in a while, even before she'd learned of Ryan's infidelity.

She'd probably get an earful tonight when she finally called him back, but Alicia compartmentalized her family problems for later. A gentle breeze ruffled the leaves on the trees and brought the scent of blooming flowers to her nose.

"I'm thirty," Henry said. "My brother says I just have a baby face."

"And an impeccable memory," she said. "You speak of college like you were just there."

"You speak of the nineteen-forties like you lived them," he teased.

Alicia laughed, because she did love the World War Two era. "I love history," she said. "Reading all the historical documents, even the fiction I like."

"History is definitely my first love," Henry said, and that topic took off, with him telling her about the various projects he'd worked on since graduation and her detailing some of the projects she'd worked on at PastForward.

They walked in silence for a while, the sound of their footsteps mingling with the distant hum of traffic. Alicia found herself relaxing again, the stress of the day melting away in Henry's presence.

When they reached a small park, Henry gestured to a bench. "Do you have time to sit for a bit?"

"Sure," Alicia said, taking a seat and leaving room for him beside her. "I love the city." She breathed in the scent of so many people, and so much life, and it simply added energy to her reserves. The streetlights started to come on, and a sense of having lived a good day moved through Alicia.

The silence between them felt as comfortable as the texting, the dinner, the walk, the holding hands.

"Do I get a second date?" Henry didn't look at her as he asked.

Her heart fluttered at his words, and warmth spread through her chest. She leaned her head against his shoulder. "Yeah, I think a second date would be nice." Excitement, anxiety, and hope mixed into a terrible cocktail inside her, and she made a bit of room on her plate for a new relationship.

"My kids are gone until the ninth," she said.

"What about brunch at my place?" he asked. "Tomorrow?"

"Your place?" Her voice pitched up with teasing. "You haven't even told me where you live yet. It's like you're guarding it, like maybe I'll show up and egg the place or something."

Henry smiled, but he didn't immediately volunteer his address. In that moment, she realized this date was almost over, and her body went cold at *how* it would end.

Could she kiss him goodnight? On the first date? He hadn't picked her up, and Alicia could admit that was one reason why she'd wanted to meet him. Then, she could simply say she needed to get going, and they could part ways right there on the street.

They sat in comfortable silence, their hands intertwined, the world around them fading away. When she got home, she'd be consumed by her calendar, her ex-husband, the work files she'd brought home to study for their preliminary plans for the kitchen.

She didn't want to go back to the apartment alone and let life tread over her. She was exactly where she needed—and wanted—to be.

After several more minutes, Henry stood. "Brunch at eleven?"

She got to her feet too, tucking her hands in her pockets. "All right. Tell me where to come."

He gave her a playful look and said, "I'll text you."

Awkwardness descend on them, the way it did at the

end of a date. Alicia wasn't sure what to do. Shake his hand? Give him a hug? She wasn't going to kiss him, not out here on the very public street.

"You'll text me?" She lifted her eyebrows and then shook her head as she laughed. "All right." She stepped into him and hugged him. "Thank you for dinner, Henry." She gasped and pulled back "Oh, no. The leftovers. We left them on the table."

This was just her luck—and her life. Things would go well for a while, and then something would get dropped. And the worst part was, she often didn't know about the sinkhole in the living room or the leftovers sitting on the table until it was too late.

"It's fine," Henry said with a chuckle. "It's just Chinese food."

"Yeah," Alicia said, though it felt like more to her. It felt like another brick in a backpack already full of them. Her kids, her job, her friends, her ex-husband, the calendar, all of it.

Henry stepped over to the side of the road and lifted his hand. "I'm not a bad cook," he said as a cab started to slow for him. "And I'm only about twenty minutes from you, so I'll text you my address, okay?"

"Okay," she said.

And with that, he slid into the cab, smiling at her through the window. He drove off, and Alicia started to make her way back to her apartment, the weight of her responsibilities returning with every step.

She had a promotion to secure, a project to perfect,

and children to care for. Henry's words echoed in her mind, and she jotted down *modern touches, appealing to today's buyers*, determined to bring it up with Mandie even if that meant one of her friend's laser looks.

"And don't forget about an intruder in the mansion." Just because she could, Alicia opened her laptop and navigated to the live feed of the cameras they'd gotten up this week. They showed nothing. No movement. She checked the archives and found the same thing.

Whoever had been sneaking into the Hampton House had stopped in the past couple of days—but that didn't mean they hadn't already gotten what they wanted. Perhaps they didn't need to come back—and neither she, nor Suzie, nor Mandie would ever know everything they'd taken.

"Or where the Harrington fortune is," Alicia muttered. She remembered her phone, and with a sense of dread she pulled it out to call Ryan.

She found a text from Henry. *I had a wonderful time tonight. Looking forward to brunch.*

A smile instantly sprang to her face, and she forgot about Ryan for a moment. Which only made her forget about her kids, and when she remembered, guilt pinched through her.

But Henry had texted again, this time with his address. Alicia stared at it, her heartbeat thrashing in her chest. "Yonkers?" she said aloud. "He lives in *Yonkers*?"

It was a charming little suburb right on the Hudson River, and she'd told him she'd put it at the top of her list as a place she'd like to someday buy a house and raise her kids.

And he lived there. No wonder he hadn't said anything.

She scoffed and then got back to texting, deciding to simply get everything out through her fingers at the same time. So she texted Mandie about the modern flourishes idea, as well as Ryan about their childcare schedule for the next month.

She could deal with the fallout once all the words came out.

Chapter Twelve

Suzie stood in the grand library of the Hampton House, now turned into the organized chaos she called their makeshift war room. Tall mahogany bookshelves lined the walls, filled with dusty tomes and ancient volumes that concealed the secrets of the past. The scent of old leather and aged paper mingled with the faint tang of wood polish, a constant reminder of the work still ahead.

The library wasn't just a repository of books they'd been steadily going through; it had become the nerve center for their operation. Maps, blueprints, and photographs of the mansion covered the large oak table in the middle of the room. Laptops and tablets hummed quietly as they provided a modern contrast to the antiquated surroundings, so any of the three of them could look up whatever they needed to with only a few taps and clicks.

Mandie had just dropped the final design and décor

plans over the blueprint, and she sighed as she pushed her hair out of her face. "We have to approve these today to get things ordered and delivered in time."

She looked at Suzie and Alicia with weariness in her eyes. They'd been working on this place for five weeks now, and this week was a short work week due to the Fourth of July holiday.

Outside the open library door, the sounds of construction echoed through the mansion. Men called out to each other, pounding echoed through the two-story foyer, and the occasional buzz of a saw sliced through the air. The ballroom, game room, and study were undergoing significant renovations all at the same time, as the construction crew moved steadily toward the back of the house—the heart. The kitchen.

Suzie in particular felt a sense of connection to the mansion that went beyond the professional. She couldn't shake the feeling that she was meant to be here, that her heritage tied her to this place in a way she couldn't fully explain. And today, as she stood among the relics of the past, she was determined to prove her worth to the team— and herself.

Alicia leaned over the décor plans and cleared her throat. Oh, boy, that wasn't good, and Suzie stopped living in her romanticized thoughts and centered herself in reality.

"I was thinking," she said. "We want to make sure we're putting a perfectly restored, historical home on the market—which is a current, modern market." She raised her dark eyes to Mandie, and Mandie alone.

"Yes," Mandie said slowly. "And?"

Alicia sighed and straightened to her full height. She stood taller than Mandie, but Suzie had an inch or two on her. "I think we can pull back on the mega-historical finishes."

Mandie narrowed her eyes and then peered at the list of décor items. "Meaning...?"

"Drapes," Alicia said. "In fact, no one calls them *drapes* anymore. They're *curtains*."

"Okay," Mandie said, but Suzie could tell she hadn't really connected the dots. "What else?"

"Maybe we could tone down the brass in the ballroom," Alicia said lightly. "And bring out some brighter things in the study. No one wants to feel like they're working in a cave for a home office."

Mandie dragged her finger down the list and reached for a pencil. Alicia exchanged a glanced with Suzie, and she made a small nudge with her chin toward Mandie. *Say something*, Alicia was saying.

Suzie cleared her throat, trying to find a way to say something tactfully. "I can see Alicia's point," she said. "The wood in the study is really dark, so bringing in some brighter, more modern accents would be really nice." She swallowed when Mandie didn't look up, didn't even seem to know she'd spoken. "A great office for someone who has important business to conduct from home."

"Yes," Mandie said almost absently. "My husband's

mother used to live in the Hamptons and work from a home office." She lifted her head then. "We have a lot of brass and Brocade on the list."

"It should all go," Alicia said. "Plus, more modern flourishes will be cheaper." She clicked a pen into action. "And we need things to be a little cheaper. I mean, just the bill for Windex for the glass in that lounge..." She whistled like she'd never seen anything like it, and Suzie grinned.

Mandie started crossing out the outdated things and writing in substitutions. "I have to have this turned in by this afternoon," she muttered, clearly unhappy with the last-minute changes. "Lish, can you help with pricing?"

"Absolutely."

Suzie had bulldozed her way through most of the rooms, but she still had a couple of outbuildings she could go through. She looked over her shoulder, needing to get outside the walls of this place.

"Anything new on the Harrington fortune?" Alicia asked innocently, but her dark eyes shot something meaningful at Suzie.

Mandie stopped scribbling and looked up. "Unless someone has been breaking the rules and coming here after hours alone, we haven't had any time to explore more on that." She looked from Alicia to Suzie, her eyebrows going up in challenge.

"I've behaved," Suzie said, her voice tinny and hoarse at the same time. "I did, however, go out to my mother's and go through my grandma's books and journals."

"Nothing on the cameras?" Mandie asked.

Alicia shook her head and turned to pick up a laptop.

"I found the title to a couple of Edmund's ships, as well as a copy of his birth certificate." Suzie lifted her chin, because she felt like no one was paying attention to her. Why had Alicia brought this up, only to move on to another task before Suzie could speak?

She threw the other woman a glare. "The Harringtons of today live in California," she continued. "As far as I know, I'm the only one still here in the New York area."

"This is great and all," Mandie said. "But I don't know how it relates to this project."

It related, because Suzie felt a personal connection to this house. She swallowed, not sure how to articulate such a thing. "I'm going to go through a bookcase," she said, and she turned her back on the other two women.

She moved away from them, to the furthest recesses of the library. She'd taken pictures of the journal in the hidden den, as well as the one she'd seen at her parents' house.

Edmund's son had apparently hidden a fortune one hundred years ago now. The journal said: *It's just a legend, but most of the Harrington stories are almost always true. William liked riddles and puzzles, and if he had something to hide, it'll only be found by deciphering something.*

Perhaps his journals.

Suzie wasn't sure if the missing journal was William's or not. She didn't know if William was the one who used the hidden den. Her heart told her it was, and Suzie needed to forward along the pictures of her grandmother's journals to Alicia and Mandie.

But they suddenly didn't seem so interested, and Suzie told herself not to be bitter. They both had super-important career goals riding on this renovation and restoration, while the importance of it to Suzie delved deeper into her heart than anywhere else.

So she kept her back turned to them, and she swiped through the new pictures she'd gotten recently. *A puzzle*, she thought. *A riddle. A clue.*

She looked up, a literal wall of books in front of her. No one had gone through these cases yet, pulling out the books and lovingly wiping them down, ruffling the pages to see if anything had been concealed within, and then cataloging them. All of that had to be done, volume by volume, and they'd each done a little bit over the past few weeks, usually when they had something to think through.

Suzie glanced over her shoulder and found Mandie and Alicia bent over the same computer, both peering at something on the screen as they redid the décor list, which included re-pricing things.

She'd always been a private person, and she looked back to the bookshelves. Just like she'd seen the slightly off seam of the shelves on the other side of the library, Suzie found an inconsistency in the books in front of her.

One of them had been pushed further in than the others. She gravitated toward it instantly and swiftly, reached up, straining to get to it. Someone several inches taller than her had put it there—and recently—and Suzie turned to get a chair.

"Guys," she said, and her voice must've carried something quivering and exciting in it, because Mandie and Alicia both looked at her. "I just found something." She pulled the chair over to the bookcase and got up on it.

The leather-bound book came out easily then, and Suzie barely needed to open it to know she'd just found the journal that had once been behind the bookcase, down the hall, and in the secret den.

She turned on the chair and held it up like she'd just won a heavyweight belt in a boxing match. "The journal."

Mandie nearly tripped over her feet she got up so fast, and Alicia practically threw the laptop onto the table. "That's it?"

"This is it." Suzie got down off the chair and held the book in front of her as the other two women arrived. "Someone put it there. I could see it had been pushed in further than the others."

She flipped open the front cover, and sure enough, there was the handwriting she had memorized. Her fingers ran along the inside cover, and the paper that had been glued down there flaked back. Gently, using her fingernail, she lifted it up, and there, she saw a name that made her gasp right out loud.

"What?" Alicia asked, crowding in closer. "William Joseph Harrington."

"He's Edmund's son," Suzie whispered. "My grandmother wrote about him in her journal. He's the one who hid the fortune." She looked up. "She thinks there will be puzzles or riddles or something to decipher if we want to find it."

And oh, Suzie wanted to find it. *If it exists*, she amended in her head. Looking at Alicia's wide eyes and Mandie's rounded-in-shock mouth, Suzie was so glad she had someone to share this with. These two women specifically.

"What kind of puzzle?" Alicia finally asked.

"I don't know." Suzie flipped the page and found a tiny, capital letter L up in the corner. She frowned, because she didn't remember seeing that in her photos. She suddenly snapped the journal closed. "Can I take this home?" She looked at Mandie for the permission she needed.

Mandie wore a stunned expression, and she swallowed. "I don't know. Do we get to—?"

"Mandie?"

They all turned toward the entrance to the library, where Carl stood half-in and half-out, an anxious look on his face. He hooked one gloved thumb over his shoulder. "You better come see this. Right now."

Mandie took off without a second thought or another word. Suzie's heart dropped to her steel-toed boots, but she hurried after her.

"What room?" Mandie asked.

"The ballroom," Carl called over his shoulder. "Listen, we knew some of the pillars in here had cracks. We took pictures of everything." He strode with purpose, and his legs had to be twice as long as everyone else's.

Suzie broke into a jog to try to catch up, and her only consolation was that Alicia was behind her.

"But there's one in the back that looks like it's been hit with a sledgehammer." Carl reached the ballroom and went through the double-wide doors, Mandie nearly on top of him. Suzie followed and came to a stop to take everything in.

The ballroom should've been an easy fix. A big open room with a grand piano where people sipped drinks and danced? They only needed to make sure everything was structurally sound and clean as a whistle.

Yes, there had been a couple of pillars where they'd discovered some hairline cracks, probably from some subtle shifting in the ground over the years. The black and white tiles had also been examined, and plenty of them had also cracked over time.

Mandie hated them anyway, proclaiming them, "Too much like the board game *Clue*. No. We're ripping all of that out and putting in something else." Suzie had agreed, and they'd found a beautiful wide-plank parquet wood in a variety of shades that Mandie had decided to lay in a herringbone pattern.

The designer had come up with a circular pattern around the round room, and the pattern would run out from the middle of the room to that.

But now, in the middle of the room lay the chandelier

that had been securely fixed in the ceiling yesterday. That morning, even.

"What in the world happened?" Mandie asked.

She'd just asked Alicia to file a filming report for the pink gems they'd found embedded in the chandelier— Suzie had been in the huddle up where it had happened. Alicia would do that; Flint would *schedule* a time to come lower the chandelier to film the uniqueness of the chandelier.

It shouldn't just be lying on the ground.

"And there's this." Carl moved to the last pillar in the room and around it. "This pillar didn't even *have* a crack in it. I pulled up all the pictures and checked, then double-checked." He looked at Mandie with something dark in his gaze.

"So, what are you saying?" Suzie asked, marching forward. She looked up, and it sure didn't seem like the chandelier had fallen. More like someone had...lowered it down for some reason.

No gaping hole. No ripped sheetrock. Nothing that would indicate the ceiling hadn't been able to hold the chandelier.

Suzie paced around it, not finding a broken shard of glass anywhere. She frowned. "This was lowered out of the ceiling." She faced Carl. "Why? We'll send in the cleaning crew once everything else is done."

"That's how it was when we came back from lunch," Carl said, coming back around the pillar. "It was up when we left. Down now." He glanced at Alicia and Mandie. "I wondered if one of you ladies had lowered it."

"No," Mandie barked. "Why would we do that? We know you're working in here today."

"I don't even know how to lower and lift this chandelier." Alicia looked up to the ceiling too, a perplexed look on her face. She sucked in a breath. "Guys."

Suzie immediately looked up as Alicia said, "There's someone there."

Nothing made sense, but Suzie definitely met a pair of eyes for the briefest of moments. Then the masked face disappeared, pulled back.

"What? Where?" Mandie joined them and looked up, Carl right behind her. "I don't see anything."

"There was someone there," Suzie said loudly. Panic tore through her. "How do we get up there?"

"Up there?" Carl repeated.

"He's up there!" Suzie scanned the wall in front of her, wondering what was behind the curved walls in the corner. "How do I get up there?" She'd bulldoze anything to get up into the ceiling. "Alicia!"

"I don't know, Suzie."

She spun to Mandie. "You have the blueprints memorized. How do I get up to the ceiling to lower and lift this chandelier?"

In the resulting silence, several hollow, footstep-like noises echoed down from the ceiling. The elation of finding the journal had disappeared completely, only to be replaced with pure panic, and heavy pressure settled onto her ribs.

Suzie could not stand here and let someone sabotage this project. Not when they were in the house. "Alicia, check the cameras! Carl, secure every door!" She ran toward the corner. She'd kick a hole in it to see what it concealed, and thankfully, Mandie darted in front of her.

"The ladder to the second floor, where the chandelier mechanism is, is in that corner." She pointed behind Suzie to the far left corner, and Suzie changed direction on a dime. "But we haven't been able to get the door open!"

Suzie wasn't going to play nice with it. She reached the wall, searching for the seam that would indicate a door there. She wasn't sure if her eyes had malfunctioned or it was that well concealed, but she couldn't see it.

But she wore boots for a reason, and she reared back and kicked the wall with everything she had. She'd earned the reputation and nickname as The Bulldozer for a reason —and it was time to demonstrate why.

Mandie yelped behind her as Suzie's foot went through the wall. She kicked again and again, desperate when she realized how much time had gone by. The door finally popped out on the fourth kick, and she ripped at it. A set of tight spiral steps led up, and Suzie threw herself at them.

Her breath came in quick gulps by the time she reached the top, and her head spun as if she'd been twirling in a circle for hours. She looked down the catwalk— empty.

She ran that way anyway, and she dropped to her knees next to the automatic mechanism that lifted and lowered the enormous chandelier. Suzie peered down and found only Alicia looking up at her.

"They're not here," she called.

"Be careful," Alicia called back. "Where else does that go?"

Suzie had no idea, and she lifted her head, her eyes taking too long to adjust to the darker circumstances up here. It would take at least an hour to get the chandelier back into position, which meant that was an hour that Carl's crew couldn't work in the ballroom.

A wave of despair washed over her. The stakes felt so high, and the gravity of the situation settled around her neck like a yoke. This adversary had access to the house.

What would they ruin next? Take next? Hide next?

She felt like the success of the Hampton House project —and their futures—lay all the way down on the ground...just the way the chandelier did.

Suzie sat back on her haunches, her mind running in several different directions. She wasn't even sure which way to go or what to do next. Her phone chimed, and Alicia called, "Mandie wants us back in the library."

Helplessness filled Suzie, and she didn't move.

"Suze?"

She leaned over and looked at Alicia. "Yeah," she said. "I'm coming." She got to her feet and moved past this opening in the ceiling. The catwalk continued, but there wasn't another ladder or way up or down.

HVAC and wiring and pipes, but no way up or down. It didn't branch left or right to go into any other rooms, and Suzie exhaled in pure frustration as she turned back the way she'd come. The saboteur had to have gone this way too, and Suzie paused at the bottom of the stairs, trying to find another way out.

Another doorway stood in front of her, and Suzie reached out with two fingers and pushed it open.

The latch hadn't closed, and her heartbeat whipped through her body. She moved into the wall, the room on the other side of this room the library, something screaming at her to tell someone where she was going.

Instead, she took the first step into the darkness.

Chapter Thirteen

"Where is she?" Mandie paced in the library, feeling more and more unsafe with every passing second. Carl's team had scattered to secure the mansion, but she wasn't sure he had enough men to cover every door. Certainly not all the windows.

And certainly not if there were more secret passageways and hidden rooms she didn't know about yet.

She hugged herself, her arms tight, tight, tight around her ribcage. The very walls of this place had so many stories, and Mandie didn't mean just the ones holding books. Every stitch in mansions like this had seen so much. Experienced so many things with different owners, heard so many conversations.

She could almost hear them whispering to her, but she turned back to the door. Suzie had not returned from the ballroom, and Mandie prayed she had not been injured. She lifted her thumbnail to her mouth. "Call her again."

Alicia dutifully did, and Mandie's thoughts turned to Candace. How much longer could she keep this a secret from her boss? She'd approved the cameras on the exterior of the property, and Mandie moved over to the laptop station.

"Maybe they'll be on here," she said. Her skin crawled at the idea of someone sneaking into the house *while they were right there* and lowering the chandelier while they were only one room away, going over fixtures and finishes.

She pulled up the window with their security camera feed on it, and she clicked on the button to show her the incidents—any movement that triggered the cameras. She didn't see anything, and tears filled her eyes.

Then, she *really* couldn't see anything. She sniffled and lowered her head. She held it in her hands and ignored Alicia when she sat next to her on the couch. "I don't want to be here anymore," she said, hating the high pitch of her voice.

Alicia put her arm around her. "I know," she whispered.

"I really don't." Mandie lifted her head. "They were here, Lish. Right on the other side of the wall from us. While we talked about—about Brocade or linen, brass or silver knobs, and looked at prices." She looked at her best friend. "It's freaking me out."

Alicia leaned into her, her own eyes wide and full of worry. "Me too."

Mandie pushed her hair back and sat up a little

straighter. "What am I supposed to do? It's going to take time to get that chandelier back up."

"Carl can move his crew into the study," Alicia said. She looked at the laptop too, hissed, and sat up straight. "What was that?"

"What?" Mandie looked too as Alicia rewound the footage. She still didn't see anything as she started it, and Alicia pointed to the top of the screen.

"Boots."

Mandie sucked in a breath. Someone was walking along the grass right at the top of the screen, as if they knew how far the cameras reached. "They still have to come into the house somehow." She couldn't comb through nine different camera feeds. She'd need a whole team of people for that.

Alicia kept searching on the laptops, and Mandie turned to her phone. She dialed Suzie and tapped the speaker icon. The ringing came through the line...and behind her on the left. Mandie twisted just as the bookcase swung into the room and Suzie appeared.

"There you are." Mandie jumped to her feet and jogged over to her. She grabbed onto Suzie and hugged her, getting a grunt and a delayed embrace in return. "What did you find?"

"This person is dressed like a member of Carl's crew," Alicia called, and Mandie once again felt like she'd been yanked in the complete opposite direction. "But they've got a hat way down over their face. It's totally on purpose."

Mandie arrived in front of the monitors, and Alicia clicked back. "Look."

They all watched as yes, a person came into view of the camera as they walked directly next to the front of the house. How they'd gotten there without getting seen, Mandie didn't understand.

Slight shoulders, head turned away, hat down. "We can't see their face."

The person stepped up onto the steps and Alicia switched to another camera. "There they are, entering the door." A moment later, the person wearing jeans and the same blue shirt as the construction crew entered the house and left the camera's view.

"Back it up," Mandie said.

Alicia didn't question her; she simply rewound the footage and started it again. Mandie paid close attention to the gait, the jeans, the movement. "Guys...I think it's a woman."

For some reason, that only made the knife in her back feel sharper and dig in deeper. Why would another woman sabotage this all-female team? It felt like such the wrong thing to do, and Mandie swallowed hard.

"I think you're right," Suzie said. "It is a woman."

"We need to figure out who they are," Mandie said.

"We need to figure out what they *want*," Alicia said. "That could lead us to who they are."

Mandie met her eyes and nodded. "So what do they want?"

"They're trying to ruin our renovation," Suzie said.

"So they don't want us to restore this house for some reason."

"But they also took the journal," Alicia said. "So maybe they're looking for the Harrington fortune."

"Those could go together," Suzie argued. "They don't want the house restored, because they think the fortune is here somewhere."

Silence flowed between them, and Mandie glanced toward the door. "Do either of you think it has anything to do with...us?" Worry filled her from top to bottom. "Like, they don't want us specifically to succeed? Or this would've happened to anyone assigned to the Hampton House?"

When neither Suzie nor Alicia answered immediately, Mandie's fears only grew another head. She looked at Suzie. "Take the journal home tonight if you think it'll help you find the fortune."

Suzie wore a grim look as she nodded.

"Mandie." Alicia nodded to the doorway, where Carl stood. She got to her feet and approached him, honestly not sure she could stay for the rest of the day. At the same time, she couldn't just run away. This was her job.

"Nothing," Carl said. "We searched everywhere. Never saw anyone."

Mandie nodded, her determination resolute. "Okay, well, can one of your guys get the chandelier back up? And maybe you can move your crew into the study and work on the...window frames and flooring there."

Carl nodded. "Yep, I've already moved most of the

crew. They'll have that floor sanded and repolished by the end of the day. We'll get the chandelier up, and I'll get the structural engineer out to look at that pillar."

Mandie nodded, because she'd forgotten about the pillar. "A sledgehammer? Really?"

"We found it in the pool," Carl said. "Like they'd run out the back door and just chucked it in there."

Her pulse bounced through her veins. "Is it still there?"

"I had one of my guys pull it out." He sighed. "The concrete there is chipped now too."

"Maybe we can get fingerprints off it," she mused, because she'd seen a few crime dramas. She gave herself a mental shake, because real life was not a crime drama. She'd seen the person on the footage, and Alicia had said they'd been wearing a full face mask as they looked down from the ceiling.

They'd most likely worn gloves when using the sledgehammer.

"It's not one of ours," he said. "So they found it here on-site, or they brought it."

Mandie nodded. "Okay. I'm going to talk to Candace about...security."

Carl ran his hand through his hair and sighed. "We can tighten up the construction site, especially when we go to lunch." He raised his hand to indicate the conversation was done, and he turned to leave the library.

Mandie faced her friends again, and she really needed

to find a way to reassure them that they were safe. She needed that for herself too. Badly.

With the holiday weekend coming up, she wondered if they could simply move their work off-site while she worked through some things. Before she returned to everyone, she took out her phone and texted Candace.

I need to meet with you ASAP. When is a good time?

Candace kept her device close at all times, especially when she had teams out in the field, and she had two right now.

Anytime but tomorrow at two, Candace texted back.

She looked up and made an executive decision. "Gather up what we need to work the rest of the week out of the office."

"What?" Suzie got to her feet. "No, we need—"

"We need a break from this house," Mandie said as she strode toward her friends. "I'm going to tell Candace everything, because if I've learned anything over the years, it's that I don't have to shoulder everything alone." She arrived in front of Alicia and Suzie. "I have you guys, but we don't have to hide this from Candace."

When neither of them agreed with her, Mandie looked at Alicia. "You have two kids. How do I call your mother and tell her that something happened to you here in this house, because someone dangerous is here, sneaking into the house in the middle of the day, and setting us back?"

Alicia's jawline hardened, but her eyes softened.

"And how do you even enjoy your heritage if this place swallows you whole?" Mandie looked at Suzie. "And I've heard nothing about your hike with Donovan, and nothing about your date with Henry." She threw Alicia a side-eyed look. "And *I* need a break."

"It's a short work week," Alicia said.

"We're done for today," Mandie said. "I'll meet with Candace in the morning, and we'll work from the office tomorrow and Wednesday." Maybe by next Monday, there would be a more permanent solution to their safety.

"Okay," Alicia said.

"Fine." Suzie folded her arms. "I guess now is as good as time as any for me to invite you guys to a Fourth picnic." She wouldn't look at Mandie or Alicia, and Mandie wondered how long she'd been holding onto the invitation.

"With you?" Alicia asked.

"You can invite Henry," Suzie said. "And Charlie is a given." She met Mandie's eyes. "Donovan and a few of his friends are having a picnic and he invited me." She lifted her head and it wobbled a little, as if she'd been turned into one of those dolls with the bobbly head.

"He invited you?" Mandie asked, something light-hearted and fizzy filling her.

"Yes."

"Did you go hiking with him?"

Suzie looked at Alicia. "This is in lieu of the hiking."

"How many of his friends?" Mandie asked.

"He said 'a few,'" Suzie said. "It's at Jones Beach State Park."

"This guy has a thing for State Parks," Mandie teased.

"It's going to be so hot on the beach," Alicia complained in a mocking voice.

"Then you don't have to come," Suzie said. "*I* would be more comfortable if I had some friends there, but it's fine. I'm going to go, because I like talking to Donovan."

"I didn't even know you were talking to Donovan," Mandie said. "You keep everything so close to the vest, Suze."

She swallowed, which meant she had more, but Mandie held up her hand. "Just text it to me later, okay? I'm so done with today." She slapped the laptop closed. "*We're* done for today. Let's pack up and go. We're not coming back here until next week, at least."

Thankfully, no one argued with her, and the three of them rolled up the blueprints, put their papers in folders, and loaded up the laptops. When Mandie left the property, the gravity of the situation lifted from her shoulders. Finally.

She wanted to feel the same magic she'd felt the first time she'd stepped through the gate. Sadness descended on her that she didn't, and that the Hampton House now held fear and worry instead of the joy, anticipation, and happiness she'd once felt.

Out in the road, while they loaded up, Mandie looked over to Suzie. "Charlie and I will come to your picnic at Jones Beach."

Suzie jerked her head up. "Really?"

Mandie grinned at her. "Yeah, really." She looked over

to Alicia. "And I think Alicia will at least talk to Henry about coming."

"I will."

And with that, they all piled into the car and left the Hampton House in their rearview mirror. She couldn't wait to get home to her husband, her one safe space, the love of her life.

Since Suzie drove, and Mandie couldn't watch that disaster, she pulled out her phone and started texting Charlie everything. If she told him now, they could go over all the happenings of today in only a few minutes once they both made it home.

Then the Hamptons wouldn't keep eating at her, wouldn't consume her, and she could continue to be Mandie Kelton, Charlie's wife, lover of chickeny noodles, and lying in her husband's arms as they watched movies, and walking down the New York City streets in search of a sweet, cold treat on a hot, July day.

This house, this project, this job was not going to consume her. She wouldn't let it.

She got the best text in return just as Suzie arrived back in the city.

You're my favorite person ever, Charlie said. *I love you so much, and I can't wait to hold you tonight.*

She smiled as she looked up, and now that she was finally away from that house, she'd started to feel human again. She wasn't sure what that said about this project she'd been so excited about, and she pressed her lips together, trying to make sense of things that didn't make sense.

Chapter Fourteen

Alicia stepped off the elevator, the luxurious glass doors of PastForward just ahead, at least an hour before anyone else should be there. She hadn't wanted to tread on Mandie's toes, but she also couldn't let her friend face Candace alone.

The woman was always better handled with a partner; Alicia knew that.

Despite the early hour, the glass glimmered in the early morning sunlight streaming from the windows within, and the automatic doors whooshed open with a quiet efficiency that Alicia found soothing.

She adjusted her purse over her shoulder and took a deep breath as she tossed a glance to Candace's back office. Her nerves tamped through her, but she focused on getting to her desk. She could put her things away, fill up her water bottle with far colder water than her pathetic sink in the apartment put out, and be ready to pounce the moment Mandie entered the office.

She'd been up late last night, talking with Henry about how to explain a delicate situation without making it seem like she, Mandie, and Suzie couldn't handle the project. She couldn't give him many details, but just having someone to hash it all out with had been a thrill.

Alicia went through her normal morning routine, and when she returned to her desk, she started on the paperwork necessary to get the items ordered for the next stage of the renovation. She had far more back-end work than the others on the team, and she'd been doing it at home, after long days at the construction site.

Relief pounded through her that Mandie had called them back to the office this week. She wasn't sure she'd have been brave enough to do that, but Mandie was fearless in a lot of ways that Alicia wasn't.

She looked up when movement caught her eye, and pure shock stamped through her when she saw the blonde bulldozer enter the office. Suzie stopped short the moment she saw Alicia, who rose slowly to her feet.

"Couldn't let Mandie go in alone either, huh?" Alicia asked with a small grin. Hope ballooned through her, widening her smile. She should've texted Suzie last night to coordinate with her.

Suzie wore a resigned look among the fierceness in her eyes as she came down the aisle of cubicles. "Nope. This project means too much to all of us."

"I just know Candace can argue with one person, but two? Who have the same story?" She shook her head.

"Candace doesn't like Mandie all that much for some reason," Suzie said. "I couldn't throw her to the Big Bad Wolf." She took a sip of her coffee while Alicia giggled. She exhaled and looked toward their boss's office. "Plus, you're right. With all of us there, telling the same story, she'll be more inclined to believe us."

"What are you two doing here?"

Alicia looked past Suzie to Mandie, who'd just arrived. She wore a gorgeous sundress, with brown leather heels, plenty of makeup, and her hair curled as it flowed over her shoulders.

"We're meeting with Candace this morning," Suzie said with plenty of bite in her tone.

"*I'm* meeting with Candace this morning," Mandie said, frowning and glaring as she moved to her cubicle.

"You're not going in alone," Alicia said, plenty of hidden meaning in the words.

"We're in this together," Suzie said.

Mandie softened as she dropped her bag on her desk with a semi-irritated sigh. She looked at Alicia and then Suzie. "Thanks, you guys." She opened her arms, and Alicia practically flew into them.

Suzie took an extra moment or two, and then she joined them in their three-way hug. "She's going to believe us."

"I've been preparing to be fired since we left the house yesterday," Mandie whispered.

"No," Alicia said. "You're not going to be fired." She might lose her promotion, but no one on the team would lose their job.

"Let's go over a few things." Mandie stepped back and plucked a folder from her bag. She glanced down the aisle that led to the door. "In private." She moved into the conference room, and Alicia and Suzie went with her.

A meticulous organizer, Mandie had put together some talking points for that morning's meeting. Alicia sat down and said, "Pretend I'm Candace."

"I don't—"

"I can't be wasting time on meetings that don't mean anything," Alicia yelled.

Mandie froze and looked at her with wide eyes. Alicia held her boss-like demeanor for as long as she could—which meant a few seconds. Then she broke down and giggled. Mandie softened too.

"Okay," she said, pacing on the far side of the conference table. Suzie didn't sit either, which only added to the tension in the room. Mandie went over how things had been progressing at the Hampton House, and then she said, "We asked for those cameras for a reason, Candace."

She took out a handful of printouts and splayed them across the table like crime scene photos. "Someone has been breaking in. Both Alicia and Suzie saw them." She looked at Alicia, then cut a glance over to Suzie. "They were in the house yesterday, and they're sabotaging our work, causing problems for Carl and his crew, and who knows what else."

She went on to outline the rest of her concerns, and she left plenty of open-ended questions that would allow Candace to be, well, Candace. The boss.

By the time she finished, and Alicia stood and faced the rest of the office, a dozen more people had arrived at work.

"All right," Mandie said. "I saw her come in about fifteen minutes ago. Let's get this over with." She collected all of her papers and went through them, putting them back in the right order.

They exchanged a nod of solidarity, left the conference room, and walked toward Candace's office. Alicia's stomach churned with a mixture of anxiety and determination. Framed photographs of previous successful projects—restored mansions, refurbished offices, and modernized historical buildings—lined the wall on her right. Each picture seemed to radiate a sense of accomplishment, but today, they only added weight to Alicia's shoulders.

"Candace?" Mandie paused and knocked on the doorframe of Candace's open office door. She turned from the window, a voice recorder in her hand. She gestured them in while she continued to talk.

They filed in, the atmosphere growing more tense with each step toward Candace's desk. The office itself held a blend of modern design and antique touches—a fitting reflection of PastForward's mission. Large windows let in natural light, illuminating the room and casting a sunny glow on Candace's serious face as she finished dictating her notes to herself and sat down.

"Good morning," Candace said, her tone pleasant but not friendly. "Have a seat."

Once they were settled, Candace leaned forward, her fingers steepled in front of her. She looked first to Suzie, then Mandie in the middle, and then Alicia. "Why is your whole team here with you?" She pinned Alicia with a predatory look that said so much. "You don't have work to do at the Hampton House?"

Mandie cleared her throat and launched into her prepared speech, recounting the events with precise detail, using her pictures and other evidence flawlessly. Alicia's chest swelled with pride to be her friend, to be on her team.

She also watched Candace's face closely, noting the way her eyes narrowed and her mouth tightened as she listened and looked at the pictures. When Mandie finished, the room held only silence for a moment.

"This is insane," Candace finally said. "We've never had anything like this happen at our restoration sites before." She looked at Mandie with wide eyes. "I want you to text Carl and have him pull his crew off today and tomorrow."

Mandie swallowed. "Okay, ma'am, but..."

"I know it'll set you back." Candace picked up one of the still images that had come from the security cameras. "It's fine. No one is going to blame anyone for that. I'll call the police department and see if they can station someone at the gate while we're off-site."

"But they came on-site while we were all there," Suzie pointed out.

Candace lifted her eyes from the photograph, her sharp expression somewhat thoughtful. "And you believe it's connected to this—this—this phantom Harrington fortune?"

Suzie leaned forward, her blue eyes shining with conviction. "Yes. We found evidence that suggests there are puzzles or riddles to solve. It seems like someone else might know about them too."

"Suzie," Mandie warned, because she cared less about finding the fortune than Suzie. Alicia did too, truth be told, but she didn't want to squash Suzie's ideas either.

Candace sighed, her gaze drifting to the window for a moment before returning to them. "All right. I'll arrange for additional surveillance through the union, and I'll see if we can get someone to analyze that sledgehammer for fingerprints."

Mandie visibly relaxed, relief flooding her face. "Thank you, Candace."

"Don't thank me yet," Candace said wryly. "We still have a lot of work to do. But I believe in you three. You've done excellent work so far, and I trust you can handle this." She looked at Alicia. "How's the budget going to fare with this?"

"Union security?" Alicia scoffed. "That's not cheap, and we're barely under as it is."

"I'll talk to Gerald," Candace said. "I know him from another project, and if he can pull some strings on the Hampton PD, he will."

Alicia had no idea who Gerald was, but it didn't matter. Candace had believed them, and she was going to help. A surge of gratitude clogged her throat, and she nodded.

"I want daily updates once you go back on-site," Candace added as she stood. She pinned Mandie with a glare. "I'll keep you in the loop as far as the additional security goes."

"Yes, ma'am." Mandie stood and shook Candace's hand while Alicia scrambled to do the same.

"Don't hesitate to ask for more help if you need it." Candace nodded, clearly ending the meeting, and Alicia nodded back.

She left Candace's office feeling a mix of relief and renewed resolve. No one spoke, and somehow, they all knew they couldn't talk here. Mandie led the way out of the office and onto the elevator.

When it was just the three of them, Alicia finally pushed the air out of her lungs. "Well, that could've definitely gone worse."

"Are you kidding?" Mandie wiped her hand down her face. "We're lucky we still have jobs."

Alicia burst out laughing, glad when Mandie joined her. They looked over to Suzie, who grinned and grinned and then finally...laughed with them.

TWO DAYS LATER, ALICIA STOOD IN HER kitchen, staring at her phone in disbelief as the cold air conditioning blew down the back of her neck, making her shiver. Ryan's text message was short and to the point: *Plans with my mom fell through. Can I bring the kids back today?*

"Today." She scoffed and glanced at the clock—it had just clicked to ten, on the morning of the Fourth of July. She already wore her bright white, recently bleached white shorts, with a bright red tank top with blue stars on it.

Red, white, and blue. Patriotic through and through.

She had plans with Henry today, who would be here in thirty minutes to pick her up for their picnic date to Jones Beach. If she suddenly had to get her two children, she wouldn't even arrive before the beginning of the holiday beach barbecue.

Her fingers ached with the number of texts she'd need to send in the next few minutes to literally rearrange everything she had planned for the day. Ryan *had* had the kids for almost two full weeks...

"But he *asked* to keep them through the Fourth," she muttered, her fingers flying over her phone.

When were you thinking? I have lunch plans with my friends, but I could come get them after that.

Her heart sank as she thought about her evening plans with Henry. A private dinner. Fireworks over the Hudson. She hadn't kissed him yet, and Alicia could admit she'd started fantasizing about a late-night kiss with showers of sparks above her head.

We're in the city already, Ryan said. *I brought them for breakfast before my mom texted me her plans had changed.*

Alicia huffed out all the air in her lungs. She had no idea if she could take her kids to the beach with her. Suzie had invited her, but she'd said nothing about the kids—she wasn't supposed to have the kids.

She sighed and tapped to call Suzie. "Pick up," she muttered as the line rang.

"Hey," Suzie said, a bit breathless. "I don't get why you can't just let me merge!"

Alicia pulled the phone away from her ear as Suzie yelled at a driver somewhere in the city.

"What's going on?" Suzie barked.

Alicia flinched as she brought the phone back into position. "Ryan wants to drop the kids off this morning," she said. "Can I bring them to the beach?"

Part of her simply wanted to text her ex-husband to bring the kids by, and Alicia would cancel everything, make them red, white, and blue drinks, order pizza for dinner, and take them up to the rooftop for the fireworks that night.

Just like everyone else would on this block.

"Yeah, sure," Suzie said in a much calmer voice. "Donovan said anyone can come."

"Will there be other kids there?"

"I don't know."

Alicia didn't know what to do, and she hated it when

she had so many options she couldn't simply make a decisions. "Okay," she said.

"Wait." Honking came through the line, but Suzie spoke over it. "Are you not coming, then?"

Alicia detected something in her voice, and it felt very important that Alicia be there. "I'm going to be there," she said. "But I'm going to have my kids, and I'm probably going to be late."

Suzie didn't say anything for a moment. Then she came in with, "So are you going to introduce your kids to Henry today?"

Her heartbeat completely stalled, as she hadn't even thought of that. "One problem at a time," she said. "I'm going to bring my kids to the beach."

"Okay," Suzie said.

Maybe Alicia could get her mom to babysit tonight, and she and Henry could still have their magical fireworks date-slash-first-kiss. "You don't even know if he's going to kiss you tonight," she muttered.

"What?" Suzie asked.

"Nothing." Embarrassment ran through her, and Alicia cleared her throat. "Okay, I have to go. I'll see you soon."

"Yep." Suzie started to yell something else, and Alicia hung up, so she didn't have to hear what some driver somewhere had done to her.

If you can bring the kids now, that would be best, Alicia said. *Or you'll have to keep them until later this afternoon.*

We're half an hour out, Ryan said.

She exhaled and tapped away from her ex-husband and to Henry. Ah, Henry. What was she going to do about Henry? She didn't want to text him this news, so she tapped to call him. He might be on his way here already.

"Hey, there," he said when he answered.

Her throat closed up, and she couldn't speak for several long moments. Long enough for Henry to say, "You have to cancel."

"No," she managed to push out of her mouth. "I mean, plans have changed, and I'm going to have my kids today." She pushed away from the countertop and paced into the living room. "If you don't mind tagging along with the single mom, I still want to take them to the beach."

It was the evening date she'd need to cancel or make arrangements for.

"Okay," Henry said slowly. "How do you feel about me meeting your children?"

"I mean—" Alicia didn't know quite how she felt. "There will be a lot of people there."

Another pause came through the line, and Alicia couldn't believe a simple text from her ex had been the bomb to blow up everything.

"I'm okay with meeting them if you're okay with it," Henry said.

"Okay." Relief sagged through Alicia, and she sank down onto the couch. She suddenly had a million more things to do to get the kids ready to go to the beach in literal minutes, and her adrenaline shot to the top of her head.

"What about tonight?" Henry asked quietly. "By the way, I'm on my way to you right now."

"We might be a little late," she said, shelving his first question. "The kids aren't here yet, and I have to get them packed up and ready to go."

"All right."

"I'm going to call my mom as soon as we hang up," she said. "I'll see if she can take the kids for our date tonight."

"We can reschedule," Henry said properly.

"Yeah, but I don't want to," Alicia said, flirting as much as she knew how. She ran her hand through her hair, the juggling act of being a mom and a girlfriend coming at her faster than she'd anticipated.

"Well, call her, then, I guess," he said. "But I'm really okay if we can't make it work."

Alicia smiled despite her frustration. At least Henry was understanding. "Okay," she said quietly. "I'll work on it."

"I'll see you soon."

The call ended, and Alicia jumped to her feet to quickly pack a bag for the kids—swimwear, sunscreen, snacks, and some toys—her mind buzzing over how to ask her parents to take the kids so last-minute.

In the end, she just had to put the words out there. She picked up her phone and tapped to call her mom.

"Hey, baby," her mom said, her voice chipper and bright.

"Hey, Mom." Alicia held her breath and then blurted out, "What are you and Dad doing tonight? I have a date, and Ryan is bringing the kids back a few days early."

"We're just going over to the Jacobs'," her mom said. "The kids can come."

"Really?" Alicia couldn't hope for this to actually be true. "Would it be okay if I brought them over after we go to our beach barbecue?"

"Yes, we'll just be home until about five-thirty or so."

"Thank you, Mom."

"Love you, baby."

That call ended too, and Alicia turned in a full circle, trying to get her bearings. No, this wasn't the Independence Day she'd been planning, but it could still be great.

Her door buzzed, and Alicia spun toward the speaker. She rushed to it and pressed the button. "Yeah?"

"It's Henry."

"Come on up." She pressed the button to open the door for him, and she turned to make sure she had her wallet tucked into her beach bag.

Henry arrived faster than Alicia thought possible, and she felt winded as she opened the door and found him standing there. He wore navy blue shorts and a white polo with the stars and stripes on the chest pocket.

Understated. And so hot.

"Hey." Alicia leaned into the doorway, suddenly nervous about having him here. With Ryan due to arrive any minute.

Henry grinned at her. "Hey." He stepped in closer to

her, puncturing her personal bubble as he slid his hand up her arm. "Wow, you're so beautiful."

"Thank you." She grinned and backed up a step. "Come in and see my little apartment." She turned, caught his hand, and pulled him into her home. "This is the living room, kitchen, dining room combo."

Since the kids had been gone, the apartment was clean. "Two bedrooms and two baths down there." She indicated the hallway that branched off to the left. "They'll be here in a few minutes."

"Okay." Henry seemed so cool about everything, but Alicia's pulse felt like it had been blown up into a basketball and was being passed from vein to vein. "Did you say a few minutes?"

"Yep." She rocked back on her heels and faced him. She smiled and loved the way his eyes lit up when he grinned back.

"I think there's enough time then," he said, his hand coming up to cradle her face. She wanted to ask, *Time for what?* but Henry was already leaning closer to her, his eyes drifting closed softly.

Alicia tilted her head back and let her own eyes close. Her pulse pounded; her hand drifted up to his chest; it took so long for his mouth to meet hers, but when it did...

Fireworks in the middle of her apartment, with the sun shining in through the window—and her children moments away from arriving.

Alicia didn't care. She hadn't been kissed like this in a

good long while, if ever, and she wanted this kiss to last, and last, and last.

Chapter Fifteen

S uzie sat in her car, trying to psyche herself up to get out on the sand. She already wore her swimming suit, with a super-cute tank dress over it. It had a hood, which she loved, and a fun tie-dye Patriotic pattern all over.

She'd paired it with white sandals, and she'd bought a brand new canvas bag just for this.

And now she couldn't get out of the car.

Why was her heart beating so fast?

"What if Donovan isn't really excited to see you?" So much self-doubt bled through her, and Suzie hated it. She'd been texting with Donovan since they'd met a couple of weeks ago, and she was pretty good in words.

She could flirt and laugh and tell him things about herself. He'd been doing the same, and they'd only seen each other in person one other time before this. A weekend lunch date, and Suzie figured she'd made it past that.

So why couldn't she get out of the car?

Her phone buzzed, and Suzie looked down into her cupholder. Donovan's name sat there, and he'd sent a couple of bald eagles, and Suzie lifted the phone to read his text. *Where are you? Still coming? I've got your favorite drink.*

As she smiled at her phone, a picture of Donovan came in. He wore sunglasses, a huge smile, and he held a can of Coke Zero right up to his face. His bare shoulders made Suzie's throat dry, and she really needed that cola right now.

She'd told him in a lengthy conversation about how Coke Zero was far superior to Diet Coke, and he'd heard her. Listened. Sure, he'd teased her a bit about it too, but Suzie had counted that as flirting.

That picture gave her the courage to grab her bag and get out of the car. Plenty of people had come to Jones Beach State Park that day, but Suzie didn't have any trouble finding Donovan and his friends.

He currently had his head tipped back, a can of Diet Dr. Pepper in his hand, laughing at something someone had said. Only three other men stood with him, and one of them turned back to the grill they'd brought.

Suzie didn't see Mandie or Alicia, and she really wasn't sure she could walk across the sand herself. In that moment, Donovan looked right at her, and before she could turn around and dash back to her car, he jogged toward her.

"Hey, you." He didn't slow as he approached, and Suzie braced herself for his arrival. He laughed as he lifted her right up off her feet. She cried out, not quite sure women her age got picked up very much.

She smiled at him as he set her down, and she didn't detect the scent of beer or alcohol on his breath.

"You made it," he said, and he easily slid his hand into hers.

"I made it." She reminded herself she wanted to be here, that anything would be better than how she'd celebrated Independence Day last year. And the year before that. And the year before that too.

Alone. Watching the red, white, and blue explode in the sky from the window in her apartment.

"Introduce me to your friends," she said, squeezing his hand. He took her across the sand to them, and Suzie put a smile on her face.

"Guys," Donovan said. "This is Suzie Paxman. Suzie, this is my brother Jeremy, and a couple of our college roommates, Eli and Liam."

She shook their hands, looking at Jeremy for an extra-long moment. "Wait a second," she said. "Are you two twins?"

"I told you she'd know." Jeremy pumped her hand and grinned at his brother. "We're fraternal twins, yes."

Suzie bumped Donovan. "You didn't tell me you had a twin."

"It's this thing he does," Jeremy said as he took the tongs from Eli. "He thinks people won't know we're twins, even though he tells them we're brothers."

"So who's older?" Suzie asked, gazing up at Donovan. She wondered if he was her boyfriend, and she decided it didn't matter if he knew he carried that label. She could call him that in her head.

"Hey, Suzie," someone called, and she turned toward Mandie. Instant relief filled her, because she wasn't sure how to talk to four men by herself. In person.

Mandie's honey blonde hair blew behind her as she approached, her husband taller than her and absolutely gorgeous. Suzie had never met him, but she knew his name.

"Hey." Suzie smiled and stepped into Mandie and gave her a light hug. Charlie smiled at her, and Mandie stepped back to his side and indicated him.

"This is my husband, Charlie. Charlie, this is Suzie."

"So great to meet you," he said, giving her hand a firm shake. "Mandie has told me a lot about you."

"Oh, brother."

"Good things," Mandie said, her eyes roaming over to Donovan. "Hey, Donovan. Good to see you again."

"You too," he said, and he introduced her and Charlie around to his brother and friends. Charlie took a bottle of beer from one of them, and Suzie grinned at Donovan as he handed her the icy can of Coke Zero.

He leaned closer to her and pressed his lips to her temple. "I can't wait to see your party dress tonight."

Confusion ran through Suzie. She didn't have a party dress for tonight. Or a date with Donovan. She'd never been very good at flirting, but she tried to imagine what someone the complete opposite of her would do.

She leaned into him too. "Oh, yeah? What would I be wearing that for?"

"Our dinner in my apartment," he said. "Rooftop fireworks at dark. My neighbor brings up a Bluetooth speaker, and we play all the patriotic music you can imagine." He grinned at her, and he didn't even ask if she could make it.

It was simply implied.

Suzie ducked her head, her smile absolutely huge, as one of his friends asked him something.

"I don't know, bro," Donovan said. "Jordan said he'd bring the meat." They all looked toward the parking lot. "He'll be here."

"I'm going to call him again." Donovan found his phone and started tapping.

"Heard from Lish?" Mandie asked, and she'd gotten a drink somewhere too. She lifted the green can of ginger ale to her lips.

"She called and asked me if she could bring her kids." Suzie popped the top on her cola too and glanced over to Donovan.

"Oh." Mandie seemed surprised by that. "Is she bringing them?"

"I think so?" Suzie took a sip of her cola. "She didn't say." And she had much more pressing problems. She leaned into Mandie and whispered, "Where do I find a patriotic party dress before a date I didn't know I had tonight?"

Mandie looked at her, eyes wide. "With Donovan?"

Suzie nodded as he took a sip of her soda.

"He didn't ask you?"

"I suppose he just did," she said. "But before I showed up? I thought today was a beach barbecue and then me getting take-out on the way home for dinner."

"What about what you're wearing?" Mandie asked.

Suzie looked down at the hooded tank dress, aghast. She met Mandie's eyes again, horrified and blinking fast. Mandie shrugged. "It's a dress, and it's patriotic."

"Mandie."

"Do you have any other options?"

"No."

"You don't have any other dresses?"

"I do, but not for Independence Day."

"Maybe one of them." Mandie shrugged one shoulder and giggled. "What did he say you'd be doing?"

"Dinner at his place," Suzie hissed as his brother came closer. "Rooftop fireworks with his friends in his building."

Mandie grinned, her eyes positively dancing with light. "Look at you, Suzie."

She couldn't help smiling too, and she tucked her hair back as she caught Donovan turning toward her. "What do you see?" she asked.

"Do you like him?"

Suzie nodded. "I mean, this is our second date. We text."

"Hey," he said, arriving at her side. "My friend is at the store. Do you guys want hamburgers or hot dogs?"

"Hot dogs," Suzie said while Mandie said, "Whatever."

"Get both, brother," Donovan said. "I'll take whatever we don't eat." He turned way and added, "Then I'll pay for it. There's a lot of people here. Get both and get here. We're starving."

Suzie's stomach growled, but she turned to chit-chat with Donovan's college roommate. His friend showed up with the meat and it went on the grill before Alicia appeared, herding her two children toward their group.

And Henry.

Suzie watched as Mandie went to meet them. She seemed to know what to say and do, and Suzie felt at a loss almost all the time. But something told her to get over there and welcome Alicia too.

So she did, and as she hugged her friend, it became painfully and wonderfully obvious that she even had friends. She gripped her hard and pulled back, their eyes meeting. "I'm glad you came."

"Is it weird with the kids?" Alicia asked, glancing around.

"No," Suzie assured her. "It's totally fine. Jeremy is grilling, and he'll make you whatever you want. Then we're just hanging out."

Hanging out. Her.

Suzie barely recognized herself, even as Donovan snaked his hand along her waist. "Oh, hello there."

"Alicia," Suzie said, leaning into his body. "This is the master puppeteer on our team, Alicia."

She grinned and then laughed. "Oh, wow. A puppeteer. Never been called that before." She shook Donovan's hand again, and he took her around to meet everyone. Suzie reached into a bag and pulled out a handful of cheddar and sour cream chips. She faced the water as she ate them, grinning when Donovan's warmth curled up behind her.

"You didn't tell me we were going out tonight," she said.

"Didn't I?"

She looked at him, knowing he was eight years younger than her. "You know you didn't."

"Do you have someone else you're meeting for dinner and fireworks?"

Suzie shifted her feet in the sand. "No." She rolled her head, stretching her neck. "I don't have a patriotic party dress."

"That was a joke."

Suzie didn't know what to make of that. "I'm—well, I'll just be honest. I'm not good at figuring out what's a joke and what's not." She sighed, because she was pretty literal. She took people at face value, with exactly what they said, and she didn't know how to deal with Donovan's more happy-go-lucky personality.

"Let me try again," Donovan said. "Are you busy tonight?"

Suzie appraised him, really appreciating the muscles in his chest and abs. "No," she admitted.

"I make really amazing red, white, and blue crepes, and I'd love to have you over to my place for dinner."

Suzie smiled, because it felt great to be asked out. And right to her face too. "Okay," she said. "I guess I have to eat."

Donovan grinned at her. "You wear whatever you want, Suzie. You look great right now."

"I'm wearing a swimming suit cover up," she said.

He leaned closer, the nearness of him making her hot in some places and shivering cold in other. "Mm, yeah, and you look amazing."

Suzie grinned out at the water, her stomach rumbling again. "After we eat, can we go swimming?"

"There's nothing I want more," Donovan said, and he turned her toward the grill. "I think your hot dog is done, sweetheart. What do you want on it? I'll get it for you."

"Uh." She glanced over to the short, stout card table that had been set up with the chips and condiments. "Ketchup, mustard, and onions."

Suddenly, she thought of what that would do to her breath, and then she dismissed the idea of kissing Donovan on the beach. Not with all these people here. Probably not anytime soon at all.

She'd never had anyone make her what she wanted to

eat, and she felt a little bit outside her body as she stood there and let him fix her hot dog for her.

"He's sweet," Alicia said as her son ran a few feet away from her and dropped to the sand to build a castle.

"He is." Suzie smiled at Alicia's son. "How old is he?"

Alicia looked at her, and then her son, and then back to Suzie. "My son?"

"Yes."

"I meant Donovan."

"Here you go," Donovan said, arriving back on-scene before Suzie could truly catch up to the conversation.

"Thank you," she said genuinely, and she let Donovan drift her away from Alicia. Once they had an adequate amount of distance, she looked over to him. "What time would I need to be ready for a crepe dinner?"

"Oh, I don't know," and Donovan was definitely less scheduled than Suzie. "Six or seven?"

That seemed like a really long time to make and eat crepes before dark, and her stomach trembled with what they might do to pass all those other hours. She took a bite of her hot dog and nodded. "Okay."

"Yeah?" He grinned at her. "I don't know what time we'll be done here, but I have to run to the store."

"Do you want to give me your address, and I'll just... come over?"

"Yeah, sure," he said, and he took a bite of his hamburger. He flashed her that devilishly handsome smile, and Suzie lost herself a little.

Don't lose your head, she told herself. She just hadn't been out with anyone in a while, but that didn't mean she needed to fall in love with the first man who dared to text her back and make her a crepe.

<h1 style="text-align:center">Chapter Sixteen</h1>

Mandie exhaled as she got out of the cab, the gate of the Hampton House looming in front of her. A police car sat there, and as Mandie shouldered her bag, an officer got out of the vehicle.

Candace had texted them all over the weekend to make sure they had their ID badges with them any time they went to their construction site, or they wouldn't be let onto the property.

Mandie dug into her bag to find her ID, which she had definitely, absolutely put there this morning. Her fingers closed around it, and she raised it to show him. "Mandie Kelton," she said.

The officer actually consulted his phone, looked up, took a good long gander at her ID, and then nodded.

"Thank you," she said, and she followed him to the gate, which he opened for her. As she walked over the mosaic and down the drive, she heard the officer locking the gate behind her. She had no idea if any of the other girls had arrived yet, and another officer met her at the top of the sidewalk, and Mandie had to pull out her ID again.

At least she felt safe as she finally gained the entrance of the Hampton House for the first time in a week. At least a dozen boxes had been delivered to the mansion while they'd been gone, and Mandie would have to go through all of that to see where it went.

The scent of coffee and chocolate met her nose, which meant Alicia had arrived ahead of her. Sure enough, she found her best friend in the library, and Mandie chirped, "Hey, Lish," as she reached the huge oak table in the middle of the room.

Alicia looked up from the laptop in front of her and pulled off her glasses. "I didn't even hear you come in."

"Haven't seen Suzie?" For some reason, Mandie looked over to the bookcase that led to the hidden den. Mandie knew Candace had hired a private security team to go through the house in the week they hadn't been here, and they'd secured everything.

They'd taken pictures of everything. Every rug. Every bookcase. Every hole in the wall. All of it. Candace had called it "gathering evidence," and Mandie honestly didn't know what she meant by that.

Was she going to go through all of those pictures at some point? And do what?

Thankfully, that wasn't part of Mandie's job. Candace had told her to get back to work, that she'd make sure the property stayed secure, and Mandie was going to take her at her word.

"No," Alicia said slowly. "She's here." She nodded to the door, and Mandie turned to watch Suzie-the-Storm blow into the library.

"Whoa," she said. "What's going on?" She almost expected a figure clad in black to rush into the room right behind her.

"Nothing," Suzie bit out.

Mandie looked at Alicia, who stayed seated on the couch. Smart, considering the wolverine-like energy coming off Suzie.

But they had a lot of work to do today. They'd already been off-site for almost three full days last week, and Mandie couldn't afford to have them on different pages today.

"Suzie," she said. "What's going on?" Her phone bleeped out the sound that indicated her husband had messaged. Alicia and Suzie knew it was him, and as Mandie rummaged in her purse to find her phone and silence it for this conversation. She could catch up with her husband and her boss later.

She tapped and silenced her phone, then dropped it back into her bag.

"Just answer your perfect husband." Suzie folded her arms and glared at Mandie.

Mandie's mouth dropped open, her heartbeat thrashing in her chest.

"Hey, now," Alicia said, jumping to her feet and positioning herself between Mandie and Suzie, neither of whom had moved. "Suzie, come on."

"What?" Suzie flicked her a glance. "I'm so sick of everyone living their perfect lives, with their perfect boyfriends and husbands."

"What is going on?" Mandie asked, folding her arms across her chest too, like Suzie's words wouldn't be able to puncture her that way.

The Bulldozer had shown up today, and Mandie hadn't seen her in a while.

"Suze," Alicia said slowly, shooting Mandie a look. But she couldn't read her friend's mind before she looked back at Suzie. "What happened?"

Suzie glared knives at Alicia. "Who says something happened?"

"Because when we left you on the Fourth of July, you were lying blissfully in a hot man's arms," Alicia said. "So yeah, I'm going to say something happened." She flicked a glance at Mandie, but she wasn't going to open her mouth and contribute. Alicia was handling things just fine on her own.

Suzie blew out her breath heavily. "You know what? This is so embarrassing." She turned around and took a couple of stomping steps before she stopped.

"Just tell us," Mandie said quietly, hoping she hadn't just made a fatal mistake. But the house sat in silence, as Carl and his crew hadn't arrived yet.

"My date with Donovan was amazing," she said. "The

red, white, and blue crepes, the fireworks, the...spending the night."

Alicia pulled in a breath, and Mandie's jaw dropped again. She searched Alicia's face, so glad Suzie had turned her back on them, so she couldn't see the pure shock pouring from her. Alicia stepped over to Suzie and said, "Oh, honey, what's...?"

"He hasn't called since," she said. "Or answered a single text." She turned to face them, her eyes filled with tears. They didn't track down her face, but Mandie's heart still grew three sizes, and then six.

She immediately stepped over to Suzie and gripped her in a hug. "I'm sure—he's—" No way Donovan ghosted her after sleeping with her. Just—no *way*.

Mandie looked over to Alicia, desperate for her to say something. Alicia shook her head, her eyes angry, but Mandie couldn't believe it. She'd seen Donovan with Suzie at the beach. He'd been kind, caring, attentive. He'd laughed with his friends and brother, and Mandie had really liked him.

Suzie had too, obviously.

"Maybe something happened," Mandie said.

"Like what?" Suzie asked, sniffling. She bent her head and wiped her face quickly, and when she looked at Mandie again, her fierce bulldozer expression had returned.

"Maybe his mom got sick," Mandie said, seizing onto the first thing that came to her mind. "And he had to leave town suddenly."

"Without his phone," Alicia tacked onto the end of her sentence, and Mandie heard how lame that sounded. She cringed inwardly, but she didn't know why else a man would sleep with a woman and then ignore her for three full days.

"Hey, hey," someone said, a man, and Mandie jolted to attention, her eyes flying to the doorway.

Brandt Bowman stood there. Sort of. He stood on one leg, the one he'd broken bent at the knee and resting on a medical scooter.

"Brandt," Mandie said, the relief at getting away from the conversation with Suzie palpable in the back of her throat. "What are you doing here?" She left Suzie standing near the oak table as she went to greet the bulldozer who'd originally been assigned to her team. To this house.

"Just came by to see how you guys are doing." He looked up to the ceiling with a smile. "Yikes. I do not envy you cleaning out this library."

Mandie grinned at him. "Oh, come on. This is what you'd be doing, and you'd love it." She gave Brandt a semi-awkward hug, as his scooter moved a little. "You want a tour?" She stepped back and looked at his scooter. "I mean, of the first floor."

"Sure," he said. "I heard you guys were ahead of schedule and way below budget." He gave her a cocked eyebrow, and then turned to leave the library. Mandie glanced over her shoulder and found Suzie coming toward her.

"I'll show him around," Suzie said, and Mandie

nodded, glad she didn't have to give details on the status of the project. Suzie paused near her. "Sorry, Mandie. I didn't mean to say Charlie was perfect."

Mandie put her hand on Suzie's arm and squeezed. "I'm really sorry about Donovan."

Suzie's jaw clenched, the muscles along the bone jumping. "Me too." She sighed as she looked out into the foyer. "But Brandt's a good friend, and I'll make him go out to the pool house with me and smash something." She flashed a smile that held no happiness, and Mandie didn't think for a moment that Suzie was joking.

She smashed things when she was in a good mood, and Mandie didn't want to know how that would intensify when she wasn't.

"Okay," Mandie said. "Alicia and I will go through the deliveries, and I'll meet with Carl before we do our morning huddle-up."

"Text me when I need to come back," Suzie said, and then she followed Brandt out into the foyer.

Mandie turned back to Alicia, raising her eyebrows at her. "Were you looking up news articles about Donovan Petrovik? Maybe he was kidnapped? Reported missing." Mandie sank into a chair next to where Alicia had been sitting. "There has to be something, and we're going to find it."

Alicia returned to her seat with a sigh. "Mandie."

"Lish." She opened a new window and typed in Donovan's name. "I'm at least looking."

"What if there isn't anything, and he's just the world's biggest jerk?"

"I refuse to believe that." Mandie tossed Alicia a dirty look. "I liked him. We all liked him. I just don't believe it." She refocused on the computer again. "Did you get any of his friends' numbers?"

"Yeah, while I was there with my kids and my boyfriend," Alicia said dryly. "I got some other guy's number."

Mandie grinned at her sarcastic wit. "Maybe Charlie did." She stretched for her phone and sent him a text. He'd asked her if she wanted ice cream sandwiches, and she quickly answered that text with, *When have I ever not wanted ice cream sandwiches?*

I got Jeremy's number, Charlie said. *We're going to go play disc golf together sometime. Why?*

"Praise the heavens," Mandie breathed, her fingers already moving across her phone. "He got Jeremy's number."

She quickly explained, and Charlie sent her the number in the next text. She could text Donovan's brother, but she decided to be a bit bulldozer-y herself, and she dialed him instead. The line rang once, twice, and then a man said, "You need to stop calling me."

"This is the first time I've called," Mandie said briskly, quickly tapping to put the call on speaker so Alicia could hear too. "It's Mandie Kelton, Suzie's friend? Donovan's... friend from the beach last week?"

A moment of silence, and then Jeremy said, "Oh, sure."

"Have you heard from Donovan?" she asked. "We're trying to get in touch with him, and—"

"I'm sitting right next to him."

Mandie's blood boiled as she exchanged a glance with Alicia. "Can you put him on the phone, please?" She'd had no idea she could be so polite, not with the poisonous thoughts running through her head.

"No," Jeremy said, and he sounded so tired. "He hasn't woken up."

"I'm..."

"Woken up?" Alicia asked. "This morning?"

Jeremy sighed. "No, since the accident."

Shock mixed with vindication inside Mandie, and she held up one fisted hand, as if she'd just won something amazing. At the same time, she couldn't believe she was talking to someone's twin who'd been in an accident at all.

"I'm sorry?" she asked. "We—we didn't know about an accident."

"Yeah, we went fishing on Friday morning, and there was a problem with the boat. Donovan got caught in some rope and dragged under. He was underwater for a long time." Jeremy's voice took on a haunted quality, and Mandie didn't want to hear this.

Her heart bled, not only for Donovan, but for Suzie. "No," she said. "I'm so sorry." What else was there to say?

"We got him out, and I resuscitated him," Jeremy said.

"He woke up for a few minutes, but he fell into a coma on the way to the hospital, and he hasn't woken up yet."

"This is just awful," Alicia said. "Can we come see him?"

"Sure," Jeremy said. "We're at Eastern Long Island."

"Okay," Alicia said. "Jeremy, we're so sorry. Thank you. We'll come by later today."

Mandie nodded along, and she added her own condolences one more time before the call ended. She sat back and exhaled. "My word," she said. "It feels like we can't catch a break anywhere."

Alicia shook her head and reached for her coffee. "No kidding."

Mandie flipped her phone over and over, then picked it up. "I'm going to text Suzie right now, and then we really do have to go through those boxes out in the foyer and make a plan for this week."

"Yeah." Alicia stood and headed that way, and Mandie grabbed her clipboard and followed her as soon as she'd sent an explanation text to Suzie about Donovan's accident. Honestly, that wouldn't be an easy pill to swallow either, but Mandie couldn't devote her whole day to this issue.

She left the library, noticing the scooter tracks Brandt had left in the construction dust. They made her smile, this unique footprint he had right now, and she glanced down the row of arched doorways but didn't see him or Suzie.

As she arrived in front of the towering boxes, the

weight of Monday morning settled on her shoulders. She flipped a couple of pages on the notebook attached to her clipboard and said, "All right. Let's see what we're working with this week."

With a lot of hard work and plenty of luck, they could get the study and the ballroom finished with these boxes. That would make three complete rooms, and Mandie didn't even want to think about how many more they had to go.

Ten bedrooms. Twelve and a half baths.

She reminded herself the lounge only had to be staged with furniture, that all the windows had been cleaned, the floor repaired and shined already, all the dead foliage and old furniture removed.

The landscape architect would be here this week, and once Mandie signed off on his plans, the outdoor work would begin too. She'd been given seven months to get this house ready for the market, and Mandie was absolutely going to make that deadline.

Starting with opening this box to see what was inside.

"Poor Suzie," Alicia said as she sliced open a box. "Did she respond?"

Mandie shook her head. "Not yet. Hopefully she knocks down a couple of walls first."

"Then she'll only be more upset." Alicia glanced toward the kitchen. "So...I kissed Henry on the Fourth."

Mandie grinned at her. "You did, hmm?"

Alicia grinned and ducked her head. "Yeah. It was nice."

"I bet it was." Mandie giggled and pulled open the box flaps she'd just opened. "These are the drapes for the ballroom." She peered down at the robin's-egg-blue-colored fabric. Not Brocade. Nothing heavy. Elegant, but lightweight. Something modern, to go with the high-end wood floor and the opulent chandelier.

"I've got the fixtures for the ballroom powder room." Alicia started a pile on the left-hand side of the foyer, as the ballroom sat right next to the library on that side. Mandie wrote down the items on her clipboard as Alicia moved the box with the curtains in it, and Mandie could admit it was good to be back in the house.

Now, she just had to keep this project on track; no more intruders. No more construction issues. No more changes to the décor.

Oh, and it would be nice if the personal problems for her, Alicia, and Suzie went away too.

Wishful thinking, perhaps, but Mandie had always had her head in the clouds a bit, and she really just wanted the next few months to be filled with good experiences, learning and growth, and exciting opportunities.

So when her phone chimed, she ignored it. She could talk to Suzie when she came back to the foyer for the huddle-up.

Chapter Seventeen

Suzie gripped Brandt's scooter handle as he used his good leg and she pulled. That way, they made it up the ramp to the entrance of the pool house. She'd been through it, of course, during their initial discovery, but all the team's focus had then been inside. First, on the parlor, and then the foyer, the lounge, the library and study and hidden room.

She panted by the time they made it to even ground, and she let go of Brandt's scooter. He could push it himself now, and she turned to open the door. The morning sun hadn't come up over the roof of the mansion yet, and the shady shadows filtered across the empty pool and expansive lawns that went beyond the pool house.

The mansion loomed in front of her, its grandeur undeniable even under the cloud of confusion and frustration that had settled over her. She sighed and looked back to Brandt as she held the door for him to enter the building.

Brandt's scooter left distinct, parallel tracks in the dust that coated everything out here. Suzie's footprints, as well as those of the film crew had come through here too, but his scooter left a different kind of mark.

Suzie found a modicum of comfort in those tracks, as if they were a tangible sign of progress, of moving forward despite the chaos that seemed to engulf her life.

"Thanks for helping me out here," Brandt said, glancing up at Suzie. "I hate this thing, but Candace is unbearable in the office."

"I bet she is," Suzie replied, forcing a smile. "You come anytime you want, but we'll probably start putting you to work." With the time they'd taken away from the house last week, they certainly couldn't afford the distraction of a team member who couldn't walk, and Suzie's smile straightened.

She didn't really want to entertain him, but he hadn't said much as she'd shown him the ballroom, the study, the bathrooms on the main floor, the two master ensuites, and the kitchen. They couldn't go upstairs, not with the scooter, and Suzie let the door fall closed as Brandt moved further inside.

The once-vibrant paint on the walls was now faded, with clear outlines of where the art had hung. Flint removed those for filming to give people a good idea of what time, sunshine, and neglect did to the simplest of things. It wasn't always about vines growing over the exterior walls. Houses needed to be cared for, or the elements really took over in the simplest of ways.

Inside, the air hadn't heated yet, but it still carried a musty, almost-chlorinated scent. Brandt maneuvered his scooter through the last door in the corner, a classic bulldozer move. Start in the corner and work back to the door.

Suzie already knew it was a laundry room, with a whole wall of high-end stackable machines. She wondered just how many towels, swimming suits, and cover-ups needed to be washed and dried at once, but the laundry room in the pool house answered that question. Five loads' worth.

She followed him, her thoughts somewhere else. She couldn't shake the image of Donovan's smile, the fiery touch of his mouth against hers, the way he'd held her close during the fireworks, the warmth of his body everywhere.

And then, nothing. Not a single word from him since he'd gone fishing the next morning.

"This place has seen better days," Brandt remarked, his eyes scanning the washers and dryers. "But everyone needs a laundry room like this, don't they?" He grinned and turned to face the long counter under the windows. They faced the broad back lawn, and Suzie stepped over to them.

She nodded, not really seeing the grass they'd been watering, fertilizing, and spraying weed control on for the past couple of months. It never ceased to amaze her how hardy grass was. Put a little water on it, and it grew right back—usually not where she wanted it.

Instead, she relived the Fourth of July with Donovan, her frustration and complete self-loathing rearing up again. "Yeah," she said as she turned and kicked an old cardboard box. "Everyone needs a laundry room like this." Her sturdy boot sent the box skidding across the floor, where it thunked into one of the washer-dryer combos.

She felt Brandt's gaze on the side of her face, but Suzie wasn't in the mood to look at him. Bulldozers didn't work together on projects, but they did have their own little pod at PastForward, and Suzie had always liked him.

"You okay?"

"Yeah." She drew in a deep breath, because she couldn't believe she'd told Mandie and Alicia about Donovan. She certainly wasn't going to tell Brandt. "I'm just peachy-keen."

She needed to do something to show tangible progress. Something big that would prove to her that she hadn't spent the day wiping down leather-bound volumes in a library while the sound of construction happened around her.

She wanted to *produce* the construction noise, and she glanced over to Brandt. "Want to help me dismantle something?"

Brandt's grin widened. "When don't I want to dismantle something?"

Suzie's phone buzzed, the sound floating through the silence. She pulled it from her pocket and saw Mandie's name flash across the screen. She'd texted a couple of times, but Suzie didn't want to see her apology.

She was the one who needed to apologize, but that wasn't the easiest thing for Suzie to do. So she shoved her phone away, intending to deal with Mandie later.

Right now, she just wanted to pull out old appliances and make a big mess. It would mirror her life, and Suzie wanted to believe that she could then clean it all up and turn it into something beautiful and worth having.

The room seemed to tilt, but Suzie took a breath and blinked it back to normal. "Let's pull these machines out. We'll have to get rid of them eventually."

Brandt scooted over to the box and picked it up. "I'll make a pile out in the main room. Maybe scoot around and see what else there is."

She nodded at him as he headed for the door. She already knew what the pool house held—two locker rooms, one for men and one for women, as well as a kitchenette in the corner, with enormous walls of glass accordion doors, so pool-goers could go inside and outside seamlessly along the side of the building that faced the pool.

Bracing her body against the middle washer-dryer combo, she pulled it out of line. It took quite a bit of physical effort, which was just what she needed right now. Her muscles stretched and groaned, but Suzie pulled out another unit, and then another.

The housekeepers here at the Hampton House had most likely kept everything neat to a fault, and Suzie found evidence of that behind the washers. Rather, nothing littered the ground there, the way they would have in a normal house. Last time she'd moved, she'd found coins, pens, and long tendrils of dryer lint behind her dryer.

Here? Nothing.

Dust, just like everywhere else, but nothing else. Nothing to show that actual people lived here and used this line of washers and dryers. Something seethed inside her, and Suzie just wanted to kick this wall right down. Having such an immaculate laundry room in a pool house only added to her ire.

She reared back and kicked the wall, expecting her steel-toed boot to at least go through the plaster. She wasn't expecting to have her whole leg go through—and then land down a step.

"What in the world?" Her heartbeat pounded up into her throat as Suzie pushed against the wall and pulled her leg back. Since she'd seen all kinds of things at the sites where she worked, her first thought was another secret passageway.

"Is the wall wide enough for that?" Suzie glanced up to the ceiling and then over to the doorway. She hadn't noticed anything odd about the size of the rooms here in the pool house, but she stepped out of the room and looked down the wall.

Yes, it was a little thicker, but Suzie expected as much when someone needed all the electrical and plumbing components to run five washers and dryers.

"These locker rooms are insane," Brandt said as he came out of the women's one down by the door. "The floors are heated."

"Are they?"

"They've got thermostats for them," Brandt said, hooking his thumb back into the room. Instead of returning to her, he pushed himself into the corner kitchenette. Suzie actually pulled the laundry room door closed behind her, not sure why, but not wanting to show Brandt the hole she'd kicked in the wall.

She licked her lips, sudden nerves assaulting her. To distract herself from telling him of a possible find, she pulled her phone out and looked at Mandie's texts.

We just called Donovan's brother to find out what we could. Suze...he's in the hospital. He got in a sailing accident on Friday morning, and he's been in the hospital since.

The very life left her body. So much so that she could barely hold up her device with both hands. "We have to go," she blurted out.

Brandt spun to face her. "Why?" He wore concern etched around his eyes.

"Donovan..." she said, though Brandt wouldn't know who he was. "He's been in an accident." She didn't have Jeremy's number, nor had she even thought to try to find it and call him. She already carried enough humiliation, thank you very much.

Brandt's eyes widened. "I don't know who that is, but—"

Suzie blinked back tears, trying to process the information. "I need to talk to Mandie," she said, striding abruptly toward the exit. "I need to know more."

She heard him following her, and she paused long

enough to hold the door so he could exit. He shot her a concerned look, but Suzie just needed to go.

Her mind raced as she hurried back to the house, and she paused to help Brandt steady himself on the few broad steps that went up to the outdoor patio outside the kitchen. He could use her and his scooter like a pair of crutches, and he managed to get up to the main level again.

"I should go," he said as they re-entered the house, and Suzie wasn't going to argue with him.

She did hear arguing in the foyer, and she exchanged a glance with Brandt and hurried ahead of him. She found Mandie and Alicia standing on one side of a pile of boxes, a much smaller one to the right, while Carl and one of his guys stood opposite of them.

"…not your job," Carl said, frowning.

"It's not that big of a deal," Mandie said.

"Nevertheless." Carl lifted his clipboard and made a mark on it. "I've got Jacob and Dalton going through the boxes this morning."

"Fine," Mandie huffed. "We want all the ballroom stuff in this pile, with the study items over there." She lifted her own clipboard. "I suppose I can stand here and make notes and check-off the things we've ordered."

Carl glared back at her. "Yes, that's acceptable," he said.

Mandie glanced over to Suzie and Brandt as they arrived. Her expression automatically changed, her eyes widening and all the fire in them going out. "Hey," she said quickly. "How—did you get my text?"

Suzie pressed her mouth together. "Mm, yeah."

"I'm going to head out," Brandt said. "You ladies are doing a great job here."

Mandie's featured registered relief now. "Thanks, Brandt. It was good to see you." Alicia echoed her sentiments, but Suzie couldn't even articulate a proper good-bye. She just needed to get Jeremy's number and call him.

Now.

HALF AN HOUR LATER, SUZIE RETURNED TO THE pool house, this time alone. Donovan had been in a coma since last Friday, and Suzie sniffled as she pushed through the door. Her heartbeat had been on a roller coaster for a full thirty minutes, getting flung up, down, and around. She was tired and it wasn't even nine o'clock in the morning yet.

She wanted to race to Eastern Long Island Hospital, crowd in beside Donovan's twin, and hold his hand. At the same time, she'd only known Donovan for about three weeks now, and she absolutely couldn't ask for work off. They'd already vacated the property last week, and Suzie was needed here.

Not right this minute in the main house, as Alicia and Mandie continued to sort the delivery items as the union workers opened and then moved the boxes. Carl and his team had gotten back to work in both the study and the ballroom today, as Candace had hired an additional half-dozen people to help them get caught up.

She sniffled even as she felt like the ground was slipping away beneath her. "You're going after work," she told herself. "Just get through today, and then go see him."

Determined in her decision, she returned to the laundry room and once again closed the door behind her. Brandt had left, and Suzie had grabbed a hammer from one of the open toolboxes in the kitchen.

With her feet standing on solid ground, and her mind shaking with nerves and worries, she faced the hole in the wall she'd made with her foot. She directed her frustration and unease by swinging the hammer and sending painted plaster exploding everywhere.

She should be wearing a protective mask and a pair of plastic glasses, but she hadn't thought to nab those from the construction crew. She didn't care right now.

This definitely wasn't an ordinary wall, as a draft of air came out of the hole as she widened it one more time. Then, to her complete surprise, a section of the wall bumped out, so much like the bookcase in the library.

A door stood there now, lilting open, with damage in the lower left-hand corner. The hinges had been completely concealed in the wall, and Suzie stared as she reached out and brought the door open all the way with only two fingers.

This was more of a panel, not a door at all, which was why Suzie's boot had gone right through it. She looked into the gaping darkness, not seeing the usual things she expected to—electrical wires, plumbing piles, or HVAC vents.

She stood there, frozen, her heartbeat pounding and pounding through her whole body. *This house*, she thought as she reached slowly for her phone. Her gaze went down the steep steps she could see, but darkness took over after only the third one.

A mix of fear and exhilaration, the promise of uncovering another secret of the Hampton House, propelled her fingers to fly over her phone, typing out an all-caps message for Alicia and Mandie.

COME TO THE POOL HOUSE RIGHT NOW. COME TO THE ROOM IN THE FAR LEFT CORNER.

She sent the text, and took a deep breath. Then, she flicked on the flashlight on her phone and shone it down onto the steps inside the secret doorway. Carefully, hesitantly, she placed one foot on the first step, her throat closing up as she tried to swallow.

It held her weight, and Suzie committed to the step down. Then another. And another. With each step, the tension mounted, the air growing colder. Suzie's foot finally hit cement instead of a wooden step, and she paused, shining her light around the tiny space where the staircase had spit her out.

The evidence of water intensified down here, almost a moldy, moist smell that told Suzie to get as far away as she could.

Instead, she breathed shallowly, about all she could do right now, and tried not to pass out.

A licia wiped her brow, glad to be back in the house but also wishing she could work out of the air-conditioned Flatiron building. The promise of a big promotion, with a much larger salary reminded her that she could sweat through anything.

Her phone buzzed in her back pocket, and since all she could do was stand there while Jacob used a utility knife to slice open another box, she pulled it out to check it. The kids had gone back to Ryan as regularly scheduled on Saturday night, but she'd have them every day next week as he went on his business trip.

Still, this text could be a question from him.

Instead, she found a shouting message from Suzie. *COME TO THE POOL HOUSE RIGHT NOW. COME TO THE ROOM IN THE FAR LEFT CORNER.*

Her muscles tightened up, and her pulse raced right to the top of her head. The room spun, but she managed to throw her hand out and grab onto Mandie. "Mandie," she gasped.

Her friend turned toward her, irritation in her expression—until she met Alicia's gaze. "We have to go to the pool house."

"What?"

"Now." Alicia held up her phone, but she didn't give Mandie enough time to read the message before she turned and marched way.

Mandie's shoes slapped the tile behind her as she ran to catch her. "What did that say?"

"Suzie needs us out there," Alicia clipped out. She dang near slammed into Wendell as he exited the kitchen with an armful of supplies, and she grunted as her eyes squished shut.

"Sorry," he mumbled as he ducked out of the way. Alicia stumbled for a moment, then got herself moving again. Mandie called something behind her, and then she moved to Alicia's side as they gained the outdoors.

"What did that say?" Mandie panted at Alicia's side. "Why are we running out here?"

"Suzie texted in all caps for us to come to the pool house."

"When?"

"Just a minute ago." Alicia went past the empty hole in the concrete and around the corner. She jogged up the ramp, almost desperate to get inside. Once there, her breath heaved as it went into her lungs, and she couldn't quite get it all out.

The door in the far left corner stood closed, but Alicia strode that way while Mandie looked at her own phone. "Oh no," she moaned behind her, and then Mandie ran once more to catch her.

"The door's closed," she said, her voice much higher than normal.

"Suzie is in there," Alicia said, though she hesitated too. She put her palm against the door, as if checking for heat behind it. Like the pool house would be on fire. Her pulse was, and Alicia swallowed, looked at Mandie, and dropped her hand to the doorknob.

It twisted just fine, and she opened the door and peered in it. In front of her, a wall of windows looked out over the back of the property, with a shelf from wall to wall. A couple of stacked washer-dryer units had been moved to the middle of the room, and more stood along the wall just inside the door.

"She's not here." Alicia entered the room, noting it felt cooler in here. Smelled wetter too. She took a few steps, then turned to face Mandie.

She froze when she saw the gaping hole in the wall. The breath all left her lungs then, leaving her lightheaded and cold at the same time.

Mandie came to her side, and the two of them stared at the black rectangle in the middle of the light blue wall. It gaped in the oddest way, while also beckoning her forward.

"Let's go," Mandie said, her bravery as a team lead shining through in that moment. She had her flashlight on before she reached the doorway, and Alicia scrambled to follow her this time. She managed to turn on her flashlight too, and she followed Mandie down a steep set of wooden steps and into a tiny compartment of a room.

Empty.

"Where is she?" Alicia asked, hoping she could get back up those steps. As it was, her legs felt like she'd cast them in gelatin and they'd collapse at any moment.

"Suzie!" Mandie yelled.

Alicia cringed away from her, alarms ringing through her. "Hush," she said. "We don't want anyone to know we're here."

Mandie gave her a pinched look and then swept her light along the cement walls of the room. "She has to be here."

"But we don't want everyone to know we're here."

"It's Carl and the construction crew," Mandie said. "And they all had to get past the same *two* security check-points we did." She definitely appreciated the safety measures, but she didn't wholly trust them yet.

"It smells like this place has been leaking," Mandie said in a much quieter voice. "We'll probably need to address that at some point."

"I didn't know this place had a basement," Alicia said. "That is not in the blueprints."

"Neither is that hidden room behind the bookcases." Mandie gave her a side-eyed look, and Alicia turned to shine her light in the opposite direction. An opening in the wall revealed another doorway, and she reached out to grab onto Mandie's wrist.

"Over here." She crept that way, sure Suzie had done the same. It barely accommodated the width of her hips, and she turned sideways as she moved through it. She didn't want to touch the stones, fearing them to be slimy or covered in grimy cobwebs.

The steps were more like slabs now, and Alicia could take a couple of steps on each one before she had to go down again. *Four, five, six,* she counted until she finally saw another doorway ahead.

This too looked like it didn't actually have a door on it, but mimicked the rooms off the foyer—large archways that led into grand rooms through shallow hallways.

Mandie gripped her arm, but Alicia kept walking. She wasn't sure how far she'd come, nor where she was in time or space in this moment, and it left her feeling unsettled and unsure.

Through the doorway, the hallway turned sharply to the right, and Alicia followed it. Mandie's breathing mirrored hers—almost short gasps of air—as they finally arrived in a much larger space.

More air. More of the same dank chill.

And Suzie.

"Suzie," Alicia breathed, and her friend turned from where she'd been standing in front of a table.

"You made it."

"Made it?" Mandie asked. "Made it where?"

Suzie hadn't turned on any lights down here, and perhaps there weren't any to ignite. "I think this is where the Harrington fortune is." She approached, the light from her cell phone illuminating her face in a freaky way. "Look."

She held her phone out, and it showed a picture of one of the pages she'd snapped of the journal. Which one, Alicia had no idea. She'd chosen not to focus on the finding of the fortune, because her literal livelihood relied on the success of the Hampton House renovation, not whether or not they found some long-lost treasure that might not even exist.

Coupled with a new summer relationship and her kids, and Alicia didn't have bandwidth for more. Mandie had agreed, and they'd both agreed not to breathe a word of their focus to Suzie.

She obviously cared more—and had a bigger personal stake—about the mysterious Harrington fortune, as evidenced by her saying, "I've been studying these pages, and look. They all have letters written up in the corners. Some of them are tiny, and some have faded away. I wrote them all down, and I've been trying to make sense of them."

"Ohhh-kay," Mandie said while Suzie swiped right on her phone. Right, right, right. She moved so fast, Alicia couldn't even see the letters in the corners, though she tried.

"I'm not sure," Suzie said. "But I'm pretty sure at least some of these letters spell out the words *pool house*." She looked up, her smile as wide as her eyes.

"Why would this person literally label where the treasure was hidden?" Alicia asked.

"It's a fortune," Suzie said. "Not a treasure."

Alicia wasn't sure about the difference, but she didn't argue. She glanced around. "So," she said. "Is it here?"

"It seems to be several tables." Suzie cast her phone around the space, and Alicia copied her. "Covered with things. We need to find a way to turn on the lights."

"So no money," Alicia said.

"They're not just going to have piles of cash from nineteen-hundred," Suzie said in a disgruntled, dry voice.

"What are you expecting to find?" Alicia asked. In her mind, she pictured something like what she'd seen in the movie *National Treasure*. A huge, underground room full of gold bars, chalices made from brass and bronze, and piles and piles of other treasures.

A treasure room.

This was no treasure room.

"I don't know," Suzie said. "Art, stocks, bonds, jewelry, maybe some bank accounts." She glanced around, moving her flashlight. Alicia combined hers with Suzie's, and Mandie did the same, amplifying their beam.

"So far, these things might be of importance to the Harrington family, but I don't see much in the way of actual dollars."

Mandie stepped over to the nearest table, which sat a few paces away. "But look at this lamp. We should take these things upstairs and see what we've got." She glanced at Suzie and then Alicia. "Maybe we can learn about their historical significance and include them in the décor."

She wore a glint in her eye that said she'd lose sleep to

do exactly that, and Alicia could admire her passion. Plus, long-lost family heirlooms from the rich and important tended to fetch quite the price.

Alicia nodded. "We need to get some lanterns down here." She thought of the steep steps they'd come down. Surely there wouldn't be anything too unwieldy to carry up and outside. Of course, she had no idea how they'd gotten this table down here in the first place. It almost seemed like someone had put all this stuff here and then built a room around it.

"Lanterns?" Suzie asked. "We're not going camping."

"They'd work," Alicia said.

"There's electricity here," Mandie said, swiveling to shine her light on the wall beside her. "We just need to find a switch."

With all of them there, Alicia started to calm a little. She spread out from the others and moved over to the nearest wall, looking for a switch. She didn't find one, but she did find a long, narrow table pushed up against the wall, and yes, items littered the top of it. Everything from a stack of old newspapers, to an antique desk lamp, to an old typewriter. Really old.

She saw an antique cigarette case and an ashtray, as if two men had sat here, talking until late in the evening. A couple of candles—with burnt wicks—stood nearby that, but Alicia couldn't see any way to light any of it. The cigarettes, the candles, anything.

No light switch among all the trinkets. She retraced her steps to the doorway, where she stepped back into the corridor. There, on the outside of the room, sat a single switch. Alicia's pulse bumped twice, and then took forever to sound for a third time as she reached for it.

With a quick press, the lights flared to life inside the room. Both Mandie and Suzie cried out in surprise, and Alicia stuck her head back inside.

The room couldn't be bigger than the swimming pool outside, and she currently stood in the only entrance and exit. Several tables had been spread throughout the space, and Alicia decided it had to be somehow strategic for whoever had done it.

A bank of filing cabinets—she counted seven—stood against the wall in front of her. She didn't see the piles of gold coins or pyramids of gold bars the way she was imagining. No, she simply saw more stuff to go through. Most of it possibly junk.

And those filing cabinets? Alicia didn't even want to think about what those contained.

She sighed mightily, like she needed to infuse more air into this room with only her breath, and looked over to where Mandie stood. She examined something on the table in front of her, but Alicia simply wanted to get back to work.

The real work they were being paid to do.

"Guys," she said. "I think we might have to put a pin in this."

Technically, it was Mandie's job to keep the team on track according to the timeline. But it was Alicia's to make sure they met the budgetary requirement. She acted in an advisory role, as well as doing all of the secretarial and administrative work on the backend. That meant a lot of paperwork, and she didn't want to try to figure out how to account for their time today if they spent the majority of it in a secret underground room, looking through things that wouldn't actually accelerate their project.

Mandie met her eyes, and Alicia raised her eyebrows. She didn't have to tell her that this wasn't part of the scope of their job—or perhaps it could be, but not right now. Right now, they needed to finish going through the foyer and get back to work on the tasks they'd have to report to Candace about.

"All right," Mandie said. "Alicia's right. We need to focus upstairs." She left the table where she stood and headed Alicia's way.

"I just don't want to have to fabricate something for Candace," Alicia said under her breath.

"Suzie," Mandie said. "We can work on this during our lunch hour."

Suzie barely turned her way, and Alicia's throat tightened. She'd seen this behavior in her son, when she'd asked him to empty his rack of the dishwasher and he didn't want to.

"Let's go," Mandie said loudly.

Suzie turned then, and as she came toward them, her jaw tightened. "I can come back during lunch."

"Did you get in touch with Jeremy?" Alicia asked as she turned and left the room first.

Suzie ground her voice through her throat. "Yes," she said. "I'm going to the hospital after work."

"I'm sorry you can't go right now," Mandie said.

"It's fine," Suzie said. "I mean, Jeremy's there. He said he'd like a break tonight, so it works out fine." She spoke in a clipped, tight voice that echoed in the narrow passageway.

Alicia labored to go up the tight incline of the steps, and she breathed hard when she finally burst out into the warmer, less dank laundry room. Sunshine poured in through the windows in front of her, and Alicia headed toward them, trying to get a good full breath.

The others came behind her, and as she turned back to them, she said, "Let's huddle up."

Mandie usually called the huddle, but Alicia had to speak her mind. The others came toward her, and with her chest still heaving, she added, "We cannot afford to let ourselves get distracted by the Harrington history."

She cut a look to Suzie. "I know it's important to you, Suze. I do. But we're barely going to make our deadlines as it is, and there's a lot on the line for all of us. We each need this project to succeed."

Mandie let a beat of silence go by before she said, "I agree. Sorry, Suzie."

"I know you're right," Suzie said. She sighed as she pulled her ponytail out and then started putting it back in. "I'll focus, and anything I do for the fortune, I'll do on my own time."

Mandie nodded. "Okay, then let's get back inside."

Her phone chimed, and she checked it. "See? There's Carl, and he wants to see me about something in the lounge."

"Let's go," Alicia said. "The last thing we need is arousing any suspicion about why we're out here at all."

Suzie glanced over her shoulder to the opening. "I'll take care of this and be right in."

"Sounds good." Mandie nodded like they could simply start the day over again by going back inside, and in fact, that was what Alicia planned to do.

She was still getting to know Suzie, so she wasn't sure if she'd really be able to focus on the job they needed to be doing, not the one she wanted to do.

Back inside, Alicia followed Mandie into the foyer. "Oh, they're done sorting," she said.

"Looks like it." Alicia turned to follow her upstairs. "I'll come with you, and then I think I'll try to get a report together on the ballroom and study. I'd love to see those rooms finished or near finished by the week's end. Then we can stage and clean, and Flint can come back for filming."

"Okay," Mandie said as they started up the staircase to the second floor.

"If we can pull that off, Candace will be thrilled," Alicia said, already doubting if they could get two more rooms done in the next week, but suddenly more determined than ever to actually do it.

At the top of the stairs, she saw tracks in the dustiness there that looked like Carl had brought up something they couldn't quite carry. So he'd used something with wheels to get it where it needed to go.

"Oh my goodness!" Mandie said in such a different tone than any she'd used that day. She walked through the open glass doors and into the magnificent lounge. "Look at this place, Carl."

Her construction manager turned from where he stood with a couple of other men, both of whom worked on hanging a piece of art on the wall. He smiled at Mandie and spread his arm wide. "Not a stitch of brass in sight. Ultra-modern, and yet comfortable."

Alicia soaked in the sunshine, all the plush, luxurious furniture—not the single-person loungers of yesteryear, but double-wide chaise chairs, overstuffed couches, and comfy bean bags—and the stunning light fixture overhead.

"Ultra-modern," she repeated. "Yet comfortable." That had to be the motto for the Hampton House, and Alicia became more determined than ever to make it so.

"It's *gorgeous*," Mandie said. "Thank you so much, Carl." As she continued to go over things with Carl, Alicia ducked back out onto the landing.

She followed the tracks on the floor to the left, wondering what his crew had brought this way. The second floor had the glorious lounge, of course, and then two wings. With the front of the house facing south, that made the wing Alicia currently meandered toward the West Wing, and she felt very much like Belle walking into forbidden, beastly territory.

The wings only contained bedrooms and bathrooms,

with cavernous closets, and a single laundry room in this wing. Perhaps Carl had decided to use that for storage, for things they'd use when they finally moved on to the second floor.

Alicia had been through the rooms up here, but they weren't anything terribly special. Big bed frames with canopies, and linens filled with dust and who knew what else. Alicia didn't even want to imagine.

The track did not go into the laundry room, and Alicia simply kept following it. The construction noise echoed up from the first floor below, but she couldn't hear Mandie anymore. The tracks veered into the second bedroom on the right, and Alicia paused.

Confusion ran through her. Why would Carl be storing anything up here, of all places? They hadn't done any ordering for the bedrooms, not even the pair of ensuites on the main floor. Without an elevator, anything being transported up here had to take some serious manpower—manpower they paid a lot for through the unionized workers.

Something wasn't right, and Alicia opened the door and went inside the bedroom to see what was going on there.

Everything seemed fairly normal for one, two, three beats of time, and then her vision went black as someone pulled something over her face. Alicia yelped and struggled, but a pair of strong arms restrained her, and a low, menacing, gender-neutral voice said, "Stop it, or I'll knock you out."

Chapter Nineteen

Mandie set the list of items needed for the game room on the pile where Alicia usually worked. She hadn't come back down to the library, and Mandie wasn't sure where she was. Suzie had been wiping down and looking through books for the past hour while Mandie went through her list.

"Should we go start doing what we can in the ballroom?" she asked, causing Suzie to turn toward her. The morning had been eventful already, and Mandie's bones carried a weariness she didn't usually feel until later in the week. Or at least until afternoon.

"Sure," Suzie said, blinking several times as if bringing herself back to the present. "Where's Alicia?'

"I don't know," Mandie said, glancing toward the door. "I guess it's possible she went in there already." Perhaps she'd been working and waiting for them all this time. They hadn't truly huddled up due to Suzie's second hidden room discovery. But Alicia knew what they needed to get done—she was the one who'd reined them in and reminded them of what they were really meant to be doing here at the Hampton House.

They weren't treasure hunters, and while Mandie found family history fascinating too, they definitely had a job to do here that wasn't about the Harrington fortune. Mandie had seen several pieces under the pool house that she wanted to bring out, polish up, and find a home for right here in the mansion.

And she would. Just not right now.

"Knock, knock," Henry said as he came through the door. He carried a large brown bag with him, and the salty scent of bacon preceded him. He smiled and added, "I brought lunch." His eyes scanned the library, and then he met Mandie's gaze. "Where's Alicia?"

Suzie came to Mandie's side. "You didn't tell her you were bringing lunch?"

"I did," Henry said slowly. He advanced and set the bag on the table in front of them. "She hasn't answered any of my calls or texts." He pulled his phone out of the inside pocket of his jacket. "Since…about nine-twenty this morning."

Suzie looked at Mandie, and Mandie looked at Suzie. Her blood felt like the molecules had grown barbs, and they ripped against her delicate veins with every beat of her heart. It continuously pushed the blood through her body, no matter how badly she wanted it to stop.

"Well, where is she?" Henry asked.

Mandie shook her head, her throat and mouth so dry she couldn't speak. "I don't know. *We* don't know."

The silence in the mansion pressed upon Mandie then. She couldn't hear any grinding or pounding, no construction noise at all. Carl and his crew had obviously gone to lunch, and her stomach simultaneously growled and lurched at the same time.

She wanted to eat the food Henry had brought while she laughed and chatted with her friends. But she needed to find Alicia, and she looked over to Suzie. The blonde bulldozer wore an equally perplexed and somewhat strained look on her face, and Mandie swallowed hard.

"Let me call her." Mandie swiped up her phone and quickly tapped to dial Alicia. She walked to the doorway of the library, almost expecting to hear her friend's ringtone echoing somewhere from inside the mansion.

She didn't, and Mandie strode toward the ballroom next door. It stood empty—very nearly ready to do a final cleaning and staging in, but empty besides the boxes that had been brought in earlier that morning.

The game room next door needed more construction work in the repairing of the cue holders and the final sealing of the floor. Then, Mandie would go over the larger purchases needed for this room. After all, pool tables were very expensive, and she'd need to make sure they had the budget for such things.

The study sat across the foyer, but Mandie checked the full bath between to the game room and kitchen before heading that way. Small construction tools like drills and sanders sat on the two sawhorses there, which had a broad piece of plywood covering them to make a work station.

No people. No Alicia.

Panic built beneath her tongue then, thickening it and making both breathing and swallowing difficult. The parlor was locked, so she couldn't be in there, and the family den took up the front of the first floor, an enormous family room they'd fill with new couches and the biggest TV they could afford.

After all, even the ultra-rich needed somewhere to watch sitcoms and family dramas.

She spun back to the foyer as Suzie said, "Maybe she's upstairs."

"Why would she be upstairs?" Mandie asked, but she was already headed that way. Suzie and Henry met her at the base of the wide staircase, and together, the three of them went up.

"Tell me what you did when you left the pool house," Suzie demanded.

Mandie's mind went round and round. "We came up here," she said. "Carl was in the lounge, hanging the art." She paused outside the door of the room she'd gone in. It was finished now, complete with everything hung exactly right, the pillows propped up just-so, and a professional window cleaning job done.

"She came in with me." Mandie's chest heaved, her imagination running away from her. Had Alicia fallen somewhere? Been hurt and unable to get anyone's attention? Why didn't she have her phone with her?

"But when I finished with Carl, she was gone." Alicia looked right toward the East Wing and left into the West. "I don't know where she went. I assumed downstairs. She always has twice as much work as the rest of us, what with all the filing and reports she needs to do."

She twisted her hands around one another. "I don't—I don't know what to do."

Henry lowered his phone again. "She's still not answering."

Mandie felt like she didn't exist inside her own body. "Okay," she said, trying to find a center spot where she could make a rational decision. "Henry, you go ask the police officers if she left the property. Would you?"

"On it." Henry started down the steps while Mandie turned her attention to Suzie.

"I don't want to split up," Mandie said. "So we're going to go through the rooms up here one by one together." She nodded, and Suzie, a woman fifteen years older than her, nodded and stepped to her side.

She linked her arm through Mandie's. "All right," she said. "East or west?"

"Let's go east first." They moved right, and Mandie led them down to the furthest bedroom. They opened door by door, calling Alicia's name. She didn't appear. Mandie's phone stayed silent, and Henry returned when they'd just entered the third bedroom.

He panted from his jog, and he said, "Neither of them saw her leave."

"Then she's here," Mandie said with authority. She

wondered if Alicia had gone back out to the pool house. If so, why? Why hadn't she texted to say where she was going?

They walked past the lounge, the three of them side-by-side. Suzie slowed and then came to a complete stop. "Wait," she said. She sucked in a breath in a loud, shocked way.

"What?" Mandie asked. Suzie stared down at the ground, and Mandie looked at it too. "What?"

"The tracks," Suzie whispered, and she looked up sharply. "This track...this is from Brandt's scooter." She looked at Mandie with wide eyes. "How did he get up here?"

Mandie's pulse positively pounded through her body. Brandt had a broken leg, and he'd stopped by this morning for a visit. "You were with him this morning." Her throat stuck to itself. "You guys didn't come up here?"

"How could we?" Suzie asked. "I had to help him up and down the few steps off the back patio. I pulled that scooter up the ramp to the pool house." Her fingers flexed and released. "How—I know this is from his scooter."

"Maybe someone brought it up to move something," Mandie suggested. Her own fingertips tingled and her hands mimicked blocks of ice. She shook them, trying to get her circulation to resume normally.

"Why would they do that?" Suzie asked. She shook her head. "No one has any reason to be up here. We're not working up here."

"Just in the lounge," Mandie said, casting a look to the

big, open room with plenty of sunshine pouring in. It sat in such contrast to the fear and anxiety pouring through Mandie.

"Come on." She stepped forward again. "We have a few more rooms to check."

Henry hadn't said anything, and now he met Mandie's eyes. He wore his worry plainly too, but they all stepped forward together. Mandie pulled out her phone as they approached the first bathroom, and she tapped to get to Candace's name.

She dialed as Suzie opened the door and peered inside. "Alicia?" she called.

"Hey, Mandie," Candace barked. "I have five minutes. What's going on?"

"We don't know where Alicia is," Mandie said, her voice shaking on her best friend's name. "We checked with the cops, and she didn't leave. But she's not answering her phone or our calls."

"Where are you now?"

"Checking the upstairs bedrooms."

"No." Candace barked. "No, get out of the house."

Mandie came to a stop. "Get out of the house?"

Suzie looked over to her, her gaze filled with fierceness. Mandie couldn't imagine leaving Alicia behind. "But she didn't leave."

"Get out now," Candace barked. "Go tell the cops you can't find her. Let them search the house."

That seemed smart, and Mandie kicked herself for not thinking of it. Her hands trembled as Suzie pulled the bathroom door closed, and the three of them stood there, silent and still.

"Mandie," Candace said in one of her harshest tones. "Get out of the house right now. I'm not asking you. I'm telling you, and if you don't do it, you're fired."

She swallowed as she nodded, but her feet still wouldn't move. "Alicia—"

"What's done is done," Candace said. "There's no sense in you and Suzie getting injured too. Go talk to the cops. Go now."

Mandie finally had enough feeling in her feet to turn herself around. With her back to the portion of the house they hadn't searched, Mandie felt like running. "Okay." She breathed out heavily. "We're going. Come on, guys. We're leaving."

"Is Carl there?" Candace asked as Mandie reached the top of the staircase.

"No." Mandie panted through the line. "The construction crew is at lunch."

"I have to go for a minute," Candace said. "I'll just cancel my meeting that's starting right now and call you back."

"Okay." Mandie landed on the bottom floor and jogged toward the front doors. The call ended, and Mandie burst out into the fresh air, sucking at it to try to get her frenzied mind to calm down.

"Hey," she called to the man at the top of the sidewalk. "One of my team members is missing." She ran toward him. "The dark-haired one? A little taller than me; she was wearing a pair of black pants and a...a pink? Was her shirt pink this morning?"

"No," Henry said. "It was peach-colored. It had all those birds on it."

"Right," Mandie said, suddenly seeing the shirt in her mind. "We can't find her. She's missing, and we need you to call in your back-up and go search the house and property."

The man in uniform stood there and blinked at her, and Mandie's irritation fired instantly. "Now," she said as she clapped her hands. "Should I call nine-one-one?"

"On it," Suzie said, and she lifted her phone to her ear.

"I can call it in," the cop said.

"I'm doing it." Suzie gave him a glare and then turned her back on them, moving out into the lane as she said, "Yes, hi, one of my team members is missing at the Hampton House, and we need some people to search the house and grounds for her."

Mandie stepped over to Henry and linked her arm through his. "When's the last time you talked to her?"

"Nine-twenty," he said promptly.

"We came back into the house about then," Mandie said, turning to look back at the Hampton House. It seemed to have so many secrets, and Mandie studied the windows, wishing they'd show her any flicker of life.

The wind blew through the branches, bringing with it the scent of summer—sunscreen and sand and sunshine. It didn't quite fit with the hulking house, and Mandie turned away from this place she'd fought so hard to be.

A wailing part of her wanted to quit right now. Just walk off-site and never come back. But she couldn't do that—she *wouldn't* do that to her friends.

Suzie returned and said, "They're on the way."

"Great," Mandie said. "Yeah, great." She startled as her phone rang, and she very nearly dropped it. She managed to hold onto it and lift it up. "It's Candace."

"Answer it," Suzie said as the police officer from outside the gate came jogging in. He said something to the other cop, and Mandie stared in horror as they barked, "Go stand on the other side of the gate," drew their weapons, and advanced toward the house.

She let Henry guide her down the lane and away from the house, and Suzie plucked the phone from her hand and said, "Hey, Candace. It's Suzie, and yes, the cops are going in now."

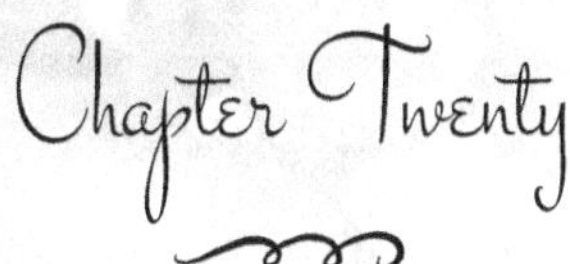

licia blinked, her eyes struggling to see something in the darkness. She had no idea how much time had passed. She hadn't been clubbed over the head or force-fed pills. But her right hand tried to lift up to rub an itchy spot on the inner crook of her left arm.

She couldn't, because her hands had been tied behind her back.

She sat on a hard chair, her heart beating, banging, booming at her to get out now. But she couldn't stand.

She could barely think.

Images of her children ran through her mind, and Alicia forced herself to take a long breath in through her nose. She'd heard two voices before she'd been dragged onto this chair, and she suspected she'd been stowed away in the bedroom closet.

She hadn't been gagged, but she didn't dare scream for help. Whoever had covered her head in a black bag, hit-man-style, had told her to stay quiet or she'd be knocked out. Alicia heard herself whimper before she pulled on that emotional thread. She tucked it away, hiding it for later.

She wiggled her hands, trying to find some give in the ties that bound her. The plastic zip ties dug into her skin, and Alicia shied away from the sharp edges and focused on her feet instead.

Their enemies were right here in the house, and Alicia wasn't sure how she could come back to work here.

Something shifted suddenly, and Alicia froze. Without being able to see, she wasn't sure if someone had entered the room or not, but then she heard shouts, and in the next moment, the bag got removed from her head.

She squinted, disoriented, and looked up at the man in front of her. Police name tag. Stripes. He lifted the radio on his shoulder and spoke into it.

His words made no sense, because Alicia hadn't found her bearings yet. She glanced away from the man, the ghost of someone's hands on her arms and hands. To her right, she found the shelves of a closet, and she looked back to the doorway as several more police officers streamed through it.

Her throat felt so dry, and Alicia coughed as she tried to swallow. She could taste fear as she licked her lips, her thoughts flapping through her mind like big, bat wings.

"You're okay," an officer said. "Jerry, let's get her out of these zip ties."

Alicia started to cry as she got cut free, and the

moment she could, she lurched away from the chair where she'd been restrained.

Despite the number of people who'd come into the room, the house echoed with an eerie silence, only the creaking of floorboards filling the air as officers inspected the closet and bedroom beyond.

Her breathing seemed loud to her own ears, and she tried to calm herself, tried to think of what to do next.

"My name is Jerry Rhinehold," the man in front of her said, and Alicia's eyes flitted to his. He wasn't her captor, as his voice was more of a tenor than a bass, and Alicia's pulse slowed. "What's your name?"

"Alicia Halverson."

"Can you tell us what happened?" He didn't flip open one of those little notebooks she'd seen detectives use on TV.

"Uh, yeah." She reached up and wiped her hand through her hair. She caught the redness of her wrist as she lowered her arm. "I came upstairs to look at the lounge with Mandie." She quickly related the few minutes where she'd seen the tracks in the dirt, followed them, and then been blindfolded.

"There were two people," she said. "They were arguing."

"What did they say?"

Her mind fogged; her thoughts wouldn't form. "I'm not sure. I could just tell they weren't happy with each other." No strands of a sentence would come forward, and Alicia shook her head. "Sorry."

"Don't be sorry," the detective said. He took her by the elbow and indicated the doorway leading out of the closet. "Where did you get intercepted? Can you show me?"

Alicia left the closet, thankfully, and found more police officers in the bedroom. They each seemed to have a purpose, whether that was looking at something on the nightstand or lifting the bed skirt and peering underneath it.

"Right when I came in the door," she said. "I think it was a man, but I'm not sure." Her hands came up and brushed against her neck. "His fingers...seemed bigger than a woman's. He told me not to struggle, or he'd knock me out."

"Did he?"

Alicia shook her head. "No, I froze. Didn't make a sound. They bound my hands and marched me to the chair. Right when they finished, that's when the second person came in." She pressed her eyes closed. "I had the bag on my head. I didn't see either of them, but..."

Her eyes popped open. "The second person said, 'we'll for sure have to leave now.'" She looked at Detective Jerry. "The other person said he knew where they could go, that it was fine. They weren't going to lose anything."

"Lose what?"

"I don't know," she said. "That's what he said. 'We won't lose anything.' The other person—I think it was a woman—didn't seem to believe him."

Jerry nodded, his expression blank, a mask with nothing

behind it. "Let's get you outside." He led the way, not walking too fast so he didn't get too far ahead of her. Alicia found herself surrounded by cops on all sides, and she wasn't sure if it made her feel more secure or absolutely terrified.

"These tracks?" Detective Jerry asked, pausing and crouching down to get a closer look at the floor.

Alicia looked down and saw the partial parallel lines on the floor. Footsteps had crowded over them, but she could still see them. "Yes," she whispered.

"Mark this off," Jerry said as he straightened again. "No one else walks over anything like this."

One of his colleagues nodded, and Jerry indicated Alicia should move in front of him now. She did, carefully avoiding the wheel tracks which had troubled her. Could Brandt be one of the people who'd restrained her?

She didn't want to believe it; she'd known Brandt for years. She'd worked with him on other renovation and restoration projects. How—?

"Sir," someone said behind Jerry. "We found evidence of someone living in the third bedroom."

Detective Jerry turned back to them, and Alicia paused too, her ears keen to pick up anything she could.

"Fingerprint everything," he said. "Bag anything that looks like it doesn't belong."

"We have pictures of the mansion before we started the project," Alicia said, drawing all law enforcement attention to her. "My team lead can provide those, so you can see what's out of place and what's not."

Detective Jerry nodded. "Excellent. Tape it off. Only forensics in that room."

"Yes, sir," the officer said, and he turned around to go back around the curved hallway to the bedroom beside the one Alicia had entered.

As she went down the grand staircase, Alicia noticed the cop cars outside, their lights flashing in the otherwise serene surroundings. The house, once filled with the noise of construction, was now a somber scene of alarm and confusion.

She hurried through the foyer, finding the air stale and hard to take into her lungs. The moment she stepped out into the fresh air, Alicia took a deep breath. Finally, oxygen filled her the right way, and she turned her face toward the bright sunshine.

Tears slipped down her cheeks, a release of her relief and residual fear.

"Alicia."

She met Mandie's eyes, and Alicia sobbed as she ran toward her friend. Mandie grabbed onto her and held her tightly. "You're okay," she said firmly. "You're absolutely okay." She stepped back, gripping Alicia by the shoulders. "Are you okay? Did they hurt you?"

"Ma'am," Detective Jerry said, giving Mandie a stern look. When he turned his attention to Alicia, he wore a softer look. "We want the paramedics to check you out."

"Yes," Mandie said. "Then, can we go?" She threw a look to the mansion, but Alicia's pulse crashed to the ground.

"Mandie." She wiped her face, all the pieces inside her settling back to their rightful place. "We need to work."

Mandie turned to Detective Jerry. "Can our construction crew get back in?" She threw a look to Alicia. "We can go over the budget and look at textiles for the kitchen."

They'd spent last week doing the same thing, and part of Alicia simply wanted to pick up a sledge hammer and start bashing something.

"My guys have to clear the house first," Detective Jerry said easily. "No one's allowed in until then."

Suzie arrived, asking, "How long will that take?"

Alicia appreciated the way she flanked Alicia on one side, with Mandie on the other. She needed their support, and while she'd felt so alone in the dark only minutes ago, that wasn't the reality of her life.

"I can't give you a timeline, ladies," Detective Jerry said. "Miss Halverson?" He indicated the ambulance with a single nod of his head, and the three of them faced it.

Mandie led the way, with Alicia right behind her. She'd no sooner arrived at the back of the ambulance when she heard the barky, demanding voice of her boss.

"Mandie? Alicia? Suzie? What's going on here?"

"Candace," Suzie said smoothly from behind Alicia. She detoured over to her and steered her away from Alicia and the ambulance and toward the house and officer in charge just outside it.

"She's good with Candace," Mandie noted.

"Yes." Alicia held out her hands to the paramedic in front of her.

"I'm going to let her handle Candace."

Alicia met Mandie's eyes, and surprisingly, a smile touched her mouth. "Smart move."

Mandie's big hazel eyes drank her right up. "Are you okay?"

Alicia drew in a breath, overwhelmed but somehow feeling solid as well. "Yes," she said. "I'm okay."

"Did you see anyone?"

She shook her head and sucked in a breath as the paramedic swiped an alcohol wipe along her wrist. "These don't look bad," he said. "I'm going to put some antibiotic ointment on them, and you should be fine. They'll heal up in only a couple of days."

Alicia nodded, and the conversation stalled while she got treated. Then, she walked away from the ambulance, and no one stopped her.

She linked her arm through Mandie's and turned her back on the activity still humming around the entrance of the Hampton House. She couldn't see Suzie or Candace right now, and she simply needed to get some distance.

They walked down the lane, past the pool house, and out onto the grounds. "Do you really think it could be Brandt?" she asked.

"Brandt?" Mandie asked, shocked. "Why would you think that?"

"The tracks on the floor," she said simply. "They think people have been living in the house while we've been there working."

"What? Where?"

"Third bedroom in the West Wing," she said. "Which is what? Right above the end of the library and over part of the ballroom." She shot Mandie a look. "Maybe there's another secret passageway that's vertical."

Mandie walked along, pure shock flowing from her. "I just can't believe this."

"There were two people," Alicia said. "I think a man and a woman." She blew out her breath and took in a fresh round of air. "We really don't need this. We're a week behind now, Suzie's off breaking down walls on a personal quest, and our overages..." She shook her head. "How are we supposed to finish on time with all these distractions?"

The enormity of the situation pressed down on her as heavy as the entire sky above. The Hampton House was supposed to be her big break, her chance to prove herself, to get a coveted promotion. Now, if felt more like a curse, a never-ending series of obstacles designed to break her down until she had nothing.

"I don't know," Mandie said. "But we're not giving up." She spoke with a fierceness Alicia wanted to feel inside her chest. But right now, she just wanted to get off the property and find something to eat—and clarity.

She sighed as they reached the end of the lane, thick trees in front of them. She turned around and faced the other way. "They're leaving."

Mandie joined her, and they watched as officer after officer moved down the lane and toward the gate. Some of them carried items with them, but Alicia didn't have the energy to try to figure out what they might be.

Their phones both chimed, and Alicia suspected that might be Suzie. She let Mandie check her phone, and she said, "Suzie says Candace is going with the police to find out what she can, and that we should go to lunch."

"She wants a huddle-up."

"We need a huddle-up," Mandie said. "We didn't ever do it this morning."

"Was it really only this morning where we were in that dungeon treasure room?"

Mandie blinked at her. "What?" She giggled slightly, then sobered again. "I think that was this morning, yeah."

"Feels like another lifetime."

"It does, but we can't let this stuff get to us. We'll get back on track with the project, and we'll figure out who's behind all of this—and why." She took the first step back toward the house. "I'm sure Suzie will have some ideas."

Alicia was sure of that as well. Her phone chimed and chimed and chimed, and she slowed her step to check it.

I'm going to call you after I'm done at the police station, Candace said.

The paramedics say you're okay, but I want to hear you say it.

And we need to talk about the overage sheet you submitted this morning.

Her chest lifted in a big breath, but Alicia had to do her job if she wanted to keep it.

But most of all, Alicia, I'm glad you're okay.

That last text told Alicia that Candace was indeed human, something she'd wondered about in the past. She fired people in such a clinical, unemotional way, and she was a ruthless leader who had never held her poisonous tongue.

She could end Alicia's dreams with a single word, and yet, she'd just expressed that she...cared.

Alicia felt like she was the one getting her floorboards ripped up and examined. She was the one getting a wall torn down to the foundation, with new insulation being sprayed on, sealed up, mudded over, and then textured to look pretty.

She'd taken other houses through complete remodels, and she'd never felt the same thing happening inside her—until this project.

"There you are."

Alicia turned toward the male voice, almost flinching away from Henry before she recognized him. He drew her into his chest without another word, and Alicia wrapped her arms around him too.

"I didn't know you were here."

"Yeah, I brought lunch."

Alicia's stomach growled again, even as she recognized how thoughtful Henry was. "Do you think we can still eat it?"

Henry looked toward the house, but none of them moved toward it. No one would stop them if they entered it, and Alicia couldn't believe they could just...go back to work as if nothing happened.

Suzie came out of the house in that moment, a large brown bag in her hand. She lifted it and offered everyone a smile. "I got the lunch Henry brought. Let's get out of here for a minute and eat."

"Great idea," Mandie said, and Alicia didn't have to be told twice. She went with everyone to Henry's car, and she found greater relief once the Hampton House sat in his rearview mirror.

It wouldn't stay there forever, and Alicia didn't even want it to. She just needed a little break, a really good sandwich, and to figure out how to talk to Candace later that day.

Chapter Twenty-One

Mandie stepped over to the stove and picked up the wooden spoon. She told herself the reason her eyes kept watering was because of the onions and garlic she'd sautéed in butter. She stirred them, deemed them soft enough, and tossed in a healthy dose of salt and pepper.

Then, she added the diced celery and carrots. The pan hissed, and Mandie mixed everything together. These would need to cook for a few minutes, and then she'd add the potatoes.

Her grandmother's recipe for chicken pot pie had always made her feel better. When she'd failed her chemistry test in eighth grade, her mother had made it and brought a smile to Mandie's face with the toasty brown dough on the top.

She'd started learning to make it for her father's homecoming party one year when he'd gone to Alaska for his summer fishing. Mandie didn't get to see his mother as often as her mom's mother, but every time she even smelled chicken broth, she thought of Grandma Grover.

With the celery and carrots softer, she added the chicken broth, the liquid immediately bubbling up and boiling. Around and around her spoon went, making sure not to stop moving. The added liquid would help cook the vegetables, and she reached to add the potatoes.

They got mixed in, and she set a lid on the pan to encourage the boiling to continue. With a timer set for ten minutes, she prepped the cornstarch slurry and set it next to the stove. Now, she just needed to shred the rotisserie chicken she'd bought on the way home from work today.

After lunch, they'd returned to the Hampton House. The staircase leading to the second floor had been taped off with a yellow police banner, and Mandie had barely been able to look at it.

"It's fine," she muttered to herself. "We don't have to go up to the second floor for months."

She had not left Alicia alone for another minute that day, even staying with her while she called Candace and talked through everything that had happened that morning—minus the "treasure room" discovery in the pool house, which they'd agreed to keep to themselves for now. They went over the overage report, and Mandie found herself stopping in her dinner prep completely.

She hadn't known their reserves had been dipped into to the tune of one hundred thousand dollars.

With a deep breath, Mandie shored up her courage

and squared her shoulders. "It's fine," she said again. "We'll make up some of that by sealing the pool instead of replacing all the tiles. We'll reuse anything we can." She immediately thought of the items in the hidden room under the pool house, as well as the more modern touches they'd put in the ballroom, study, and game room.

Those items, while luxurious, cost less than historical replicas and rare fabrics. "I'm not giving up the textured hardware in the kitchen," she vowed.

Gold was so two-thousand-and-late, and yet, Mandie had just submitted the order list for golden fixtures—everything from the kitchen faucet to the drawer pulls to the lighting options in the kitchen.

"It's going to be glorious," she told herself. "And gold is cheaper than any other finish right now."

Maybe because no one wanted it, but Mandie pushed that out of her head as she picked up her knife and chopped up the chicken she'd pulled off the bones. The timer went off, and Mandie turned back to the stove to silence it.

She lifted the lid and stirred her vegetables, testing the doneness of the potatoes with the tip of her knife. Not quite done, but only minutes away. She quickly picked up her whisk, poured in the slurry, and started swirling, swirling, swirling as the chicken broth thickened as it boiled.

She picked up the chopped chicken by the handful and put it in, then cut off the top of the bag of peas and added them too. She stirred everything together, noting the filling had thickened to perfection.

After pouring it into the prepared casserole dish, Mandie worked quickly to roll the dough she'd already prepared over the rolling pin. Then, she carefully laid that over the casserole dish, the pot pie filling steaming as she did.

She tucked the edges down into the pan and slid the whole thing into the oven. In forty minutes, she'd have her comfort food, and she'd just picked up the whisk and the wooden spoon when the door locks behind her clanked and jangled.

Mandie tossed the used utensils in the sink, wiped her hands on her apron, and beelined for her one safe place. Her anchor. Her very heart.

Charlie.

"Hey, babe," he said. "What are you—?" He grunted as Mandie flew into his arms. It took him a moment to wrap her in his arms, and Mandie had started crying by them. "Hey." He stroked her hair once, then again, and again. "What's wrong?"

She had no idea what he saw in the apartment, but just the fact that she'd beat him home spoke volumes. He didn't ask her question after question but simply let her cry for a minute or two.

When she finally stepped back, he asked, "You made chicken pot pie?"

She nodded, sniffling, and wiped her face. "Yes." She

took a deep breath. "And I just want to eat and lay in bed with the TV on tonight."

"All right," he said, his eyebrows up.

"And I got us tickets to the cove this weekend."

Charlie's curiosity flew off the charts, lifting his eyebrows. "Did you lose your job?"

She shook her head. "No." Her voice broke. "It just—everything's going wrong with the Hampton House, Charlie, and I don't know how to right the ship." She turned away from him and went back into the kitchen to get cleaned up.

He joined her, saying nothing, and together, they simply worked in silence. Charlie finally said, "Smells good, babe."

"Thank you," she murmured. "Did you have a good day at work?"

"Yeah," he said. "I mean, there was this one instance where that guy John came in again, but Doctor Flashburn called security, and they got him out before he made it to the window."

Mandie flashed him a smile. "I love that name. Flashburn. I wish that was our last name."

Charlie smiled too. "Right? Kelton is so pedestrian."

Everything felt lighter as they played this old game about names. He'd started it years ago when he'd said he wished he had a cool name instead of Charlie. Mandie stepped into him and held on to his strong shoulders as she looked up to him.

"I can do this, right?"

"What's derailed?" he asked.

"We're a hundred grand into the reserve."

"Okay," he said. "But you have half-a-million. That's nothing."

"We haven't gotten to the kitchen yet."

"You can still do this."

"The police got called in today."

Charlie's eyes searched hers then, and the story spilled out of Mandie while the chicken pot pie finished baking. She removed it from the oven when the timer went off, and then she and Charlie moved to set the table for the two of them.

He didn't immediately reassure her, but opened a bagged salad and mixed it up while Mandie placed the golden brown pot pie in the middle of their tiny table. She put ice cubes in their glasses and got out the peach Fresca and lime powder packets.

They sat down together, and Charlie met her eyes. "Is the project continuing?"

Mandie nodded as she picked up the big serving spoon. "They've doubled the police presence, and it's twenty-four hours a day now. They didn't find anyone in the house, and they took everything out of the bedroom where they thought unauthorized people were living."

She took a scoop of the pot pie and put it on her plate. Then she handed that to Charlie and took his plate to serve herself.

"It's going to be fine," he said. "You're brilliant, and Alicia won't let you go over the budget, I just know it."

"Yeah," Mandie said, deciding she was done talking about work. With her steaming chicken and veggies on her plate, the saltiness of the filling wafting up to meet her nose, Mandie looked at Charlie. "Can we have Alicia and Henry over for dinner?"

"Sure," Charlie said, his blue eyes seeing right through her.

"Oh, and Suzie found out today that Donovan got in a boating accident." She forked up a bite of pot pie. "That's why I texted you about his brother's number."

Charlie's expression changed to one of surprise then. "Are you serious?"

"Yes," she said. "She headed to the hospital after work, and I told her if she didn't text us all before we go to bed, I'd call down the fires from heaven." She trilled out a laugh, starting to feel a little better now that she'd been home, in a place of comfort and safety, and now that Charlie was here with her.

Her husband chuckled. "I bet you will, too."

"He's been in a coma," Mandie said.

"This is really serious," Charlie said, displaying his concern.

"Yes," she agreed. "We're just getting hit with things left and right." Mandie felt like she'd lived through times like this before, but not as an adult. She'd seen her parents struggle financially, through sicknesses, with job changes, family members, and difficult situations with friends. Hurricanes, tsunamis, hail storms, big waves that came— both figuratively and literally.

But now, as the adult inside all of that raging water, Mandie realized things held more weight. They meant more, and it certainly felt like she might drown with the next big wave that came along.

Charlie reached across the table and covered her hand with his. "But Mandie, hey."

She looked at him, so much inside of her shaking. "Yeah?"

"We can do this," he said earnestly. "*You* can do this. It's just a house, and you're Mandie Kelton. Nothing beats you."

A tiny smile graced her face. "Thank you, Charlie."

"I love you, sweetheart."

"I love you too." She took her first bite of chicken pot pie, and that creamy richness, with the tang of salt and the pop of green peas comforted her all the way. "I just feel...I feel like I'm getting renovated at the same time as this mansion."

He grinned at her. "Yeah?" He took a bite of his dinner too and moaned immediately afterward. "I love this stuff." He chewed and swallowed. "Well, you're already awesome, just like that mansion is, and maybe, by the end of this, you'll both come out spectacular."

She smiled back at him, hoping and praying with all she had that he was right. And that Alicia and Henry could come for dinner soon.

Oh, and that Suzie would text or call with good news about Donovan very, *very* soon.

Chapter Twenty-Two

Suzie pushed through the revolving doors of Eastern Long Island Hospital, her heart galloping in her chest. This day had felt like four hundred all rolled into one, and as the sterile scent of antiseptic hit her nostrils, mingling with the faint aroma of cafeteria food, Suzie wanted nothing more than to walk back out and go home.

However, she also wanted to be here for Donovan. Jeremy had texted an hour ago that his brother had awakened, and Suzie had been the one to break up their mid-afternoon work and get them all out of the mansion early.

She paused for a moment, taking in the bustling activity around her: nurses darting in and out of rooms, doctors conferring at counters, and voices coming over the PA system practically on top of one another. It was controlled chaos, and Suzie felt a pang of sympathy for all those caught in it.

She navigated her way to the information desk, where

a young woman in a crisp white blouse and navy blazer sat typing furiously on a keyboard. "Hi, I'm here to see Donovan Petrovik," Suzie said, her bulldozer personality in full-force.

The woman glanced up, her eyes bleary for a moment. She clicked around on the computer, said, "Donovan... Petrovik..." She hit the enter key hard and read the screen. "Room three-twelve, just down that hallway and to the right." She gestured to the hall on her left-hand side.

"Thank you," Suzie murmured, her legs already carrying her in the right direction. Every step brought her closer to the man who had occupied her thoughts incessantly for the last few days.

She had a somewhat addictive personality, she knew, and she needed to put things in perspective. She'd only known Donovan for three weeks. It wasn't like she was in love with him, nor him with her. That reality slowed her steps and allowed her to breathe as she approached the appointed room.

A nurse came out of his room, laughing, and Suzie figured things couldn't be too bad inside. She steeled herself by taking a breath and holding it, then she pushed open the door. Donovan lay in the bed, his eyes open and his smile sitting good-naturedly on his face.

His gaze switched to hers, and she took in the soft beeping of the heart monitor and the way his chest rose and fell in a steady rhythm. He had good color, even though the pale blue hospital robe he wore did him no favors.

"Donovan." Suzie's voice came out as a whisper, barely more than a breath.

"Hey, you," he said, and she wondered if he knew her, if he could remember her name. He reached for her. "Jeremy said you'd be coming by."

To her horror, tears sprang to her eyes as she rushed to his side. "You're really awake."

"I am," he replied, squeezing her hand as she laced her fingers through his. "They say I'm part fish." He grinned, as if almost getting drowned and then spending a few days in a coma could ever be laughed about.

And for some reason, Suzie did laugh. Right out loud, the sound releasing all the pent-up anxiety she'd held in her chest, her shoulders, her mind. "I've been so worried."

"I bet," he said. "In fact, I bet you thought I'd ghosted you."

Her teeth pressed together as her smile faded. "Honestly? Yeah, that's what I thought." She shook her head, brushing away the last of the tears. "But it's not your fault. I'm just so glad you're okay."

He shifted slightly, wincing as he moved under the thin blanket. "They're keeping me here for observation, but I'm out of the woods. I should be okay."

The rush of Suzie's adrenaline faded. "Jeremy went home?"

"He's been here for three straight days." Donovan's eyes danced with amusement. "I told him it was his body odor that called me back from the other side." He chuckled, and Suzie marveled that he could be so normal after being so sick.

"Ready for some good stories, then? Did he tell you any while you were out?"

"I don't know," Donovan said. "I was asleep."

"They say you should talk to coma patients," she said, not really knowing. It wasn't like she was a doctor or anything.

His eyes drifted closed. "Tell me your stories, sweetheart."

So, with his hand in hers, Suzie filled him in on the happenings of that morning. That whole day. By the time she finished, her throat felt like someone had smoothed it with sandpaper.

"So I'm trying to figure out what to do with the stuff in the room. There are *so* many filing cabinets down there." And she couldn't go onto the property without at least a half-dozen police officers knowing. So the middle of the night was out.

"Maybe they'll be empty," he said, his eyes still shut.

"Maybe." She lost herself to thinking about what was in them for a few moments, then blinked her way back to the sterility of the hospital. "I think I'll try to go in early tomorrow and go through some things before everyone else shows up."

"I can't wait to hear about it." Donovan's grip on her hand tightened slightly. "And Alicia is okay tonight?"

"She's...I think she'll be okay." Suzie's concern for Alicia surprised her still. "She did okay this afternoon, but we worked outside on the back patio, in the shade. It was like...none of us wanted to be inside very badly."

"Understandable," he said. "And tomorrow?"

"We'll be there," she said. "We have to get back on track. Mandie and Alicia aren't saying, but I can see the anxiety in their faces. They're the ones with budgets and timelines. My job is to literally kick things down and help rebuild them."

He smiled and opened his eyes. "Mm, yeah. That's sexy."

She grinned back at him, though the weight of her situation hadn't lessened. Several moments passed, each one taking with it some of her light-heartedness. "I don't know who to trust. We've worked with Brandt for years. *I've* worked personally with him. He's my friend."

She'd spent the morning with him—alone—in the pool house.

"Do you really think it could be him?" Donovan asked as he searched her face.

"I don't want to believe it," Suzie admitted. "But those the tracks on the floor...I saw them out in the pool house too. It's all so confusing."

"Could be another wheeled thing," he said. "A wagon. Whatever."

Suzie nodded. "Yeah, that's what we all said too. Without simply marching up to him and asking, I don't know how we'll know." And Suzie had never shied away from such a conversation. But with Brandt? What would she do? Text him and ask him if he'd been living in the second-floor bedroom of the Hampton House?

She scoffed under her breath. No, she wasn't going to send any texts like that. She prided herself on always knowing what to say and being the one to say it. But with this? Suzie felt like someone had tied her tongue in a knot.

Donovan stayed silent too, and when Suzie looked at him, she found him deep in thought. "What are you thinking?" she asked, reaching over to brush a lock of his hair off his forehead. She'd never touched a man like this before, and it felt personal, intimate.

Their eyes met, and he smiled at her. "I didn't realize the Harrington's owned the house," he said.

"They're the original owners," she said. "It's changed hands four or five times in the past hundred and fifty years."

"I know a Harrington," he said. "Well, I mean, maybe. There's a guy who's come into Chelle's a couple of times. He's said he's related to at least half of the rich families who built the Hamptons. I'm pretty sure he said Edmund Harrington."

Suzie's interest reached for the atmosphere. "Maybe I should talk to him." Or maybe she'd just meet up with a nutter, who would then want part of any fortune she found. She couldn't believe she even thought there might be a fortune. Families like the Harringtons knew how to protect their wealth, passing it along from generation to generation.

"Where does he live?" she asked.

"I…don't think he has a place." Donovan's eyes widened. "I think he's sort of a couch-surfer."

Suzie read between the lines. "So he could be staying anywhere." Like inside the Hampton House.

"I honestly don't know," he said. "As a waiter, we overhear a lot of conversations, talk to a lot of people. But it's just a snapshot of time. A blip of a conversation. It's never the whole piece."

"Sure," she said, but she'd never waited tables. Not even in college. She sighed as she laid back against the raised mattress. "Do you know his name?"

"Uh, Dustin…uh…Dustin something." He looked over to her. "You need to be careful. Sounds like there's a lot going on at that mansion."

"Yeah," she said, because that was the understatement of the year. She gave him the best smile she could, her eyes dropping to his mouth. "I'll talk to Mandie and Alicia about it. Off the clock. We need to get this project back on track, but we also need to figure out what's going on."

At least she did. This mansion was more personal to her than the others, she knew that. She'd tried to distract herself over the weekend by going through the journals, the family trees, all of it.

"You're so pretty," Donovan said again, and warmth filled Suzie. A smile spread across her face, and she leaned toward him for a kiss. "Thank you, Donovan. I needed to hear that."

He looked tired, and Suzie definitely felt weary all the way to her bones. As she sat there, holding his hand and feeling the warmth of his presence, Suzie absolutely knew she wasn't alone.

She didn't have to hole up in her apartment with dusty old records, searching for the familial connection she craved.

She had her friends; Mandie and Alicia meant something to her, and she wouldn't move on from them the way she had all the others she'd worked with. She didn't have to fly solo, not anymore.

A glimmer of hope shone through her in the quiet serenity of this hospital room, and it wasn't until her phone buzzed that she remembered she'd promised her friends that she'd let them know how Donovan was doing.

She'd told them she'd let them know before bedtime, and she still had hours until then. So she laid her head against Donovan's shoulder, listened to his breathing even out, and even closed her own eyes.

She didn't fall asleep, though. She simply let her mind work through possibilities—any possibilities—that didn't include one of her friends and co-workers being the one ruining the Hampton House project.

Chapter Twenty-Three

Alicia stood in the grand ballroom of the Hampton House, her eyes scanning the ornate chandelier hanging from the ceiling, the gold-leafed trim along the walls, and the polished hardwood floor beneath her feet—laid perfectly in the herringbone pattern. She couldn't help but marvel at the transformation that had taken place over the past few weeks. The room now exuded an old-world charm blended with modern elegance, thanks to the meticulous efforts of the team, the construction crew, everyone assigned to the Hampton House.

Today was a big day; Flint would be here any minute to film the transformation of the ballroom, and a flutter of excitement winged through her.

The constant presence of the police had become almost routine, and they hadn't had any other problems with the renovation. August had just dawned, and Alicia had high hopes that they could get back on schedule and stay under budget after all.

"All right," Flint said as he entered. He whistled through his teeth. "Wow, would you look at this?" He scanned the room, taking several long moments to look at things. Alicia had been in here dozens of times, and she saw something new every time. From the richness of the blue and white patterned wallpaper, to the gleaming grand piano, to the ivory and blue drapes. They had a pattern to them, and everything sang together, all of it creating a perfect symphony for the soul.

The chairs bore blue with bright, sunshine-yellow accent pillows and beading around the tops of them. The whole room screamed opulence, but also invited everyone inside, where a grand party would surely be happening.

Flint's gaze landed on her. "Look at you. How's everything here?" He approached as his crew came in behind him, carrying all their gear. "I've never seen wallpaper like this."

"It almost looks vintage, right?" Alicia stepped into him and gave him a light hug. "Did you see Mandie when you came in?"

"Nope, she wasn't out there." Flint turned in a slow circle, his eyes on the ceiling now. "This is incredible."

"It's wallpaper," Alicia said. "Made to look like a fresco." Just like the cathedrals and churches of old Rome had painted ceilings, so too did this ballroom.

"It's incredible," he said, and Alicia basked in Flint's praise. He worked on a lot of projects and had seen a lot of amazing renovations. Definitely more than her, and his approval carried a lot of weight.

"So where did Mandie want us to focus?"

"The color palette," Alicia said. "I think we all decided that has to be the focus."

Flint slid his boot along the perfectly polished floor. "I think it's this."

"And how it plays with the blues and yellows," Alicia said. "It has an air of royalty, making anyone who comes here feel like kings and queens."

Flint grinned at her. "I like that angle."

She smiled back at him. "It's so good to see you."

He chuckled and shook his head. "I've been here a lot lately. You guys are flying through rooms."

"We just have a few almost done," she said.

"We're filming the kitchen floor tear-down today too." He reached for the camera his assistant held for him. "So let's do this first, because I love getting all the angles of a finished room far better than zooming in on Carl sliding a crowbar under a piece of wood and seeing what's underneath."

"We think there might be an original floor in the kitchen," Alicia said, giving him the side-eye.

"Yeah, I heard," he said. "I still hate the fake shots, like we don't know what's under there."

She nudged him with her hip. "We *don't* know what's under there."

Flint started to film, and Alicia faded out of the way.

Mandie met her in the doorway and said, "Oh, good, he's here."

"Yeah, and he's about to pan this way." Alicia backed out into the foyer, but Mandie didn't.

"Flint, we need to talk about this video you sent."

"Later," he said in a distracted voice, and Mandie frowned as she joined Alicia in the foyer too.

"What video?" she asked, watching Mandie's facial expression. It took her a long moment to look up from her phone, and when she did, her brows stayed furrowed.

"What?"

"What video?"

She moved closer to Alicia. "Flint's been texting me about some piece of footage he swears he didn't shoot."

"Of somewhere here?"

"Yeah." Mandie handed her the phone and started gathering her hair into a ponytail. The summer heat had only intensified, and without functional AC here, Alicia went home a sweaty mess most of the time.

She focused on the phone, and tapped on the link Flint had sent to Mandie. This footage definitely didn't match up with the quality of Flint's. It looked like it had been taken with a cellphone, not the professional equipment Flint had access to at PastForward.

She frowned too, and Mandie said, "Do you recognize it?"

"No." Alicia looked up, though the clip went on. "It's the second floor." They hadn't gone up there since her incident, though the police tape had been removed. They had gotten prints, but they didn't match anyone in any of the systems. All that meant was that the person or persons who'd been in the house hadn't been arrested and didn't have their prints on file.

"We only took pictures of the rooms," Mandie said. "Flint is the only one who does recordings."

"Maybe someone on his crew."

"They all say no." Mandie took her phone back and together, they looked back to the door leading into the ballroom. The exterior walls in the foyer had been completed, and they glowed with the same ivory as they'd been draping the windows with.

The doorknob glinted with silver and crystal, and Alicia couldn't help smiling at it. Such simple details gave her such a thrill. "Flint said they're shooting the kitchen flooring reveal today."

"Yeah." Mandie sighed. "The kitchen...tell me that's not going to bankrupt us."

Alicia gave her a smile. "It won't. I think the last family who owned this house redid the kitchen."

"Maybe."

"It's the most modern room in the house." Alicia was sure of it, but she also understood Mandie's hesitancy. She tended to wait and see what came to fruition instead of making predictions. It was actually something Alicia really liked about her.

"How's the study coming along?" Mandie asked.

"Almost done," Alicia said, her soul lighting up. "We're putting the finishing touches on it this week. Suzie wanted you to go down to the treasure room and pick some things to complete the staging."

"Okay."

Alicia didn't hardly ever go down the steep steps that led under the pool house either, because then, she didn't feel as guilty when Candace asked questions about the rare and unique pieces they used to put that final flourish on each room.

She fully expected to get a text once Candace saw the footage from the ballroom, for they'd put two vases on an end table that had come from the treasure room. She'd want to know where they got them, and how they matched a bygone era so perfectly.

And if Alicia didn't go down into the treasure room, she didn't have to know what else they might pull from there. She'd told Candace that Mandie had worked her magic on the pieces she'd seen in the study, though the room wasn't finished yet.

"And I signed off on the pool table. It's waiting in the game room for Carl to put the legs on and move it into position." Pride stole through her. Despite the setbacks, they'd made great progress in the past few weeks.

"You guys," Suzie said from the direction of the kitchen, her voice a touch labored. As Alicia looked over, she saw why. The blonde bulldozer carried an antique clock, and it didn't look light.

"Look what I found for the den," she said. "It'll be perfect on the mantle in there."

Oh, that mantle. They'd had to bring in an engineer to

construct a solid steel frame for the white marble show-piece that came in four separate parts. Each one weighed four hundred and fifty pounds, and steel rods had gone into the wall to provide the frame of support for them.

The mantle currently still sat in pieces in the den, but the steel support was almost finished—and they'd paid for it out of their overage fund. Six hundred and seventy-five dollars gone from their reserves.

But the mantle and fireplace would be exquisite, even if they could never light a fire in it, due to the possibility of the whole house going up in flames if someone did.

Alicia hurried over to help Suzie, taking the clock from her and setting it gently on a long table that housed a variety of other items they'd ordered but hadn't placed yet. The clock had brass hands and Roman numerals for the numbers, and while it didn't currently tick, Alicia knew Suzie would get it back in working order. The woman never took no for an answer, that was for sure.

"It's beautiful," Alicia said. "We'll have to see if we can find some other pieces to go with it." She smiled over to Suzie. "You never answered about dinner at Mandie's."

Suzie's glow lessened, and she suddenly could only look at the clock. "Yeah, uh, well, I don't know about that."

"What don't you know?"

"Donovan and I…I'm not sure I'm going to keep going out with him."

Surprise shot through Alicia. "No?"

Suzie shook her head. "I mean, he's a nice guy, but...I don't know."

Alicia put her arm around Suzie. "I know what it is."

"Do you?" she bit out. "Please, tell me."

"He's too...golden retriever for you."

"Golden retriever?"

"Yeah, he's like, always smiling and bringing you whatever you want and...he's a nice guy," she finished lamely. "I just think you'd like someone a little more—like you."

Suzie settled her weight on one foot and pushed her hip away from Alicia. "And what does that mean?"

"More serious," Alicia said. "That's all I mean. Someone who isn't going to be a waiter his whole life and who wants to do more than spend every weekend at the beach."

"I want to spend every weekend at the beach," Mandie said.

Alicia blew out her breath, realizing no matter what she said, it could be offensive. "That's not what I meant."

Suzie held her glare for a couple of seconds, and then she softened. "I know what you meant." She switched her attention to Mandie. "There's more down there, and I want you to help me pick things to go with the clock. For the den."

Mandie nodded. "All right, but I won't be able to get down there today. There's too much going on here."

"I can take pictures for you while Flint is filming."

"Perfect."

Alicia nodded along with Mandie, a sense of camaraderie swelling within her. They made a good team, and she smiled to herself as Mandie said, "All right, Lish. I want you to go get the kitchen flooring staged for Flint. Suzie, we need the bathroom demo done today."

"Yep," Suzie said.

"I'll have everything ready for you in the kitchen," Alicia promised, and they dispersed to their various jobs. Alicia, however, took another moment to appreciate the clock, wondering where it had come from. And when.

It was a beautiful piece, intricately designed, and it would add a touch of historical authenticity to the den. A mix of old and new. Historical and modern. She loved such things, and as she left the clock there to tend to the task she'd been assigned, her phone rang.

Candace.

Alicia's pulse pounced through her body, her first instinct to answer the call. It was her boss, after all. But she didn't want to lie to her boss, and if she didn't answer, then she didn't have to do that.

"You can't avoid her forever," Alicia muttered to herself as she entered the kitchen. The room spanned the entire back of the mansion, an absolutely massive space that would house a sixteen-foot island, a dining nook, and a wet bar around the corner.

It flowed seamlessly into the dining room, which could hold a table large enough to seat sixteen. In fact, the table and chairs for this room sat out in their storage pod, and Alicia couldn't wait to see the bright pink in the mansion. They certainly wouldn't have used that color in 1875.

Her phone bleeped, meaning she'd gotten a voicemail message. She ignored it as she moved over to the corner where they'd decided to shoot the flooring reveal. She cleared away the tools that already sat there, as they'd already done a board or two. Just to get started. Just to have a little taste—enough to know what to have Flint come in and film.

Once she had everything moved where it needed to be for Carl, Mandie, and Flint, she pulled out her phone. Candace had texted too, and Alicia tapped to read those first.

Flint just sent me a ten-second clip of the ballroom. Gorgeous!

I got the final budget report for it too, and I have to say, I'm impressed you only had a $1000 overage.

Alicia grinned right there in the kitchen, because they'd done really well on the ballroom, and she expected similar results from the study, game room, and den. It was the kitchen she needed to monitor carefully...

I need to know where you got that standing lamp in the corner, Candace had said next. *It's exquisite, and I've never seen anything like it.*

Alicia knew why. Suzie and Mandie had brought that lamp—which stood just over six feet tall—up from the treasure room. Alicia herself had polished it and chosen the low-wattage bulb.

We might want to use something like that in an upcoming project, and I want to make sure I start scouting the supplier.

Alicia's stomach churned. She still hadn't told Candace about the underground room and the possible Harrington heirlooms. She knew she needed to, but the thought of revealing that secret filled her with dread. She quickly typed a response.

We found a few things stored here in the mansion—the lamp is one of them. I'll give you a full inventory soon.

She hit send and slipped her phone back into her pocket, hoping it would buy her some time. She couldn't afford to lose Candace's trust, but the team had agreed to tell their boss about the treasure room together—and only if necessary.

"You ready in here, Lish?" Mandie called, and she shoved her phone away. But Mandie had the eyes of a hawk, and she slowed as she neared. "What's going on?"

"Nothing," Alicia said quickly. "Just texting Candace." She forced a smile to her lips. "She actually complimented me on the overage in the ballroom."

Mandie nodded, but Alicia still found worry in her eyes. They both knew how precarious their situation was. One wrong move, and they could lose everything they'd worked so hard for.

"What's she pressing you about?"

"The extra items." Alicia saw no point in hiding it. "She wants to know where we're getting such idyllic, vintage pieces." She paced away from Mandie and then turned back. "I told her we'd found that floor lamp here in the mansion."

"It's not exactly a lie."

"It's not exactly the truth either."

"All right," Flint said in his boisterous voice as he entered the kitchen. "We ready in here?"

Alicia held Mandie's gaze for another harrowing heartbeat. Then she said, "Yep, I'll go get Carl." She went to do just that, her mind racing. They couldn't keep the treasure room hidden forever. Sooner or later, Candace would find out, and when she did, Alicia honestly couldn't predict how she'd react.

She stood out of the way while Carl and Mandie went through the script of pulling up the wooden planks of yesteryear. Mandie even hammered the crowbar underneath one and broke it off, exclaiming about the deeper, darker hardwood underneath.

Carl said they could reclaim it, polish it up, and use the "antique floor," as long as it was mostly in decent condition. With a room this big, anything could happen, and dread settled in Alicia's stomach.

She hated kitchen renovations. They tended to cost so much more than budgeted, as there were a lot of things that could need fixing—plumbing, electricity, appliances, windows, doors. And this kitchen also had a hearth.

"Oh, look at this," Mandie said, and she grinned right into Flint's camera. "There are old newspapers stuck in the walls here." She pulled out a crispy, weathered newspaper. "They used to do this to use as insulation and to level things."

The paper crinkled mightily as she tried to smooth it in her hands. "This will tell us when this floor was last redone." She swiped her thumb across the paper, and Alicia went to examine it with her.

"November," Mandie said. "Nineteen-forty-two." She turned the paper toward Alicia. "Look at the headline."

She could only see part of it, since the paper had been ripped in half. The latter part of the headline read "Nazi Germany today" in all capital letters.

A shiver ran through Alicia's shoulders. "Wow," she said. She took the paper from Mandie and held it up for Flint's camera. "Pieces of history like this are priceless."

"And now we know these floors are from the forties," Mandie said. "Not quite as old as the house, but still a beautiful antique."

Alicia happened to agree, but she bent to get more newspapers out of the wall. This kind of stuff fascinated her, and perhaps she could use it as a distraction today. No matter what, they always kept items like this and tried to preserve them. In fact, these old newspapers could become art for somewhere in the home. Perhaps even the kitchen.

Her phone rang again, and this time, Henry's name sat there. Alicia smiled and breathed easier as she left Mandie, Carl, and Flint in the kitchen and went outside to take her phone call.

"Hey," she said, basking in the morning sunshine. She breathed in deep and then let it out. "What's going on?"

"Candace just called me," he said. "Sent me a video clip and asked me about a floor lamp."

Alicia's pulse plummeted, and she couldn't even take

in the grandeur and progress the grounds crew had made in the backyard. "Of course she did," she said dryly.

"I've never seen a lamp like that," he said.

"No?" That couldn't be true. Henry was a historian, for crying out loud. He'd seen everything.

"No." Something shuffled and crinkled on his end of the line. "Where did you guys get it?"

Alicia sighed, but she didn't know how to lie when asked such a direct question. So she didn't.

Chapter Twenty-Four

Mandie fidgeted on the subway, her eyes glued to her phone. She always lost service for several minutes before she arrived at the station, and she cursed the underground reception.

She should be on the sidewalk in front of her building, waiting for her cab out to the Hamptons. Instead, the texts from Flint had become increasingly alarming, and Mandie had decided to add a stop by the Flatiron building on the way out to the construction site.

She flipped her phone over and over, glancing at the black screen every time it came up. No texts, of course.

The ones she'd seen before stepping onto the subway made her heart thump hard, stall, and then race forward again. Last week, Flint had sent her a confusing clip from the mansion. She hadn't filmed it; Alicia hadn't; Suzie hadn't; no one on Flint's team had done it.

And yet, it had been shot after Mandie's team had met

Henry here and entered the mansion for the first time in almost a decade. A single question had plagued her since she'd seen the original footage: Who had taken it?

And a second one: How had Flint gotten it?

The subway began to slow, and Mandie got to her feet, because she needed to get off and get upstairs as soon as possible. Flint had sent her another clip with the words, *Found another one. Look at that and tell me who it is.*

Mandie hadn't been able to do that, because the video had not come through before she'd boarded the subway and started her journey to the Flatiron District. She was the first off the train and she strode toward the exit, her destination singular.

She didn't get a text as she rode the escalator up, nor when she exited to the street. She tapped quickly as she kept walking. *The video didn't come through. Send it again.*

She'd be at the office in five minutes, but the next three hundred seconds might be her complete undoing.

You must almost be here, Flint said. *Don't go up to the office. I'll meet you in the lobby on the second floor.*

Mandie frowned at that text. PastForward wasn't anywhere near the second floor, and in fact, Mandie had no idea what enterprise took up the second floor. She wanted to ask, but a horn sounded very near her head, and Mandie looked up.

She better focus on getting to the building alive before anything else. She did that, and she bypassed the elevator completely, opting for the stairs instead. She came out onto the second floor, which seemed to be empty.

Mandie shouldn't be surprised, but she was. A lot of companies had moved to at-home work, and she'd known several of the tenants in the building here had moved out and moved on.

She walker to the nose of the Flatiron building and looked out into the city. When she heard footsteps behind her, she turned to find Flint coming her way. "What are we doing here?" she asked.

Flint, who usually wore joviality on his face and always maintained a positive outlook on life, wore a grim expression. Mandie couldn't handle that. She'd relied on Flint to keep her spirits high too many times at work.

"A couple of things," he said with a sigh as he came to stand beside her. He gazed out the same windows she'd just been, and she turned to do the same. "One, they're putting this building up for auction again."

"Again?" Mandie wasn't sure what this had to do with the video footage, or Flint, or PastForward, but she'd give Flint a couple of minutes to explain.

"Mm hm." Flint tucked his hands into his pockets. "Word around the office is that Candace is going to contact the owner and offer restoration services in exchange for free rent forever."

"Restoration services?" Mandie turned to face him. "What? For the whole building?"

Flint's eyebrows went up, but he nodded.

Mandie couldn't make sense of it. "That's—that's insane, that's what that is."

"It would be PastForward's biggest project."

"By like a multiplier of twenty," Mandie said. "This building has to be what? Two hundred thousand square feet?" She shook her head and faced the window again. She couldn't really see anything outside now, not with her mind as full as it was. "The biggest restoration project we've ever done is twenty-one thousand."

She shook her head. Trying to take on a twenty-two story building? Pure insanity.

"Something like that," Flint said. "No matter what, she's already looking for new commercial space for Past-Forward. So we'll have to move the office at some point."

"Joy," Mandie said. "I hope it's while I'm still out in the Hamptons." That way, she wouldn't have to do much more than pack up her own cubicle.

"I hope we can finish out in the Hamptons," Flint said, his voice taking on an undercurrent of darkness.

Mandie's chest squeezed around her lungs. "What do you mean?"

He pulled out his phone, silent, and swiped and tapped to get into it. "I found another piece of footage." He touched the screen and handed her the phone without another word.

Mandie took it, her eyes glued to the moving images that showed, once again, the interior of the Hampton House. She had that foyer memorized, and she sucked in a breath as this recording showed delivery men piling boxes up in the foyer.

"Those—" She couldn't be absolutely certain, but she and Alicia had gone through the pile of boxes. Carl had gotten after them, because of the union contract. She snapped her mouth closed as the video continued.

The delivery people finished up and left. The front door closed, if the lack of morning light coming in told her anything. And then...the screen brightened again. The door had been opened.

She expected to see herself, or Alicia, or Suzie. Instead, a figure entered right at the top of the screen—someone very clearly not walking.

Someone very clearly pushing themselves on a scooter, though Mandie couldn't see more than the blocky shape of it in the shadows. She didn't see another leg take the right-hand step, because Brandt had broken his right leg.

The footage continued, but Brandt had exited the scene, and no one else came in. He'd left the door open, and the light continued to slant across the floor.

Her mind caught up with her eyes, and she sucked in a breath. "Brandt," she whispered. She looked at Flint with wide eyes. They stung, because she hadn't blinked in so long. "So it was him."

Flint shrugged one shoulder, obviously not going to say anything, as he continued to look out the window.

She tried to put the pieces together, but she still didn't have them all. "Where is the camera that filmed this?"

"Has to be on the second floor," he said.

Mandie pulled out her phone and handed Flint's back to him. "I'm going to call Suzie, and see if she can find it." She did that, saying, "I can't explain right now. Go up to the West Wing and see if you can find a camera out in the hallway that could film the foyer where we get our deliveries."

"Fine," Suzie barked at her. "But if you know something—"

Mandie pulled the phone from her ear and hung up. "Another question: Where are you finding this footage?"

"It's getting uploaded to the cloud at PastForward." Flint finally turned toward her, and Mandie searched his face.

"That means..." She trailed off. Having Brandt involved had already shocked her. Now there was someone else? Maybe everyone else? Maybe that was why Flint had told her to meet him on the second floor.

"It's someone at PastForward," Flint said. "Specifically, someone who knows how to upload big media files to the cloud server."

"Well, I don't do that," Mandie said.

"Nope."

"Who does—?" She cut off again, the answer coming into her mind. "Only videographers need to do that."

Flint nodded and said, "Yep."

"So..." She actually took a step away from him, because she had no idea what might happen next. No idea what might come out of Flint's mouth in the next moment. She swallowed. "We don't even have that many videographers."

"And we're down one," he said. "Well, we were when the Hampton House started."

Mandie pulled in another breath so sharply, it actually hurt. "That's when Jo Ann quit."

"That's when Jo Ann *got fired*," he corrected her.

"Wait—she got fired?"

"I met with Candace this morning," he said. "She still hasn't hired anyone to replace Jo Ann, and we're dying on the production side."

"Yeah," Mandie said, because Flint had complained about that.

"She said she couldn't help it if Jo Ann had decided to, and I quote, 'hook up with Brandt," when they both know inter-office dating is grounds for dismissal."

"But Brandt—got the very next assignment," Mandie said, confused.

"Jo Ann volunteered to leave PastForward," Flint said. "But Candace would've fired them both if she hadn't."

Irritation and anger started a slow burn through her. "And Brandt got an assignment." She shook her head. "I thought Candace was at least fair."

"I'm pretty sure..." Flint trailed off, which only made Mandie's curiosity rear up and thrash around.

"You're pretty sure—what?"

"I'm pretty sure Candace told him to do something so he wouldn't be able to work on the Hampton House."

"What?" exploded out of her mouth. It took several long seconds for her to find a spot for that piece. "He broke his leg on purpose?"

"I don't think so," Flint said. "That was a lucky accident. I think he'd have come in and said he was sick or something." He looked at her again and rocked back on his heels. "But he didn't have to."

"This is wild," Mandie said, her brain buzzing. She needed to huddle up with her ladies and figure out what to do next. *If anything*, she thought. This was all office gossip, sure, but she wasn't sure how it affected her project.

She drew in a deep breath, her frustration over Candace's supposed sexism fading away. "So Jo Ann quits, then goes to the Hampton House and sets up a hidden camera. Somehow, some of the footage is getting uploaded to the PastForward cloud. And we know Brandt's been at the mansion."

Maybe even on the second floor, when no one had known he'd gone upstairs.

"The question is why," Flint said.

"Right," Mandie said, frowning out at the city again. "And it can't have been Brandt who grabbed Alicia and put a bag over her head."

"No? Why not?"

"She said that person was taller than her, and Brandt's shorter because of the scooter. His gait isn't normal either, and she said the person *walked* behind her—using both legs." Mandie shook her head. "It couldn't have been him."

Flint remained silent for several long moments. "Let's assume it's the two of them, and they're still seeing each other."

"Which isn't against the rules anymore, now that Jo Ann's gone."

"Right." Flint nodded at her and checked his phone as it chimed. He ignored it and looked at her again. "They're both at the Hampton House, living out of the second-floor bedroom."

"Okay," Mandie said, catching on. "Again—why?"

"Why?" Flint echoed. "What are they looking for? What is their goal?"

"Maybe they're both bitter and upset and want to sabotage the project?" Mandie guessed.

"Maybe," Flint said, but he clearly didn't believe that. "Brandt's never struck me as a vengeful guy. And Jo Ann—she can barely swat a fly."

Silence from the empty second floor pressed down on them, and Mandie didn't know what to say into it. She finally sighed and said, "Okay, so...I guess I'll head out to the Hamptons and see if Suzie's found the camera."

"Mandie, be careful." Flint put his hand on her forearm, and Mandie froze. He didn't normally touch her, and again, his seriousness surprised her.

"Will there be footage on the camera?" she asked. "If we find it?"

"Maybe," he said. "The PastForward cameras upload to the cloud every evening."

"So she'd have to be erasing the footage before it uploads?"

"That," Flint said. "Or transferring it off the camera. Or she could've disabled the data chip, so it doesn't connect to the Internet."

"There's no Internet at the mansion. How could the camera even upload the snippets it did?"

"I don't know," Flint said. "Hotspot, maybe. Or it

found a connection somewhere, if they're traveling or taking it back and forth."

"I gotta say, I hate the fact that they're going back and forth. They shouldn't be there."

"That footage is old, right?" Flint asked, and Mandie nodded. "So it's possible they haven't been there since the cops came in and cleared the house."

Mandie nodded again, though she knew the house had hidden hallways, secret rooms, and underground areas. She hadn't told Flint or Candace that yet, because she didn't see the point. They couldn't add those areas to their renovation budget, and they weren't shown on the blueprints.

"Okay," she said. "Thank you, Flint." She stepped into him and hugged him lightly. "The ballroom segment looks amazing."

He gave her a smile that reminded her of the friend she had in the office pre-Hampton House.

"You gave me a lot of amazing stuff to work with at the mansion," he said.

"I'm gonna head out there," she said.

He sighed heavily. "I better get back upstairs."

Mandie wasn't sure why his voice sounded so gravitational, but she left him in front of the elevator as she pulled open the door to go down the stairs. She surely hailed a cab, and she told the driver where to go.

She existed a little outside herself until she found herself getting out of the car in front of the Hampton House. She showed her ID, the real world launching itself at her as she stepped through the gate and onto the grounds.

In the library, she found Alicia—and an extra cup of coffee. "Is that for me?"

"Yep." Alicia looked up, plenty of questions riding in her eyes. "How was the office?"

"I didn't go inside." She pulled out her chair and sank into it. A sigh moved through her body with the first sip of coffee. "Where's Suzie? Did she find that camera?"

"She went upstairs a bit ago," Alicia said, her gaze wandering over to the doorway behind Mandie. "But she yelled that she was leaving about fifteen minutes ago."

"Leaving?" Mandie slowly lowered her to-go cup of coffee, a new kind of electricity running through her veins. "Where did she go?"

"I don't know," Alicia said. "I assumed you'd called her somewhere."

"I did not." Mandie blinked at her best friend, her pulse continuing to accelerate, and accelerate, and accelerate.

"What are you thinking?" Alicia asked, her voice mostly air.

"What if—?" Mandie shook her head. "Never mind."

"No, you better say it."

She swallowed, the bitter taste of coffee not the only unpleasant thing in her mouth. "What if Suzie found the camera, took it down, and...left to get rid of it? Because she's the one who put it up?"

"Because she's the one behind all the delays and catastrophes around here," Alicia filled in, and she wasn't asking.

Mandie nodded, her eyes wide and dry all over again. She didn't want to say Suzie's name out loud with any sort of accusation at all, but it ran through her head quietly. Then louder and louder until it screamed.

But the same question emerged from Mandie's chaotic thoughts, and that was— *Why?*

Why would Suzie ever do anything to jeopardize her own project?

Chapter Twenty-Five

Suzie's heart pounded as she strode into the bistro Candace had named, her heels clicking decisively on the tiled floor. She hadn't planned on coming here today, but after finding that camera hidden in the Hampton House, she could barely keep herself in the mansion.

She found the blonde bombshell sitting in the corner, and of course she hadn't gotten anything to eat. She had two cups of coffee on the table in front of her, and she nodded to the one across from her, her blue eyes blazing fire in Suzie's direction.

She almost turned around and walked right back out. Suzie said nothing as she pulled out the chair at the tiny table, glared at the seat next to her—only a foot away and empty—and looked back to Candace.

"What am I doing here, Suzie?" Candace stirred her cappuccino with a silver spoon, something dangerous in her demeanor, her sitting stance, all of it.

Suzie took a deep breath. "There are things going on at the Hampton House you need to know about." Her vision blurred slightly, but she'd made the call and left the mansion. She'd come here.

She'd committed to this conversation, and it needed to happen.

She pulled out her phone and brought up the photos she'd taken. She set it closer to Candace, who held Suzie's gaze for a moment before dropping her eyes to the screen.

Without her boss's sharp, pointed, laser-gaze on her, Suzie could breathe easier. "First, we found a hidden room full of antiques and valuables that may or may not have belonged to the original owners."

Candace's eyebrows shot up as she scrolled through the images. "And you're just telling me this now? Why wasn't this in any of the reports?"

"We...we weren't sure what to do," Suzie admitted. "But that's not all. I found a hidden room behind the library, which was exciting for me, because I'm a distant relative of the Harringtons."

Candace glanced up, her chin still down, but her eyebrows high.

"I've let that part of it distract me a little bit," Suzie admitted. "But I'm still wholly committed to this project. But someone—maybe more than one person—is trying to stop us."

"I know that," Candace said. She surely hadn't been able to look through all of the photos, but she didn't return her attention to the device.

"I think it's Brandt," Suzie blurted out, a tsunami of guilt cascading down over her.

Candace didn't immediately speak into the silence hovering over them at the table.

Suzie didn't normally carry a purse, but she'd brought along her backpack. Now, she dipped down and unzipped it. "I just found a PastForward camera on the second floor at the mansion," she said, pulling it out and putting it on the table between them.

It felt like a bomb sitting there.

"Flint didn't do that," she said, her voice quieter, almost getting covered up by the din of other patrons chatting in the restaurant.

"Let me get this straight," Candace said before Suzie could finish, her voice dangerously low. "You've been concealing valuable assets, failing to report major security breaches, and now you're accusing a long-time employee of corporate espionage?"

"We reported all the security breaches," Suzie fired back. "That's why we've been operating under the watchful eye of police officers for weeks."

Candace pursed her lips and lifted her mug. Without taking a sip, she said, "I assume you have more to say."

Suzie should have more to say, yes. "We think it's Brandt," she said. "We found evidence of his scooter tracks upstairs. I'm not even sure how he *got* up there with a broken leg."

"Indeed," Candace said.

"He's stopped by the mansion. Seemed suspicious."

"This is your evidence?" Candace nodded to the tiny camera Suzie had found positioned on the banister outside the last bedroom in the West Wing. "A camera that could belong to anyone, and Brandt has stopped by the house of the project he was taken off of?"

Suzie swallowed, because it sounded like nothing.

"In fact, it sounds like Alicia's been hiding things from me, Mandie's lost control of her team because you're here, and you've been wasting company time on personal endeavors."

"No," Suzie said, but her ribcage collapsed in on her vital organs.

Candace glared at her, and this woman could make a unicorn cry. "I'm thinking I better pull you guys out of there and get a new team in."

Horror filled Suzie. "No, you can't do that. This project is important to all of us."

She leaned forward and reset her cup on the matching saucer. "I can do whatever I want, Suzette."

Suzie had made a terrible mistake in coming here. How had it felt like exactly the right thing to do only a half-hour ago?

"Your personal attachment is clearly a problem."

"But it's not," Suzie said, a pleading quality in her voice. "I've done everything necessary for this project. I've been way more contributory creatively than on any other project I've ever done. We're catching up, and we've finished three rooms now with almost no overages at all."

They'd been doing good work at the Hampton House.

Surely Candace knew that. Surely she'd *seen* it in Flint's footage.

Suzie opened her mouth to provide more evidence, but desperation clogged her throat. She hadn't taken a single sip of the coffee Candace had bought. "I'm not a videographer, but even I know that camera belongs to PastForward, and it's one of the new ones you bought last year." She took a deep breath. "It's been used on one project and one project only."

"And which project would that be?" Candace sat back and took a sip of her coffee, using both hands to hold onto the coffee cup only on the rim.

Suzie glared back at her this time, and she leaned in the way Candace had. "The Mountain Manor."

Candace blinked, because she knew every detail of every project, and they both knew who'd been the videographer at the Mountain Manor.

Jo Ann Lloyd.

And the bulldozer?

Brandt Paulson.

Suzie's blood ran hot and cold, and she knocked lightly on the table in front of her. "Take that camera. Check out what's on it." She stood and pushed her chair back in, meeting Candace's eyes again.

Everything in her life wavered. She hadn't been able to trust her decisions as much as she normally did, because she'd started a relationship with a man who was all wrong for her. She'd gone too far with him, and she'd ended things with him this past weekend.

Perhaps she wasn't in a good emotional state to be making such rash decisions—like calling the boss within ten seconds of pulling down a hidden PastForward camera from her renovation site.

"I have to get back to work," she said, and she didn't wait for Candace to fire her on the spot. She walked out, panic building behind every breath, every step, every moment of time.

What did you do? she asked herself as she burst out into the sunshine here in the Hamptons.

"And what will happen to Alicia and Mandie?"

If the team lost the Hampton House because of her... Suzie had no idea what she'd do. She knew she couldn't swallow as she tried to find a cab that would take her back to the Hampton House.

Then she turned and paced away, wondering if she should even go back. Her phone rang, and she nearly jumped out of her skin.

Mandie's name sat on the screen, and Suzie swept the call to voicemail. She couldn't face talking to her right now. And she didn't even have the hidden camera anymore.

She breathed as she put more distance between her and the bistro where she'd met Candace. Between her and the camera she'd left behind. Between her and simply everything.

With the added oxygen, Suzie could think better. She arrived at the corner, and to her right, a boardwalk went down to the sand. She followed it, almost desperate for the waves to wash through her, rip out all the things she'd done wrong, and clean everything up in her life that she'd made a mess of.

Only a few minutes later, she stood on the cusp of the sand, the waves in front of her rolling ashore. The water went on and on and on, seemingly without end, and Suzie tried to draw calming energy from something so large, so deep, that held so many secrets.

Finally settled, she realized she had to go back to the mansion.

She had to tell Alicia and Mandie what she'd done and why. "Hopefully they'll understand," she murmured.

She'd only gone about a mile from the Hampton House and the ride back took less than ten minutes once she'd found a cab.

The house loomed over her, imposing as ever. The second-story windows mimicked dark eyes watching her every move, and she once again thought about turning around and simply leaving.

Then, she took a deep breath and approached the second officer who had to check her ID before she could gain entrance to the house.

She could only pray her friends would forgive her if they all lost the Hampton House.

licia's heart pounded as she made her way past the still-empty pool to the paved entrance to the pool house. "I can't even believe I'm doing this," she grumbled to herself. She wasn't the one who came out here, moved aside a stacked washer and dryer, squeezed herself down a narrow set of steps, and picked out artifacts from a hidden treasure room.

Mandie and Suzie had been doing it.

But Suzie had run straight to Candace and told her everything. Well, that wasn't quite true. In fact, Alicia wasn't even sure what Candace knew.

She'd sent a text with a threat attached to it.

I just spoke with Suzie about everything going on at that mansion, and I want to meet you in the pool house in ten minutes. If you don't respond in the next sixty seconds, I'll assume you're resigning.

So Alicia has answered as fast as possible. So fast, all she'd sent was a single word: *Okay.*

She'd shown her phone to Mandie, who'd sworn and then called Suzie. Alicia had left her in the library, and with every step she took, worry wormed its way through her. "I need this job," she muttered to herself. Surely Candace wouldn't fire her over this.

They'd gotten several great pieces from the treasure room, after all, and that had saved on the budget and provided an irreplaceable historical artifact to the renovation.

A cool breeze rustled through the trees, but it wasn't enough to dull the August heat. She did love the grounds here, and the grounds crew only had a few more things to do. The pool needed to be filled and staged, and they'd been working to redo the raised beds surrounding the front of the house and those that lined the lane.

The unexpected summons from Candace had her pacing inside the pool house. They hadn't moved out here yet, as they still had to finish the kitchen, the outdoor patio, and the den on the first floor.

The demo crew had moved into the upstairs bathrooms, but the pool house remained untouched. They'd huddled up about it already, and Mandie wanted everything out here to be done in shades of blue and white. Alicia hadn't argued, because she'd seen some beach houses, and they did exist in waves of azure and fields of cornflower.

She'd arrived ahead of Candace, and surprise punched

through her when the taller, blonde woman came in only a few minutes later. Alicia faced her, her pulse pinging against the back of her tongue. "You must've been close by."

"Yes," Candace said, letting the door close behind her. "It's warm out here."

Alicia nodded, because it was. She leaned against the bar in the kitchen that ran along the far side of the pool house. They'd likely debate over the flooring here, if they should replace it, what they still had in the budget for such things, and if it was even necessary in a pool house.

"I just had a very interesting conversation with Suzette."

Alicia's stomach dropped to the heels of her boots. Suzie had left in a hurry earlier, calling to her that she was "going out," but not saying where. "I was going—"

Candace held up her hand, effectively silencing Alicia. "I can't believe you've been hiding valuable Harrington heirlooms."

"Hiding is not the right word," Alicia said.

"Why is Suzie spending time on…on—side quests instead of focusing on the renovation?" She glanced around, the look on her face as if the whole pool house smelled like a dead carcass. "And where the devil is Mandie?"

"She—I didn't know you wanted to see her."

"She'll get her turn," Candace said, and it so sounded like a threat. Alicia wanted to protect Mandie, but she wasn't sure how. Suzie had really not done them any favors but going to Candace without consulting them first.

"I don't see how I can promote you to assistant director if I can't trust you."

Anger flared in Alicia's chest, pushing against the guilt and fear. "And what about you, Candace? You want to talk about keeping secrets? How about your plans to renovate the Flatiron building?" The words left her mouth before she could stop them, and Alicia immediately wished she could take them back.

Candace's eyes widened in surprise, then narrowed dangerously. "Where did you hear about that?"

Alicia lifted her chin, refusing to back down now that she'd started. She certainly wasn't going to throw Flint—or Mandie—under the bus. "It doesn't matter. The point is, I —as the person living this reality every single day—made a judgment call to protect this project and the team. And for the record, we haven't been wasting time. Those 'side quests' as you call them have been integral to understanding the history of this house and doing justice to its restoration."

She couldn't believe she'd just stood up for Suzie and her family history obsession.

Candace studied Alicia with an unreadable expression. Finally, she said, "Show me the treasure room."

"Yes, ma'am." She moved toward the laundry facility at the back of the pool house, Candace flowing toward her like an angry storm gathering strength over the warm, open ocean. She said nothing as she moved the appliance blocking the doorway, and she only glanced at Candace before disappearing into the yawning darkness.

At the bottom of the stairs, Candace said, "This is incredible," and she didn't sound nearly as angry anymore. "This is why I love old houses."

"The creepy secret passageways?" Alicia asked, hardly in agreement with her boss.

"The history of them," she said from behind her. "Thinking about who built this. Why'd they build it? What were they hiding? And from whom?"

Alicia could appreciate that, sure. She still didn't like being underground. But dutifully, she led Candace down the wider slab-steps to the treasure room. Mandie had brought in a couple of electric lanterns she'd had in her camping supplies at home, and they sat waiting for Alicia right by the door.

She picked one up and turned it on, then handed it to Candace. She switched on the second one, and the room bloomed under the light. Alicia sighed out as she took in the space. "I don't come down here very often. Mandie picks the pieces, and Suzie's been going through the filing cabinets."

Stacks of old paper sat on the table across the room, near those filing cabinets, and Alicia let Candace go ahead of her.

"There are some art pieces," Alicia said needlessly. Candace had eyes; she could see.

"This is incredible," Candace breathed, her anger seemingly forgotten as she took in the wealth of historical artifacts. She moved from item to item, and Alicia wondered what she saw in the pieces. Despite the negativity swirling within her, Alicia couldn't help but feel a surge of pride. They had protected these treasures, ensured they would be preserved and honored.

After what felt like a long time, Candace turned back to Alicia. Her expression still broadcasted some sternness, but she'd softened too. "Come look at this."

Alicia hesitantly stepped toward the back of the room, where Candace bent over the stack of papers. Suzie had been working through those, and Alicia hadn't heard anything newsworthy about them.

Her emotions ran between relief and lingering anxiety, and she wasn't sure what she should say, if anything. She turned at the sound of footsteps, and Suzie filled the doorway abruptly, Mandie right behind her.

"Alicia," she said.

Mandie crowded into the doorway too. "Candace."

The two women looked at one another, and Alicia felt like she'd just ridden a roller coaster to the top of a tall hill, and the car was about to spill over the crest.

Suzie moved in her long, powerful, afraid-of-nothing strides. "I've been going through those."

"These would be amazing if some of the more important things got framed." Candace picked up one of the pages. "I mean, this one just looks like some sort of inventory sheet." She set it down. "But there's so much here."

"I've been putting the important documents in a folder." Suzie stepped over to a filling cabinet and opened the top drawer. "I've found a few birth certificates, death certificates, even a couple of land deeds." She lifted a folder out, and her throat worked as she swallowed.

Alicia's ire rose up until all she could see was Suzie's hair flaming red. "Why haven't you told any of us?" She snatched the folder from Suzie's triumphant hand. "And why did you call Candace without huddling up with us first?"

Suzie lifted her chin, but she didn't argue back.

"This isn't helping," Mandie said, stepping up to the group. "Suzie does not work through the documents during her work day. She comes before work, works through lunch, or stays late."

She moved her gaze between Suzie, Alicia, and Candace as she spoke. "We have made up great time with the rooms on the first floor, and though we had to do some extra plumbing work in the kitchen, we got right back on track."

Her hazel eyes fired, and she glared at Suzie. "You should've told me about the camera first. *We* should've made a decision about it together."

Suzie nodded in tight bursts. "I know," she said. "I found it, and I just got so—so—so mad. And I looked at the oldest shot footage on it, and you know what it was?"

"Of course I don't," Mandie said, planting one hand on her hip and gesturing with the other. "Because you ran out with it before I got here from the Flatiron building."

"What were you doing in the office today?" Candace asked.

That sucked the air right out of the room. Alicia threw a glance to Mandie, because she hadn't gotten that whole story yet either. In fact, she hadn't even known that Mandie had asked Suzie about a camera.

She suddenly didn't know who she could trust, and she hated that feeling with every cell in her body.

"I talked to Flint," Mandie said, her eyes shooting lightning at Candace. "He found footage of this house being uploaded to the PastForward cloud server, from a camera that he didn't install." She dropped her hand from her hip. "We know there have been unauthorized people in this house, supposedly *living* here for the first few weeks, and honestly, I think, as does Flint, that you have a problem with some of your employees at the firm."

She indicated Alicia and then Suzie. "And it's not us."

"It's Jo Ann and Brandt," Suzie said.

"We don't know that," Alicia said, mostly because she truly didn't want to believe that one of her colleagues could do this.

Candace set down the paper she'd been holding all this time. "I want this room catalogued and a list of the items here in my inbox by the end of the week."

"Yes, ma'am," Suzie said, and she'd obviously take on that job.

Their boss pinned Alicia with a look. "I want to get out of this room and talk. Take me to the library."

"Gladly," Alicia said, the word sliding out of her mouth in sort of a hiss. "I hate this room."

"It's not that bad," Mandie grumped at her.

Surprise cut through Alicia as she looked at her best friend. "I'm allowed not to like it."

"Let's huddle up in the library." Mandie spun on her heel and marched toward the doorway. Alicia went with her, because she really didn't like this underground room.

By the sound of the clicking heels, Candace followed Alicia, and it wasn't shocking that Suzie, the bulldozer, brought up the rear.

The lanterns went out behind Alicia about the time she reached the corner, and she fumbled with her phone to get the flashlight on. She navigated the narrow steps, and she finally took a full breath when she burst out of the pool house completely.

"These documents are *incredible*," Candace said from behind her, and Alicia fell to her side. "We'll definitely frame some, but the others that mean something need to be preserved too."

"Okay," Alicia said. "Suzie loves that kind of stuff." She shot a look to the other woman who'd just come up beside them.

"It was the Mountain Manor," Suzie said. "On the camera. You know who shot that?"

Mandie turned back to them, her eyes searching Suzie's face. Alicia knew, but she held back, wanting to see what Mandie did. How she handled this.

"Of course I do." Mandie swallowed and blinked rapidly a couple of times. "You still shouldn't have removed it from the premises and called Candace on your own."

"I know that."

"Do you?" Mandie huffed and started angry-walking toward the house again. "We've been working through things together for months, Suzie. The three of us. Not you on your own—which I have let you do plenty of, by the way." She tossed the words over her shoulder as she went past the pool.

To Alicia's surprise, Candace didn't try to cut in. Didn't try to be the boss in this situation.

"I'm close to finding the fortune," Suzie said. "I'm sure of it. I can just feel it."

"Suzie," Alicia said, almost under her breath. "Can you just leave it for a minute?"

Suzie fumed at her side, but after a couple of steps, she said, "Yes, all right."

Alicia nodded at her, cast a look to Candace, who wore the strangest look of...satisfaction on her face.

Sinister satisfaction? Alicia thought, a shiver running down her spine though the sunshine burned brightly overhead. Then they all entered the mansion, and Alicia had no idea what this huddle up would bring.

Chapter Twenty-Seven

Mandie didn't go to the big oak table in the library. Nope. She kept walking over to the bookcase, and she indicated it. "Open it, please."

"Mandie," Suzie said.

"Now." Mandie was done with the games. She folded her arms and gave Suzie a meaningful look.

Suzie did as asked, moving the chair she always used to press the button and release the bookcase.

"You've got to be kidding me," Candace said.

"I found this one early on," Suzie said, keeping her eyes straight ahead on the entrance of the hallway that led back into the secret room.

"We're doing our huddle up back here," Mandie said, and she stepped past Suzie and headed for the room with the two desks. "Bring your A-game, ladies. Our boss is here."

She didn't care if they wanted to stay out in the library;

she needed a tight, enclosed space to ensure no one overheard this conversation. For the house felt like it had eyes and ears everywhere, and now that she knew a hidden camera had been found in the mansion, she just wanted to leave.

Since she couldn't do that, this secret room with only one way in and one way out would have to do. She came to a complete halt, remembering how Suzie had gotten into this hallway and the secret room from the ballroom.

She turned around, finding Alicia practically on top of her. "What's going on?" Alicia asked.

"I just—" Mandie cut off, because she didn't want to display any weakness in front of Candace. "Nothing is going to bring down this project. We have already worked too hard for that to happen."

"Are we huddling up in the hallway?" Suzie asked in her barky tone.

"If I say we are, we are," Mandie shot back at her. She regretted the words the moment they left her mouth. She needed to pull herself together. Fast, before Candace saw something that would get her fired. She blew out her breath and wiped her bangs back.

"I just want somewhere private and enclosed for us to talk." She cut her eyes over to Candace. "Because I have a wild idea I don't want anyone to overhear."

"The only way into this room is through this hallway," Suzie said. "Either from the library or the ballroom, but only this hallway." She wore something bright in her big, round eyes.

Mandie nodded, starting to feel a little more grounded. "Okay," she said. "Then, yes, back here." She turned and continued on, her steps not really a march or a stride anymore. In fact, her legs felt like they might not hold up her body weight for much longer.

Thankfully, this room had two desks facing one another, and they each had a chair situated behind them. Mandie veered left and took the chair at the desk, not sure if anything had been moved, taken, or changed in this room. Suzie explored the house more than any of them, her spirit restless and her need for adventure insatiable. If she wasn't finding secret passageways, kicking down doors or through walls, or discovering the history in the mansion, she wasn't happy.

"Okay," she said as the other three women filed into the small, square room behind her. "Raise your hand if you think Brandt or Jo Ann is going to show up here at the mansion again."

Suzie gazed evenly back at her from the end of the desk where she'd perched, but Alicia and Candace exchanged a glance with one another. None of them moved to lift their arm.

"Right." Mandie looked down at the desktop in front of her and then over to the trio who'd lined up in front of the opposite desk. Mandie liked how she could speak harshly and the words didn't echo through the air.

"So, we need to brainstorm why they've set up secret cameras, why they lowered the chandelier in the ballroom, why they thought they could live in the upstairs bedroom, all of it."

Several seconds of silence shredded her nerves, but she hung on. She refused to be the first to offer an idea, and she cocked her eyebrows at Suzie and then Alicia.

"The cameras suggest they were watching for something," Alicia said slowly.

"It was focused on the foyer," Suzie added. "Where our deliveries get put."

"Right," Mandie said. "So why would they be interested in curtain rods, boxes of tile, or whether we're getting shipment from Goldman's or Target?"

She'd made it this far on her own, but she couldn't take the next step. The path in front of her, the reason why Brandt and Jo Ann were doing what they did, sat shrouded in pure blackness.

Again, no one said anything. Alicia studied the floor while Suzie turned toward the painting of Edmund Harrington. Candace looked from one woman to the other, and Mandie finally planted her palms against the cool wood and stood up.

"I think they're looking for something in the mansion," she said. "Something they think is valuable." Her mind whirred with possibilities, but she didn't know how to organize them all into coherent thoughts.

"The chandelier," she mused. "Brandt going with Suzie out to the pool house…" She met Alicia's gaze, a measure of hope filling her for the first time that day. "I don't know what it is, but I think if we want to find out, we have to…"

"Go on," Candace prompted.

"We have to draw Jo Ann and Brandt to the house."

"How are we going to do that?" Suzie asked. "They haven't been back in weeks, and I don't think they'll come back." She tossed a worried look down the row of women beside her.

"I agree," Mandie said as she sat back down. She felt completely in control of herself now, calm, and absolutely rational. "So, we need to create a reason for them to come back—when they think we're not here."

"Are you suggesting some sort of sting operation?" Candace asked.

Mandie fixed her with a steady look. "Yes, that's what I'm suggesting, and we have the personnel and power to do it."

So she was going to do it—with or without Candace's approval.

A WEEK LATER, MANDIE PACED THE LENGTH OF the library, her footsteps muffled by the old carpet they hadn't ripped out yet. She didn't even want to consider the depth and breadth of the library yet.

They'd been going through the books one by one. Well, mostly Suzie had been. But once they finished the kitchen, they'd simultaneously move to the library and the second floor. The plan was to only redo the flooring in here, with restoration instead of redoing for the bookcases, art, and fixtures.

In essence, the library would be the oldest room in the mansion, almost a museum for the Hampton House.

As the light faded, Mandie stilled. Alicia watched her from where she'd sat at the large oak table, but Suzie paced further in the library. The tension hung like a taut, tight clothesline in the room, and Mandie felt like she might get choked by it at any moment.

"Are we sure about this?" Alicia asked, her voice barely above a whisper. "It seems... risky."

"Crazy," Suzie barked out, her blue eyes blazing with determination. "But we need to know for sure."

"I'm kind of hoping they don't come," Mandie admitted, her hands winding around one another in a rare show of her nerves.

She faced the two women she'd done so much with. "Thank you guys for coming tonight," she said. "Detective Rhinehold is on speaker, and he'll move in the moment they show up." Mandie leaned over. "The *very moment* they show up."

She imagined the grumpy detective agreeing, though Mandie couldn't hear him. She'd muted the call, so nothing on his end of the line would come through accidentally. They didn't exactly have Candace's permission to do this "operation," either, but Flint had been in that day to film the cabinet transformation in the kitchen—and install some PastForward hidden cameras of his own.

Mandie had leaked news of an amazing find in the Hampton House. A gem from the early twentieth century, rumored to have come across the Atlantic on the Mauretania, an ocean liner which didn't hit an iceberg and sink, but that brought many wealthy people across the sea.

People, and their money, their family heirlooms, their gems.

Specifically, Mandie had invented a sapphire, deciding to stick with the suspicion that Brandt and Jo Ann had been trying to get a better look at the pink diamonds in the ballroom's chandelier when they'd lowered it intentionally nearly two months ago now.

Mandie nodded. "Then the team is ready." And not just hers. Flint had said he'd handle Candace, and he'd texted ten minutes ago to say they'd holed up together in her office in the Flatiron building, with the live feed from his cameras on in front of them.

"Let's get out of here," she said. "They won't come if they think we're here." She met Suzie's eyes. "Suze?"

"Going." She opened the bookcase and disappeared into the wall. This plan just had to work, and Mandie truly believed it would. If she'd learned anything from living in New York City and watching crime documentaries, it was that money and greed fueled more people than she'd care to admit.

The Hampton House took on an eerie quality as

Alicia stood, her eyes fixed on Mandie. They moved toward the door leading into the foyer, and as they arrived, Mandie pealed out a string of laughter. "I just can't believe it," she said in an overly loud voice. She almost cringed as the sound echoed back to her from the high ceilings.

"That sapphire is going to catapult us to the top," she said, leaning into Alicia like they'd had a little too much to drink. Celebrating their find, and all.

"Maybe Candace will let us sell it," Alicia said. "The way they did that art from the Moorfield Mansion." She laughed too. "It would really help the budget." She came to a complete stop, and while they'd rehearsed this, it sounded pretty real to Mandie. "Maybe we really could push out the kitchen and do those marble columns around the pool."

"With a gem that size?" Mandie grinned right up to where Jo Ann's camera had been repositioned. "We could do that ten times."

They laughed again, and Mandie turned out all the lights in the mansion the way she always did. "Suzie's putting it in the treasure room in the pool house right now," she said loudly. "Candace will be here tomorrow to take it for appraisal." She said the last sentence as she reached for the handle on the front door.

They walked out, and Mandie's smile and joviality immediately dropped. She and Alicia had to appear to be leaving the property, and since neither she nor Alicia knew what Jo Ann and Brandt could see, they were legit leaving.

They'd circle back to the house next door, then sneak back onto the property from the northeast, steal across the lawn, and join Suzie in the pool house.

This had to work. It absolutely had to.

Literally everything Mandie wanted in her life rested on it.

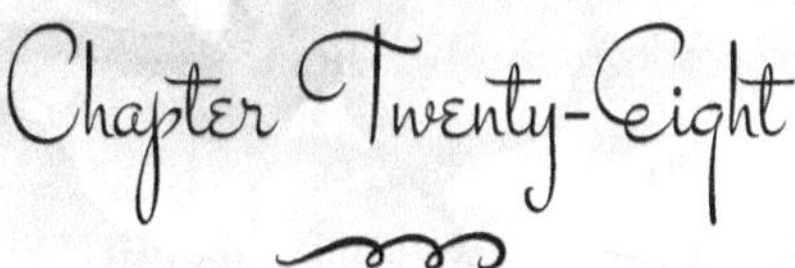

Chapter Twenty-Eight

Alicia stood in the women's locker room in the pool house of the Hampton House, her fingers nervously twisting the hem of her shirt as she watched the screen of Mandie's computer.

Mandie stood to her left, arms crossed tightly over her chest, while Suzie flanked her right side. Alicia's heart raced, a mix of anger and disbelief coursing through her veins.

She was an accountant, and nothing exciting, or strange, or off-script ever happened to accountants.

Everything about a sting operation put together by an anthropologist and a historian was strange, off-script, and yes, a little exciting.

"I can't believe what I'm seeing," Suzie whispered. "He has a key." She swung her attention to Alicia. "How does he have a key to *our* mansion?"

"I have no idea," ghosted between Alicia's lips as everything else inside of her quieted and came to a rest.

Brandt finished unlocking the front door of the Hampton House, and he scootered straight inside.

Shock coursed through Alicia. "How did he get past the officers?"

"They let him in, remember?" Mandie whispered.

"Yeah, this time," Alicia said. "What about the other times?"

"They haven't been back since we put up our twenty-four-hour surveillance." Suzie glared at her. "It isn't chatting time, ladies."

Alicia gave her attitude right back to her, because it wasn't like she'd been silent this whole time. They'd been hanging around this un-renovated pool house locker room for three hours now, and Alicia wanted nothing more than to go home to her tiny apartment.

They'd waited to do this until tonight, a Monday, so she could stay as long as necessary for this operation.

Jo Ann entered the mansion behind Brandt, her stride sure and strong. Even. Purposed.

"Strange they didn't just skirt around the mansion and come into the pool house," Mandie said.

"It has a different key," Suzie said.

"Maybe they don't have that one," Mandie mused, leaning forward as Brandt and Jo Ann crossed the lobby toward the steps, and then veered to the left and into the ballroom.

Alicia couldn't help wondering how Brandt and Jo

Ann had come to be working together. They disappeared, and Suzie quickly clicked over to the camera that had been put in the ballroom.

"They're going straight toward the hidden corner," she whispered. "That only goes into the library."

"Does it?" Alicia asked, and that simple question got her heartbeat pumping hard again.

Brandt and Jo Ann disappeared into the concealed corner compartment; it was freaky watching the wall seal back into itself, erasing all the evidence of their presence in the Hampton House.

"Look." Alicia pointed to the camera Suzie had minimized and put in the corner. "The cops are coming." They moved like silent soldiers, at least seven of them, their weapons drawn. Their knees never straightened as they prowled closer to the front door.

A small contingent of them moved along the side of the house toward the backyard, and Alicia wondered—not for the first time—what she was doing here.

She shouldn't be here at all. She should be at home, sitting up anxiously for news, or watching this from a remote location like Candace and Flint.

The cops eased into the mansion too, but nothing happened. No firestorm of shots being fired from the ballroom, and Mandie leaned over her phone. "They went in the ballroom, Jerry."

The detective couldn't answer, but Alicia saw the evidence that he'd heard her as he motioned his guys toward the left-hand side of the grand staircase. Most went that way, but not all, and Alicia could appreciate the way they fanned out, searching every nook and cranny of the house despite the report they'd gotten.

She jumped when Suzie gasped and then yelped. "They're here." She clicked away from the ballroom and right there in strange, eerie, unsettling grays and blacks and blown-out whites appeared Jo Ann and Brandt.

"They're in the pool house." Alicia swallowed.

"There's obviously a secret way in," Suzie whispered. "I didn't see where they came from." She swore but didn't rewind the feed.

Alicia lifted her phone and nodded as Mandie moved hers closer too. "I hope you heard that, Flint; Detective. They're in the pool house, and the last time we saw them was in the ballroom. We can't rewind from here, and we don't know where they came into the pool house."

The very air seemed to be holding its breath. Alicia certainly couldn't get enough oxygen, especially when Mandie's voice shook as she repeated, "They're in the pool house, Detective," and then added, "And we're out here alone."

Brandt and Jo Ann had paused in the middle of the room where families would share light, laughter-filled lunches and summer-sunshine-drenched dinners once the pool house was renovated.

He spoke to her, but they didn't have the sound up here in the locker room. Alicia's legs ached, but she didn't dare move lest any resulting sound alerted Brandt and Jo Ann to their presence.

To her horror, Jo Ann turned toward the women's locker room door, an awful, determined look on her face.

"They're coming this way," Mandie hissed. "Get out here."

"Hurry," Alicia added. They didn't actually have a sapphire down in the treasure room. She didn't think Brandt could move the stacked washer and dryer himself, but she'd also never pegged the quiet, kind, somewhat-geeky Jo Ann as someone who'd dress in all-black and break into a mansion.

She hadn't seen Brandt or Jo Ann carrying a weapon, but that didn't mean they didn't have one.

"There are no cameras in the locker rooms," Suzie said needlessly as Jo Ann reached for the door and pulled it toward her.

They'd set up in the only enclosed room in the locker room—an office of sorts. It held shelves with dusty towels and a table and nothing else. Well, now the three of them, their phones, and the laptop.

Suzie darted in front of the table and peered through the window. "Close the laptop," she whispered. "Now."

Alicia reached out and slapped the computer closed. Her eyes blinked as she tried to get them to adjust to the darkness faster, to get that blue light out of her retinas.

A thump out in the locker room had Alicia yelping right out loud and stumbling back against the shelves full of towels. She grabbed one, her thoughts racing through how she could protect herself with a *towel*.

She twisted it and twisted it as a figure—Jo Ann—

approached. *Where are they?* screamed through her head and made her hands tremble.

Where are they? Where are they? Where are the cops?

"Suzie," Mandie whimpered from where she'd pressed herself into the wall a few feet from Alicia.

Suzie had frozen closer to the window, and if Jo Ann took a few more steps, surely she'd see her out of her peripheral vision—if she didn't look through the window into the only room where someone could be hiding to catch her.

The ghastly light moved as Jo Ann carefully, slowly stepped forward. Alicia assumed she'd turned on the flashlight on her phone, but the light disappeared. Then, a moment later, it came back. Her mind misfired, not sure where Jo Ann's light came from.

Without thinking, she moved to Suzie's side, dancing on her tiptoes to do so. She passed Suzie the towel, who looked down at it before raising her head and turning it as if in slow motion to look at Alicia.

They'd been working together for a few months now, but Alicia didn't have to explain in a long conversation. She stepped over to the door and whipped it open, and Suzie the Bulldozer let loose a primal yell as she barreled out of the office, towel swinging.

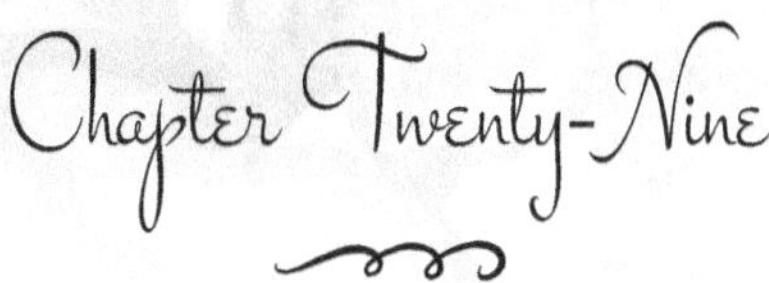

Chapter Twenty-Nine

Suzie had never had so many things crackling through her as she did while crashing into another woman. A former colleague. Someone she'd worked with on projects in the past.

Her breath felt like volcanic ash in her chest; her ribs sparked as she landed on top of Jo Ann, her hands automatically moving to pull off her face mask. "Hold still," she commanded, pinning Jo Ann beneath her weight and cinching her knees against the smaller woman's hips.

"It's over," Suzie said next as Jo Ann kept thrashing. Alicia scrambled out of the room behind her, and she carried another towel. She managed to grab Jo Ann's flailing hands and wrap the towel around her wrists, pinning them above her head while Mandie talked and talked and talked behind them.

Shouting and banging happened outside the locker room, and then everything shot inward, right at Suzie.

Cops came toward her, their flashlights far brighter than whatever Jo Ann had been using to light her way, and Suzie straightened and raised both hands. "Right here! She's right here."

Alicia got out of the way, and for one terrible moment, Jo Ann's hand came free. Suzie braced for the punch that never came, as the officers arrived on-scene.

Suzie's adrenaline blitzed through her body, but she allowed herself to be pulled off Jo Ann. They started reading the Miranda rights, and then she got led out of the locker room in handcuffs.

"That's it?" Mandie asked. "Oh, no way." She marched after the officers, calling over her shoulder, "Come on! We have to know why they're doing this."

"Mandie," Alicia called after her, but Suzie only hesitated for a moment. Then she launched herself after Mandie.

THEY ARRIVED AT THE POLICE STATION SEVERAL minutes after the police, and Suzie did what she was known for: she bulldozed her way past secretaries and gatekeepers until the three of them stood outside an interview room with a couple of detectives.

Two more sat in the room with Brandt, and Suzie's stomach recoiled at how much she'd trusted him. How much she'd enjoyed his company. Detective Rhinehold said, "So you went there to get the sapphire."

Brandt pinched the bridge of his nose like this line of questioning irritated him. "Yes. We just wanted one big-ticket item. No one would've gotten hurt."

Next to her, Mandie shifted her feet, but Suzie held very still as she asked, "One item?" She couldn't imagine being so desperate as to spy on her friends and sneak into a secure property after-hours. Did they need money? For what?

"The Hamptons are full of old money," Detective Jerry said. "Why this place?"

"Access," Brandt said. "And we saw their press releases. Some of those items weren't coming *into* the mansion, and we figured they'd been found within. The Harringtons owned shipping vessels."

"Of course," Suzie said.

"Ships and trains and all kinds of things," Detective Rhinehold said. "Big deal. Who cares?"

"Everyone should," Brandt said. "They were one of the richest families in the Hamptons, and they're rumored to have a collection worth millions."

"A collection of what?" the detective asked nonchalantly. Like he didn't care at all. Suzie had moved closer to the window, her breath fogging it up as she breathed out.

The Harrington fortune. She'd learned nothing more of it. Found no documents. Nothing but the treasure room, which held plenty of paper and historical items, but nothing worth millions. No collection of anything.

"No one knows," Brandt said, leaning back in his chair. "But Jo Ann is the great-great-granddaughter of old

Edmund Harrington's mistress, and the legends were passed down through family stories."

"Did you hear those stories too?" Mandie asked.

Suzie nodded. "At least a whisper of them." She realized with a jolt that she'd been doing the same thing as Jo Ann and Brandt—looking for the Harrington fortune. For very different reasons, but still.

"She feels entitled to it," Brandt said in a tired voice. "She'd just lost her job, and well…"

"You're in love with her," Detective Rhinehold filled in.

Brandt only nodded, his eyes hooked on the detective's.

"How'd you get a key?"

"Made a copy of the copy at PastForward."

"How were you planning to sell the sapphire?"

"Jo Ann has a buyer lined up."

"Who?"

Brandt's eyes turned dark and dangerous, glittering with all kinds of unspoken secrets. "I want full immunity," he said. "No charges at all. I work for PastForward. It's not trespassing at all. I needed to go there and check on the status of something for the team."

Suzie faced Mandie, seeing her own disbelief staring back at her. Jo Ann had a buyer lined up for some mystery artifact she'd convinced herself existed in the Hampton House.

"Unbelievable," she said.

Detective Rhinehold came out of the room, looked at them and said, "I'm going to get his immunity."

"Where's Jo Ann?" Alicia asked quickly.

Detective Rhinehold looked past them all, focusing on somewhere down the hall. "I don't know." He nodded in that direction, and Suzie and Mandie spun as a unit. Alicia caught them on the second step, and they found Jo Ann's interrogation room two down, where two cops looked like they'd just been standing to discuss last night's baseball game.

Three cops were in the room with her, and Suzie arrived just in time to hear her say, "I was going to sell it."

"To who?" one of the officers asked.

"Sebastian Blackwood," she said, and Suzie cried out. Mandie and Alicia both gasped, sucking the oxygen right out of the hallway.

"Who's Sebastian Blackwood?" one of the cops outside the room asked, while inside, the officers only looked confused.

"Sebastian Blackwood owns ReviveWorks," someone said, and Suzie once again got whipped toward the voice.

Candace stood there, still wearing her black pencil skirt and heels, and oh, boy, she did not look happy. "They're the number one rival to PastForward."

An odd sense of relief and betrayal filled Suzie. She wasn't sure why. Perhaps because they'd finally caught Jo Ann and Brandt and knew the reasons behind their sabotage. Maybe because Candace was here, and she didn't have to be the strong one anymore. Maybe because she finally had friends to stand beside, and fight for, and confide in.

She'd lost track of the conversation in the interrogation room, and she startled as the door opened. "No more questions," the man said who exited. "She's asked for a lawyer."

Suzie squeezed back into Mandie and Alicia as all the cops exited the room, and everyone walked away.

"Corporate espionage," Mandie whispered.

"Let's leave it to the cops, ladies," Candace said in her *do-not-argue-with-me* tone. "Come on. You've all had enough excitement for one night."

"Forever," Alicia said.

"Exactly." Candace started walking away from them, her heels clicking against the tile. "And I expect the project to stay on time and under budget, ladies."

Suzie stood there, gaping after her.

"Come on," Mandie said with plenty of authority. "I'm exhausted, and my husband is about to call the cops to bring me home." She linked her arm through Suzie's and looked at her. "You can stay with us tonight."

"I'm—"

"Staying with us tonight," Mandie said firmly. She swiveled her attention to Alicia. "You are too. Let's go."

Chapter Thirty

S uzie stood in the library, surrounded by the familiar scent of old books and polished wood. The room had become her sanctuary over the past few months, a place where she could lose herself in the history of the Hampton House and her own family's connection to it. Today, however, she hadn't come to pore over dusty documents or search for hidden clues.

No, today she would put everything back in order.

Her workload had doubled since their late-night sting a month ago. Candace had been brutal in her demands for an inventory of the treasure room, as well as the hidden room behind the bookcase here in the library, and updated blue prints for every secret room, hallway, passageway, and staircase.

Most of that work had fallen to Suzie as Alicia and Mandie labored in the kitchen—which was nearing completion. That meant Suzie needed to have the library ready for the demo crew to come in to do the flooring.

She'd been cleaning every book, volume by volume, polishing every shelf, and then covering them with protective plastic. She only had two shelves left to finish, and she expected to be done by the end of today.

Suzie wanted nothing more than to prove her worth to the team, to Candace, to PastForward. To herself. She'd made a mistake going to Candace behind Mandie's and Alicia's backs, but she'd apologized.

They'd accepted, and Suzie had been trying to put it all behind her. She had to shove the happenings that had gone on here at the Hampton House into the past from time to time, but today, she simply let her mind wander.

"One day at a time," she whispered to herself, picking up a stack of leather-bound volumes she'd already pulled out and needed to lovingly clean. She swept the dust from the covers, smiling softly at the gold lettering on the spine and the way the gold-leafed pages stuck together on the edges.

As she began to place them back on the shelves, her mind wandered to the fortune she'd been so sure was hidden somewhere in the house. Hearing Jo Ann speak of it only confirmed to Suzie that it existed. But despite all her searching, she'd found nothing but a few interesting historical tidbits and a lot of dust, useless documents, and dead ends.

Maybe she should let go of that particular dream.

She removed the dust-free gloves and took snapshots

of the title pages of each book, as she'd make a master catalog of all the titles. She'd numbered all of the shelves, but she wasn't alphabetizing or categorizing anything. Perhaps she'd have to later, but she simply didn't have time right now.

So with everything clean and caught in her phone, Suzie bent to put the books on a lower shelf she'd already cleared. Then the shelf in front of her would hold the books of the shelf above it.

She slid three volumes onto the shelf, but they wouldn't go all the way back. She frowned and leaned lower. "Strange," she said. She'd just pulled books from that shelf, and they hadn't had their spines hanging out over the edge. Perhaps these books were simply bigger, taller, wider.

Still frowning, Suzie set the books aside and bent to examine the shelf. It wasn't the lowest shelf, but only one below eye-level. She didn't have to stoop far, but she did fold her shoulders forward to look at the shelf.

It ran in a straight, smooth grain of golden wood, and Suzie detected nothing amiss under her fingertips. She glanced up, and yes, this shelf was definitely shallower than it should be, given the depth of the bookcase—and the shelf above it.

She rapped gently against it, the semi-hollow sound echoing in her heartbeat as it started to speed through her veins. Excitement bubbled up inside her, but she forced herself to stay calm. How many times had she thought she was onto something, only to be disappointed?

Too many.

Suzie ran her fingers along every edge and corner, slowly, meticulously, going over a section once, twice, three times when it felt a little...off.

She moved from side to side, starting at the bottom and moving toward the top corners. Her arm started to ache, and of course, it took a couple of minutes before she reached the top right corner.

Where the tiniest of bumps registered against her finger. She pressed in gently, her breath stalling in her lungs completely. For a moment, nothing happened. Then, with a soft click, the false back of the shelf popped open.

Suzie's eyes did the same, as if they could take in more the wider they bulged. She lowered herself further as she bumped open the long, plank-like door to reveal a hidden compartment.

Books, just like the ones she'd been removing from the shelves she could see, stood there like soldiers. A flicker of fear moved through her, and Suzie quickly reached for her gloves again.

With trembling hands to match her winged heartbeat, she carefully extracted the first book. The cover bore disembodied eyes and a mouth over a blue skyline with images of naked women reflected in the irises, and Suzie knew this book instantly: *The Great Gatsby* by F. Scott Fitzgerald. It seemed to have its original dust jacket, which only made it more valuable, and she carefully opened the cover...and very nearly screamed.

This wasn't just any copy, for the title page had been signed by the author himself, dated 1925.

Suzie panted, her breath unable to be more than a shallow suck in and a quick puff out. This couldn't be real. But she held it in her hands, the weight of it very, very tangible.

She barely wanted to let go of it, so she reached into the compartment and extracted the next book, already knowing she'd stumbled onto something incredibly valuable here.

The Harrington fortune, she thought, and she gazed at the dust jacket of this book. It had weathered very well in its hidden spot and showed a beige color with delightful gold images of a honey pot and Christopher Robin pulling Winnie the Pooh out of a tree.

"Winnie the Pooh," she breathed out. She hardly dared to hope it could be signed, but she opened the cover to find out anyway. A.A. Milne's signature sat there—Candace would want that authenticated, of course—and a yellowed paper slipped toward the bottom of the book too.

Suzie managed to catch it, and she read the verification letter from an auction house here in the Hamptons quickly.

"Mandie," she called over her shoulder. *Winnie the Pooh* had been published in the 1920s too, and this seemed to match up with the journal entries from the hidden office she'd found. "Alicia."

Of course they didn't come running. They had to be

in the kitchen with Carl today, going over every square inch of what needed to be done in what they called their "finishing walk-through."

Then, the three of them would stage the kitchen with era-specific pieces, as well as all the new items Mandie and Alicia had chosen. Suzie loved the turquoise, white, sandy, and clear dishes, plates, cups, and bowls they'd picked out, because they echoed the beach and the pool just beyond the kitchen windows. She couldn't wait to see it all come together, but right now, she needed her friends in here.

She set aside *Winnie the Pooh* and *The Great Gatsby*, and hurried to get her phone out of her back pocket. Mandie and Alicia would want to see this, and Suzie was done keeping secrets.

Come quick to the library! I found something amazing.

Then, as much as she wanted to dive right back into that compartment, Suzie actually backed up a step to wait for her friends. It didn't take long, because Mandie had to keep her phone close by for literally everything, and as her team lead came through the library door, her eyebrows high and her gaze seeking Suzie, she realized how much she loved Mandie Kelton.

"Come on," she said, gesturing them forward. "I think I found the Harrington fortune."

"You did?" Alicia asked, and she did a half-jog to keep up with Mandie.

Suzie picked up *The Great Gatsby* and *Winnie the Pooh*. "Signed, first editions, with the original dust jackets."

Both Mandie and Alicia came to a complete stop. No one spoke, but Suzie knew that would wear off quickly. She grinned and grinned, bouncing on the balls of her feet. "I found them in a hidden compartment."

She moved out of the way to show them the long plank poking out of the bookshelf. "I've only taken out these two."

"I'll get some gloves," Alicia said, and she bustled over to the oak table to do that. She returned and handed Mandie a pair of the soft white hand wear, already pulling one glove on. Suzie handed her the two books and turned back to the bookcase.

The next book she pulled out had dark red stripes on the top and bottom, with a white middle, a semi-abstract picture of a man and a woman done in black. "The Sun Also Rises." She turned and held it up for the others. "Ernest Hemingway's first major bestseller."

She gazed down at the book, marveling at just these three books. This amazing collection of American literature from a century ago. Upon opening the cover, she found the book signed, and joy burst through her.

"The Harrington's were obviously steeped in the literature scene," she said, handing the book off to Mandie, who'd finally gotten her gloves on.

"Ulysses." Suzie stared at the teal cover, hardly daring to believe it could be real. "This was first published in Paris." She heard her voice filled with awe and wonder and softness. "James Joyce."

Mrs. Dalloway by Virginia Woolf followed, as did a

couple more classics in children's literature—*The Tale of Peter Rabbit* by Beatrix Potter, and *Peter Pan in Kensington Gardens* by J.M. Barrie and illustrated by Arthur Rackham.

Every book existed in pristine condition, with dust jackets and signatures. Some had letters of authentication signed by auction houses and other witnesses.

The three of them seemed to know what an amazing find they had literally in their hands, and they spoke very little and only in low voices.

All told, Suzie found nine volumes, and she had Mandie and Alicia hold them as best they could as she snapped a picture to send to Candace.

"These need to go in dust-proofing bags," Mandie said. "And taken to the office for authentication. And we'll need to do the restoration and cleaning on these in a more controlled environment."

"I'll get the bags."

"I'm sending this to Candace. She's going to freak out." Suzie grinned as she completed that task, and then she swept her hand into the compartment one last time. She certainly didn't want to miss anything.

At the very back left of the compartment, where the door hinged open, her fingers bumped up against another volume. She pulled it out and found a leather-bound journal. The dark brown leather cover curled up and had faded along the edges. It had no title, but Suzie opened the book and found a name written there.

Elizabeth Harrington.

Her great-great-grandmother.

Neat, flowing handwriting filled the pages inside, and Suzie sank into the nearest chair to read, cradling the journal in her hands. With shaking fingers, she opened to the first entry and began to read.

My dearest descendants,

If you are reading this, then you have discovered the true fortune of the Harrington family. It is not gold or jewels that we have hidden away, but something far more precious—knowledge and history, preserved in the pages of some of our favorite books.

For generations, our family has sought out, collected, and protected these volumes, as we believe in the power of words and ideas.

Suzie read on, tears forming in her eyes as Elizabeth's words painted a picture of a family dedicated to preserving literary history. During times of war and social upheaval, the Harringtons had used their wealth and influence to purchase literary bestsellers and rescue rare books from destruction.

The journal went on to detail the provenance of each book in the collection, along with Elizabeth's hopes for their future. She wrote of her dream that one day, these books would be shared with the world, inspiring new generations of readers and thinkers.

As Suzie reached the final page, she felt a profound sense of connection to her ancestors. This was the legacy she'd been searching for all along—not a hidden pile of gold, but a priceless contribution to literary history.

"Suzie," Mandie said. "Candace is calling you, and she's irritated you haven't picked up."

Suzie closed the journal, her adrenaline climbing as she picked up her phone. Candace had indeed called three times, and she tapped to return her boss's call. "Sorry," she said in lieu of hello. "I found a journal from one of my ancestors with those books, and I was reading it."

"I—" Candace started and stopped just as quickly. "From one of your ancestors?"

"Yes, but it was part of those rare first editions."

"Was it...what you hoped for?"

A smile came to Suzie's face, because her boss had never really showed any emotion to her employees. She'd never really opened up about anything personal at all, so the fact she'd paused her lecture about Suzie's personal ancestors meant something.

"Yes," Suzie said. "It honestly feels like this is exactly what I've been looking for."

"Those books need to be behind glass," Candace said. "I'm thinking like a museum-type display, perhaps outside the library, with a beautiful, matching case."

"Sure," Suzie said. "We can house them in the library too, or perhaps it can be moveable, so whoever purchases the house can put them where they'd like."

"Maybe a special built-in," Candace mused, and Suzie realized she wasn't even listening to her. She didn't even care, because she'd found an amazing, amazing...fortune.

Chapter Thirty-One

Six Months Later:

Alicia herded the kids off the elevator and said, "Out the door, guys." Her heartbeat boomed like a kettle drum in a symphony—the holiday one she'd attended with Henry last week. They'd been dating for a very solid six months now, and Alicia expected to see him waiting for them outside on the sidewalk.

Gray pushed through the door of their building first, but Alicia stepped only a pace behind him. She could look over his head, but she didn't see Henry.

"Mama, I'm hungry," Lily said. "Can we get a hot dog on the way to the subway?"

"No, princess," Alicia said. "We're going to dinner at Mandie's tonight, remember? We'll eat there." She looked left and right as she exited the building, and she found Henry down the block about four strides in the direction they needed to go.

Her son had already turned to go that way, and Alicia drew in a breath of the chilled night air. The sun had already set, because it was winter in the Northern Hemisphere. Alicia tucked her gloved hands into her coat and met Henry's gaze.

He grinned in her direction, seemingly at-ease with the whole situation. He'd wanted to meet her children as her boyfriend for weeks now. Months, even.

On the trip to the beach, she'd introduced him as a "work friend," equal to say, Mandie or Suzie.

She'd wanted to make sure their relationship had real wings, good teeth, before she brought him into her children's lives as a boyfriend.

"Guys," Alicia said in the moment before Gray would walk right past Henry whom he hadn't seen in six months and clearly didn't recognize.

"Remember I told you about someone I'd started dating?" That conversation hadn't been terribly easy, but even her five- and eight-year-old seemed to know what dating was.

"Yes," Lily said, skipping past Henry.

Alicia stalled in front of him and reached for his hand. "This is him. Henry."

Lily and Gray both turned back to face them, and Alicia turned her smile on her children. "Henry, these are my kids. My son, Gray, and my daughter, Lily."

Her kids blinked and stared, and Alicia's chest narrowed. "Come say hello," she said. "Happy New Year. Something."

Gray stepped forward and stuck out his hand, the way Alicia had taught him to do. "Hello," he said. "Happy New Year."

Henry chuckled as he pumped Gray's hand. "Happy New Year to you too." He shifted his attention to Lily. "And to you too, princess."

Lily pressed into Gray's side and said nothing.

"We've got to catch the next train," Alicia said. "We don't want to be late to dinner, do we?"

"I'm starving," Lily said.

"Right." Alicia grinned at her and took her hand too. "So let's go."

Henry started talking about the ball dropping later that night, and Gray said, "Mom doesn't let us stay up that late."

"It's really late," Henry said. "I can barely stay up that late."

"Tomorrow's just another day," Alicia said, as she didn't really get the allure of New Year's. To her, it just meant another night where people had an excuse to party. Since she wasn't much into partying, she'd rather stay in, stay safe, and watch the festivities from her couch.

"Well, that's where you're wrong," Henry said. "Maybe in other years, but this year, you're starting a brand-new job tomorrow." He beamed his pride at her, and Alicia could admit everything inside her warmed at the thought of her new job.

Assistant Director of PastForward.

The Hampton House wasn't quite finished yet. They

currently ran nine weeks behind, and Mandie had sched-uled the unveiling of the mansion for three weeks from now.

Alicia could only pray they'd be ready.

They had to be, because she wasn't sure Candace would tolerate them going into a fourth month of delays. She also wasn't sure she, Mandie, and Suzie could have the mansion ready for an unveiling in only three more weeks.

She had new duties at PastForward to attend to, but Mandie and Suzie had insisted they could pull extra hours to make sure the house was staged, decorated, and camera-ready.

The date had been set. Mandie's parents were coming from Five Island Cove. Henry and the kids would be there. Candace, the construction crew and their significant others, Suzie and her mother.

"I think it got colder while we were on the train," Henry said as they came up from the subway.

"Maybe it's colder in Manhattan," Alicia said almost absently.

"Mama, it's snowing!" Lily ran ahead of them, her arms outstretched.

Alicia clued in then, and sure enough, fat white flakes had started to drift lazily down through the sky. Every-thing felt brighter with the addition of the snow, but the wind still sang through the tall buildings.

She hunkered down into her collar and coat and hurried the kids along. They arrived at Mandie's building, and thankfully, the heat blew with a fierceness that would ward off the winter cold. "Ninth floor," she told Gray, who pushed the button in the elevator.

Up they went, and Alicia gave Henry a tight smile as they followed the children off the car. "Nine-G, Gray."

"Like my name," Gray said, and he led them to the door.

"Knock, bud," Alicia said, and her boy did.

The door opened almost instantly, and Mandie stood there, a bright-as-Christmas smile on her face. "Well, hello there."

Lily cheered and ran at her, and Mandie laughed as she wrapped her up in a hug. "I gotted you a present," Lily said as she pulled back. She reached into her pocket and extracted the box Alicia had helped her wrap. And that meant Alicia had done it all, and Lily had put on the last piece of tape.

It was a small box, and Lily didn't have the best dexterity, and Alicia didn't truly mind.

Mandie crouched down in front of Lily while Gray said, "Hey, Mandie," and went by her. Alicia and Henry waited in the hallway just outside the door while Mandie pulled off the sparkly silver paper to reveal a small jewelry box.

She glanced up at Alicia, who only gave her an encouraging smile. Mandie lifted the lid and pulled out the necklace made of rainbow-colored yarn. It held a dyed-macaroni heart charm, and Mandie's whole face lit up. "Wooow," she said. "This is stunning."

She looped it around her neck and reached out to

boop Lily's nose. "I have gifts for you and Gray under our tree." She straightened and backed up a few steps. "Come in, guys."

"Is Suzie here yet?" Alicia asked.

Her answer came in the form of a loud round of laughter from the kitchen. That meant yes, Suzie had arrived. She claimed to be functional in the kitchen, but she didn't enjoy cooking, so sometimes didn't pay attention—and Alicia had seen first-hand evidence of that when she'd attempted to make pancakes the morning following what they'd all started calling "the hoax heist."

She'd just...stopped in the middle of it, her mind obviously somewhere else.

Mandie had brought her and Suzie back to her house after they'd set up Jo Ann and Brandt in the Hampton House, and Alicia had never been more grateful to not have to go home to an empty apartment.

In the kitchen, Charlie wore an apron, and Alicia found Suzie pouring drinks. She stepped over to her best friend's husband and gave him a quick hug. "Thanks for cooking for us tonight."

"I'm just putting on the finishing touches," he said with a grin. "Mandie's the one who got up early to put in the roast."

"I peeled the potatoes too," Mandie said as she arrived in the kitchen. "Don't go giving him the credit because he put on an apron to make gravy." She gave her husband the same wide smile she had for her guests and plucked the pastry brush from his hands. "And he's pulling out the rolls and buttering them, and you all think he's the one who's been slaving away."

"Hey, now," Charlie said good-naturedly. "I have been." He glanced over to Alicia, his blue eyes bright. "I'm studying for the NAPLEX, and that thing isn't easy."

"A pharmacy test?" Alicia guessed.

"He has to do three of them," Mandie said as she finished with the rolls. "I can't wait until we're done with the Hampton House. Then my life will just be supporting him through all these exams."

Alicia loved the way Mandie and Charlie loved one another. He'd been there for her every moment, every step of the way, since Mandie had been assigned the Hampton House. Even when he'd started his classes again at the end of the summer, he'd still given her all the attention and support she needed.

Now, she'd mirror that back to him while he prepped to become a full-fledged pharmacist. Dr. Charlie Kelton, and his beautiful wife.

"Mama," Gray said, and Alicia blinked away from her best friend.

"Yeah, mm?"

"I asked if we could open our presents."

"Of course, baby." Alicia smoothed down her son's hair and glanced over to Suzie. "Hey, you." She moved into the blonde powerhouse who'd become a very, very good friend and hugged her.

"I brought your kids a little something too," Suzie said as she squeezed Alicia back.

"You didn't have to do that."

"They're children," Suzie said. "Of course I did."

"Mama, there's two with my name on them!" Lily yelled, holding a gift in each one of her hands.

"They must both be yours then," Alicia said while Henry moved over to say hello to Suzie, then Mandie and Charlie. This wasn't the first time the five of them had spent time together, and Alicia sincerely hoped it wouldn't be the last.

These women meant so much more to her than simply co-workers. She'd told them personal things she hadn't shared with anyone besides her mother. Both Mandie and Suzie had gone to bat for her with Candace to help her get her new job, and Alicia loved them so much.

"Big day for you tomorrow," Suzie said as Lily ripped into the smaller present.

"We technically don't go back to work until the fifth," Alicia said, though a tremor of nerves ran through her. "And look who's talking. You finally got Mister Only-Wants-Phone-Dates to ask you out to dinner." She gave Suzie a knowing grin, almost not quite sure what to expect.

With Suzie, anything was still possible.

But tonight, Suzie grinned and grinned. "Finally, right?"

"Where are you going?"

"Since I might only get one date," Suzie said. "I suggested a couple of places I've been wanting to try. He picked Slender's."

"Ooh, we've wanted to try that too," Mandie said. "I want to know how it is."

Alicia knew they'd both get the complete run-down on Suzie's date once it happened, because Suzie didn't have others to talk to about this kind of stuff. About anything, really.

"It's a princess coloring book!" Lily yelled, drawing Alicia's attention again.

"Amazing," Henry said, and he swept into the room to pick up the discarded wrapping paper. He sat down on the couch, and Alicia went to join him. She let him hold her hand; she leaned into his bicep; they both watched Gray grapple with the blue-and-gray snowman paper on his gift.

"Yes!" He held up the box he'd just unearthed. "It's those superhero shoes!" He scrambled to his feet. "Look, Mom." He shoved the box in her face like she had to have it two inches from her eyes to see it.

She grinned even as she flinched. "Say thank you, baby," she told him.

Gray ran into the kitchen, saying, "Thank you, thank you, thank you for the shoes."

"They're from both of us," Mandie said. "Suzie and us put our money together for them, okay? That's why you only get one present."

"They're awesome." Gray wrapped his arms around Mandie and hugged her tightly, and Alicia's throat narrowed. Seven months ago, she'd never dreamed she'd have friends willing to buy her son a coveted pair of sneakers.

And now, she was living the dream.

Lily finished unwrapping her second gift, and she squealed so loud, Alicia squished her eyes shut. "Mama, Henry, look!"

She opened her eyes and found Lily showing Henry something pink and puffy and positively perfect for a princess dress.

"I can wear it," Lily sang as she turned to Alicia. "I go change right now."

She ran off down the hallway just as Charlie said, "Okay, we're ready."

"Lily," Alicia called after her, but her daughter was already gone. She sighed as she got to her feet, adding, "I'll get her."

"Leave her to change," Mandie said. "We can start without her for a minute." She indicated a seat at the table, and Alicia gratefully took it. Henry settled in beside her on her right, with Lily's empty seat on her left. Gray then took the next seat, and he wanted Charlie to sit beside him.

She'd seen the way Gray always gravitated toward men. Her father. Charlie. She glanced over to Henry, hoping he'd be the next male that would mean something good in Gray's life.

Mandie sat opposite of Alicia, and Suzie closed the circle. "Okay," Mandie said. "I know you guys hate it when I get all sentimental." She shot a dry look at Suzie. "Especially you, Suze, but it's a New Year, and I think we should say one thing we want to work toward this year."

No one said anything, and Alicia met Suzie's eyes. Of

course Alicia had thought about her New Year's resolutions, but she'd only written them out for herself. Some of them she had control over, and some she didn't.

"I want to finally become a pharmacist," Charlie said as he reached for the creamed peas.

"That's too easy," Suzie complained.

"Then you say something," he fired back, and Alicia ducked her head and smiled.

"I will," Suzie said. She shook her hair over her shoulders and lifted her chin. "I am going to go out with a new man every week until I find one I can stand for longer than that."

Alicia's breath caught in her throat—thankfully, because it stifled the laughter threatening to burst out.

Mandie did fill the apartment with her laughter, and Henry joined in.

"That's great, Suzie," Charlie said with an overly large grin on his face. "Hon? What about you?"

"I'm going to visit the Cove every month and make sure I'm still myself." Mandie gave everyone a smile, but Alicia saw how it trembled in the corners. Charlie put his arm around her, squeezed, and kissed her temple.

"I want to go to the Cove with you," Alicia said as she took the basket of buttery, hot rolls. She put one on her plate and handed them on to Gray.

"I'm in on that," Suzie said. "You both talk about it like it's amazing."

"It is amazing," Charlie said.

Food continued to go around the table, and after

Henry had taken some of everything, he said, "I'm going to apply for a curator's job at the Liverpool Auction House."

Alicia pulled in another breath, her gaze swinging to him. "You are? When?"

"Rumors are that they'll be opening up applications in February," he said, obvious pride in his expression. He also wore nerves there, and Alicia reached across Gray and squeezed his thigh.

"You'll get it, of course."

"Yeah," Mandie said. "No one knows more history than you."

"Mama," Lily chirped as she came skipping into the room in her pretty pink princess dress. "Look at me."

Alicia got up to help her pull the skirt down all the way, and she kissed her daughter on the cheek. "You are so pretty. Come on and eat. I've got your favorites."

She helped her daughter into her seat, where Alicia had loaded her plate with mashed potatoes and gravy, a soft roll, and only a pinch of meat. Sometimes she argued with her kids about what they ate, and sometimes she just let them carb up in the hopes she could get some veggies and protein in them at some point.

"Lish, that just leaves you," Mandie said, a bite of mashed potatoes, gravy, and beef roast on her fork. She slid the food into her mouth as her eyes met Alicia's.

"I don't know." She told herself not to look at Henry. "I have some goals, but some of them are outside of my control."

"That's okay," Suzie said.

Alicia supposed it was. "I want this year to be…joyful." She looked around the table, with her handsome boyfriend, her two kids, and her best friends in the world. "Yeah, that's what I'm going to work toward. Joy. At work, at home, with my family."

She did dare to meet Henry's eyes then, and oh, she saw plenty in his expression now. Softness, sure, but also a male edge that told her so much of how he felt about her. He'd stayed the night several times while the kids were in Jersey with their father, and Alicia tore her eyes away from her boyfriend.

Suzie lifted her glass of champagne. "To joy."

"To joy," Mandie and Charlie said together, both of them reaching for their wine glasses. Alicia was the last to lift hers, and she first clinked against Mandie, as she sat directly across from her.

Then Henry, and they all said, together, "To joy."

Chapter Thirty-Two

Mandie felt like she might be sick at any moment. Not from the movement of the cab—Suzie wasn't driving, thankfully—but because she sat next to Charlie, who sat next to her mother in the back seat. Her dad sat up front, and they'd arrive at the Hampton House in only a few more minutes.

Her phone chimed, and she expected it to be Alicia or Suzie. She couldn't stop herself from looking at it, and she had the very real thought to give her phone to Charlie when she finished reading this text. Only then would she be free from it.

We're here! Alicia had sent. She'd included a picture of her, Henry, and the kids, the Hampton House looming in the winter sunshine behind them. The tree branches, bare and eerie, clawed up into the sky, which today, was a cold, chilly, cornflower blue after this week's storm had blown through the state and out into the ocean.

Final budget number, Alicia said next. *We have $74.54 left, and I got Candace's approval to use it on dinner following this unveiling.*

In the Hamptons? Suzie asked. *That'll pay for one of us, so I'm calling dibs on the budget excess.*

You can't call dibs, Alicia said. *I have the company card.*

Mandie smiled at the banter between her friends, but she didn't have anything to add. So she handed her phone to Charlie without an explanation. He knew what to do with it—simply silence it and keep it from her for a while.

He tucked it away and then took her hand in his. "This place is amazing, babe. Don't be nervous."

Mandie hadn't realized she was nervous until then. "It feels like this is my whole life," she said. It had been for so long—eight months of living, breathing, worrying over, talking about, and working on the Hampton House.

Which light fixture to choose? Were those drapes too heavy? That piece not historical enough? The wrong era?

"Yeah, it feels like that," he said. "But it's not true." He lifted her hand to his lips, and whispered, "Will you look at me?"

Mandie swung her attention from the landscape going by outside to her husband. "Sorry," she murmured.

"You are so much more than your job," he said.

"Charlie's right, sweetheart," her dad said from the front seat. He twisted and looked at her, and Mandie nearly lost her grip on her composure. Dad smiled and smiled. "We're so proud of you, even if we show up and the house is trashed."

"Dad, don't say that." Mandie reached up and wiped her eyes.

"It's not going to be trashed," her mom said. She covered Mandie and Charlie's joined hands and squeezed. "It's going to be amazing."

The cab made the left turn, and Mandie's heartbeat bobbed up into the back of her throat. She turned away from everyone in the car and took in the magnificent gates of the Hampton House. Today, they'd been thrown open, and the cab went right up to the main sidewalk.

Dad paid while Mandie climbed out of the car, Charlie right behind her. He wore a black suit, complete with a pink and gray paisley tie and his hair combed just-so. Mandie had bought a new dress for this event, as she had to do an interview, and as the team lead, she'd be in the spotlight for the next couple of hours.

She'd never minded the attention and eyes on her, but this felt so different. She'd never been in charge of something so big, and she paused and looked at the sixteen-thousand-square-foot mansion she'd personally taken from abandoned and forgotten about to vibrant, alive, and beautiful again.

Charlie took her hand again and led her toward the front door. Mandie moved with him in her heels, her dark blue dress swirling around her calves as she walked as his side. He paused at the door, her parents crowding in behind them.

"Ready, babe?"

"One more breath," she said, and they looked at one

another. Then, they breathed in together, Charlie grinned, and he opened the door.

Mandie released her breath in a slow, measured, controlled way as she entered the house. Her parents had taken the trip to the Hamptons from Five Island Cove just to be here with her.

She'd taken one step inside the house when the applause started, and Mandie froze. Everyone from Past-Forward had gathered onto the staircase leading to the second floor, and she saw smiles and laughter for miles.

Charlie stepped away from her and indicated her like she was the main event, and then he started clapping too. Her parents squeezed into the house too, both of them grinning and applauding too.

Mandie couldn't hold back her tears then, and she let them trickle down her cheeks despite the attention she'd given to her makeup only a couple of hours ago.

She'd been the one in the crowd when big projects like this finished, but for some reason, she hadn't anticipated this. Candace had given her no indication that the entire office would be here today, but at least forty people stood on those steps, and then Suzie stepped off the bottom one and came toward her.

She wore a cute flowered sundress—with her steel-toed boots—and a smile. Alicia had dressed more like Mandie, her dress a gorgeous swirl of stripes in pink, blue, green, and purple that fit her like a glove.

"Let's huddle up." Mandie opened her arms, and her two teammate hugged her, all three of them laughing.

"All right," Candace called, and that got everyone to start to settle down. She waited several more moments while people came down off the steps and gathered in front of her, as she stood just outside the library.

Candace wore a beaming, bright smile, and she held a cordless mic in her hand. She lifted it to her mouth again, and the crowd of co-workers quieted further. "We love every project we take on at PastForward, but the Hampton House has a special place in our company history now."

She indicated the display case she stood next to. "We found nine first edition novels in the shelves of this house. With original dust jackets and family letters about the books. It's something so rare, and so exquisite, and we have the careful dedication of Suzette Paxman to thank for that."

She lowered the mic, indicated Suzie should go forward, and started to clap. Everyone else did the same, and Suzie strode with her usual confidence toward Candace. To Mandie's surprise, they embraced, and Candace handed Suzie an envelope.

"We've gotten her a massage, because she's worked tirelessly over the past several months to tear down the old and weathered, the moldy and abandoned, and then rebuilt it all back up."

More applause, and Mandie teared up again while Suzie's face turned pink.

"This is the first project in five years that has come in under budget," Candace said, her eyes fixed on Alicia now. "And with something this vast, with all the twists and turns and setbacks here, that's a testament to an amazing accountant on the team. Ladies and gentlemen, your Assistant Director, Alicia."

The roof got raised, as Charlie whistled through his teeth, and Henry whooped like they were at a football game and not standing in a ritzy mansion in the Hamptons. Alicia grinned and grinned as she moved into Candace. They hugged too, and Mandie's throat turned dry.

She'd gotten along with Candace quite well while working on this project, but now that it was over...Mandie wasn't sure what she'd get from her boss. She'd like to believe she'd proven her worth to Candace. She'd seen this project through to the end, even with two co-workers trying to steal from the house for a competing company.

And under budget?

No one did that.

True, she was three months overdue, but honestly, the timeline for this mega-mansion had been ridiculous to start with. And it didn't matter, other than she, Suzie, and Alicia couldn't work on other projects.

Two more had been assigned a couple of weeks ago, which meant Mandie wouldn't get something outside the office for at least another six months; maybe longer.

She didn't mind. She did need a reset, something to get her mind and heart out of the Hamptons and back to who she truly was. Though she'd fought it, Charlie's mother had been right when she'd said the Hamptons could consume a person.

Mandie had felt herself getting nipped at, bitten here and there, while she'd been working on this project. Relief rushed through her that this project was finished, for so many reasons.

"Alicia has poured her heart and soul into this house," Candace said, and Mandie brushed at her eyes again as her vision had gone blurry. She didn't want to miss a moment of her friends' glory.

"And she's gotten more than just an immaculate ledger with her numbers." Candace's grin turned a little predatory, but it quickly morphed back to something friendlier. "She's been seeing a historian here in the Hamptons, who's been an advocate for this house for as long as I've known him. So we put together a date night for you and Henry."

She handed Alicia an envelope too, and Mandie saw she held one more. It had to be for her, and she had no idea what Candace would've put together for her. She wasn't sure she believed Candace was behind the gifts at all, as a date night felt more like something Flint would suggest.

"And your team lead here at the Hampton House," Candace said as a few people continued to chitchat. They stopped, and all eyes were either on Candace or Mandie. She ignored them all, her gaze fixed on her boss.

"Someone who saw things others couldn't, even in the most stressful, tense situations—that's what a team lead does. They come up with unique and interesting ways to accomplish the goals for the project. They call audibles when things don't seem right, and they manage an enormous construction crew, as well as their own co-workers."

All true, but Mandie wasn't sure where Candace was going with this.

"When I gave this project to Mandie Kelton, I expected her to fail. I just knew she'd be in my office within two weeks, crying and begging for someone to take over for her." Candace finally looked at Mandie, and her smile rivaled the wattage put off by the sixty-four light bulbs in the chandelier hanging above them.

"But she didn't come in. With every mishap that happened, Mandie had a solution. Despite her age, she's been one of PastForward's most innovative and successful team leads." She held up her hand to wave Mandie forward. "To many more projects together; everyone give it up for Mandie Kelton!"

The crowd went wild again, and Mandie ducked her head, embarrassment running through her. She looked at Charlie, who cocked an eyebrow at her. They'd talk about Candace's speech later, but for right now, it had sounded pretty perfect.

So Mandie stepped forward while her friends and colleagues and loved ones cheered for her. She moved into Candace's embrace and said, "Thank you, Candace," as diplomatically as she could.

She wouldn't call the woman a friend, but at least she wasn't an enemy anymore. She fell to Candace's side and smiled out at all her friends. Flint wore the biggest grin, and she sincerely hoped Candace had something for him.

He put in so many hours behind the camera, getting just the right shots, then editing it all together to make a beautiful, flawless, end-product.

"Now, because of Mandie's tireless efforts to keep everything in line here in the Hamptons, we know she hasn't gotten a good night's sleep in eight months. She hasn't thought of anything but flooring or lighting or what dishes to display in the open cupboards in the kitchen."

The crowd twittered, but Candace wasn't wrong.

"So we put together our heads and our money, and we got a couple of airplane tickets for Mandie and her husband Charlie, so they can take a much-needed vacation." She brandished the envelope toward Mandie, who's mouth fell open as she took it. "Anywhere in the world," Candace added with a bright grin. "Just make sure you submit your request for time off at least two weeks in advance."

Several people laughed, and the applause started up again. But Mandie could only stare at the envelope, and then Candace. Then she hurried back to Charlie in her heels and let him wrap her up in a hug and swing her around.

"Anywhere in the world," she breathed as he set her back on her feet. "We can go after your graduation, after you pass all of your exams, this summer." She looked up at him, such hope streaming through her whole body.

"They probably have an expiration date," he said.

"This summer," she said, giving him her full confidence that he'd pass off of his exams and become a pharmacist by summertime.

"And lastly," Candace said. "A house is just a house. The renovation is only seen by those who are rich enough to come through the real estate open house. But at Past-Forward, we create legacies through film, and we have the best videographers with extraordinary vision for taking the very best pieces of something so huge and so intricate. So come on up, Flint."

He jogged forward, his camera up and supposedly recording. He turned and scanned it along everyone, and Mandie cheered harder when he faced her.

"Flint's worked back-to-back projects, with endless hours of film to go through for this project, most of it outside the scope of actually putting together footages of the before-and-after shots of the mansion."

Flint lowered his camera, and the crowd noise calmed enough for Candace to continue without yelling into the mic. "So we're giving him two extra weeks of paid time off and a cruise to the Caribbean, so he can escape this New York winter and work on his tan."

He snatched the envelope from her and lifted Candace right up off her feet. She yelped and the mic reverberated as she smashed it into his shoulder. He set her down, yelled into the crowd, and jogged back to his spot in the crowd.

Candace's face flushed a dark red as she smoothed down her hair and tugged her blouse back into position. She lifted the mic and spoke, but no one could hear her. She looked at the mic, then lowered it.

"The house is open for the next couple of hours," Candace yelled, but again, no one seemed to be paying attention to her anymore.

Mandie strode forward and lifted both of her hands above her head. "Everyone, the house is open for the next couple of hours," she yelled, and her voice caught their attention when Candace's wouldn't. "Explore it at your leisure, and be sure to stop by the den, where Flint has part of his film playing on the big screen there."

"Be sure to stop by the pool house for drinks!" Suzie yelled, and that definitely got a better reception than Mandie's announcement.

She didn't care, and she simply grinned her way back to her parents and husband and said, "Come on. Let's start in my favorite room...the library."

Read on for the first 2 chapters of **THE YACHT CLUB**, the next book in The Hamptons trilogy, which features Mandie, Alicia, Susie, and Candace as they embark on their next journey at PastForward!

Learn more about it and preorder by scanning the QR code below:

Sneak Peek! The Yacht Club
Chapter One:

Mandie Kelton swung her husband's hand, not wanting to let him go. But he had to get going to take his final exam to become a pharmacist, and she needed to get to work.

The view from Madison Square Park showed her the iconic—and crumbling—Flatiron building, and she exhaled out into the summer morning. "I can't wait to go to Aruba."

"Thirteen more days," Charlie said, his smile flashing on his face for only a moment. There, then gone. His nerves wouldn't allow it to stay for any longer than that.

"Hey." Mandie stopped near the bubbling fountain and turned her back on the building where she worked. "The Hampton House is going to sell, and you're going to pass the state exam. You've already aced the NAPLEX and the MPJE. What is the State of New York going to throw at you that those national tests haven't?"

He wouldn't look at her, but Mandie held very still and cocked her eyebrows. When he did look, he'd get her dubious expression in full force.

"Charles," she finally said, and that got him to cut her a look out of the side of his eye. She grinned at him, and he enveloped her in a hug instead of holding her gaze.

"Thank you for believing in me," he said.

"I'm not the only one, you know."

"I know." He pulled back. "You're going to be late, and I'm pretty sure you used the last of your Hampton-House-credits by putting in our vacation when your office is moving." Charlie grinned at her, and he was so good, so hard-working, and so handsome.

They'd been working so hard for so long to be where they were. Mandie loved living in the city, but the constant noise, hustle, and cut-throat attitude of most people here had started to wear her down.

She was just a simple woman from a small-island town, after all. Part of her longed to go back to Five Island Cove and find a way to pay their bills there. Her daddy had done it. Plenty of people did.

They had pharmacies in the Cove, and Charlie was literally one test away from everything he'd been working for over the past eight years.

"I love you," she murmured. "Thank you for putting up with my intensity. For—"

"Mm, I love your intensity." He leaned down and kissed her, and Mandie lost herself to his sizzling touch for a few moments. Then, he pulled back and tucked her against his heartbeat—right where she always wanted to be.

"Go on," he said. "I need to go find a dozen doughnuts to stress-eat my way through, and you've got a meeting with your boss."

With a groan, Mandie stepped out of her husband's arms and faced the Flatiron building. She stepped away from him and inhaled deeply, savoring the familiar scent of New York City in summer—a blend of hot asphalt, food cart pretzels, and the faintest whiff of the East River.

She adjusted her tote bag, the leather cutting into her shoulder. She couldn't wait to pack it full of sunscreen, strappy sandals, and a swimming suit cover up and take it to the beach in Aruba.

She needed a vacation from the city that never slept. From the pressures at work. From working behind walls, in a cubicle that felt too small for her most days.

Construction workers exited the building as Mandie started to go in, and she gave the first floor cellphone company sign a cursory glance as she headed for the elevators. Hardly anyone remained in the Flatiron building, though it had once been a coveted, expensive, and beautiful place to work.

But the building needed major renovations to even be safe, and no one had purchased the two-hundred million dollar building, only to have to sink many more millions into preserving it, getting it up to code, and making it beautiful again.

Her phone went off, and Mandie pulled it out while

she waited for the elevator. It had slowed over the years, but she wasn't going to take the stairs, she knew that. She pulled her phone out and saw Alicia's name get sucked back up into the top of the phone.

She hadn't been able to see any of the message, but she tapped to put in her passcode, and then she opened the texting app. Candace had texted a couple of times, but Mandie ignored those and went to her best friend's texts.

To be honest, she kept expecting Alicia to announce her engagement any day now. Or maybe a confession that she'd finally told her boyfriend of the past year that she loved him. But Mandie wasn't sure Alicia had even admitted that out loud to herself yet.

She could see it every time she saw Henry and Alicia together. Every single time.

The boss is in rare form this morning. The bear literally just poked her head out of her office, bellowed your name, and then retreated.

She'd included a laughing emoji.

Now the door is just hanging open, but no one dares to go close it or tell her you're not here.

So get here quick!

Mandie's heartbeat whipped through her veins, and her thumbs flew across the screen. *Waiting for the elevator now. Our meeting isn't for another fifteen minutes.*

Still, Alicia sent back, and Mandie looked up as the elevator dinged and the car arrived. Construction workers piled off of it, and Mandie couldn't wait to get on and see what scent remained behind from all of them.

She put a polite smile on her face, and when she could, she got on the elevator. Yep, the smell of too many varieties of cologne mingled with maybe...tar filled her nose. Now she got to ride with that up to the PastForward office.

When the doors started to slide open, Mandie turned sideways to get out, and she took the biggest breath she could, trying to clear her nose now that she'd arrived in the lobby outside PastForward.

The glass doors glittered at her in their usual fashion, and Mandie moved toward them the way she had many times in the past. Inside the office, she found a few people who'd gotten there ahead of her. All eyes came to her, as if they'd been waiting for her arrival.

Alicia rose from her desk, her head sticking up above the divider that separated her cubicle from the one next to it. Mandie glanced toward Candace's office, noting the slightly ajar door, as she went down the row of cubicles.

The conference room sat on her left, and she nodded politely to the few people in the cubicles before she reached Alicia.

"Things are tense here," she murmured.

"Yeah, no kidding."

Mandie unshouldered her tote and set it on her friend's desk. "No news on where we're relocating?"

If anyone would know, it would be Alicia. She'd been acting as the Assistant Director of Operations here at Past-Forward for the past five months. Brilliantly too, as she had a real eye for detail and could organize anything.

She put every piece of herself together and showed up

to work on time—early, even—despite being a single mom to two kids under the age of nine. Mandie could barely get herself here on time, and she didn't even eat breakfast.

She liked sleeping in, that was for sure, and Mandie sometimes wondered if Alicia slept at all.

"No news," Alicia said.

"Anything on the Hampton House?" Mandie tried not to be a jerk and ask about it everyday. If it sold, she stood to earn a very healthy six-figure bonus. Three percent of the sale price, to be exact.

Half the realtor fee, with PastForward pocketing the rest.

It was close to a half-million dollars, and Mandie could practically taste the powdery, inky, dirty taste of money in her mouth almost all the time now.

With that money, she and Charlie could buy a really nice place in a city-suburb, where they could raise their family. She was only twenty-six-years-old, but she and Charlie had been married for six years now, and she could admit—only to herself—that she'd started dreaming of becoming a mother.

Candace Ewing, her boss, seemed to frown on such things, and Mandie wasn't sure why. Candace could run hot or cold, and the worst thing about her was her unpredictability. No one ever knew which version of Candace they might get, Mandie included.

Her phone buzzed, her calendar reminding her she had a meeting in ten minutes.

Taking a deep breath, Mandie straightened her shoulders and left her bag on Alicia's desk. "Let's go." She looked down the row toward Suzie's cubicle, but she didn't see the blonde.

"Where's Suze?"

"She got sent up to Rhode Island for the week." Alicia blinked, something clearly confusing her. "I'm not going into the meeting."

It was Mandie's turn to be confused. "What do you mean?" She searched her friend's face. "We were all supposed to meet with her this morning. The team from the Hampton House. I—I assumed it was about a potential buyer or a sale or…"

Alicia shook her head. "I didn't get notice of a meeting."

"Well—" She exhaled heavily. "That makes no sense, Lish. Candace told me she was meeting with all of us this morning."

"Is Mandie here yet?" Candace yelled, and Mandie whipped her attention to her boss's office.

Their eyes met, and Candace motioned her forward with a violent flap of her hand. She disappeared into the office again, and someone somewhere coughed. Then it sounded like they were trying to stifle a laugh.

Mandie smoothed her hands down her blouse and started toward Candace's office. "Oooh, someone is in troub-ble," Hailey said, and Mandie flicked her a wicked look. Hailey only kept on smiling, and Mandie ignored everyone else as she approached the office.

Candace's door had blinds covering the window, and

they knocked against the wood as Mandie pushed it open with two fingers. "Good morning," she said as cordially as she could as she entered.

"Close the door."

"We're not waiting for the others?"

Candace glared up at her for a moment. "No. This is a private meeting."

Mandie swallowed and moved to close the door behind her. "Okay," she said. Her mind went into overdrive as she tried to figure out why Candace would want to see her and not Alicia.

She was nothing at PastForward. A woman who'd begged her boss for a team lead position she hadn't quite earned yet, and somehow Candace had given it to her.

Through a myriad of ups and downs, sabotage attempts, hidden passageways, budget overages, and one late-night sting, Mandie had somehow found a way to keep her team together and successfully finish the project.

But now that the Hampton House was finished, Mandie had gone back to answering phones, scheduling restoration projects, and consulting on historical art pieces whenever the opportunity arose.

New projects had been assigned in January, but she hadn't been finished with the Hampton House yet. She wouldn't have gotten another one so soon anyway. Now, the only thing on anyone's radar was the move. Candace hadn't even put out any dates for future meetings, though she constantly scoured the Eastern Seaboard for properties to renovate, restore, and resell.

Candace sat behind an imposing mahogany desk, looking as polished and put-together as ever. Her office showed no signs of being boxed up and labeled, though those things existed out in the main part of PastForward.

"Sit." She jabbed at the chair in front of Mandie.

"Why are you in a bad mood?" Mandie couldn't believe the question had crossed her vocal cords, but she couldn't swallow them down now. All she could do now was stare at her boss and hope she didn't get fired.

To her surprise, Candace's shoulders softened, and she sighed in frustration. "Things are a bit hectic, that's all." She flipped over her notebook, revealing a sloth in a hammock on the back of it.

"I'm sorry," Mandie said, swallowing after speaking. "Anything I can do to help?" Her heart raced for a reason she couldn't name. She glanced around Candace's office, taking in the neatly stacked files on the corner of the desk, the framed photos on the walls of various completed projects, and the large window behind her, offering a beautiful view of Fifth Avenue. The tension in the air choked her, making it hard for Mandie to breathe.

"Mandie," Candace began, her tone shifting to something more serious again. "I want you to coordinate our move."

She blinked and tried to come up with a response that wasn't whiny. "I...well, ma'am, I'm sure you remember I'm going to be in Aruba over the move."

"Right, but you can coordinate all of it before you go."

Mandie's mouth fished, and she really wanted to ask why Candace couldn't do it. "It's not done yet?"

"No." Candace folded her arms and leaned back in her luxurious desk chair. "Which is why I need you."

"Okay," Mandie said, because she didn't see another way through this. "I'll need dates and a location."

"Yeah, uh."

Mandie was absolutely sure she'd never heard her boss use the word "uh" before. She never hemmed nor hawed. She was a shark of a woman who'd grown up in the city, still lived in the city, and could probably conquer this city.

She dressed in designer clothes, never had brassy blonde hair though the color obviously came from a bottle —or rather, a salon—and Mandie hardly ever saw her eat.

So "Yeah, uh," did not fit with the picture Mandie had of Candace Ewing. At all.

"I don't have new office space." Candace cleared her throat, creating another riddle in Mandie's universe.

"You don't have...office space," she said, the words there but making no sense. "We have to be out of this building in fifteen days."

"I'm aware of when we have to vacate this space."

"Where are we going to go?" Panic built inside Mandie, and she reminded herself she didn't own PastForward. This wasn't truly her problem.

Candace ran her hand through her hair, and Mandie wondered what she'd been doing since they'd gotten the notice about vacating the Flatiron building. It had been two months. She still came to work, though she had been working behind a closed door more often.

Heck, if Mandie could work behind a closed door, she would too.

Her overactive imagination ran away from her in the silence. Were there financial troubles here that she hadn't been aware of? Was Candace quitting? Was a huge restructuring coming? The uncertainty gnawed at her, each scenario worse than the last.

When Candace continued to massage her temples with one hand, her fingers going round and round, Mandie found one train of thought and boarded that.

"Let me get this straight," she said. "You need me to find office space large enough for fifty employees, rent it, and then coordinate our move from here to there. All before I leave for Aruba in thirteen days—and that includes weekends."

Candace dropped her hand and opened her eyes. She gazed evenly at Mandie as she said, "Yes. That's what I need you to do."

Candace Ewing massaged her temples, willing the tension headache to subside. She'd barely slept last night, tossing and turning as her mind raced with a thousand thoughts. The impending move. The lack of new office space. And most pressingly, the email from Lana Cutler.

Her daughter.

The word felt foreign, even in her thoughts. For twenty-one years, Candace had pushed away any thoughts of the baby girl she'd given up for adoption. She'd buried herself in her work, building PastForward from the ground up, focusing on restoring beautiful old buildings rather than dwelling on the past she couldn't change.

Rather than trying to rebuild or restore anything in her life that had been broken by her college relationship and pregnancy.

But now, that past had come knocking, demanding her attention.

She forced herself to focus on the present moment, on Mandie sitting across from her desk, waiting for a response. The young woman's brow furrowed with concern, her bright eyes missing nothing, and Candace realized she'd been silent for too long.

"I have—" Her voice caught on itself, and Candace cleared her throat to get all of the emotions, all the thoughts, all the things out of the way. She reached for a folder on her desk, grateful for something tangible to focus on.

"I have some leads," she tried again, sliding the folder across to Mandie. "I've been looking into potential spaces, but I haven't had time to follow up on any of them."

Mandie opened the folder, her eyes scanning the contents. "These all look..." She paused, and Candace wasn't sure what she saw in the folder. It only contained a few sheets of paper, and at the moment, she couldn't remember what she'd put in there.

Candace's stomach growling at her for something to eat. She couldn't actually remember the last time she'd put anything of substance in her mouth. Could someone live on coffee, Diet Coke, and saltines?

Maybe for a few days, as she'd been doing. But her hands shook as she pulled them back and hid them under her desk. She couldn't believe she was exhibiting such nerves and such a show of weakness in front of Mandie Kelton of all people.

She'd disliked the young woman since the moment she'd met her, though Candace was a pragmatic and smart businesswoman. She knew talent when she saw it, and she'd hired Mandie with the intent to use her history knowledge and leadership skills as much as possible without really giving her a chance to shine.

The Hampton House had changed that. Everyone in the office adored Mandie, and that only made Candace dislike her even more.

At the same time, she admired so much about the young, honey-blonde woman across from her. The relationship confused her greatly—very much like her biological daughter's request to meet.

Meet?

Candace felt like she didn't even know the meaning of that word right now.

"...club?"

She blinked and met Mandie's eye. They both knew Candace hadn't been listening, but Mandie didn't lift her eyebrows or challenge Candace. "Is there really enough room for us in a yacht club?"

Candace struggled to remember the yacht club rental listing. "I don't know," she said crisply. "I'll leave that to you to figure out." She rose from her desk, needing this meeting to be over.

All at once, she remembered the old yacht club in the Hamptons. "Oh, they're turning into yacht storage," she said. "It too needs some work, and I'd put in a bid on doing the renovation."

Mandie's eyes scanned the paperwork. "But they want tenants during the transition."

"Yes," Candace said, relieved that her brain seemed to be working again. "We only need a temporary location until we find the perfect office space for PastForward."

A Yacht Club was certainly unconventional for an office space, but it had potential. And right now, potential was all they had.

"We may need to think outside the box," Candace said. "Our current situation calls for creative solutions."

Mandie nodded slowly, still reading the listing. "I'll do my best," she said, finally slapping the folder closed. "Ma'am..."

"Oh, just spit it out, Mandie." Candace sat back down, her headache intensifying. Her first inclination was to hold her breath, but she forced her lungs to expand.

Mandie glared back at her, and Candace would give her points for determination and boldness. "Alicia is the Assistant Director." She folded her arms. "Not me. I won't step on her toes."

Candace shook her head a bit impatiently. "Alicia is swamped coordinating the actual move with the movers and all the employees. I need you to focus on finding and securing our new space."

"So I don't need to coordinate the actual moving."

"You can coordinate that with Alicia."

"Does she know we don't have a new location?"

Candace pressed her lips together, her mouth so dry. "Not yet."

She didn't mention that she simply couldn't bear to put one more thing on Alicia's plate. The woman already juggled so much, between her work responsibilities and being a single mother. And with the way Mandie wiped her hand through her hair and sighed... Guilt twinged through Candace as she wondered if she'd been pushing her employees too hard lately.

But she set the thought aside. They all knew what they'd signed up for when they joined PastForward. This was New York City. If Mandie couldn't handle the pressure, she didn't belong here.

"Okay," Mandie said as she got to her feet. "I'll get started on this right away. Is there anything else you need from me?"

Candace shook her head. "That's all for now. Loop Alicia in and keep me updated."

As Mandie turned to leave, Candace suddenly wanted to say something more, to acknowledge the enormity of the task she'd just handed over. But the words stuck in her throat. She was the boss. She didn't need to explain herself or coddle her employees.

The door closed behind Mandie, and Candace let out a long breath. She swiveled her chair to face the window, gazing out at the bustling street below. From up here, the people looked like almost like robotic figurines, scurrying about their day. She wondered how many of them carried secrets, how many grappled with life-altering decisions, how many had hidden their true selves behind carefully constructed façades, and how many, like her, stood at the precipice of a new beginning, uncertain and scared out of their mind.

Her hand moved unconsciously back to her desk, where her phone sat. She'd read the email from Lana so many times she practically had it memorized, but she tapped and swiped and pulled it up again now, her eyes scanning the words that had turned her world upside down only a few weeks ago.

Dear Ms. Ewing,

My name is Lana Cutler. I believe you may be my birth mother. I've recently turned twenty-one, and I've been searching for information about my biological parents. Through DNA testing and some help from a search angel, I've traced my lineage back to you.

I want you to know that I'm not looking to disrupt your life or make any demands. I simply have some questions about my medical history and would love to learn a bit more about where I come from—and get to know you, if possible.

If you're open to it, I'd like to meet.

I understand if this is overwhelming or if you're not interested in contact. Please take your time to consider. I'll respect whatever decision you make.

Sincerely, Lana Cutler

CANDACE SIGHED AND LOOKED UP FROM THE screen. Her fingers absently traced along her lips as her mind wandered into the past. She'd spent two decades convincing herself she'd made the right choice, that giving up her baby had been the best thing for everyone involved. She'd been young, still in college, with big dreams and bigger ambitions. A baby would have derailed everything.

And yet, reading Lana's words, seeing the name she'd never known, a hollow pit opened in Candace's chest and expanded, grew bigger, and threatened to drown her from the inside out.

She hadn't answered Lana yet, and it felt like a giant clock followed her around everywhere she went, ticking away, reminding her of just how long it had been since the email had arrived.

Too long.

Tick, tock. Tick, tock. Tick, tock.

What should she say? How did one respond to a daughter they'd never known?

A knock at the door startled her out of her reverie. "Come in," she called, quickly turning her phone over and lamenting that she didn't swallow some painkillers in the few minutes since Mandie had vacated her office.

Alicia poked her head in, her dark hair braided perfectly. She wore an ivory blouse with a navy blue skirt, heels, the exact right earrings. She reminded Candace so much of herself, though Alicia possessed a compassion and softness that Candace had actually worked hard to eradicate from herself.

"Sorry to bother you," Alicia said as she straightened right there in the doorway. "The bid from the moving company I'm working with won't touch artwork worth more than three thousand dollars."

Candace frowned, then rolled her eyes, though her mind had already shifted gears to problem-solving mode. This was what she was good at, what she'd built her career on. Logistics, planning, making things happen against all odds.

"Yes," she said. "You have to contact Goodwin's. They have specialty moving services, specifically for artwork."

Alicia made a note on the tablet in her hand. "Got it. I'll reach out to them today. See if they can get us on the schedule."

"They do storage too," she said. "You'll need to work with Mandie on if we'll have room in our temporary location for the artwork we have here. If not, we can store it."

"Yes, ma'am." Alicia nodded, her fingers tapping on the tablet, which gave Candace a chance to study her face. The younger woman looked tired, with faint shadows under her eyes that even her expertly applied makeup couldn't quite hide.

"How are you holding up with all this?" she asked, surprising herself with the question.

Alicia looked up and blinked, clearly caught off guard by the personal inquiry. "Oh, I'm...managing," she said with a small smile. "It's a lot, but I'm used to juggling multiple priorities."

Candace nodded, a mix of pride and guilt parading through her. Alicia was exactly the kind of employee she valued most—hardworking, efficient, able to handle pressure. She'd never worried about what her employees did outside the walls of the office, but the Hampton House had shown her that she should.

Two of her former employees were still waiting to go to trial for their part in a scheme orchestrated by a competitor. Sebastian Blackwood at ReviveWorks had been trying to steal valuable assets from a property that Candace owned. He'd put her employees up to it, and other employees in danger.

And Candace had never even thought something like that could happen. Not to her, at least. She'd lost plenty of sleep last year during the Hampton House renovation, and in the weeks and months since.

She had to deal with lawyers now, court hearings, and constant worry for her teams out in the field.

"Make sure you're taking care of yourself," Candace found herself saying. "We need you at your best."

Alicia's smile appeared slightly. "Thank you, Candace. I appreciate that."

As Alicia turned to leave, Candace's eyes fell on the only framed photo on her desk. It had been taken during last year's company Christmas party, and it showed Candace standing with Alicia, who had gathered her children in front of her, all of them beaming at the camera.

A pang of missing, of hurt, rang through Candace's chest as she thought of the family photos she'd never taken, the holidays that has passed, the milestones she'd missed with Lana.

She shook her head, trying to clear the thoughts away.

This was why she'd avoided thinking about her daughter for so long. It opened up a Pandora's box of emotions she wasn't equipped to deal with.

She'd made her decision long ago. She'd made that bed, and she'd been lying in it ever since.

Turning back to her computer, Candace tried to focus on work. She had emails to answer, reports to review, decisions to make about ongoing projects. But her mind kept drifting back to Lana's email, to the possibility of meeting the daughter she'd given up.

What would Lana be like? Did she have Candace's drive, her ambition? Or was she more like her father, with his easy charm and laid-back attitude?

Bradley Short. There was a name Candace hadn't allowed herself to think about in years. Their relationship had been intense but short-lived, a whirlwind college romance that had ended as abruptly as it began. When Candace found out she was pregnant, Bradley was already gone, off to chase his dreams of becoming a professional bull rider.

She'd never told him about the baby. It had seemed pointless at the time, just another complication in a situation that was already overwhelming. But now, with Lana reaching out, Candace wondered if that had been the right decision.

The ping of an incoming email jolted her back to the present. It was from Mandie, already following up on the potential office spaces. Candace skimmed the message, impressed despite herself at Mandie's quick action.

Maybe she'd made the right choice in assigning her this task.

She gave Mandie an affirmative and complimentary email, then scrolled down, down, down to the one that had been haunting her. She needed to answer. Today.

Candace stared at the message, her fingers hovering over the keyboard. Before she could overthink it yet again, she found herself typing:

Hello Lana,

Thank you for reaching out. I have read your email and given it a lot of thought. I would be open to meeting. Perhaps we could arrange a time next week?

She hit send before she could change her mind, then sat back in her desk chair, her heart racing. What had she just done? Was she really ready for this?

But as the initial panic subsided, something else moved forward. A sense of...anticipation? Hope? She couldn't quite name it, but it sat there, unfurling like a flower after a long winter.

Her phone buzzed almost at the same time her computer chirped a notification of an incoming email.

From Lana.

That would be wonderful! I'm free most evenings next week. Is there a day that works best for you?

Emails flew back and forth as Candace worked out the

details of meeting her biological daughter for the first time. Next Wednesday. Almost a week from today. A quiet bistro in the Upper East Side of the city. Seven o'clock.

Great! Lana's last email said. *I'll be there with my boyfriend, Mark. I can't wait to meet you, Candace.*

Candace sat back again, then lunged forward and closed her email window. She silenced her phone. She just wanted to sit with this for a minute.

What would Lana think of her? Would she be disappointed? Angry? Or would she be understanding about Candace's decision all those years ago? Would she want to know who her father was?

Her stomach clenched and her blood turned to ice as she realized Lana might already know Bradley was her father. Had she reached out to him too?

"She can't have," Candace whispered to herself. If Lana had contacted Bradley and told him he was her father, Candace would've heard from him by now. For sure.

Wednesday seemed both impossibly far away and alarmingly close. She had no idea what that meeting would bring, how it might change her life. But she knew one thing: She needed to find Bradley and tell him he had a daughter.

Her fingers shook, because Candace didn't know how to run her company, move the office, maintain her reputation, and deal with all the personal things after hours. She'd always prided herself at compartmentalizing, keeping work and home life separate.

But she'd been doing a poor job of that here, and Candace didn't see it changing anytime soon.

Not even come Wednesday, when she looked into her daughter's eyes, searching for her own.

She startled when she realized she'd once again drifted off inside her own mind. She had no idea how long it had been this time, but she leaned forward and pulled her keyboard closer. She needed to find Bradley and get in touch with him quickly, and since she had others getting things done here in the office, Candace could devote her morning to doing exactly that.

Now, she had to simply pray that she could find him before Lana did—and that he wouldn't be absolutely irate with her once he found out about their daughter.

OH, A SECRET BABY! PREORDER **THE YACHT CLUB** now by scanning the code below with your phone!

The Hampton House, Book 1: Mandie Kelton, Alicia Halverson, and Suzette Paxman are drawn together by the allure of forgotten elegance and the shadows of the past. They'll have to learn to get along if they have any hope of keeping their jobs, and as they restore an abandoned mansion in The Hamptons, they'll also discover the lost and hidden parts of themselves that make them into the women they're meant to be.

The Yacht Club, Book 2: Mandie Kelton, fresh from the triumphant restoration of the Hampton House, faces a new challenge when her boss, Candace Ewing, reveals their next project: restoring a famous historical yacht once owned by a legendary figure. Tasked with breathing new life into the venerable vessel, Mandie,  along with her trusted friends and colleagues—Suzie, Alicia, and the enigmatic Candace—embarks on a journey that will test their skills and uncover long-buried secrets.

Books in the Five Island Cove series

The Cliffside Inn, Book 3:
Spend another month in Five Island Cove and experience an amazing adventure between five best friends, the challenges they face, the secrets threatening to come between them, and their undying support of each other.

Christmas at the Cove, Book 4:
Secrets are never discovered during the holidays, right? That's what these five best friends are banking on as they gather once again to Five Island Cove for what they hope will be a Christmas to remember.

The House on Seabreeze Shore, Book 5: Your next trip to Five Island Cove...this time to face a fresh future and leave all the secrets and fears in the past. Join best friends, old and new, as they learn about themselves, strengthen their bonds of friendship, and learn what it truly means to thrive.

Four Weddings and a Baby,

Book 6: When disaster strikes, whose wedding will be postponed? Whose dreams will be underwater?

And there's a baby coming too... Best friends, old and new, must learn to work together to clean up after a natural disaster that leaves bouquets and altars, bassinets and baby blankets, in a soggy heap.

The Seafaring Girls, Book 7:
Journey to Five Island Cove for a roaring good time with friends old and new, their sons and daughters, and all their new husbands as they navigate the heartaches and celebrations of life and love.

But when someone returns to the Cove that no one ever expected to see again, old wounds open just as they'd started to heal. This group of women will be tested again, both on land and at sea, just as they once were as teens.

Rebuilding Friendship Inn, Book 8:
Clara Tanner has lost it all. Her husband is accused in one of the biggest heists on the East Coast, and she relocates her family to Five Island Cove—the hometown she hates.

Clara needs all of their help and support in order to rebuild Friendship Inn, and as all the women pitch in, there's so much more getting fixed up, put in place, and restored.

Then a single phone call changes everything.

Will these women in Five Island Cove rally around one another as they've been doing? Or will this finally be the thing that breaks them?

The Glass Dolphin, Book 9: With new friends in Five Island Cove, has the group grown too big? Is there room for all the different personalities, their problems, and their expanding population?

The Bicycle Book Club, Book 10: Summer is upon Five Island Cove, and that means beach days with friends and family, an explosion of tourism, and summer reading programs! When Tessa decides to look into the past to help shape the future, what she finds in the Five Island Cove library archives could bring them closer together...or splinter them forever.

The Holiday House, Book 11:
Revisit Five Island Cove at
Christmastime! Join the women in
the cove as they come together for
a wedding, the holidays, and new
ideals to what it means to be a
mother, daughter, sister, aunt, and
friend.

The Cottage on Nantucket, Book 1: When two sisters arrive at the cottage on Nantucket after their mother's death, they begin down a road filled with the ghosts of their past. And when Tessa finds a final letter addressed only to her in a locked desk drawer, the two sisters will uncover secret after secret that exposes them to danger at their Nantucket cottage.

The Lighthouse Inn, Book 2: The Nantucket Historical Society pairs two women together to begin running a defunct inn, not knowing that they're bitter enemies. When they come face-to-face, Julia and Madelynne are horrified and dumbstruck—and bound together by their future commitment and their obstacles in their pasts...

The Seashell Promise, Book 3: When two sisters arrive at the cottage on Nantucket after their mother's death, they begin down a road filled with the ghosts of their past. And when Tessa finds a final letter addressed only to her in a locked desk drawer, the two sisters will uncover secret after secret that exposes them to danger at their Nantucket cottage.

About Jessie

Jessie Newton is a saleswoman during the day and escapes into romance and women's fiction in the evening, usually with a cat and a cup of tea nearby. She is a Top 30 KU All-Star Author and a USA Today Bestselling Author. She also writes as Elana Johnson and Liz Isaacson as well, with almost 200 books to all of her names. Find out more at www.feelgoodfictionbooks.com.